As others ha leaped onto came up. It hissed a challenge. Tyressa roared back, the stepped on its throat and thrust the fishing spear straight through the larger eye.

The ogre thrashed, ripping the spear from her hand and tossing her into the crowd. Its death throes crushed one man and broke several others. The people withdrew, weapons ready, as the monster thrashed out the last seconds of its life, then cheered as it lay still.

Tyressa emerged from the bloodthirsty throng bruised but otherwise unhurt.

Jerrad stared at her, and wasn't alone. *You're my mother, but are you my mother?*

Tyressa bent, resting hands on knees. She breathed heavily for a moment or two, then let her skirt hem slip down and straightened up. She looked around, then nodded.

"This is a terrible night, but you've all done well. See to yourselves. See to our wounded. Then we shall attend to our dead." She wiped her bloody hands on her skirts. "This is a night we mourn now, but shall celebrate in the future. And because of you, Silverlake will *have* a future."

The Pathfinder Tales Library

The Crusader Road

Michael A. Stackpole

paizo

Cover art by Steve Prescott.
Cover design by Emily Crowell.
Map by Robert Lazzaretti.

Paizo Inc.
7120 185th Ave NE, Ste 120
Redmond, WA 98052
paizo.com

ISBN 978-1-60125-657-7 (mass market paperback)
ISBN 978-1-60125-658-4 (ebook)

Publisher's Cataloging-In-Publication Data
(Prepared by The Donohue Group, Inc.)

Stackpole, Michael A., 1957-
    The crusader road / Michael A. Stackpole.

    pages : map ; cm. -- (Pathfinder tales)

    Set in the world of the role-playing game, Pathfinder and Pathfinder Online.
    Issued also as an ebook.
    ISBN: 978-1-60125-657-7 (mass market paperback)

    1. Aristocracy (Social class)--Fiction. 2. Exile (Punishment)--Fiction. 3. Acquisition of territory--Fiction. 4. Good and evil--Fiction. 5. Pathfinder (Game)--Fiction. 6. Fantasy fiction. 7. Adventure stories. I. Title. II. Series: Pathfinder tales library.

PS3569.T137 C78 2014
813/.54

First printing June 2014.

Printed in the United States of America.

To the Memory of Aaron Allston
A great storyteller, and a greater friend.

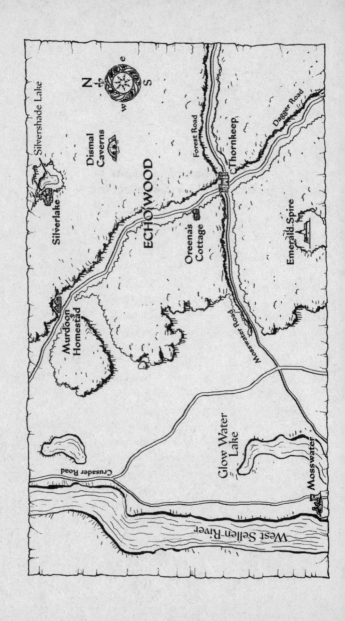

Chapter One
In The Court of Baron Blackshield

Jerrad's back itched. Right there, right where he couldn't get to it. His green woolen tunic scratched *everywhere*, but just not *there*. He wanted to do something, just twist or rub against a door jamb, but he couldn't.

He didn't dare move. He barely dared breathe. He really hoped everyone would forget he was there. *I'll just be as quiet as a*—his cheeks burned—*mouse*.

Tension filled the dark and close castle room. Thornkeep's sneering master, Baron Tervin Blackshield, stretched his lithe form across a throne woven of antlers and covered in animal skins. Mounted heads of other animals hung in a glassy-eyed gallery, half-hidden in the shadows near the ceiling. Even the most placid of the beasts had a sinister look, and the predators all flashed fang.

Jerrad could feel them watching him. He couldn't shrink back to escape them. They'd be hunting him in nightmares.

And the baron will lead the pack. Tervin Blackshield had a lupine cast to his features and hard eyes. Flesh tightened around them as he listened. He clad himself in fine clothes—not as fine as the ones Jerrad and his mother and sister had donned—but he wore them uncomfortably, as if they were woven of nettles. He seemed the sort of man who'd only be happy following a blood trail.

Less a man than an animal in a man's skin.

Lady Tyressa Vishov, Jerrad's mother, stood tall before Blackshield. Her dark hair had been plaited into a single, thick braid that rested between her shoulder blades. Unlike Lord Maraschal Sunnock, who had dropped to a knee beside her, Jerrad's mother showed no sign of subservience to the castle's master.

"Your kindness in receiving us so late in the evening is appreciated, Baron Blackshield." Tyressa nodded toward the slender, wizened man hunched in the shadow of Blackshield's throne. "Your man Cranstin made clear your desire to see us without the least bit of delay."

Irritation flickered over Blackshield's face, then retreated behind a facade of affected boredom. "He is good at stating in diplomatic terms that which I put in more direct language. But pleasantries, like noble visitors from Ustalav, are rare in my court. We must cherish them."

Tyressa nodded briefly. Jerrad had seen her do that many times. *She thinks he's lying.* She would never trust him, but for the sake of form, she would accept the lie.

Blackshield's right hand flicked up idly, a finger pointing at the severe woman standing near his right shoulder. "You are acquainted, Lady Vishov, with my wife, Lady Ivis Druscor. She's told me you met at court, years ago."

Lady Ivis smiled cat-like, her skeletal fingers clawing the back of the throne. "When you were still welcome at court, my dear."

"I do remember you, Lady Ivis. You were most talented at the dance." Tyressa's voice took on an edge. "I recall you being very popular with the prince's officers. And here you are, with your own court and, as I have been told, two beautiful children. I actually hope that your children and mine will be able to pass time together."

Ivis's eyes widened. "And be tainted? I think not."

Jerrad's cheeks flushed and burned, a sensation contrasting sharply with the chill running down his spine. His sister, Serrana, likewise blushed, but raised her chin and stared hard at Ivis. Jerrad waited for the woman to burst into flames or die—which is what he'd thought would happen to him whenever his sister locked her incendiary blue-eyed stare on him.

Ivis didn't, but Lord Sunnock, who knelt halfway between them, did waver as if faint. Jerrad wouldn't have minded if he dropped twitching. The steward of the Vishov holdings in Ustalav, Baron Creelisk, had sent Sunnock to spy on them—though he told everyone he was an *advisor*. The youth hadn't heard a joke from the man that he considered the least bit funny, and Sunnock was less inclined to physical labor than Serra. *This is the first I've seen him being quiet, however.*

Tyressa cocked her head ever so slightly. "I am certain I don't understand what you mean, Lady Ivis."

Before his wife could comment, Blackshield silenced her with a glance. Smiling coolly, he rose from his throne. "We may be on the east bank of the river, deep here in Echo Wood, but news reaches us faster than you might imagine. Within six months of his execution, we heard of your brother's treason. To think a Vishov could seat himself on Ustalav's throne is as silly as believing your brother's gallows confession exonerating your family and accepting full blame for his crimes."

Blackshield raised a hand to forestall a rebuttal. "And we had copies of Ailson Kindler's *Winds of Treason* within a month of publication. My wife is devoted to her books. Though she fictionalized things, the name Urshov is so close to Vishov that even a fool could read the book for the history it was."

The chill which had run down Jerrad's spine now spread out and started him shivering. Kindler's novel had taken facts from his uncle's trial as a start, then built around them a huge conspiracy to create a political backdrop for her novel. She turned his mother's friendship with Prince Aduard into a torrid and illicit affair that implicated the prince in the death of Jerrad's father. It was all one big pack of lies, but the prince's political enemies used it to force him to act against the Vishovs, and Blackshield clearly understood that.

Tyressa opened her arms. "M'lord, I'm pleased to see that news travels quickly. This will make what I've come to do so much easier."

Blackshield gave her a half-smile, then settled back amid skins and antlers. He offered his right hand to his wife, who took it, then he nodded to Tyressa. "Enlighten me." His words came as a lupine growl.

"What that scurrilous novel did was not reveal *truth*, but libel a noble man—that being Prince Aduard. Your wife will recall how gracious he was at balls and fetes—a man who saw intellect as a desirable form of beauty. His enemies thought that a weakness, and used the novel to attack him.

"As you noted, only a fool would not see that the Vishov family, and my friendship with his Highness, was the dagger with which they stuck him. Because he is my friend—and remains so—I came to him with a plan. To prove our loyalty to the crown, my family and I would come here, to Echo Wood, and establish a new town, Silverlake, on the shores of Silvershade Lake. We would maintain it and grow it for twenty years. At that time, having proved our worth and innocence to the prince, the Vishovs would return to Ustalav and resume direct control of our lands. Until them, Lord Sunnock's master, Baron Creelisk, will administer our holding in service to the court. Lord Sunnock will see to it that we are true to our mission here."

Sunnock smiled, opening his hands. "I'm not here to be any bother, really, I merely clerk for my master."

Blackshield stared at him until the man cast his gaze down and folded his hands together, then threw his head back and laughed aloud. "Oh, bravo, Lady Vishov. You spin a fiction worthy of Kindler herself. The prince exiles you, tossing you a tiny bone suggesting a return to honor if you can do the impossible. I have no doubt you wish me to believe that's the truth. What I wish to know is if you believe it yourself?"

Tyressa shrugged. "Belief is immaterial, my lord. Were your children's future ransomed, would you hesitate to act to secure it?"

Blackshield raised an eyebrow. "You have a fair point."

"I'm glad you see that, my lord. So I can count on your help in this matter?"

"Ha!"

Tyressa brought her hands back together. "And this means?"

"Cranstin."

The castellan crept from within the throne's shadow. "Your party consists of sixty individuals. You have fifteen warriors, a few artisans, their families and apprentices. Not enough to do what you want. You're doomed."

"He's telling you only half of it, Tyressa Vishov." Blackshield released his wife's hand and sat forward. "You and your party haven't been fallen upon only because *I* have proclaimed you inviolate. So far. Your fighters are insufficient to defend you even here in Thornkeep. We have goblins here that would go through them like grass through a goose. I'm sure they're all loyal retainers, but they're too young to be good, or too old to be great. Echo Wood will swallow you utterly."

He rose from his throne. "Likewise, you have poor food stocks—hardly enough to see you to winter, much less through it. You do have trade goods—nails, hinges, finer things we don't often see. I believe my wife likes the gown your daughter's wearing, for example."

Tyressa stiffened. "You're saying you can be bribed into cooperation?"

Sunnock raised a hand, halfway bent, as if to ward off a blow from Thornkeep's master. "What Lady Vishov meant to say was . . ."

"Quiet!"

The fact that Tyressa and Blackshield had snapped the command at the same time appeared to surprise and briefly unite them.

Tyressa glanced down at Creelisk's minion. "I said what I meant to say. Bribery. Extortion. Consideration. Protection. I have not deluded myself as to the reality of Echo Wood and your demesne, Baron Blackshield. We are more than prepared to pay fair market value for supplies. You'll find us a good trade partner."

"And I'm afraid you'll find little fair in what we consider market value." Blackshield shrugged. "Tell me why I don't just take what you have? Your fate means nothing to me. My wife is happy to see you humiliated. And your family already has debts run up here. I believe you already owe me ten gold."

Tyressa shook her head. "For?"

"Oh, did I not tell you?" Baron Blackshield reached up and parted black hair, revealing a jagged scar over his left ear. "Ten years ago, when your late husband came through, we had a discussion much like this one. The courts awarded me a judgment against him for assault."

"Only ten gold? You must not have gotten up after that first punch."

Ivis hissed, but Blackshield smiled. "Shall I lie to you and say I was sorry to hear he died at the Worldwound, in the Crusades?"

"He's not dead."

"Cling to threadbare hope if you will, but the rest of the world knows the truth." The man shrugged. "I didn't like him, but there were things to admire about him."

Tyressa nodded. "I shall see to it you're paid your ten. Twenty, even."

"In case you wish to hit me as well? Or perhaps Garath's get will do it. Not your daughter. Your son, maybe?" Blackshield stared past Tyressa at Jerrad. "For him, it would be five. And only if he hit me twice."

Jerrad ducked his head, cringing, his shoulders rising.

Tyressa moved to eclipse Blackshield. "Touch either of my children and you get two coins. One for each eye as they lower you into a grave."

"Ah, the Vishov temper—that which got your brother into trouble. Very good. Now that's we've shed pretense, perhaps we can reach agreement." Blackshield began to pace. "Your Silverlake will send all goods through Thornkeep. There will be a ten percent transfer tax—and our assessors will determine the value of the items."

"Seven percent, and I only pay on what is delivered to Silverlake. Theft and wastage prior to arrival are not taxed. I also reserve the right to hunt down bandits and their associates who steal from me. Their antics will profit neither of us."

"Eight and a half, and I believe banditry can be curbed."

"Agreed." Jerrad's mother tapped a finger against her chin. "Is anyone here worthy of their hire? Talented artisans?"

"I know you don't mean to disparage my citizens."

"I beg your pardon. The question stands."

"Cranstin can locate laborers. You'll pay him, he will pay them."

"Will he supervise?"

"He will send someone." Blackshield's smile broadened. "You'll want lumber. You can negotiate with the timber men yourself. Enjoy it. If you were wise, you'd build your own lumber mill. Then you would be a good trading partner."

"I shall take that under advisement." Tyressa lowered her hand. "Will the harvest be good this year, or shall I have to send to Ustalav for provisions?"

"That would be a wise course regardless." Blackshield folded his arms over his chest. "The land is fertile, but little is cleared—before or after planting."

"I'm not certain I understand."

"This I will give you for nothing, Tyressa of Silverlake: These lands have woven into them Azlanti sorceries. The *where* of big things—like rivers, lakes, and towns—is simple, but all else is confusing. Perhaps, when a child, you played a game where you spun about quickly, then tried to chase after another. You knew where you wanted to go, but could not get there."

He spread his arms wide. "So it is here. Farmers may clear land, plant it, but then never find it again. This is what makes the timbermen so prickly. They harvest a hillside, create a wood yard, and yet it hides itself. Not always malignly—often playfully—but frustrating regardless."

Tyressa glanced up at the gallery of animal heads. "I should think that would make hunting especially difficult."

"I've found the magic quite accommodating when it comes to bloodletting." Blackshield smiled slowly. "Blissfully accommodating."

Jerrad shivered first at the joy in the man's voice, but more as he considered the enchantments Blackshield described. The Vishov estates in Ustalav had been in the family for centuries, and Jerrad had spent a lot of time alone wandering through field and forest. He'd spent hours and days drawing maps and writing up stories of what had happened there. The idea that a land could be essentially unmappable intrigued and terrified him.

If I were to get lost . . . The prospect frightened him, yet not as much as the idea of someone like Blackshield hunting him. Jerrad got the distinct feeling the man would revel in the chase first, and consider the consequences of killing him later. Much later. *If at all*.

"We shall do our best to make certain our people don't wander off. There will be enough work at Silverlake to keep them close. Is it worth creating a fishery?"

"Yes, do that, if you're able." Blackshield stared at her for a handful of heartbeats, then stroked his chin with a hand. "There are rules, Tyressa. Abide by them, and we need have little trouble—trouble of the sort which accountants cannot repair."

"Please, my lord."

"You'd do well to keep shy of the Broken Men. Your husband led brave men to the Worldwound. Broken Men are soldiers the Crusades destroyed, but did not kill—not all the way. Many are scarred, but not all demon-caused scars are visible. There are camps of these men out there. Leave them alone and they'll pass you by."

He raised a finger. "The primary rule, and one which carries dire consequences for all who violate it, is this: stay away from Mosswater. Ignore the tales of riches to be found in that ruin of a settlement. The ogres took the town fifty years ago and are not inclined to give it up. They patrol constantly and guard it jealously. They have been known to strike at those who disturb them. The last thing any of us want is to earn their ire."

Tyressa nodded. "I understand, my lord. I appreciate the warnings, and will see to it that no one violates Mosswater."

"Good." Blackshield's eyes narrowed. "I believe, then, we have but one last issue to settle. That would be the matter of tribute."

"Indeed. Your thoughts on the matter, my lord?"

"I thought two hundred gold a month would be suitable."

Tyressa bowed her head for a second. "Baron Blackshield is most generous."

"Am I? We can't have that." Blackshield smiled at Jerrad's mother. "Three hundred, then, the first installment due now, shall we say?"

"Excellent, my lord." Tyressa's head came up. "And you will deliver further tribute to us at Silverlake, then?"

Blackshield's backhanded slap spun Tyressa around and down to a knee. "Insolent cow!"

Mother!

Lord Sunnock sought to protest, but a kick to his breastbone dropped him onto his back.

"You dare demand tribute from *me?*"

Jerrad ran forward, skidding to his knees beside his mother. "Leave her alone!"

Blackshield snorted. "So, the boy emerges from his mother's shadow. Not a good time to grow a spine, child. Echo Wood will rip it right out of you."

Jerrad did his best to ignore Blackshield and hoped his involuntary shiver didn't betray him. He rested hands on his mother's shoulders. "Are you hurt?"

"No, pet." Tyressa's left hand covered her cheek, but could not hide the blood from her split lip.

Jerrad turned quickly, his fists balling, but stumbled and fell beside his mother.

Blackshield's cold laughter filled the chamber. "Oh, the Vishovs have fallen even further than I could have imagined. I suppose you would have me admire your arrogance, but it's as hollow and rotten as your family's future. A daughter cowers, and this one, your husband's weak seed, comforts you, then collapses when he turns to face me. Clearly it was not friendship that prompted the prince to send you east. He pitied you."

Jerrad started to rise, but Tyressa grabbed his left arm. "No."

"That's right, boy, listen to her. I would not visit more humiliation upon you tonight, save that you give me cause." Blackshield snorted. "Did we say three hundred? Four, I think, and if gold is scarce, it can be taken in trade."

Tyressa rose slowly, smearing blood over her chin with a hand. "Four it shall be then, and you *will* pay.»

Blackshield raised his hand again. "'Ware, woman, lest your deafness cost you even more."

Tyressa's eyes tightened. "Here is *why* you will pay, my lord: You remember that Thornkeep was created by Antun Druscor. Lord Sunnock here can bore you with the family history, since the Creelisks are related to the Druscors—as, obviously, is your wife. Of import is the fact that only ninety years ago did the holding pass from the hands of an Ustalavic lord. After you took possession, you came to Ustalav, shopping for a wife with a specific pedigree. Through Ivis's Druscor blood, you've legitimized your claim to this holding.

"The prince is aware of this. He is likewise aware that the Druscors have *never* paid taxes or tribute, or even showed common courtesy to Ustalavic envoys and citizens. Your own experience with my husband is proof enough of that. But the prince's patience has run out. I have but fifteen soldiers. The prince has fifteen *thousand*. Do you really wish him to lay siege to your home?"

Blackshield's hand slowly fell. "You're bluffing."

"You have choices, Baron. You can believe whatever your wife has told you of me—and I'm certain no matter what she's said, she never said I was either stupid or out of favor with the prince. You can believe what was written in that fictional tripe and accept that the prince and I were lovers and that Jerrad here is his son." Tyressa shrugged. "It matters not what you believe, save that you understand that the prince has as much at stake in my success as my family does. If you or Thornkeep prove an impediment to Silverlake's success, do you imagine Ustalav's finest soldiers would hesitate to level your home?"

Emotions flashed over the man's face faster than Jerrad could read. Blackshield clearly didn't like what he was hearing, but he couldn't dismiss it out of hand. Tyressa had struck a nerve when she revealed Blackshield's true motive for marrying Lady Ivis. More importantly, it struck Jerrad, Blackshield wasn't used to someone standing up to him so directly. He wasn't sure how to react to that.

"It would seem, Tyressa of Silverlake, mistakes and misapprehensions have clouded our discussions. This issue of tribute should be mooted for the nonce."

"It's clearly too important a point to be disposed of quickly."

"My thoughts exactly." Blackshield spun and seated himself again on his throne. "Cranstin shall draw up an agreement on the other points we discussed and present it to you in the morning. Until then, I hope you'll enjoy Thornkeep's hospitality."

"Given the taste of it I've had already, my lord, I'm certain it is a place of infinite surprises. Good evening to you. And you, Lady Ivis. When the time comes for you to visit," Tyressa said, her tongue tip probing her split lip, " I'm certain you'll find Silverlake equally inviting."

Chapter Two
Unexpected Danger

Sleep had teased Jerrad and nightmares had ambushed him. All the animals from the walls had chased him. He scurried hither and thither like a mouse, yet they found him. Each creature backhanded him, spinning him around and bouncing him off walls. He woke countless times with a start, then forced himself to get back to sleep. He didn't want his mother worrying that his night had been less than restful.

She has enough to concern her.

It hadn't helped at all that Baron Blackshield had provided accommodations in a part of the barracks wing of his keep. The holed roof meant the large hall served better as a cistern during the rain than it did as dry quarters. The Vishov party pitched tents as best they could within the wing, and soldiers took turns in the castle grounds to make sure their supplies and live-stock didn't get *borrowed* during the night.

Whenever he did finally get to sleep, all Jerrad saw was Baron Blackshield slapping his mother. As she fell, spittle and blood spraying, Jerrad got a good look at the pure delight on Lady Ivis's face. During their journey from Ustalav he'd seen plenty of people happy that they were going, but it hadn't been the same. Those people were pleased that traitors were paying a price. Their disapproval was born from their love for Prince and country.

With Lady Ivis, it was purely personal. Jerrad couldn't understand that. He'd never seen his mother act cruelly to anyone—unless they'd earned her ire, that was. He couldn't believe she could have done anything to hurt Ivis that much, but supposed it was possible. Adults had ways of feeling slights and bearing grudges that he couldn't really comprehend.

His sister snarled furiously—proving she was closer to being an adult than he wanted to give her credit for. She emerged from a large tent, her blonde hair tangled, a comb buried deep in her locks. She glanced about, clearly expecting to be the center of attention, and her eyes narrowed as the servants all wisely avoided her gaze and continued working.

He hoped she'd find her maidservant, Aneska, before she saw him, but luck was not with him. "You, Mouse! This is all your fault!"

Jerrad swallowed. "No it's not."

"It is. Every bit of it." She tugged at her comb, and when it wouldn't slide through her hair, she slowly drew it out as if a dagger emerging from a sheath. "If not for your nattering on about the history of Thornkeep and its curious political situation, we never would have stopped here. It never would have rained. I never would have been frozen in this wet tent and my hair wouldn't be tangled. All. Your. Fault!"

"But I didn't!"

She pointed the comb at him. "Don't try to squirm out, Mouse."

"I'm not." Jerrad cringed out of habit, and hated himself for it. He looked around, hoping someone would come to his rescue, or that a lightning bolt running late for the previous night's storm might just flash through the roof and kill him. "I don't even know what you're talking about."

"No, of course not. You read all the time. You always show off how smart you are, but when it counts, you're worthless." Her face—which others said was very pretty—puckered sourly. "You want to know the real reason we stopped here? Do you?"

Jerrad blinked.

"Serra, be quiet now."

"No, Mother. He has to know." Serrana turned back to him, venom filling her gaze. "We stopped her because mother thinks the wilderness will be too tough on you. Because you're a weakling. A mouse. You're nothing like my father!"

Jerrad's jaw dropped open, but he said nothing. He couldn't speak past the lump in his throat. *Why can't the earth just swallow me up?* He snapped his mouth shut, grinding his teeth and willing himself not to cry.

"Serrana Aleksandra Viktoria Vishov, you will apologize *now!*"

"No! I hate this place. I want to go home."

Tyressa, head held high, ignoring the stares from servants, strode briskly toward her daughter. "One more outburst, young woman, and all of your gowns and combs and ribbons and mirrors—every bit of finery you own—will be packed up and dumped in the river to float home."

Serrana's nostril's flared. "Every bit? Most of it is back there now!"

"You're not going with it, no matter how beastly you act." Tyressa matched her daughter's hard stare, and Serrana retreated just a little. "You call Jerrad a weakling, but last night he advanced where you recoiled. He may not be his father—but at his age, Garath wasn't the man he'd become either. More importantly, your antics would sorely disappoint your father. They're unworthy of him and the Vishov family. Do you understand that?"

Serrana stared at the dark wooden floor. "Yes, Mother."

Tyressa looked over at Jerrad. "Your things are packed, I see. You should take them out to the pack animals. We'll be leaving for Silverlake by noon. Return by then."

Jerrad nodded and retreated as quickly as he could. Holding tears back while in his mother's shadow hadn't been easy, but he'd managed it for her sake. *She has enough to be worried about.* He hung a bedroll, small pack, and folded ground cloth over his shoulder, then scrambled out through a narrow doorway into the castle's courtyard.

Though he was pretty sure he'd never get used to his sister's tantrums, he did his best to understand them. Serra had always been smart, and she applied her smarts in ways that charmed most people, but concealed a hint of cruelty. He saw the cruelty more often than anyone. His mother had told him that his uncle had always teased her, too—that was just the way of brothers and sisters. No matter what, however, blood was blood, and Tyressa convinced him that Serrana would defend him and the family when things got difficult.

The trip east made that idea almost impossible to believe. Serrana had always been a creature of court. She delighted in gossip and intrigues. She devoured Ailson Kindler novels, and easily imagined herself as the heroine of those gothic tales. Then their uncle was arrested and hung, and Ailson Kindler turned on the family. Disgrace flowed into exile, crushing Serrana and stealing her from the only world she'd known.

For Jerrad, who'd always been quiet and solitary, the move east was just one big adventure. He told himself that every single day. It wasn't that he didn't miss Ustalav. He did, but that was because he knew how to hide well there. He could stay out of trouble pretty easily. *Shouldn't be that hard to do that here—if I can't lose myself, the wood will do that for me.*

Serra loved being the center of attention. She'd been that at court, but the expedition came with priorities higher than gossip and noticing her. This had become ever more apparent every mile from Ustalav, and she'd not taken it well. The morning's outburst hadn't been the first since they set out, but was certainly the most volcanic.

And it had really hurt when she'd referred to *her* father. Garath Sharpax had gone off to fight when Jerrad was barely three. He couldn't remember his father at all, and only knew him through stories others told. Serrana regaled him with tales of how Father had taken her riding or had bought her anything she wanted, or returned from trips with presents for her. To hear her tell it, she'd been the jewel in his crown.

Jerrad, while he'd been told he had his father's strong jaw and quick wit, lacked any other serious—*or useful*—resemblance to Garath. Their father had always been larger than life and, in the death his mother refused to acknowledge, had become even more legendary. Within the borders of Ustalav, Garath was a hero; and Tyressa's belief that he still somehow lived added a tragically romantic note to his fame.

Despite what Mother had said, there *were* stories of Garath having performed miracles when he was Jerrad's age. *And younger.* A favorite tale told around winter fires was about how Garath had slain a bear with nothing more than a long dagger before he'd ever had to shave. Jerrad didn't know if it was true or not, but the expedition sorely needed a man of whom it was true.

And that's not me.

Past the gatehouse, Jerrad piled his stuff with the things being loaded on the expedition's beasts and carts, glanced skyward to note the sun's position, then headed south toward Thornkeep's town. The sojourn took him through a small grove, then into a motley collection of tired buildings and sluggish bogs that masqueraded as streets.

He paused, taking stock of the scene. With a practiced eye he measured the streets and took note of how deeply wagon wheels sank in the mire. He sorted new buildings from old, prosperous from poor, and well-run from suspicious. He cataloged everything which, later, he'd transfer to his journal.

A burst of melancholy caused his shoulders to slump forward. Even very young, he'd known he'd not measure up to his father. While people would share Garath stories and tell him, to his face, that he'd grow up to be just like his father, in private they'd agree in whispers that the reverse was true. They never meant Jerrad to hear, but like the mouse his sister claimed him to be, he often went unnoticed. He remained invisible and overheard many things he shouldn't.

The suggestion, in Kindler's book, that he wasn't even his father's son took on a certain currency in some circles. Still, that was just one final victory in a campaign that had long since been won. To many, the sun had set on the Vishov fortunes, and dusk had come when Garath never returned from the Worldwound.

Jerrad knew he'd never measure up to his father's legend, so he resolved to make his father proud in other ways. The problem was that few enough people saw drawing maps and scribbling history as heroic. An old sergeant in his grandfather's guard had once showed him how to use a knife to good effect in a fight, but Jerrad had realized that getting close enough to use it was foolishness itself. Ultimately, the best he could do to honor his father was to stay out of trouble.

Serra is more than enough trouble for mother right now.

Jerrad headed toward the town green. After the recent rains, it could have been called the town *brown*, but the mud didn't get much past his ankles as he squelched his way through it. He stepped carefully, both to avoid slipping and to prevent a shoe from getting sucked off his foot. While his family might be in exile, he was a

Vishov from Ustalav, so it didn't do to give the locals anything to laugh about.

Off to the northeast stood a trading post—recognizable from the mangy old skins tacked to the walls. Jerrad headed that way, figuring that goods flowing to and from Silverlake would likely head through it. Getting an idea about the wares and ownership would give his mother an advantage. At least, that was his hope.

Before he could get halfway there, he heard a half-strangled mewing sound coming from an alley due east. The piteous sound came again, definitely from the alley beside a stone barracks bearing a sign of a blue basilisk. If the slovenly men lounging on the porch were any indication, the Blue Basilisks were a mercenary company. Their lack of interest in the noise or his approach suggested strongly why they were unemployed.

Without thinking further than checking that his knife still rode in his hip sheath, Jerrad headed toward the alley. He would have sprinted, but the mud slowed him—especially when he reached the road at the green's edge. He splashed his way across, spattering himself with what he hoped was mostly just mud, then plunged into the alley and back around past the Blue Basilisk.

As he turned the corner, he realized how foolish he'd been. He tried to stop, but the greasy ground betrayed him. His heels flew up instead of digging in. He landed on his back in a great sploosh of mud, and skidded to a wet halt halfway down the alley—straight into the midst of three of the most hideous creatures he'd ever seen.

He was pretty sure he'd count them as hideous even if they weren't glistening from the wave of mud his entry had washed over them. They blinked big red eyes in oblong heads. Triangular ears, some notched, others pierced, stabbed out, further broadening their heads. Brown peg teeth blossomed in broad grins.

Goblins!

The one at his feet tossed aside the kitten he'd been squeezing to make the noise that attracted Jerrad. "And what has we here? Can't be a man."

"Not a golem."

"Not a giant."

Jerrad drew his knife and brandished it.

"He has a knife."

"A long knife."

"He has, he has." The goblin at his feet half-closed his eyes. "Three of us. One of him. But he has a knife."

Jerrad tried to draw his feet up and stand, but they slipped out from under him. "A *long* knife. I'll use it."

The goblin on the left drew back. "He'll use it."

The one on the right's eyes grew wide. "A *long* knife he'll use."

"Can't have that." The goblin leader's face scrunched up, then he hocked, pursed his lips, and spat.

Green mucus blinded Jerrad. The boy swiped at his eyes with his left hand, but that just splattered mud over his face. Then hands grabbed his ankles and pulled him forward. They twisted, rolling him, and a heavy weight landed on his shoulder blades. Hands drove his face deep into the mud.

His lungs burned. He tried to buck and throw the goblin off his back so he could get a breath, but the leader hoisted his ankles up. Jerrad tried to kick, but the goblin dug claws in and hung on tight. Then a foot stepped on his right wrist and he lost his grip on his knife.

Jerrad wanted to scream. He wanted to cry. He wanted to die of embarrassment. He'd rushed unthinking into a situation that called for a hero—*and I'm a mouse*—and that decision would kill him. *I'll drown in mud, horse piss, and goblin spit.*

Then the pressure on his chest vanished. The goblin released his ankles. Jerrad arched his back, clearing his face from the mud. He sucked in a loud, welcome breath. The sound all but covered a heavy thump and the painful screech that followed it.

His fingers found the hilt of his knife. He rolled over, then grasped it in both hands. He shook his head, clearing his eyes and ears of mud.

"Hey, stop that."

Jerrad blinked.

A young woman in homespun brown trousers and a buff woolen tunic wiped spatter from her forehead. She smiled despite the dirty stain it left behind. She had light brown hair and brown eyes. Her smile lit the whole alley up. Then she started laughing.

Jerrad's face burned, but he guessed the mud coating him hid that fact. "I'm sorry."

"Sorry? Bit o' mud won't hurt no one." She pointed the stout cudgel in her right hand at his dagger. "Goblins is gone. I'm the onliest one still in cutting range."

He lowered the knife and scraped mud off his face. "I didn't mean . . . I mean . . . I didn't know . . . They had a kitten . . ."

She offered him a hand. "Kitten cries have lured many to worse. My brother Five, he's got scars."

Jerrad shifted his knife to his left hand and took her hand in his. She proved to be surprisingly strong, and despite his slipping, she had him upright easily. "Thank you. I mean, for helping me up and, you know, saving me."

She canted her head to the side for a second. "You didn't long hesitate saying that. Not from around here, are you?"

"No. Ustalav. I'm Jerrad Vishov." He braced himself for a comment.

"Pleased to meet you, Jerrad. I'm Nelsa Murdoon. We live north of here, halfway between Silvershade Lake and the river."

"Silvershade Lake, that's where we're going to build the town of Silverlake."

"Are you, now?"

"Well, not just me. My mother and, you know, people."

Nelsa gave him a sidelong glance. "These people much like you?"

Again, he blushed. "Well, no. Some are soldiers."

"No, no, I meant brave and considerate, like you. Ain't many plunge in to help."

"I wasn't much help."

"Helped me have some fun." Her full smile returned. "Goblins don't come much out near our place, and tend to be scarce when the Murdoons come to town. But, answer me. Are your people brave?"

Jerrad nodded solemnly. "Braver than I am."

"Glad to hear that." Nelsa's smile drained away. "Building a town at the lake, brave ain't something you want in short supply."

Chapter Three
New Friends

Tyressa reined her horse to a halt twenty feet from the modest cottage. The daub-and-wattle building with a thatched roof more closely resembled a giant mushroom than it did human habitation, but seemed appropriate for the wooded glen at the end of the narrow path. The cleared land around it had been planted with herbs, flowers, and vegetables, all well tended and heading toward a bountiful harvest.

Please let this go well.

She dismounted even before being given leave to do so by the elderly woman at the cottage's front door. The woman sat in a chair, pedaling a spinning wheel up to speed. She fed wool into the thread with the easy economy of long experience.

Tyressa approached slowly, casting her gaze down. "I beg pardon for disturbing you, Mother Oreena."

The white-haired woman slowed the wheel with a hand. "It's good you came alone instead of with your whole troupe. With the Murdoon girl along, they'll fare well until you rejoin them."

Tyressa arched an eyebrow. "You're very well informed."

"I know the things I'm meant to know, Lady Vishov. All else matters not to me." Oreena stood. "Please, come in. I'll make tea."

"You're very kind."

"Leave your horse. She won't go far." The older woman smiled. "And nothing will trouble her here."

Tyressa forced herself to smile in return, then dropped the reins and followed the druid into her cottage. In contrast with the previous evening, Tyressa had chosen to wear utilitarian clothes. Her skirt and blouse were newer than the robe Oreena wore, but of the same undyed woolen color. Serrana had vehemently opposed Tyressa's choice, which convinced Tyressa she had absolutely made the correct choice.

Lord Sunnock's objection to her side-journey had revealed more about the man than even he could have guessed. He'd promoted the strategy of choosing one of the local leaders and cozying up to them, instead of trying to reach an accommodation with *all* of them. He'd chosen to remain in Thornkeep, in theory to await messages from Baron Creelisk, but truly waiting for Tyressa to return defeated to the town. By then he'd have a political arrangement with Blackshield or someone else and laugh at her mistake.

He cannot be right. Silverlake can't afford for him to be right.

Tyressa ducked her head and entered the cottage. Drying flowers and herbs hung from rafters. A low fire burned in a river-stone hearth and a small pot of something savory bubbled above the coals. A straw-stuffed pallet nestled in a corner, trapped between a curtained wardrobe and a wooden chest.

Oreena already sat at one of two chairs to either side of a small round table. She poured steaming tea into a pair of earthenware bowls. "Please, join me."

There's no way she had time to make the tea. Unless . . . Tyressa smiled. "What I've heard of you is not incorrect, then."

Oreena set the teapot down. "You're certainly wise enough to know that most tales have a kernel of truth and a skin of lies. Things which are said about an old woman living alone and unmolested in the forest— especially Echo Wood—are prone to greater exaggeration than most other stories—just as are the tales originating in Ustalav, I should think."

Tyressa picked up her tea and breathed the steam in. It carried a hint of jasmine and other herbs. She felt herself relax and almost allowed herself to succumb to that sensation.

"What I understand of you, Mother Oreena, is that you care for Echo Wood. Some say you're the avatar of the wood itself. Others say you're married to the spirit that is the wood, or in thrall to the same."

"You make my point."

"I would make another—Echo Wood is as important to me as it is to you. That's not to raise my cause to the level of yours. Before the prince and I struck the bargain that brought me here, I studied this place as best I could. The stories differ on many points, save for one: if you do not become part of Echo Wood and live with it, Echo Wood will destroy you and everything you hold dear."

The old woman's eyes opened, but focused far behind Tyressa. "This makes me wonder then, Lady Vishov, why you chose this place for your exile. Surely the prince would have allowed you to go elsewhere. Somewhere safer. Was it because your husband passed through here before he was taken from you?"

Tyressa shivered and hoped it went unnoticed. "That would have been a foolish reason for my choice. Had I been that foolish, I doubt I would be sitting here. I probably wouldn't have even seen the path to your home, would I?"

Oreena's eyes focused on her again. "Probably not. Now, if you would answer my question . . ."

"If I had chosen a safer place, or agreed to work for far fewer than twenty years, the prince would have agreed to it. However, his critics would have devoured him for his kindness. And his enemies now know the sort of punishment they'd face if they fail, so that will cool their ardor. I hope." Tyressa sipped the tea, letting it linger on her tongue until it became bitter, then swallowed. "It's the only way I can undo the evil my brother did."

Oreena nodded. "I see that for you. And for the prince. But your children? They're not safe here."

"Ustalav would not be safe for them, especially not at court or back in Ardis, at the Creelisk demesne." Tyressa shook her head. "My brother was never the most intelligent of men. Those who put him up to what he did have gone unpunished. They would happily use my children in the same way they used him. Echo Wood may be dangerous, but no more so than the realm we have departed."

"You underestimate the wood, my dear, woefully so." Oreena bid her finish her tea with the flick of a finger. "What is it you would have of me?"

Tyressa drained her bowl and returned it to the table. "I would not presume to your friendship, though I hope that can be earned. I wish your advice in how we create Silverlake. How can we do that so it will thrive?"

The old woman did not reply. Instead, she reached out and took Tyressa's empty bowl, swirled the lees, and overturned it, plopping it down on the table. Tea dripped down through space between planks. Oreena plucked the bowl up with a liver-spotted hand, then studied how the leaves had pasted themselves to the sides.

She set the bowl down again, but the shadow of its lip hid the leaves from Tyressa. "Lady Vishov, I must ask you this: if Silverlake thrives, in two decades will you return to Ustalav?"

It felt as if a cold breeze had cut at Tyressa's spine. She looked around the cottage, then at the woman across from her. The place was unlike any she had known. She and Oreena had little past gender in common, yet in that one heartbeat she understood. *I am she, and she is me.*

"I see your answer in your eyes, m'lady." Oreena smiled warmly, then poured more tea into Tyressa's bowl. "You understand that, one way or another, Echo Wood *will* consume you. Who you were outside, if you are to thrive, will barely be a memory. You will owe your life to this place, and you will give your life for it. In return, it will give you life."

"Does that bargain scare you?"

The older woman nodded. "Every day."

The future demands a hefty price. Tyressa's flesh tightened. "Then I shall give myself to this Wood."

"Good. Then I shall help you." Oreena drank, then tightened her eyes. "To the west of the lake is a meadow full of goldenstar and bluepeas. You should camp there for the first week. There is a better pasture closer to the lake itself, but some might see that as an invasion. If you harvest the flowers and herbs, I shall be happy to trade with you for them. I shall bring you and your daughter cloaks, woven of wool I've spun myself. Few are the tricksters who would welcome my ire by inconveniencing either of you."

"And my son?"

"Well, that may be out of my hands." Oreena's eyes sparkled. "The story of his goblin encounter has preceded him into the wood. Now, few of the creatures hereabouts have any use for goblins, but they do appreciate a good jest."

Tyressa raised an eyebrow. "If not for the intervention of the Murdoon girl, I doubt they would have stopped at jest."

"There's less value in killing than there is robbing—not that goblins won't do the former to accomplish the latter, but they'd rather shear sheep than skin them." Oreena shrugged. "Nelsa's arrival plays well here. The Murdoons have earned respect within the wood. Your son, however, has been the butt of goblin joke, and there are others who might wish to play even bigger jokes on him."

"I'll keep Jerrad close to me, or have a guard with him."

"And make obvious your fear that he cannot handle himself? That would make him far more precious to you, and therefore that much more of a target."

"You don't understand . . ." Tyressa's left hand curled into a fist. "He's not his father. He has great heart, and is loyal and intelligent."

"You fear he's too little for the wood."

"I fear he's too little for the world." She rapped her knuckles twice on the table. "I doubt there's a mother alive who doesn't harbor the same fears for any of her children, but Jerrad . . ."

"There are mothers, Lady Vishov, who have driven their children *into* the wood in hopes it devours them. People get lost here; but people also find themselves. You will urge your son to be cautious because you must, but he's long since off the teat. You can't do much more for him."

"I'll tell you here and now, I won't lose him. I won't."

Oreena reach out and settled a gentle hand over Tyressa's fist. "Take care making oaths, for this place has a way of testing your resolve. Sorely testing it."

Tyressa opened her hand, turned it, and grasped Oreena's. "I'll trust your understanding of the wood."

"Good. Then perhaps the wood will help you find yourself."

Tyressa almost shot back that she knew who she was, but caught herself. That might once have been true, because her life roles had been simple and expected.

Daughter—headstrong and adventurous, but dutiful— then wife and mother. After Garath had gone away, she served her father as keeper of his household, caring for him. Then when her father died, she'd done the same for her brother. *Before he sought to destroy Ustalav.*

After that, the roles changed. Her role as mother remained, but redefined itself as her daughter grew rebellious and her son grew as quiet as Serra was loud. The role of rebel had been thrust upon her by her brother's actions, and exile was something she picked for herself. *And now I'm an explorer on a mission that the most charitable see as difficult and the rational see as suicide.*

"Echo Wood, Lady Tyressa, will see you as no one else does."

In Oreena's comment she found clarity. Save for explorer, all of those roles had been dependent on others. Parents, siblings, husband and children—they had all been the defining factor in who she had been. It wasn't that she had minded, or chafed in those roles; but they had been thrust upon her, never the result of study and planning.

Explorer *was* the result of study and planning. She had made the choice after due consideration. *Perhaps Oreena is right. Perhaps the wood is where I'll learn who I truly am.*

She looked up. "How did you come to be here, Mother Oreena?"

The old woman patted her hand, then sat back and laughed. "That's a story which is too long, too old, and of so little consequence that one cannot justify the breath to share it. At least, not at this moment."

"Perhaps after I've earned it?"

"There, to be told when you have made a home here." Oreena nodded solemnly. "One thing concerning your son . . ."

"Yes?"

"Tunk Murdoon is Nelsa's father. He's head of the Murdoon clan. He's gruff and distant. And that's on his good days. But the sun rises and sets on his youngest, Nelsa. You'll be wanting to thank him for her help."

"It will be done, thank you."

"You'll need friends and allies."

"Is that just general wisdom, or did you read something specific in the tea leaves?"

"The leaves are never specific, my dear." The older woman shook her head solemnly. "But in your case, they suggest you have one fewer friend than you imagine."

The only thing about the Blue Basilisks which Maraschal Sunnock liked was that their red-headed leader, Ariane Redderfin, evidenced the same wide-eyed appreciation for his gold as had the last whore he'd had before the company had abandoned civilization on the River's far bank. This didn't surprise him—mercenaries and whores were really one and the same, save for dress and methodology.

Tyressa is the worst sort of whore. Her willingness to lead a dangerous expedition had impressed Sunnock—at least until his master had sent him from Ardis to join her. Even knowing that he would be the conduit for any supplies Silverlake was going to get from Ustalav, Tyressa had offered Sunnock neither civility, or familiarity. She thought herself his better, and was utterly

43

ungrateful to him; which made her an uppity whore in his mind.

Which is why her downfall will be so delicious. He sighed happily. *And I'll rejoice in my role in making it swift and painful.*

By way of contrast, Ariane embraced her whorishness openly. She overcharged him for the tasks he required of her, but she was quick in their accomplishment. Sunnock had only just finished his second flagon of sour ale in the back room before two of the mercenaries dragged a struggling goblin in and tossed him at Sunnock's feet.

The goblin sought to rise, but Sunnock got to his feet faster and pressed a boot heel to the creature's throat. Sunnock wasn't certain if it was his heel or the presence of the mercenaries that restrained the little beast, but he didn't care.

"You may wait outside. I'll call out if I need you."

The mercenaries shrugged and departed, all but completely closing the door behind them.

Sunnock looked down. "It's your choice. I can summon them back to free you, or to slide your corpse out to the street." The Ustalavic noble fished in his purse, then pulled out a silver coin and tossed it in the direction of the door. "That can be yours. And more."

The goblin closed his eyes and nodded, letting his hands fall slack at his side.

"Good." Sunnock returned to his chair. "You may kneel."

The goblin rolled over, got onto his knees, then prostrated himself. "Didn't mean harm."

"To the boy?" Sunnock laughed. "I certainly hope you did. Pity he lived. The sooner he dies, the sooner I get to leave this pesthole."

The goblin twisted his head and looked up with one eye. "The boy dead is good?"

"It would have been wonderful, but likely not enough." Sunnock frowned. "You have a name?"

"Welinn."

"It would appear, Welinn, I am in need of an agent. I need someone who can keep me informed. I also may need someone who can gather muscle as needed." Sunnock half-smiled. "Would that be you, or shall I send condolences to your widow?"

The goblin glanced back at the coin. "Welinn is yours. I know everything, or know those who know."

"Good. Very good." Sunnock pressed his hands together. "We can start by you giving me the lay of the land—or the wood, in this case. I need to know who is without scruples, who can keep his mouth shut, and exactly what his price is."

Chapter Four
No Place Like Home

It didn't take Jerrad long to realize that as arduous as the journey from Ustalav had been, it was nothing in comparison to the hardship of founding a town. Before their arrival at Silvershade Lake, the town had been an abstraction. He'd helped compile lists of things to do, from clearing the land to gathering the building materials needed to make basic housing and workshops. He knew dimensions for same and had worked out the needs for grading the land and using gravel to help drainage. He had even taught himself how to estimate the board feet he could get out of a tree, just by knowing its diameter and measuring for length.

What became instantly apparent to him was that while he could think of all the jobs that needed doing, he was suited to doing none of them. Everything required more of a strong back than sharp mind, and his inexperience with Echo Wood meant his mind wasn't as sharp as it could have been. His first attempt at splitting wood resulted in the axe almost taking his right leg off at the knee. About the most dangerous thing folks would let him do after that was hauling water in buckets—and they cautioned him not to fill them too full.

He quickly resolved to find other ways to make himself useful. His goal was to become more useful than Serrana or Lord Sunnock. Granted, that wasn't aiming very high in either case. Serrana occupied herself by imagining what Silverlake would look like when completed. Jerrad heard her efforts summarily dismissed by an old farmer, who noted, "No field ever got plowed by turning it over in the mind."

Lord Sunnock wasn't much better. He'd remained in Thornkeep for several days until the weather turn drier, then arrived and wondered why the settlement wasn't already finished. It was true that his servants worked a bit harder when he was on site, but he demanded most of their efforts be directed toward him, so their contribution to the settlement remained minuscule. He clearly thought himself the most important person in Silverlake, but most people wouldn't have given a bucket of warm spit for him.

Jerrad, with his mother's blessings and an admonishment not to go too far, set about gathering deadwood for fires. While doing that, he proceeded to map out the area surrounding the settlement. He took great pains to pace off distances between landmarks. Between delivering armloads of wood to the cooks, or mixing mud to caulk cabin walls, he recorded his discoveries in his journal. Every night he read things over and planned out what he'd be doing the next day—hoping he'd figure out something critically important to Silverlake's success.

Within the first week, his efforts bore fruit. He discovered that things in Echo Wood *moved*. It wasn't the way frost heaves in the winter might cause boulders to shift, or the way a storm might drop trees. It seemed as if something brushed over the landscape, like a hand over a wrinkled blanket, smoothing it here and ruffling it there. And whatever this force was, it didn't do these things in huge ways, but more subtly. A mud bog wouldn't vanish, it would just slither sideways. A boulder wouldn't shift from where it stood, but might turn a degree or three this way or that.

He even went so far as to construct an experiment. He took two dozen stakes and sank half of them into a circle in a clearing. The others he used to make a cross in the middle. He sighted them at noon and noted their relationship to the lake and nearby hills. He wanted to see if the magic would slowly twist the structure in a manner that could be predicted.

He checked for three days running and found the circle remained constant, but the cross slowly twisted around to the right. He measured and made notes, even did calculations. He was certain that he'd found a rate of twisting that matched seasonal change.

And then on the fourth day he found the cross back in its original position in the circle.

But in another meadow a hundred yards north. A meadow which had not existed previously.

His heart sank. He thought he'd found something special, something that would allow him to contribute to the settlement in a way no one else could. Echo Wood had teased him and thwarted him. For a heartbeat, he thought it would do the same for everyone in the Silverlake expedition, and he lost heart.

Pathetic, Mouse. Really pathetic. Tears began to well, but he refused to cry. *I can hide my hurt from everyone, including the wood.*

He lifted his chin and narrowed his eyes. "No. I'm not going to let you beat me. I'll figure you out. I'll win, I swear it."

A cloud blanketed the sun and the air went cold. The meadow's bright green grasses dulled and stiffened, each becoming a little blade tugging at his trousers. Crooked tree branches pointed accusingly at him. Berries withered in bushes, and the thorns guarding them grew longer.

Jerrad swallowed hard and tried in vain not to shiver. A thicket surrounded the meadow and appeared to be tightening like a noose. He spun, pointing himself back in the direction of the lake, but it had vanished. Instead, giant piles of stones he'd never seen before formed a phalanx, cutting him off from the settlement. *At least in the direction where I think it is.*

He dropped to a knee and gathered up the firewood he'd collected. Thorns and splinters raked his flesh through his tunic, but he refused to surrender his prize. He stood slowly, forcing himself to be calm. Despite having lost sight of the lake, he knew where it had to be, so he started steadily marching in that direction.

The grasses snagged and pulled against his clothing, slowing him. A cool breeze rustled them. The snake-like hissing rose to a crescendo, but couldn't mask the snap of a branch crushed underfoot. It came from the right, between two hulking oaks. He'd not noticed them being so close until he heard that sound. Wind-buffeted branches clutched at him.

Then another sound, this from the left, from across the meadow. A low growl—challenging, yes, menacing, yes, but still quiet. Jerrad imagined he'd heard it by accident. It wasn't meant for him, but meant to warn others off. Possessive, that was it. The creature wanted others to know that Jerrad belonged to it.

He crouched and forced himself to be still, very still. His heart raced, but he fought to slow his breathing. He did his best to be utterly motionless and quiet, though his drumming heart had to be audible all the way back in Silverlake.

Dead ahead, eyes burned gold and red in the gloom. He caught one pair first, then another. He looked toward the growl. A gray blur, low and fast, slithered through shadows. Then more eyes appeared past it. They flanked him on the right, too. He didn't look back. He didn't need to see the rest of them there.

He dropped the firewood in one clattering bundle, then snatched up the thickest piece. It would have been a twig compared to the cudgel Nelsa had used on the goblins. He shifted it to his left hand, and drew his dagger with his right.

What would my father have done?

In an instant he knew, and just as quickly knew he could never do the same thing. His father would have run toward the nearest boulder and leaped to the top. Garath Sharpax could have done that easily. Then he'd brandish the cudgel and challenge the creatures. He'd insult their lineage. He'd laugh at their growls. He'd meet snarl with snarl and fang with crushing blows. Bloodied and broken bodies would spin away to twitch in the grasses. His laughter would drown out Jerrad's pitiful whimpering, and then he'd challenge the gods to send him more worthy enemies.

I'm not my father. Jerrad measured the distance to the boulder. *No matter how fast the mouse, that's a race he can't win.*

The gray blur burst from the thicket at his left. Red tongue lolling, the wolf drove straight at him. It came fast, but almost playfully, fangs visible only because its mouth was open, not because of a snarl. It came quickly, but not as fast as it could.

Jerrad tightened his grip on the club. Then he shifted his gaze from the wolf back to the stone. *Too far. No time.*

The youth twisted toward his attacker. He swept the club around, aiming for the beast's slavering jaws. He missed. He'd been close enough to see dripping saliva stain the wood as the club swung past; and the dagger, coming up in something halfway between a stab and a slash, would accomplish neither.

Mice don't kill, they just die. The wolf's breath heated his flesh. Its stink filled his head. Acid burned in his throat as Jerrad stared into its black maw. He waited for the crunch of his face being crushed between those teeth.

Then the wolf spun away. It was as if an invisible giant had grabbed its tail and yanked. It rolled through the air, spittle glistening in long lines and darker fluid spraying. The beast crashed down in the grasses, hidden save for the sound of its thrashing.

"They have your scent. To me, boy!"

Jerrad looked to the left, back along the way he'd run. A tall man stood there—no, more than a man. He fitted a black-fletched arrow to a compact horse bow, drew, and let fly again. He moved as fluidly as did his long white locks on the breeze. The arrow took another wolf through the chest, whipping it around as if it meant to chase its own tail.

Jerrad needed no other urging. He darted toward his savior, slashing at grasses with club and knife. Not to be denied, the wolves focused on Jerrad. Arrows flew, transfixing throats and piercing bowels. Jerrad ducked as the archer aimed straight at him. An arrow hissed past, then thunked solidly into something at his heels.

A dozen paces and a handful more arrows later, Jerrad fell at the archer's feet. The youth's chest heaved. Jerrad wanted to vomit, but he refused. He tried to climb to his feet, but his knees gave out. He caught himself on his hands and found his whole body trembling.

"They've broken. You can get up now."

"Are you certain?" Jerrad narrowed his eyes, staring into the darkness surrounding the meadow. "There could be more out there."

"I hope you're wrong, Jerrad, because my quiver is empty."

The boy whirled and stared up. "How do you know my name?"

Bow still in his left hand, the archer jerked his right thumb back to the west. "News of the Vishov mission here is not in short supply. Unreliable, most of it, but the tale of a youth being drubbed by goblins is a staple."

Jerrad glanced down, his cheeks burning. "And you assumed I was just prone to finding trouble?"

"The dagger got mentioned in the story. And finding trouble isn't a vice, it's an *art*."

Enough kindness rolled through the archer's words that Jerrad looked up again. The archer stood taller than most men, and had pointed ears like an elf. Still, he was broader of shoulder than most elves, suggesting he was of mixed blood. Though he'd never before seen a half-elf, Jerrad figured that what the archer was.

That created another problem, though, because the elves and even their brethren of mixed blood were supposed to look ageless. The archer didn't look ancient, but he did look older. *The weariness around the eyes. And the scars.* One started on the archer's right cheek, just below his temple, and disappeared raggedly back into his hair.

The youth slid the dagger back into its sheath and offered the archer his hand. "I *am* Jerrad Vishov. Thank you for saving me."

"My pleasure. I'm known as Kiiryth." The half-elf smiled politely, but did not shake his hand. "You must learn to take more care in the wood, Master Vishov."

"I . . ." Jerrad turned to point past the stacks of stone, but they'd vanished. A distant vision of the lake shimmering silver in emerging sunlight had replaced them. "I didn't think I'd come that far from the lake. I mean, I've been out here before."

Kiiryth nodded toward the stakes. "They stink of you, you know."

Jerrad closed his eyes for a moment, then hung his head. "The wolves. They waited for me."

"You made it very easy to find you." Kiiryth patted him on the shoulder. "That, in and of itself, is not a simple task here in Echo Wood."

"You found me."

"But I wasn't really looking." Kiiryth squatted stiffly, catching himself on a hand. His empty quiver slapped against his right hip. "You're unhurt?"

"Scratches, nothing big."

"Good."

Jerrad smiled. "If you're going to skin those wolves, I can carry the skins back to Silverlake."

"That's a kind offer." Kiiryth stood again. "I'm afraid, however, there isn't going to be enough time."

Jerrad glanced up at the sky. "It's barely past noon. It shouldn't take that long, should it?"

"That particular task, no." The archer slowly shook his head. "I should have been more clear."

"Yes?"

"*You* don't have enough time." Kiiryth stepped back. "There's nothing I can do right now. I'm sorry."

In the gloaming surrounding the meadow, a rainbow of lights sparked. Some burned brightly. Others flared and some sputtered, but none of them gave off warmth. Figures moved in the shadows around them, advancing. Some lights hovered, resolving themselves into tiny winged creatures. Others, humanoid and more lithe even than Kiiryth, came forward with the lights on the ends of wands. And then those who bore no light emerged, laden with lethal weaponry.

A tall figure stepped forward and doffed a black leather helmet. It freed her hair to tumbling in a cascade over her shoulders and a dark doublet. She studied

Jerrad with eyes of gold, then glanced at Kiiryth. She spoke to him in an alien tongue.

"Yes, barely a morsel for the wolves. It doesn't mean they wanted him any less than you do."

Jerrad's throat clenched. "I don't understand, Kiiryth."

The fey band's leader looked him up and down, then laughed. The rest of the motley assembly joined her. Their mirth scourged him. He almost drew his knife, but could imagine what he'd look like if he did. Bared steel wouldn't hide his fear, and would only make them laugh all the harder.

He stared at Kiiryth. "You should have let me die."

"That was never an option." Kiiryth slung the bow over his shoulder. "As much as the wolves wanted you, Echo Wood wanted you more. They were content to let the wood have you."

Jerrad's eyes tightened. "But I don't . . ." Reality dawned on him. "The wood didn't move my stakes—not to this place. They did it."

"Every trap has its bait." Kiiryth shrugged. "In this case, you supplied it yourself."

I'm just a mouse in a trap. Jerrad's stomach collapsed in on itself. His left hand opened and the stick fell to the ground, not even heavy enough to beat grasses into submission. He dropped to his knees. "Help me, please?"

When silence answered him, Jerrad looked up. Kiiryth had disappeared. Slowly, inevitably, the fey closed in.

Chapter Five
Not As Simple As It Seems

The fey swarmed over Jerrad. Sprites blinded him with intense flashes of light. Other creatures tripped him and pounced upon him. They didn't treat him as roughly as the goblins had, but they bound his ankles tightly with woven grasses. His wrists they tied to a length of pole, forcing him to hold arms at right angles to his shoulders. A second pole ran beneath the first and snagged his ankle's bindings.

Finished with trussing him up, Jerrad's captors lifted him from the ground and his head lolled back. All he could see of the creature holding one end of the pole by his head was shaggy, goat-like quarters, though from belly up he appeared human enough. Actually, Jerrad only saw a bit of his lower body, but the goat-scent couldn't be mistaken for anything else.

Utter hopeless wrapped chains around Jerrad's chest. He sank within, letting despair drown any notion of resisting. He had no idea what the fey intended to do with him, but killing him would be a mercy. *If they kill me, I won't have to endure my sister's criticism.*

While they appeared to want him alive, they really didn't care how beat up he got. Bound in that awkward cruciform position, he wasn't easy to transport through the forest. His captors twisted him left and right, up and down, squeezing him between trees and dragging him over rocks. From their grunts and groans he gathered Echo Wood wasn't happy to give him up to them, and so made their job far more difficult than they had anticipated. He couldn't understand the things being said, but tone and vehemence conveyed a great deal. They snarled and cursed at the forest in general, visiting none of their ire on him.

He focused on their discomfort, and that started him thinking. *If the wood doesn't want them to have you, little Mouse, it might help you escape.* He focused even harder, drinking in every bit of information he could. Water splashed as they walked through a stream, feeling cool and tasting clean. Though he saw everything upside down, he caught sight of herbs and flowers. As if to reward his effort, even the sun came out, imparting color to what had previously been a gray world.

Jerrad's shoulders and wrists hurt, but he pushed past the pain. At some point he realized he wasn't scared any more. His situation hadn't become any less dire, but his understanding of things had increased. *As long as I'm thinking, I don't have time to be scared.*

That thought brought a smile to his lips. He might not be his father's son. He might not have a warrior's skills or strength. His only weapon might be the ability to think, but that was a most potent weapon against fear. It occurred to him that in many stories, courage is counted as little more than a refusal to panic. Even if he didn't have courage, he could still stave off panic.

A brave little mouse I will be.

Their path squirmed between trees and wound around hills, so Jerrad had no real idea how far they'd come from the meadow. Even when they reached the fey encampment, the sun refused to be cooperative in hinting at time traveled. Jerrad had the impression they'd not come that far. Their camp provided him few clues as to where he truly was.

The fey eventually put him down, cut him loose and stuffed him into a wicker-walled hut that more closely resembled a cage than it did proper shelter. The thatched roof would keep rain from dripping down in, but if the wind whipped raindrops along sideways, he might as well be standing out in a field during a downpour.

Rubbing his wrists, Jerrad surveyed his captors and their domain. They made their home in deep forest, with thick-boled pines in a semicircle on one side. On the other, the camp had carved tiers into a hillside. Burrows provided homes for some creatures, while smaller homes hung from branches of younger trees. Circles of blackened stones marked where fires would light the night, and the unnatural shadows between some of the trees suggested where some others might live.

The myriad dwellings spoke to the varied nature of the band. Sprites occupied the elaborately woven homes. Slender diminutive creatures with bright red caps appeared to live in the burrows. Satyrs and fauns gathered on grassy stands, while nixies splashed in a stream to the southeast. The band's leader, who appeared to be elven, disappeared into the shadows, but did so casually. Everyone in the band appeared to pitch in for work, and Jerrad felt certain the armload of wood dumped near the main fire was composed of wood he'd gathered.

Part of him took pride in being able to identify his captors, but putting a name on them didn't help much. All he knew of them was information gleaned from old books and folk stories. He considered both sources of equal reliability, though recalling the most dire tales did send a shiver through him.

Look as he might, he couldn't find any sign of Kiiryth. He'd though the half-elf had sold him out to the fey, but he didn't seem to be one of their number. Kiiryth had risked injury to save Jerrad from the wolves, then abandoned him with no recompense. *I don't see the sense of that.*

Kiiryth's departure was really the smaller of the mysteries Jerrad needed to solve. Even before the archer had intervened, something odd had happened. Jerrad had said aloud that he wouldn't let the wood defeat him, and things immediately became threatening. The day had darkened, the landscape shifted, the wolves came for him, and the fey waited in case he survived.

Jerrad checked himself. The fey had been there first. They'd moved his stakes. They'd set a trap for him. They'd intended for him to end up where he was all along. *It was only after I said I'd win that the wolves came to spoil their plan.*

His mouth gaped for a moment as the various implications warred in his mind. The first and most spectacular was that Echo Wood had some level of consciousness about it. Jerrad's experiment had been intended to detect some sort of natural process, like the tide or the wind. He thought he'd found that, but when he'd vowed to win, things changed.

But how *did they change?* Jerrad's despair at seeing his stakes transplanted had been what prompted his oath. But the wood had not done the transplanting. Had it reacted to his oath because it was disappointed that he blamed a fey action on it? Was his transgression less a matter of being defiant than it was of underestimating the subtle beauty with which the wood could act? *Stupid Mouse.*

The answers to either question had implications that could change forever how he saw the wood. *Or if the wood will forgive me.* Part of him shivered, wondering at the wisdom of imparting that high a level of consciousness to the wood. *Even so, it can't hurt to imagine it to be that wise.*

Jerrad squatted and pressed both palms firmly against the cage's dirt floor. "I'm sorry for offending you. I only wanted to understand."

It had to be a trick of the light, but something flashed off to the northwest, between trees. *Sunlight off water, maybe?* The nixie stream wound round and flowed generally in that direction. *The lake, then. I could follow the stream to the shore and on home.*

Deciding to hope he'd reached some sort of peace with Echo Wood, Jerrad considered the fey band. Because they'd laid a trap for him, they clearly had some use for him. Kidnapping usually resulted in ransom demands. His heart sank. The Vishovs hadn't come away from Ustalav with much. Despite his mother's negotiations with Baron Blackshield, they weren't likely to get much more any time soon. Even a modest demand would tax the settlement beyond its ability to pay.

A faun female trotted up toward the cage. She thrust a feathered cloak and cap between the slender sticks which made up the door. "Put these on. Now."

In her hands the cloak and cap shone with brilliant greens and blues, and the hint of red here and there. As he took them from her, they shifted to dull pigeon gray and sparrow brown. The thinly woven cloak provided no warmth, and the feathers stunk of a soiled nest. Jerrad imagined mites and midges crawling beneath the feathers and shifted his shoulders uncomfortably.

The faun smiled. "Now crow, cockerel."

"What?"

"Crow!" She withdrew a step and raised her hands. They began to glow faintly. "Do it or I'll make you do it."

"Cock-a-doodle-do?"

"Louder?"

"*Cock-a-doodle-do!*"

Various of the fey ceased their labors, looked up toward him, and laughed.

"Crow again, and flap your wings. Strut, cockerel, strut!"

His face burning, Jerrad folded his arms with his hands in his armpits and crowed while flapping. He got up and strutted around the cage. He met every demand, scratching at the earth, pecking at it until his face was brown with dust. Throats grew raw—theirs from merriment and his from harsh calls.

"You're a horrible cockerel. How ever did you amuse those goblins?"

A sprite flashed over in a hum of wingbeats. "They had mud. He was a mackerel for them, not cockerel for us."

The faun turned toward the nixies. "It's not feathers we need, but scales. Fit the mackerel-cockerel out!"

The nixies giggled, then plunged into their pools. They went deeper and stayed under longer than their pools warranted. Jerrad wondered about that, but didn't wish for their quick return.

Why are they doing this to me? Just for fun? Is there something more?

The promise of future amusements alone seemed enough for the faun. She turned from him with a disgusted snort and galloped back over to her patch of green. The others, too, ignored him, save for a tiny bearded man who paused in the entrance to his burrow every so often, plying a whetstone to a wickedly curved blade. He'd stare and nod once, then turn away and keep working.

"The redcap won't harm you, Jerrad."

Jerrad came around and found Kiiryth crouching in the shadows between the trees and the cage. Hope made his heart pound, but then he noticed that Kiiryth's quiver hadn't been refilled. "You aren't going to help me. You betrayed me to them."

"No, I saved you *for* them."

"I don't see a difference."

"They would have let the wolves have you. I couldn't stop the fey, but my stopping the wolves amused them."

"I don't like their humor."

"I'm not too fond of it myself." The half-elf held up empty hands. "There were too many of the fey, and they were united in their goal. I couldn't have prevented them from taking you."

Jerrad chewed his lower lip. He didn't like what he was hearing, but he couldn't fault the archer's logic. "There's more of them now. Why are you here?"

"They're no longer united. The fauns have had their fun. The redcaps won't until the depths of the night when they can terrify you. In between we might see about getting you out."

"You don't have any arrows."

"This isn't a problem we'll solve by killing." Kiiryth's eyes tightened. "I can get you out of the cage, but then . . ."

The youth jerked a thumb toward where he'd seen the flash of light. "The lake's that way."

"How did you . . . ?" He stopped, then smiled. "Ah, clever boy. You've amused the wood."

"Does that mean getting out of here will be easier?"

Kiiryth shrugged. "Won't be harder."

"The fey don't want me dead, do they?"

The archer shook his head. "Unlikely, but if you die, no tears will be shed."

Jerrad wasn't certain how he was supposed to react to that news. It didn't particularly surprise him. If the redcap slipped and fell on his own knife, Jerrad wouldn't be the least bit upset.

He frowned. "Is this your home? Are you one of them?"

"No and no."

"Then why were you out there?"

Kiiryth half-smiled. "Blame it on the wood. I set out to find something curious. One of the Vishov invaders was curious."

"We're not invading. We've come here to live. We'll make the place better."

"Those words have echoed down through the ages." Kiiryth's light chuckle barely made it to Jerrad's ears. "If the fey had come to Ustalav to make it better, would their action be an invasion?"

"That's different."

"It always is." Kiiryth's head came up. "Quiet. Ellesaara comes. I'll be back."

In the blink of an eye the archer dissolved within shadow. At least, that's how it appeared to Jerrad. Not wanting to betray Kiiryth, he forced himself to turn in the direction the half-elf had been looking.

The fey leader had returned, having shucked her armor. In its place she wore a black skirt of wool and a sleeveless leather vest. She'd tucked a dagger into her belt at the left hip, and wore black leather boots. Her raven hair framed a pale but beautiful face, though the grim expression robbed it of its full effect.

She approached the cage and studied him with golden eyes. "You *are* the Vishov scion."

"Yes, my lady."

The elf laughed. "We have no titles here among us. We would not be so arrogant, nor would we vest power in something as meaningless as a title. Why encourage the greedy to fight and scheme?"

"Your pardon. I meant no offense."

"A statement offered by those who believe the errors of ignorance spill less blood than willful actions."

65

Her nostrils flared. "Do you pride yourself on your ignorance?"

"No." Jerrad glanced down. "My circle and cross were meant to help erase it."

"But instead, they revealed the greater depths of your ignorance." Ellesaara tucked a lock of black hair behind her right ear. "You have been taken as a prize, not a prisoner. There are things which must be understood by your community. Your mother needs to comprehend some very important things. Therefore, we needed to get her attention."

"And you've done so, Ellesaara." Tyressa stepped from between two ancient trees. An older woman flanked her. "And now that I have *your* attention, you will free my son this instant. If you don't, your ignorance of the Vishov way will spill blood, and that's a reality that will benefit neither of us."

Chapter Six
Dance And Diplomacy

Tyressa fought to keep her expression stern and gaze hard. She looked past the fey leader to the bramble cage in which they'd trapped her son. *The cloak, the cap... he looks so* small. She wanted to run to him, free him and hug him tightly. Though Oreena had assured her that she couldn't have prevented his being taken, guilt still sank claws into her heart.

"Steady, Lady Vishov." Oreena patted her left forearm and moved forward. "I had thought, Ellesaara, you had grown past mischiefs."

"If that's what you perceive this to be, then you've grown into senility, Oreena." The elf opened her hands easily. "She brought her children here. She placed them in jeopardy. Had we not watched her son, greater mischiefs could have befallen him."

Jerrad stood within his cage. "I'm not hurt."

You say that, but I know there are unseen bruises. "You said, Ellesaara, that I need to understand some very important things. These would be?"

The various fey emerged from their homes and approached. Most came slowly, forming a crescent behind their leader. A few sprites darted in close enough for the breeze from their fast-beating wings to buffet Tyressa's hair, but she made no moves to fend them off.

Ellesaara spread her arms wide. "You should understand that there is a balance struck here in Echo Wood. A delicate balance. It allows the wood to survive. We are part of that balance. We maintain it. Your presence upsets it. This our council has decided."

"How does Silverlake do that?" Tyressa looked about, meeting fey gazes openly. "You speak of balance. I understand this from Mother Oreena. You do not address *capacity*. You suggest our arrival upsets the balance, but Echo Wood is capable of providing a home for all of us. As you live in balance, so shall we."

The elf's eyes sharpened. "A claim for which there is no support, and plenty of evidence for condemnation. Have not lumbermen and their wasteful ways devastated vast swathes of the wood?"

Oreena leaned on her staff. "They've learned."

"And have to *relearn*." The elf pointed toward the northwest. "What of the travelers along this so-called Crusader Road? They've corrupted that artery, and the Broken Men are proof of this poison. This Vishov settlement will encourage them to establish more camps. Their venom shall kill the wood."

"That's the last thing I want. It's the last thing I'll permit."

"You presume, Tyressa of the Vishovs, to have greater control over your people than any before you."

Tyressa stepped forward into the heart of the fey camp. She turned slowly, not surprised to see more fey had appeared and surrounded her. Some were creatures that only existed in fable as far as the courts of Ustalav were concerned. Others only lived in nightmares.

She should have been frightened. *They want me to be.* Tyressa refused to succumb. She would not have Jerrad see her afraid, and even a hint of fear would lose the day.

"I presume, Ellesaara, because I do not come here as others have. They come to Echo Wood to escape, or to find treasure. They come to take. I come to build."

"And destroy while building."

"Now you argue from a lack of evidence." Tyressa pointed toward her son. "You watched him, blood of my blood, flesh of my flesh. What did you see him doing? Noting, planning, yes; but killing, destroying? No. He sought to understand the wood, to understand the balance you say we're here to upset. But we aren't. We're here to live, not to take and take *away*. We know that means we must become, as are you, agents of the balance."

"Humans have not been such before." Ellesaara bowed her head. "You being an exception, Oreena."

Tyressa shook her head. "Humans are not always the agents of upset, either. Southwest of here, at Glow Water Lake, ogres destroyed the town of Mosswater."

The elf snorted. "A *human* town."

"But its destruction had nothing to do with balance." Tyressa had studied all she could learn about Echo Wood, and the vicious attack which laid waste to the town two generations previous had almost decided her against traveling east to secure her family's future. She had no doubt that the accounts she read—all of which came from survivors—were longer on hyperbole than fact. Even so, were one to study the slaughter as emotionlessly as possible, the horror could not fail to elicit shivers.

As she stood there, smoke from a fire swirled toward the settlement's heart and congealed as a gray fog. Phantoms moved through the fog, resolving themselves into men limping, children running, mothers turned to delay pursuit in hopes their children might escape. The fog conveyed no sound, but somehow that made things worse. A scream would end eventually, but to see a face contorted in a scream, then watch it vanish as a club pulverized flesh and bone shards pierced skin, suggested the torment went on forever.

What manner of magic is this? Tyressa fought to suppress a shudder. Fey magic, obviously, but magic which pulled images from her mind. She'd imagined those same images as she read of Mosswater and other tragedies within Echo Wood. *She invades my mind. Does she see? Do they all see? Will my son see?*

The fog placed her in Mosswater, as if a ghost. Large, misshapen, lumpen things charged through twisted streets. A pair of them might grab a man and rip him in half. A tableau that choked Tyressa with horror made the ogres laugh uproariously. As they overran the city, mercilessly slaying anything within arm's reach, the ogres would scoop up guts and mud and handfuls of squishy tissue to throw at compatriots or to smear on themselves. Others slumped against walls, well-gnawed limbs devoid of meat, resting across bulging stomachs, their digestive stupor rendering them all but senseless.

Is this the future of Silverlake? Will I fail and others perish because of it?

Tyressa lifted her chin. "I notice that among *your* number, Ellesaara, there are no ogres."

The elf appeared within the mist, as much a spirit as Tyressa. "They barely live in fellowship with other ogres. They are not our friends. Your settlement will draw them here. You've learned nothing from Mosswater's tragedy."

"I've learned much from it." Tyressa steeled her gaze. "Do you think I would have brought my children here if I hadn't planned for the possibility of ogres attacking?"

"Your precautions shall prove inadequate." The elf snorted. "The victory over you will embolden the ogres. They'll come for us next."

"Silverlake will be strong enough for more than humans." Tyressa extended a hand toward Ellesaara. "You and yours would be welcome there. In times of strife, or plenty. To trade, to live, to join us in maintaining the balance."

The elf threw her head back and laughed. "Do you think us that simple? You're not the first human to offer friendship."

As Ellesaara spoke, the scene in the fog changed. Thornkeep appeared, in older times and better times. The baron's keep appeared to be in much better repair, and the old Druscor family crest flew from flags and had been carved from stone. All the humans appeared short and thick and brutish. They hooted and laughed as they threw stones and rotten fruit at any fey creatures even approaching the town.

They treat the fey as the ogres treated humans. That realization told her that Ellesaara now controlled the vision in the fog. *This is how she sees us.*

Ellesaara's vision shifted. The humans remained unkempt and uncouth, but the scene shifted to the camps of Broken Men along the road. The humans treated the mangy curs that limped along with them better than the fey at the furthest glimmer of firelight. As humans had no use for the fey, so Ellesaara and her people had no use for humans.

Tyressa stared at the fey's vision of humans. Her guts twisted, not out of revulsion at how her people appeared, but because she had no doubt they had earned those images. At her worst, in her darkest hours, she'd seen her brother as being that warped and cruel. What he'd done to the Vishov family made the fey's treatment seem trivial.

The fey's vision of the Broken Men tore at her heart. Ellesaara might have warped their physical presence, but the desperation and pain that came through their eyes spoke of pure humanity. Broken Men shuffled along war-weary, eyes unfocused, mouths hanging open. They ate and drank only when urged by their compatriots. The lame aided the halt. Soldiers with only one eye remaining saw for blind comrades, and those who could barely walk carried stretchers bearing those who could not.

Yet before Tyressa could ball her fists and screw her eyes tight shut against bitter tears, she caught a glimpse of a tall man with golden hair. Somehow Ellesaara could not twist him, for it was his stern glances that stopped humans from beleaguering the fey. He walked as a god among children, and then he turned and smiled at her.

Her heart caught in her throat. *Garath. My Garath.*

Tyressa reached a hand through the vision, fingers trembling.

He came to her, his large hand swallowing her slender one. Warmth flowed from his calloused palm into hers. His fingers closed gently but firmly, and he drew her toward him. Just as he had when they first met at the prince's ball.

The vision shifted. The squalid human camp melted into a palace hall full of crystal and candles and mirrors amplifying the light. Musicians played in the corner. Tyressa heard faint strains of the music—not because it was truly faint, but because the drumming of her heart all but shut it out.

Garath's smile grew. He was not the man he had been at the dance, but an older version—the age he would be if he returned today. Gray had grown into his blond locks, but his hair had not thinned nor lost its luster. More lines tugged at the corners of his eyes and mouth, and a scar she'd not seen before curled up lazily from throat to beneath his left ear.

That cannot be true. That cut would have killed him.

They closed, and his right arm encircled her, pressed firmly between her shoulder blades. He drew her close, not crushing her in a hug, but holding her as he had when they danced. She luxuriated in his touch, feeling pressure here or there, moving with it, the two of them perfectly matched. As he led the dance, she followed—knowing he would lead her through steps that would make her smile and laugh.

Tyressa didn't know if it was her imagination, or even if she was moving, but Garath felt real, and she wanted him to be real. His arms encircling her became fortress walls which kept fears at bay. She drew warmth from him and relished the press of his body against hers once more.

She laid her cheek against his shoulder for a second, then pulled back, looking into his eyes as they spun round and round. He returned her smile. She knew the expression well. Bemusement mixed with disbelief at his fortune. He'd worn it the night they met, the day they wed, and both times he was introduced to his children. What they were sharing was impossible, and yet neither of them wished to deny it.

He lowered his mouth to hers. She felt his breath on her cheeks and the soft, moist touch of their lips. She kissed him urgently, wanting to share the love she still had for him. The love kept alive by seeing him in his children every day.

Then she completed a circle and he was gone. His warmth lingered, but the palace and finery evaporated into wisps of smoke swirling away from her. Once again she stood in the middle of the fey camp, and came around to face Ellesaara.

She saw. They all saw.

The elf eyed her closely. "You have no idea, do you?"

Oreena stepped between them. "It's not what she's done, Ellesaara, but what she and her family represent to the wood."

The elf thrust a finger toward Jerrad. "The wood meant to have him slain."

"But it allowed another to balance that outcome." Oreena's eyes half-closed. "The wood sees the Vishovs as balance for other outcomes."

"I think, Oreena, you credit the wood with more wisdom than is prudent, and more prescience than it could ever possess."

"I merely credit it with compassion and caution." The old woman shrugged. "Still, were the Vishovs the threat you believe them to be, would not the wood have already swallowed them whole?"

The elf shifted her gaze to Tyressa. "The man in the vision was your husband?"

"Is. Yes."

"Do you understand what the vision means?"

Oreena shook her head. "What it *may* mean."

"The wood showed him to you because you have love for him. You agreed to abide with him. The wood wishes this same commitment from you. As you became one with your husband, so you will become one with Echo Wood. You *and* your family."

Tyressa glanced down at her hands. They still felt warm from Garath's touch. "My husband told me that the only reason he dared go off to war was because he had no fear for our children. He told me he trusted me to keep them safe and to give him a reason to return, and a place to return to. I will keep our children. I will make Silverlake that place. If Echo Wood demands that commitment from me, and will keep my children and my people safe, then we have a bargain."

She held a hand out toward Ellesaara. "The wood cherishes you. If I'm to succeed, it will only be through the wisdom you share with me. Can we reach accord on that point?"

The elf made no move to take her hand, but turned toward Jerrad's cage. "Free the boy."

Tyressa smiled as Jerrad emerged. As he did so, the feathers on the cap and cloak became a riot of color. A smile blossomed on a dirty face, and Tyressa's chest eased. The fey withdrew quickly from around the hut and spread apart along his path.

Jerrad came running down the hill. Tyressa half expected him to throw his arms around her in a hug, but he drew himself up still several steps off and turned toward Ellesaara.

"Thank you for the lend of the cap and cloak." His fingers plucked at the knot at his throat. "I don't think I lost any feathers."

The elf raised a hand. "They're yours. An offering." She nodded toward Oreena. "An apology. And, perhaps, the basis for future discussion."

Jerrad bowed deeply toward her, then looked back up the hill as if seeking someone else. As he turned back around Tyressa read concern on his face, but it vanished with a shrug. "I'm sorry for any trouble, Mother."

"I only care that you're safe." Tyressa draped an arm over his shoulders and steered him back in the direction from whence he had come. "Nothing else matters."

Later that evening, as the expedition's camp settled for the night, Tyressa took herself to the edge of the hill. She stared out at Silvershade Lake and the silvery ribbon moonlight splashed across it. Though weariness made her bones ache, she forced herself to smile at the lake's beauty. It, the beauty of her children, and the kindnesses and hard work of her people made hardship easy to forget.

She hugged her arms around herself, seeking the last bit of Garath's warmth. Melancholy lurked at the back of her mind, but she forced herself to remember him and smile. *You kept your promise. You came back to me.*

She studied the lake a bit longer, then sensed a presence. She spoke to the night. "Are you the one to whom I owe my son's life?"

"From what I saw, *you* saved your son's life." The deep voice matched the gentle undulation of the water and seemed woven into the fabric of the night. It came welcome to her ears, carrying with it a weariness she could fully understand.

"He told me how you killed the wolves, then returned to the fey camp to rescue him." Tyressa turned toward the half-elf sliding from darkness. "He called you Kiiryth."

"At your service.»

Tyressa took him in with a measured glance, reading him as father had taught her to do. The half-elf had a bow and arrows slung across his back, and a long knife at his left hip. She had no doubt another knife rode at the small of his back, and the hilt of another protruded from the top of his left boot. He wore leather, which would suit him well in the wood, with enough patching to attest to his skill at leatherwork, and to hint at a legion of well-hidden scars beneath.

She cocked her head. "What's your family name?"

Kiiryth shook his head, then smiled. "If I had a family, I'd have a use for a family name."

"I see. Well then, Kiiryth, I offer you my thanks." She waved a hand back toward her camp. "And I invite you to join our family here. You've done me a great service, and allowing you to enjoy our hospitality, though meager, is the best reward I can offer."

"I'm not ungrateful, but I must refuse."

"Please, reconsider. We need people like you." She frowned. "What am I missing?"

"Your offer, though generous, is not mine to accept. I am not my own master."

Is he a spy? "Who is he? I would speak to your master."

Kiiryth held up both hands. "My master bears you no ill will, my lady. He would not inconvenience you with a parlay."

"But you will convey my best wishes to him?"

"It would be a pleasure." The archer watched her closely. "Did you truly mean what you said amid the fey? You are creating a home here. You will not be persuaded to do otherwise?"

"This is our home. My family's future is Silverlake. There is no *otherwise*."

"So I thought." Kiiryth gave her a tiny bow. "Let us both hope that neither the wood nor other forces suffer from a differing opinion."

Chapter Seven
Familiar Territory

The two days following his rescue from the fey dawned gray, and got darker and a whole lot wetter. It seemed to most of the folks in the Silverlake camp that the clouds were just some sort of big waterwheel, taking water from the lake and dumping it on them in buckets. Fires struggled to stay lit, the campground became a swamp, wagons got mired to their axles, and tents collapsed into soggy messes.

The only thing that stopped it from being completely intolerable was that the weather didn't turn cold. The rain remained warm—not near a bath, but warm enough that Jerrad could be out in it a while before shivering set in. Most men in the camp did what he did, which was to strip down to trousers and not worry about mud that would wash off in the next cloudburst. The difference was that they looked like men, whereas he looked like a skinny, soaked, half-drowned mouse slipping and sliding through every boggy bit of ground there was.

Because of the deluge, everyone kept largely to camp. Jerrad's mother used the weather as an excuse to keep him close, and he didn't mind too much. The fact that she let him run around half-naked like the other men meant he could pretend he was more grown-up than he really felt inside.

He'd fought being afraid while a captive, and tolerated a lot of good-natured ribbing upon his return. There were even times when he forgot all about his ordeal. Those moments came when he was laughing about someone else slipping in the mud, or was eyeballs deep in it himself and being laughed at.

At night, though, in the dark and trying to fall asleep, the fear slithered in, silent and shiny. People might laugh at him when he fell in the mud, but that was because he'd been careless. The fey had dressed him up and commanded him to act foolishly. Had he refused, they would have *forced* him to act foolishly. They'd granted him no illusion of freedom, no real dignity, and there'd not been a single thing he could do about it.

He'd never had that experience before. Throughout his life, he'd been a Vishov. In Ustalav he had people looking out for him. Even if there weren't retainers around—as with his long rambles through the estates—all the shepherds and crofters knew who he was. His being a Vishov protected him.

But here, that's what made me a target.

Jerrad wasn't so naive that he imagined his Vishov blood might not have made him a target in Ustalav. Though he'd not read as many of the Kindler adventuring novels as Serrana, in several of the ones he had read, at some point some young noble gets kidnapped and held for ransom, just because he's from a noble family. *And because it gives an adventurer someone to rescue to get noticed at court.* Somewhere in his head, he knew that portions of the world might act against him—he'd just never seen evidence of it.

He'd also never felt it in his heart. Being held captive and helpless mocked who he thought he was. Sure, he'd never be the hero his father was, but at least he could become a man his father might have liked. The fey proved he wasn't anywhere near grown.

I'm really just a mouse. It didn't matter that he was smart. All the intelligence in the world hadn't helped him elude them or escape. Echo Wood wasn't a civilized place where Jerrad could do well. He'd gotten lucky so far, and was pretty sure the wood wouldn't be as forgiving the next time.

After the rain let up, Jerrad forced himself to go back out exploring. He set aside his grand plans for figuring out how the wood's magic worked and confined himself to more useful tasks. He started out to catalogue as many of the flowers, herbs, and berries as he could find, but made a few other discoveries of note.

The biggest was that the heavy rains had succeeded in widening and deepening a stream. They washed away rocks and dirt right down to bedrock, creating a ten-foot drop into a broad pool. The stream, which before had meandered down a hillside, now provided a perfect place to build a small mill.

The flooding had also washed a considerable amount of wood down to the lake, and retreating tides had left plenty of it stacked up on the shore for the taking. That made collecting firewood a job that didn't require much travel.

Jerrad, who did a fair bit of firewood harvesting, also noted that the piles didn't shrink as fast as they should have. The settlers made no concerted effort to clear one specific area of the beach, but piles that had shrunk before dark recovered fairly well by dawn. Though he looked for signs of who or what had done that, he found no tracks in the sand.

He decided that nixies were responsible and took that as a hopeful sign. Still, he had no solid evidence that this was true. He did ask around for what people knew of nixies, seeking a way he could reward them, but no one knew much at all about the aquatic fey folk.

As much as they might be helpful, the sprites were not. They bedeviled him on his scouting expeditions. If he bent down to look at a mushroom or a flower, a pine cone would bounce off his skull—and that with the nearest pine a hundred yards away. Jerrad became convinced the sprites taught squirrels to drop acorns on him. Every time he tripped, little laughs echoed. Branches would spring around to smack him in the face and nettles managed to get lodged in all sorts of interesting places.

By the end of two weeks his patience had been tattered beyond recovery. Walking over level ground, he tripped and sprawled face-first in the loam. He tried to heave himself up, but the earth gave way beneath his left hand and knee. He rolled down a hill, snapping deadwood branches and getting whipped in the face by ferns.

And somewhere in there, in a whooshing of wings, something stuffed a bramble down his back.

At the bottom of a muddy depression, reeking of rotted leaves, needles, and mud, he reared up and shrieked. Cold muck oozed into his shoes. He ripped off his tunic, then tore away the bramble. He went to flick it away, but the needles stuck in his fingers.

"Stop it, stop it, stop it, damn it, stop it!" He swatted at the bramble with his shirt, catching it in the cloth again, and tearing it free of his flesh. Most of it, anyway. He could feel the needles still there, but they remained hidden in the dark mud coating his hands. "Just stop it!"

"Got a problem?"

Jerrad spun at the sound, but his feet remained mired. His legs twisted around and he sat abruptly in the mud. He pulled the shirt up to cover himself, sticking the bramble into his chest.

Nelsa arched an eyebrow at him. "Ain't the best mud for sitting in, is it?"

"You going to laugh at me, too?"

"Maybe, if you do something funny." Nelsa dropped to a knee and grabbed a stick of wood which was taller than she was and mostly straight. "You might find this handy."

Jerrad caught it when she tossed it. He shifted around, hating the squelching sound the mud made, untangling his legs. He pulled one foot free, but the mud kept his shoe. The foot's coming up fast caused him to lose what little balance he had, and he splashed down again.

He looked up at Nelsa Murdoon, hoping the mud would just drag him down completely. "It's okay, you can laugh."

She gave him a half-smile. "You meaning to tell me you ain't down there on purpose?"

"Why would I be down here deliberately?"

"The way I hear it told, you work at finding the best mud around. As I said, that ain't the best mud for sitting or caulking. That's a sprite bog."

"A *spite* bog, more like." Jerrad chucked his muddied tunic in her direction. It didn't make it, landing shy of the hill in a bubbling puddle. "Great."

"Been called a spite bog more than once." Nelsa found another stick and fished around for his tunic. "The sprites, they gather the stinkiest weeds they can find come fall—soured berries, other things, too—and just mush it all around. Hollow like this fills with snow and melts slow. If it were spring, you'd be wishing you was a fish long about now."

"And they just chase people into these things for fun, right?"

"I've heard that opinion before. My aunt's husband Yarnin, he's in these bogs more than he's out of them. But I tell you what . . ."

"Yes?"

"See that green leaf plant there, with the purple edging?"

Jerrad reached over and lifted up a trio of leaves. "This one?"

"Yeah. You don't want to be touching that."

Jerrad's hand recoiled. "What is it?"

"We call it roast-weed. Makes your hand feel like it's on fire."

The youth stared at his hand. "What do I do?"

"See, like I was telling you, the mud there in the sprite bog, it's good for quenching that fire. You won't so much as get an itch. None of them pustules, cuz they ain't pretty, and when they bust open and run . . . well, that stink, you'll be thinking this mud is flowers by comparison."

Jerrad immediately plunged his hand deep into the mud. "What did your uncle do to make the sprites mad at him? I mean, they hate me."

"Oh, this don't mean they hate you." She started wringing his tunic out. "See, sprites, they have a wicked sense of humor, and they like someone can make them laugh. Now, they got you in here to show you this sprite mud. It's obvious to them you're learning the wood, and as far as they're concerned, sprite bogs is the most important thing to know about because of roast-weed."

Jerrad fished around for his shoe and pulled it free with a great sucking sound. "Really? The sprites like me?"

"Well, that's what my uncle says." Nelsa stood. "Of course, he ain't been right in the head since the horse kicked him."

"If this is liking me, I don't want to see hate."

"Ain't any that do." She came halfway down the hill and anchored her foot on a stone. "Give me the dry end of that pole and I can help you out."

He did as she requested and shortly thereafter, soaking wet and smelling like something which had spent a long time composting, Jerrad cleared mud from his shoes. "Thank you."

"I wouldn't thank me. Seems like the only time I come around you, mud up and puts you at a disadvantage."

"Maybe someday I'll be smarter than mud."

"Be a big help if that comes sooner rather than later."

Jerrad stood. "I guess I should go wash myself off."

"Lye soap and a brush. Clothes you'll have to boil." She smiled. "I can fetch you back a quick way."

"I'm pretty sure I know how I got here."

"I don't doubt it. I cut your track three-four times coming along."

"Ah, *not* the quick way."

"Not exactly."

Jerrad frowned. "What *are* you doing out here? Not that I'm not glad to see you—sprite bog or no."

"I was sent to fetch you." She started trudging through the wood and he followed. "My pa, couple of my brothers, an aunt, and some cousins came to see your Silverlake. Word got around you weren't washed away, so pa figured it was right to visit."

"Word got around?"

"It does in the wood."

"Was it Kiiryth?"

Nelsa glanced back over her shoulder. "Don't believe I know that name."

"Half-elf, good with a bow, white hair worn long." Jerrad clapped his shoes together, knocking mud off them. "He killed some wolves that were after me."

"Can't say he's known to me." She shrugged her broad shoulders. "But there's all kinds come through the wood. 'Nother uncle named Qant says he's found another Broken Man camp up north. That would make for four in the wood. Could be your Kiiryth was one of them, or something else entirely."

"He didn't seem friendly with Ellesaara."

"That don't narrow it down much."

"Not really a surprise." Jerrad scraped more mud off his shoes and was about to ask Nelsa another question when he looked up and found himself at Silverlake. "Quick way I guess."

"Ain't so much about knowing where you want to go, as avoiding where you don't want to be." She winked at him. "Those there are my people."

At the settlement's heart stood a tall, beefy man, florid of face, with a bulbous nose and thick mane of wavy white hair. Two men flanked him, clearly his sons, with one looking twenty years younger and the other looking barely twenty years old. A woman and three children hung back near a small goat cart piled high with things hidden beneath a shroud.

"The big one, he's my pa, Tunk. Then my brother, Five, and my brother, Mulish. He got that name on account of he's always been a bit stubborn. Mind you, among the Murdoons, for us to take note of that means he's *real* stubborn."

Tunk Murdoon stood opposite Tyressa. "And again, Mister Murdoon, I can't thank you enough for your daughter's intercession on Jerrad's behalf in town. In fact, it looks as if she may have rescued him again."

Tunk sniffed the air. "Gots boggy, did he?"

"Sprites was engaged learning him things."

Jerrad shrugged and remained downwind. "I'm just soggy, Mother."

Tunk nodded once, solemnly. "Well, now that the man of the clan is here, we can commence our parlay."

Jerrad's mother smiled. "While it is true that my son is the eldest male in our family, Ustalav allows for women to head up a clan."

"I be aware of that, Lady Vishov, but I ain't gonna have it be said that Tunk Murdoon done bullied a woman into anything." He jerked a thumb over his shoulder at the cart. "Now, we done brung along some things, cheeses and bacon, some cloth bolts and skins, and a basket of apples from the cellar as crisp as the day they was picked last year. And if your folks here don't mind it, I can be bringing by a cask of hard cider."

"Your generosity is appreciated." Tyressa spread her arms. "As you can see, I'm afraid we don't have anything to trade."

Tunk ran a big hand over his jaw. "Mayhap you don't, not right now. Didn't really expect you would have anything. But us Murdoons, we don't mind thinking further down the road. See, we do think you have something of value here, and I'll pay a fair price. Three goats and a milk cow. Ain't going to get a better offer around here."

Tyressa's eyebrows arrowed down. "I'm sure that's a fair price. Generous, even. What would it be for?"

The Murdoon patriarch slapped his younger son on the back. "This here is my boy Mulish. He needs himself a wife, and I figure your daughter will suit him just fine."

Chapter Eight
Forging Alliances

Jerrad looked from Tunk Murdoon's earnest face to his mother's expression. It approached placidity, but only after a flash of widened eyes and flared nostrils. Jerrad managed not to gasp, and closed his throat against a laugh—though a bit of it escaped in a snort.

Mostly, though, he listened. His sister's screams could be sharper than a dagger, and her words could shatter shields and rend mail. *If she heard this offer. . . .*

His mother glanced back toward the lake, then smiled. "Mister Murdoon, that's an incredible offer. I can truthfully say that I never imagined Serrana fetching that much. And while I'm happy to consider your offer, I have to tell you, I'm not certain my daughter is worth that much. Not here in Echo Wood. Not yet, anyway."

"As I allowed, Lady Vishov, it's something to be considered for the future. I know you're all still settling in. Mulish—the map." Tunk walked over to a small table upon which Jerrad's mother had laid out a map of what would become Silverlake. Tunk only grunted as his younger son handed him a scrolled map, then he unrolled it and let his sons hold the corners down.

Jerrad approached the table and stood opposite his mother and Tunk, which put him beside Nelsa. The Murdoon map showed Echo Wood in greater detail than the maps they'd gotten in Ustalav. In addition to landmarks and towns appearing on the parchment, areas had been shaded different colors. Blue marked the area around the Murdoon compound and sent tendrils off within the wood.

Tunk tapped the heart of the blue area with a thick finger. His nail had split, but had much less dirt under it than either of his sons had under theirs. "This here is our land. These bits here, those are our traplines. You can get fox, hare, muskrat, and beaver. You'll see we don't have anything down by the lake here. You can get good fish: cutthroat, bighead, gnawfish. Some of the gnawfish run long as your arm, and have teeth sharp enough to take a finger. Take as much as you want, but don't be netting. Nixies hate nets. Leave them some of the fish heads and a half-share of the gnawfish, they'll leave you be."

Tyressa nodded. "We'd thought to set up a smokehouse . . ."

"You'll be wanting to set up two. The one for fish down to the shore. I'll have Mulish show you the high point of spring floods. The other you'll put over toward the west. Winds come from the north in winter, south in summer. Don't want hungry beasts wandering through Silverlake to get what you're smoking."

"Excellent point, thank you." Jerrad's mother ran a finger down the stream leading to the lake. "The storms eroded the bed. We were thinking of putting a mill here. Baron Blackshield suggested we make it a lumber mill."

"Short term likely a wise idea, being as how finished lumber has to come from Thornkeep."

Jerrad's brow knotted. "Why would he suggest we do something that will cost Thornkeep money?"

"Sharp mind in that skull." Tunk gave Jerrad a nod. "Belike he's having a squabble with some of the lumbermen. More like if you were to make it a grain mill, you'll open some pastures, start raising corn and wheat, and the money he makes off that trade would collapse. Us Murdoons, we do for ourselves and a bit more, but a sack of meal coming out of Thornkeep might as well be gold-sand."

"Mister Murdoon, do you run sheep on your land?"

"Two dozen. We do for ourselves, as I said."

"And Mother Oreena." Tyressa smiled. "She was spinning thread when I met her."

"Could have been our wool. Or spider silk. Never know with her." Tunk folded his arms over his chest. "Wool can go dear in Thornkeep. I'll allow as how we sell a bit here and there, mostly for nails and hinges, that kind of thing."

"Of course. I've brought a smith and I understand there are iron deposits in the area."

"We know where one or two are." The Murdoon patriarch gave Tyressa an appraising stare. "You're asking the right questions, seems to me. Your boy 'pears to be bright when he ain't bog-bound, so I'm going to be making you this offer: I'll give you the lend of a couple of my boys, and some nephews and some cousins what have sense. They'll make some things apparent to you. Winter will be blowing in here faster than anyone wants. You'll be wanting to be ready for it."

"Again, Mister Murdoon, you're being very generous. I don't know that I can repay you."

"Well now, here's the thing: you'll repay me in kind. Come fall, we'll be clearing some space for Mulish and he's going to need a barn raised and a house built. You have strong backs here, and folks what know the hitting end of a hammer from the grabbing. I've a feeling you'll be around then, so I'll wager my sweat now against yours later."

"I appreciate your confidence in us. And value your help." Tyressa smiled. "I also suspect that we'll have smoked fish to barter before we have much of anything else."

"We'll talk about that. And as fall comes, maybe we'll we wanting some folks to be picking apples in our orchards, and gathering nuts in the forest. Won't pay in gold, but in shares."

"I believe, Mister Murdoon, we have a working agreement." Tyressa extended her hand to the man.

Tunk stared at it for a moment, then took it delicately before dropping to a knee before her. "Honored, my Lady."

Jerrad's mother closed her hand on Tunk's and tugged, compelling the man to rise. "No, sir, no titles. This is not Ustalav, and I'm no longer ennobled. Here we are equals, and it pleases me to imagine I've earned that status."

The older man's eyes tightened, then he nodded. "Well now, Lady Vishov, I'll be proud to be your equal, but I must be mannerly. My wife would cut my throat while I snored if I didn't address you as proper. You may not be in Ustalav, and some foolishness might have stripped you of your title, but we Murdoons are brought up right. Just as owning a castle don't make Tervin Blackshield a baron, don't living in a tent make you less than a lady."

"You're very kind."

"That ain't often said of me." Tunk smiled. "And my wife, she done told me that when it's convenient, she would be calling on you."

"It will be my pleasure to meet her. Any time is convenient."

"We'll be taking our leave, then." Tunk patted the goat on the head. "I'll be sending the girl to bring the cart back. No hurry. Goat might need some milking until then."

"Thank you, Mr. Murdoon."

Jerrad smiled at Nelsa. "Thanks for helping me out of the bog."

"Better I acquainted you with roast-weed and the cure." She winked at him, then turned to follow her family home.

Tyressa slid her arm over his shoulders, warming him despite the wet. "Curious people, but good people. There *is* nobility in Echo Wood."

"It's good to have friends." He glanced up at his mother. "Are you going to tell Serra, or can I do it?"

"Why would a mouse want to anger a cat?"

Jerrad's guts flip-flopped. "So, *when* are you going to tell her?"

Tyressa laughed. "Does it matter? You'll hear her reaction no matter how far away you get."

"Yeah, but with warning I can get further than she can throw."

The moment of reckoning became delayed when Serrana returned from the lakeshore. She'd not liked gathering firewood, but had located some very pretty stones. Jerrad didn't think much of them, but he'd seen their like in streams or on shores back in Ustalav. Granted these might glitter a bit more, but they'd been worn smooth by the endless washing of waves. That they amused her was more than enough reason for him to keep his mouth shut.

And while he washed himself off in the lake, he found a few more pretty stones to distract her in the future.

The next morning he got up early, finished his chores as quickly as he could, and headed back into the wood. His previous journeys had been meant for exploration, but the Murdoon intervention pointed out that general exploration wasn't going to be of much use to Silverlake. The things he dug up would be valuable later, but the settlement had more pressing needs.

Jerrad started south of the camp and noted all the stands of hard woods and straight trees. He located beeches and chestnuts, as well as the overgrown remnant of an orchard. The apples might be a bit mealy, but they'd do just fine feeding the pigs. He also found deer scat, which made sense since they'd come to eat the apples, too. The settlement's huntsmen or the Murdoons could make good use of that information.

He also looked around for signs of rabbits and other varmints that could be taken for meat and fur. He found some tracks in mud, but they changed as he followed them. *Either this creature shifted shape, or the sprites are having fun with me again.*

"You started with a marten's track, but lost it on the other side of that log."

Jerrad whipped around. "Kiiryth?"

The half-elf took a bite of an apple, then got a sour look on his face as he chewed. "Horrible, but beggars can't be choosers."

"My mother said you didn't want to join us."

"Want is different from ability, Jerrad. You have obligations. So do I." The archer smiled. "Silverlake has made strides."

"We could be further along if you joined us."

Kiiryth swallowed another bite of apple. "You're persistent. That's good."

"But not convincing?" Jerrad sighed. "We need someone like you. Someone with your experience. A hero."

"A hero, like your father?"

Jerrad blinked. "You've heard of my father?"

"I've traveled a great deal. Rumors in the wood have allowed me to connect names with stories." Kiiryth tossed the apple core over his shoulder. "I am, alas, nothing like your father."

Jerrad arched an eyebrow. "But you have to be a hero."

"Why? Because I saved you from the wolves?" Kiiryth nodded once. "That may have been a heroic act, but it doesn't make me a hero. On the other hand, choosing to come here to form Silverlake—that's the stuff of heroes. Your mother, she's a hero. She saved you from the fey. And I tell you what, if she hadn't, you'd have saved yourself."

Jerrad's gaze hardened. "I couldn't have escaped."

"You were halfway to freedom, Jerrad. You'd found the Lake."

"Finding the path isn't making the journey."

"I may have underestimated you. New tactics." The half-elf played a hand along his jaw. "Let me ask you: why is your father a hero?"

"Because, you know, he was big and strong and could use an axe like no one else. He was a fearsome warrior."

"Dig a bit deeper. Do you think the first time he used an axe was to hew down men? Or was it to split wood?"

"Wood, I guess."

"And he grew tall and strong, and did so in a place where he was more highly valued as a warrior than he would have been here, say, as a woodsman."

"What are you saying? That he's not a hero?" Jerrad balled his fists. "He was."

"You won't hear me disagree. Garath Sharpax did many heroic things. That doesn't mean he started life as a hero, though. It doesn't mean he intended to be a hero. He started out using an axe, and found more ways to use it." Kiiryth gave Jerrad a quick grin. "And what I would suggest of you is that you're in the same situation."

"Great. I'll get an axe and start chopping down trees."

"Not my point." The half-elf's chin came up. "When you decided to test the magic in the wood, why did you use a circle and a cross."

Jerrad shrugged. "It seemed the easiest way to track things."

"Good. Among some people, it's believed that to control magic or evil after a person's death, it's best to bury the person at a crossroads. That way he can't follow anyone home. More importantly, if that cross is surrounded by a circle road, the spirit will forever wander within its confines."

"I didn't know that."

Kiiryth pressed his hands together at his waist. "Did you notice that when the fey moved your sticks, they planted them the way you first had, with no rotation of the cross or the stakes themselves?"

The youth's face scrunched up. "Yes."

"They did that not to trick you, but because they didn't see the shift. You did, but to anyone else, the stakes hadn't moved at all."

"But that's not . . ." Jerrad's stomach began to knot up. "What are you saying?"

"One other thing. What did the feathered cloak look like to you?"

"It was all bright and colorful, but when it passed into the cage it became dull."

Kiiryth raised an eyebrow. "When it passed into the cage, or when it passed into your *hand*?"

Jerrad stood stock still. He reviewed the events in his mind. The cloak lost *some* color when it passed into the cage's shade. *But it retained it until I touched it.*

He looked up at Kiiryth. "Enough games. What are you saying?"

"Different people have different talents. Your father's size and strength and courage made him perfect to be a great fighter. You don't have those things. What you do have, however, are all the signs of being talented at wizardry."

"What? No. That can't be." Jerrad shook his head. "No one in my family has ever been a wizard. That takes training, and I've never . . ."

"Training, certainly, but evidencing an affinity for magic is often how students are chosen."

"But I didn't." Jerrad frowned. "You're wrong. I can't be."

"I know what I saw, son. You *were* on the way to rescuing yourself from the fey. When they saw the cloak lose color, and then regain it with your joy at seeing your mother again, they understood. You have *talent,* and the wood favors you. Had your mother not intervened, Ellesaara's speech would have ended with her taking you back to Silverlake so she could speak with your mother there."

"The fey would be more afraid of the wood than they would be of my being a wizard."

"You're likely not wrong, but that doesn't mean you're right, either."

Jerrad dropped to his knees, his mouth hanging open. "Even if what you say is true, it's wrong. Silverlake doesn't need a wizard."

The half-elf's smile broadened. "You're a wise lad. If Echo Wood was a battlefield, then Silverlake would need a hero like your father. But who's better suited to dealing with a land steeped in magic? A wizard, or your father?"

"A wizard, of course, but I'm not a wizard." Jerrad glanced down at his open, impotent hands. "I can't do anything."

Kiiryth opened a pouch at his right hip and pulled out a small, leather-bound volume. A leather thong, slightly darker than the book's cover, had been knotted around it. "This is something I think was meant for you. Study what's within. I think you'll find it useful."

"What if I can't understand it?"

"That wouldn't be good." Kiiryth tossed him the book. "If this doesn't work, chances are a whole legion of heroes couldn't save Silverlake from what the future will bring."

Chapter Nine
Bargains Good and Bad

T hree cows and a *goat*!"

Tyressa, her head beginning to pound, thought better than to correct her daughter's impression. "Serrana . . ."

The young woman stabbed a finger accusingly at the goat tethered at the edge of the camp. "You even kept the goat as a down payment! You're going to marry me off to some half-wit cheese maker so I can have half a dozen grubby brats running around eating mud, grunting and picking lice off each other. No. No! I hate you. I hate this place. I want to go home!"

Tyressa forced her fist open. "Lower your voice, Serrana!"

"No, I won't! I want everyone to know!"

"You'll lower your voice, or I'll marry you off to one of Blackshield's get—and do without the cheese." Her blue eyes narrowed. "If you thought for a moment—thought as I know you're capable of doing—you'd understand the true importance of the offer."

"You can't seriously be considering . . ."

"One more word out of you, and I'll trade you for a handful of beans and a promise of a sunny day next spring."

Serrana stared at her mother, her lower lip trembling.

Cold claws closed around Tyressa's heart. *I don't want to hurt you, my child, but better a tiny sting than having your flesh torn off.* She took in a deep breath, then forced herself to exhale slowly.

"Whether or not you marry a Murdoon is immaterial. When Tunk Murdoon came here, he had a map of the area. He pointed out where his family set traplines, which told me where our trappers can put their lines out—to avoid a conflict with the Murdoons, and to get a good yield. He suggested a fishery."

"You were already doing that."

"I was, but he agreed to trade for smoked fish. Plus he told me how to handle the nixies." Tyressa nodded toward the forge just west of where the goat bleated. "He offered to show us iron deposits and suggested we might want to plant corn and wheat, as well as raise sheep. Now, you're a smart girl. Why would he do that?"

Serrana shook her head. "I don't know."

"You do know. It's your strength, reading social politics."

"He probably doesn't like the Blackshields any more than you do."

"Good." Tyressa nodded. "And his offer to marry you to his son—forget the price—what did that offer portend?"

The young woman sighed heavily, half-deflating as she did so. "He was offering you an alliance, cheese lord to an Ustalavic noble."

"Out here, you're not a noble."

"I *know*, Mother. I have one servant. *One*. All my good things remained home. I have no friends. You wouldn't let me bring my books. I have nothing."

"You are what you do here, Serrana."

"And I can't do anything." The girl's gaze sharpened. "I wasn't raised to *do* anything."

Tyressa's heart caught in her throat. The girl was right. From the moment she'd taken her first breath, Serrana's life had been determined. She'd been taught the important things—the things she'd need to know as an Ustalavic noblewoman. She could dance. She could sew a bit, and could be charming. Growing up in her mother's shadow, and later as her aide in the Vishov court, she'd learned to navigate political rapids. She could soothe ruffled feathers or find the heart with a stiletto-ish comment.

But here, she's been robbed of all that. Tyressa still saw politics in the way she had to deal with settlers or the fey or the Murdoons. The same games got played, but the stakes were so much lower that Serrana saw it all as being beneath her. She'd been torn from the only environment she'd known. She'd thrived there. Here, she would wither and die.

Tyressa crossed the open-walled tent to her daughter and reached out to caress her cheek. "Serrana . . ."

The girl turned from her. "Isn't it enough that you've taken me away from everything, Mother? Telling me that talking to farmers and fishwives and bandit lordlings is the same as being at court is disgusting. *You* may choose to believe that, but I know it's not true. I hate it. I hate being here. I hate *you*."

Before Tyressa could start in again, commotion to the west interrupted her. One of the fishwives came running toward the tent. "What is it?"

"Men. From the forest. They have axes."

"I'll be right there." Tyressa turned to her daughter. "This isn't over, Serrana. You hate being here. I understand that. But hating this place, hating me, isn't going to return you to Ustalav. Accept that."

Tyressa stalked from the tent, keeping her head up. She wore simple clothes—a thin woolen gown gathered at the waist by a belt. Most days she wore boots, but she hadn't put them on that morning. The skinning knife she normally kept in the right boot she'd transferred to the small of her back. Aside from her bearing, and the fact that her clothes were in better repair than those of most others, no one would have picked her out as special in the settlement.

A small crowd had gathered at the western edge of the camp. A half-dozen tall men in leathers and well worn tunics formed a semi-circle behind a rotund man. He'd not shaved in a while, making his toadish aspect even more grotesque. His being bald, save for a few liver-spots, and his propensity for blinking, did nothing to approve his appearance.

"I am Tyressa Vishov of Silverlake."

The big man took one look at her, then spat at her feet. "Pine Callum."

"What can I do for you, Mister Callum?"

The men backing Pine smiled through thick beards. "It's what I'm doing for you." The man pointed at four men. "I'm taking them to join my crew. They'll be cutting wood for me."

"Indeed." Tyressa kept her face impassive. "And what makes you think they want to work for you?"

"I don't think that, and don't much care what they think." Pine spat again, shifting a bulging lump of something from inside one cheek to the other. "You folks here got the fey all riled up. Went out to find one of my crews and they was gone. Only found their tools, so I need men to work 'em. Yours will do."

"I see. And why is it that you think I'll agree to this piracy?"

"Being as how I got my biggest men with me, and another twenty working the woods, and you ain't got spit, I guess I can take them." He smiled at her with teeth stained green and spotted with vegetation. "I got me a contract with the mill in Thornkeep. Iffen I'm late, I don't get paid but a quarter what I get if I'm on time."

"I understand your motive. What does Silverlake get out of this?"

The man's blinking sped up. "What do you get? Nothing. I ain't paying you nothing." He stepped forward and grabbed her chin in a fat hand. "Course, when we get paid, we might just come back here to celebrate. Your menfolk ain't much, but your women are kind of easy on the eyes."

Tyressa tried to shake her head, but Pine hung on tight. "You might wish to reconsider, Mister Callum."

"You can't honestly be that dumb."

"Not dumb." Tyressa shifted her right hand forward. "What you feel pressing hard against your loins is a skinning knife with a very sharp hook. If you pull back, or I pull up, you'll lose bits I think you consider precious. You'll want to let go of my chin."

"You wouldn't dare."

Steady, Tyressa, steady. "Do you know the story of how I grew to love my husband? Garath Sharpax. He may be known to you."

Pine's grip remained firm. "I don't recollect hearing that name. Or yours, before today."

"I can't expect River Kingdoms bandits to know much of the world, can I?" Tyressa stared into his piggish eyes. "When I was young, my father decided his children should be able to defend themselves. My brother didn't take to it much, but I did. My father entrusted me to Garath for training. This began a strange courtship. Do you want to know what we did for fun?"

"I don't . . ."

"Of course you do." Tyressa raised the knife a hair. "We used to go hunting. Hunting highwaymen and other unsavory creatures. I wasn't much older than my daughter when I gigged my first bandit, and I have to say, you're not even half his size."

She heard gasps from among the settlers, but ignored them and looked at Callum's men. "Your master has decided *his* fate, but yours is still open. Silverlake's going to be a good town. You may like living in the woods now, but is your life *now* the one you want for your children? Do you really have a future out there? If a tree doesn't drop on you, or a blizzard freeze you, or lightning kill you, you know Callum's just waiting to cheat you out of a fair wage."

As she spoke, Tyressa slammed her right shoulder against Callum, knocking him back over the leg she'd hooked behind his. He crashed flat on his back, both hands going for his groin. She held the skinning knife aloft, a swatch of brown homespun caught on the hook.

"How about it, Pine? How much for the wood in Thornkeep? How much was your share?"

"I have costs, you know. They eat."

Tyressa looked past him. "And he charges you for that food, yes, and for your tools? Docks your pay if something goes missing, and *something* always goes missing, yes?"

One of the woodsmen nodded.

She shook her head. "Highwaymen treated their hires better."

"I take care of my men. Better care than they take of themselves."

"Here's the offer: You come to Silverlake. You cut wood for us. You learn to build—giving you some skills you can take anywhere. You can winter here, stay longer if you want. As long as you're peaceful, we won't have a problem."

Another of the woodcutters took a step forward. "What he said about the fey be the truth. They got some of ours."

"Taking wood where they shouldn't have been?"

The man shifted his shoulders. "Might could be. But one of 'em's my little brother."

This really isn't your fight. "I'll see what I can do. No promises." Tyressa exhaled slowly. "You'll want to speak to the others."

"Beg pardon, my Lady, ain't no others." A tall man leaned forward on his axe handle. "Pine don't have no problem lying as needed."

"Apparently. If you want to join us, you'll need to gather your things. Let Pine go where he will. If you know the mill with which he had the deal, I'll send Lord Sunnock to renegotiate." She resheathed the skinner at the small of her back. "Is that acceptable?"

The woodsmen exchanged glances, then nodded. Two came forward to drag Pine Callum away.

Tyressa turned and found Serrana standing there, not ten feet away, wide-eyed, arms hugging her stomach. She wanted to speak to her daughter, but wasn't certain what to say. The pounding in her head prevented coherent thought, and the look of surprised horror on the girl's face sickened her. Shaking her head, Tyressa walked past, back toward her tent.

"Mother."

"Not now."

Serrana darted after her, catching her right forearm. "Mother, how much of that was true?"

It felt as if spring melt had slushed through her guts. Tyressa turned. "Why don't you ask the question you really want answered?"

The girl glanced down. "Would you have done it? Could you have done it?"

"Could, yes. Would, absolutely."

"But how?"

"How could I?" Tyressa flung her arms wide. "How could I do any of this? I do it because I *must*, Serrana. You haven't fully comprehended what's happening here, have you? This isn't some game. We're not hiding here, waiting for the prince to decide it's safe for us to come home. Your uncle committed *treason*. He was convicted of it. The prince had every right to order the Vishov name effaced from every monument and erased from all books. Our home could have been shattered, the stones scattered, the forests burned, wells poisoned and land salted. We could have been killed or sold into slavery or given as playthings to monsters worse than anything you've seen in a nightmare."

Blood drained from the girl's face.

"Well, here we are, because the prince was my friend, and because of his profound respect for your father. Here I am, someone trained to oversee estates now having to *build* one from nothing, in a land with few friends and a bumper crop of enemies." Tyressa forced her hands open. "Yes, your father trained me to defend myself. I'm thankful for it. This place will demand everything of me *and* everything of you and your brother."

She pointed back out to the settlers. "Those people trust us. They came believing I would keep them safe because Vishovs have always kept them safe. I have no title anymore. I have no fortune to pay them. They came because they *trust* me. That means I have a sacred duty to them. So, geld a man at high noon, without a second thought, yes. Marry you off to some local, or keep you unmarried so I can use you as a prize to play one enemy off against another, yes, I would do that."

Serrana's face fell. "Mother?"

No, no. Serrana stood there, face ashen, shoulders slumped and arms limp. She barely breathed, and her eyes couldn't have gotten wider. Tears began to well.

Tyressa gathered her daughter into her arms and stroked her hair.

"Shhhhh. I don't want to do that, child. It breaks my heart to think of it. The reason I came here was so you and your brother would have the chance that will be denied me. *I* will never again see our home. I won't walk the halls. I won't see the sun set . . ."

Tyressa's voice failed as she recalled standing on the battlements, her belly swollen with her daughter, leaning back against Garath. His strong arms enfolded her. His breath warmed her cheek. They stood there, silently drinking the majesty of a golden sunset.

Serrana's arms circled her mother and she hung on tight. "I'm sorry, Mother. I don't know . . ."

"Quiet, girl. Not knowing is part of being young." *And innocent. How I wish I could have kept you innocent.*

Serrana sniffed. "Did you and father really hunt highwaymen?"

"That story could very well be true. It was before you were born." *Mostly.*

"Why didn't I know that?"

"It wasn't important you know." Tyressa kissed her daughter's head. "My mother died shortly after your brother was born. I became her social surrogate at your grandfather's court. Your father went to war. Your grandfather would have died had he known what Garath and I had done, so it just became part of a past that should have remained hidden."

"But now everyone knows."

"Its probably for the best." Tyressa hugged her daughter tightly. "Echo Wood has enough secrets. It doesn't need ours."

Chapter Ten
New Secrets

The influx of woodsmen significantly changed Silverlake. Jerrad's mother successfully negotiated with the fey to return the captives. Her ability to do that won the woodsmen's loyalty. With it came their knowledge of the area and a willingness to work hard.

Jerrad more sensed the change than could quantify it. With more lumber coming in, construction went faster. The first of the longhouses—big enough to house everyone in the settlement—neared completion. People realized that even if the winter came early, they'd be sleeping in something more substantial than a tent. That give them heart, and made the first piece of his mother's vision for Silverlake substantial. Because the longhouse had once just been a rectangle on a map, now *all* the rectangles could become houses and stables and barns or smokehouses.

The woodsmen, because of their familiarity with the wood, canceled the urgent need for Jerrad to survey the area. They cleared a lot of space. Jerrad and other younger folks went over the cleared fields gathering firewood and anything else of use. The work didn't require any serious lifting and really didn't require that many hours.

Even Serrana pitched in, though with far less enthusiasm than Jerrad thought she should be showing. She seemed to react to very little for good or ill—save to avoid Mulish Murdoon as much as possible. Even so, she just excused herself from his presence politely, whereas Jerrad was afraid she'd flay him with the sharp side of her tongue.

The only person who didn't contribute that much to the effort was Lord Sunnock. The man would listen to his mother's plans, make notes, and say he would think about things and offer suggestions later. Had Jerrad's mother listened to him, Silverlake's progress would be slowed to nothing. It came as a great relief when he left on a mission to Thornkeep to check on supplies and to negotiate a lumber contract with the mill there. Even his household servants smiled when he was absent, and seemed to enjoy pitching in to help.

Jerrad had debated whether or not to show his mother the grimoire Kiiryth had given him. While he didn't want to deceive her, he also didn't want to waste her time. She had enough to think about. What he decided to do was to read the book and practice, just to see if anything Kiiryth had said made sense. Once he knew, one way or the other, his mother could decide whether or not he should continue.

That's exactly how he thought of it, but as he wandered to a quiet glen on the other side of Silverlake from where the woodsmen plied their trade, he realized he was lying to himself. There had never been—to his knowledge, at least—any wizards in the Vishov family. If Kiiryth was right, he'd be the first, and that would make him special. *As special as my father was*. Learning magic was Jerrad's chance to be a hero.

Of course, the second he realized that was what he was truly thinking, he immediately told himself he was being stupid. Wizards weren't made overnight. He might have thrilled to stories of adventuring wizards slaying dragons and winning treasure, but those were just *stories*. Stories mattered little in the events of real life.

But it was a story that put us here.

Jerrad sighed as he slid to the base of a birch and nestled between two moss-blanketed roots. "There are times, Jerrad Vishov, when you think too much."

He opened the booklet. At first, the lettering looked like gibberish—reading marten tracks had been easier. Then things blurred for a moment, and resolved themselves into words written in a stylized but legible form of Taldane.

That process repeated itself on each page when he first looked. Jerrad shivered. There was no doubting magic was involved. He was pretty sure he wasn't doing anything, but he thought the same about the cloak. *Can Kiiryth really be right?*

He began to read. The book itself appeared to be part memoir, part instructional text written by a wizard who didn't identify himself. Jerrad couldn't be certain that it hadn't been written by a woman, but his sense of it was that the author was male. The book had been written as a response to something another wizard had claimed. The author believed that a wizard's connection to magic wasn't—as others erroneously taught—a monster to be conquered, but a talent the wizard had to embrace. In the author's opinion, in viewing magic as something that could consume him, a wizard limited his use of power. He constantly dwelt in a state of fear, wondering when the beast would turn on him. Whether or not this philosophy was true, he asserted, fear would always interfere with magic, so should be avoided at all costs.

The text ended halfway down a left page, facing a blank on the right. It ended with an exercise in which the student was instructed to close his eyes, slow his breathing, and then—only when calm—turn the page, paying close attention to what happened.

Jerrad closed his eyes. He felt kind of silly, but something in the author's tone pleased him. He drew in a deep breath, then let it out slowly. He did that several more times, then turned the page.

Nothing.

He opened his eyes.

The page spread was blank save for one word written in big letters on the left. "Again."

Jerrad closed his eyes again. He settled himself back against the tree. He felt a cool breeze on his cheek, and heard the buzz of an insect. A bird called from across the grove. The earth felt cool and a bit moist. The birch's roots pressed on his hips.

He turned the page.

Again, nothing.

Or was it nothing? He looked at the page and read once more the word, "Again."

He composed himself, forcing away annoyance. The fact that the pages changed indicated something was happening. The book wasn't failing him, he was failing the lesson.

Prepared again, he turned the page.

And got it.

Jerrad smiled, not yet opening his eyes. The previous turn he'd caught a note, a quiet whistle. He'd attributed it to the bird, but that hadn't been it. Hearing it again, absent any bird call, the note stood out, despite its being faint.

He looked down at the page. The instructions read, "Turn back three pages."

He flipped back to where the exercise had begun. Letters emerged in the empty space as if black bubbles surfacing in a parchment sea. A piped tune accompanied the words appearing. He couldn't match a note to a letter or even a word, but it struck him that they might match phrases or concepts. What amazed him most was that the text congratulated him on hearing the sounds, because he imagined it would have delivered an entirely different message for a deaf student.

Setting the book down for a moment, he thought back about his time in the woods, and as a fey captive. He couldn't remember hearing any particular notes or sounds, but he couldn't be certain there *hadn't* been any. In the fey camp he would have put things down to someone unseen playing music; and in the wood, he was absorbing so very much that odd sounds would have been put down to a bird or bug or something else.

He returned to the book, waiting for the world of magics wonderful and terrible to open up for him. He flipped forward several pages, but heard nothing and couldn't make any sense of the lettering. Frustrated, but understanding why the author might have exercised caution in teaching a student, Jerrad went back to the point he'd finished reading.

The first bit of magic he got to learn didn't involve any spells, just simple sleight of hand. The author carefully explained how to manipulate cards and dice, all without using any magic at all. The student was admonished to go off and practice things until he could perform them perfectly, without anyone being the wiser.

This made no sense to Jerrad. That wasn't magic. It was just trickery that beggars and bards performed to amaze or swindle the unwary. The idea of learning such deceit disgusted him, and he almost threw the grimoire away.

Then he read the line that materialized, accompanied by an ominous buzz. "Be forewarned: Magic can always be detected. Using it to do that which does not require it is to warn your enemies of how truly dangerous you are—and to show them how terribly foolish."

Maraschal Sunnock, despite spending an inordinate amount of time in Thornkeep in the company of the Blue Basilisks, had not warmed to their company. He had chosen to place them on retainer, which their leader took to mean that Sunnock had designs on Thornkeep or Silverlake. He let her think that was true because it kept her occupied figuring out how she would betray and slay him, making herself Lady of Echo Wood, once he'd given her enough money to finance a proper rebellion.

The only thing the Blue Basilisks had going for them, aside from being one of the better-trained private armies in the region, was a wine cellar filled with bottles looted from a number of decent cellars. Sunnock had always had a fondness for Nirmathi black wines, and the mercenaries discounted the wine well below its market value in Ustalav. Its availability and their generous pours were the only things which made life livable in Echo Wood.

He would have explained that to his guest, but Pine Callum quaffed a sour ale and fingered the small sack of gold coins Sunnock had handed him. Sunnock wanted to assure him the veneer would not rub off, but the man would not believe him. *Callum is disinclined to be trusting. Fortunately, I can trust to his greed.*

"As I was saying, Mister Callum, when you reach Ardis, you'll convey my message immediately to Baron Creelisk. He'll give you two more of those purses, and a chance to double your fortune yet again by returning with a message for me."

Callum squinted at the bulging purse, then raised his gaze to Sunnock's face. "You're doing this for her. Get me away, so's I can't get my men back."

Sunnock laughed easily, then sipped his wine. "I can assure you, I was appalled at how she treated you. Were my report not ciphered, you could read that there in the packet. I have little interest in having your life, or anyone else's, upset. It's best for me, and for my master, if the Vishov initiative fails. Her stealing your men has made it more likely that it will survive the winter.

My master needs to be informed of this, so he can take steps. Since you hate Tyressa Vishov nearly as much as my master does, you'll find your alliance with us to your advantage."

"Two more of these?"

"At a minimum." Sunnock nodded solemnly. The chances of Anthorn Creelisk giving the man money were fairly good. He might even reward him further, if Callum were to provide extra insights or prove trustworthy. Failing those two things, however, chances grew that the baron might subject the man to a variety of painful amusements—ostensibly to gain information, but not always effective.

And yet, my master always seems to be happier after such work.

"He gonna be coming here, to see to that woman proper?"

"It's possible, though he might leave her to you."

Callum nodded, not so much with his head as with the whole of his upper body. His unshaven jowls became quite animated. "I'm your man, then."

"Very well. You'll want to leave in the morning. Early."

Callum stood, not the least bit unsteady, and thrust a fat finger at Sunnock's face. "Just so you know, I weren't always like this. I've had better days. I understand things."

"Contrary to what you imagine, Mister Callum, I've assumed that all along." Sunnock sipped wine so its scent would cover the man's reek. "Were that not true, you would never have seen my gold, much less had a chance to earn it."

Callum plopped his tankard on the table. A bit of the beer slopped out. He straightened his spine, raised his chin, and walked out like a honorable man bound on a mission of mercy.

Sunnock waited for the door to the private room to close before he glanced at a shadowed corner. "You may come out now. How much of what you heard do you understand?"

Welinn emerged from beneath a tangle of stacked chairs and shards of broken tables. He darted to Callum's seat and grabbed his mug. The goblin's facile tongue darted out, licking up the dregs of the ale. "You gave the man money. Gold money."

"I did."

The goblin looked wide-eyed over the rim of the tankard. "Will you give gold money to me?"

"Of course."

"How much?"

"That will be determined by how good a job you do." Sunnock's eyes half-lidded. "Two weeks from now, on the night of no moon, I want you to stage a raid on Silverlake. Your people can keep what they carry away. You will be paid twenty gold for the raid, and more—much more—if it's terrifying enough that the settlers leave. I want them terrified."

Welinn set the mug down. "I've seen Silverlake. They're making walls."

"Except on the lake side. That will be last, and a month off. You'll come in from the east." Sunnock opened a pouch on his belt and pulled out a torn blue tunic woven of finely spun linen. "There is only one person you cannot kill. The girl, Serrana. She must live. If you can carry her off, so much the better, but she must not die. You can get her scent from this. Do you understand?"

"You want it terrifying. The girl cannot die. We keep what we loot."

"And the night of no moon."

"Yes, in the dark." The goblin chuckled. "The dark for humans. It will be very dark for humans."

"And golden for you." Sunnock smiled. The progress at Silverlake had given the settlers heart. The goblins would take it away. *And ever closer comes the end of the Vishovs and the advent of my master's pleasure.*

Chapter Eleven
Suspicion and Honor

Serrana's scream froze Jerrad's heart in his chest. He looked around, turning toward her scream, but seeking a fallen tree or clump of thick bushes behind which he could hide. He spotted a hollow between the roots of an old tree and almost started toward it.

No, stop. You can't hide. This isn't the time for hiding.

A second scream echoing through the wood, pinpointing her location. His basket fell from his fingers. The roots and herbs he'd gathered spilled out as he started running. His sister sounded more frightened than hurt, and he found himself more afraid of not going than any trouble he'd face in helping her.

If this is her idea of a joke . . . He shook his head. One scream would have been a joke, but two—that was trouble.

He raced through Echo Wood, leaping over windfall trees and sliding down a leaf-carpeted hill. He half expected to end up in the sprite-bog at the bottom, but his feet hit a stone and he vaulted himself over the mire. On all fours he scrambled up the opposite side, never slipping, and making enough noise to be a victorious army traveling with tons of jangling treasures.

He reached the top of the depression and gasped. He had to look every bit a nervous squirrel, eyes wide. *Oh, this is bad. Very bad.*

A warrior clad in brown leathers chased with wolf fur had a thick handful of his sister's hair. Another, taller and blond, had similarly forced Aneska—his sister's handmaiden—to her knees. Baskets half-filled with roots and fungus had spilled near both women. Feral children squatted, inspecting the contents, lifting up bits to show to a toothless crone leaning on a fetish staff.

Between the two women stood a barbarian warrior in a halter and skirt made of skins, with feathers braided into her dark hair and scars on the left side of her face, shoulder, and flank. The scars came in parallel sets of four and had to have been inflicted by a great cat or bear. The woman bore a spear and had a throwing axe sheathed over her left hip. Brown leather boots rose to her knees, and leather bracers protected her forearms.

Jerrad forced himself to his feet. He really wanted to vomit, but figured that would not be much of a help. *Though I could use an illusion to hide it.* He forced his fear down and made his expression impassive.

He bowed solemnly toward the warrior. "I am Jerrad Vishov of Silverlake. That is my sister and her companion."

Serrana sobbed, covering her face with her hands.

The woman rested the butt of her spear on the ground. "I am Darioth, Chieftain of the Wolfmanes. You're in our Wood."

Jerrad suppressed a shiver. The Wolfmanes were one of the many Kellid barbarian tribes who had transplanted their nomadic lifestyle south. Jerrad took it as a good sign that neither of the Silverlake women had been slain yet, as the Kellids had a reputation as fierce fighters. He had learned little of the Wolfmanes—just enough to know they had several small villages scattered through the wood and that avoiding them was best.

But we aren't near any of their villages.

"I beg your pardon. I didn't know you had claims on this area."

Darioth snorted. "This is *our* Wood. All of it. You and your village are within our grounds."

Aneska's captor yanked her head back, baring her throat, and drew a knife.

Jerrad opened his hands. "I can convey a warning to my mother. She is our chieftain. Or I can conduct you to her, and you can work out your differences."

Darioth nodded once. "Lead."

Serrana screamed again when she was yanked to her feet. Aneska smothered her outcry behind her hands. They fell into step with their captors. Behind them, the children gathered up all the things they'd harvested and brought the baskets along. The crone came last in the procession, with bones and beads on strings rattling against her staff.

Jerrad opted for the direct route, which he had thought was one thing, but proved to be another. He knew where he'd intended to go, and watched those landmarks go by on his right or left. Terrain that had seemed impassible before opened to him, and the lack of comment from the Wolfmanes suggested they weren't seeing anything out of the ordinary going on.

Once the group broke into the cleared land west of Silverlake, people in the settlement spotted them through gaps in the wall. Moving as swiftly as Jerrad had yet seen, Lord Sunnock ran to where Tyressa was inspecting the longhouse shell. He gesticulated wildly, but Tyressa turned calmly and walked toward them.

The two groups met inside the first ring of tents past the palisade wall. "I am Tyressa of Silverlake. I thank you for returning my children to me. The Kellid reputation for honor and their compassion for the helpless is well known and obviously well deserved."

The Wolfmane leader's face remained impassive. "I am Darioth of the Wolfmanes. Your children had strayed onto our lands."

"And they shall be disciplined for that." Jerrad's mother waved a hand toward her own tent. "If you would care to join me, I'll prepare tea. I have a map, and would appreciate your advice so encounters of this sort could be avoided in the future."

Darioth nodded curtly, then followed in Tyressa's wake. The two warriors released Serrana and her servant. Aneska gathered Serrana in her arms and led her off to her tent. The children set the baskets near the crone. Jerrad smiled at her, but she raised an eyebrow and stared at him with an icy blue eye.

The children squatted and brushed dust from the ground. Using short sticks, they quickly excavated a half-dozen bowl-like holes. Two of them pulled pouches from their belts and dumped out eighteen rounded pebbles. A third produced a pair of six-sided dice, and the two players faced off over the line of holes.

They paid Jerrad no attention, but he picked up the rules to the simple game. A player rolled the dice. Starting at the hole on his left, he moved one stone the number of holes equal to the value on the lowest die. Then he did the same for the higher value. Each continued to do this, putting as many of his stones as possible into play. Holes could contain any number of stones of either color. If a player picked up a stone and the die roll was greater than the number of holes left, he'd reach the final one and work his way back to the left. If one player had three stones in a hole where the opponent had none, the opponent could not place a stone in there, and would forfeit his roll if that was his only move.

When a player rolled doubles, he would move, then look at the corresponding hole. If he had more stones in that hole, he captured the enemies stones. An equal number of his own stones left play, but could reenter with another die roll. If the stones matched equally, nothing happened. If the player had fewer stones than his foe, both players put their stones back in their play pool. It seemed clear to Jerrad that the winner would be the player who captured all of his opponent's stones, or prevented any of them from entering play.

"May I?" He dropped to a knee beside the children. "I've not played before."

The Kellids jabbered back and forth, then one child picked up his stones, and another tossed down a handful of wood chips he'd scavenged from near the longhouse. The Kellids laughed, but Jerrad shrugged it off. He counted out eighteen chips, snapped them into rough squares, and indicated his opponent should throw the dice.

The Kellid snorted and threw. Though he'd only watched one game, Jerrad recognized the phases things had to go through. The initial deployment would lead to the conquest or avoidance of holes in the middle game. The end game would involve pouncing on orphaned stones and fortifying holes so no stone could enter the game.

The Kellid nudged the dice his direction. The bone cubes didn't weigh as much as Jerrad had expected they would—and they weren't matched like the ones with which he'd been practicing his magic skills. *These would be so easy to magic.*

He didn't. He tossed the dice, counted his chips into holes, and passed the dice back to his foe. The dice clacked and bounced. Stones shifted from one hole to another. The Kellid won some chips, but Jerrad won some stones. By the time his mother returned with the Wolfmane chieftain, Jerrad had lost because his foe had all the holes blocked, but he still had a half-dozen chips in his play pool.

Darioth studied the gaming area, then spoke to the crone. She answered with no emotion, but punctuated her remarks with a rattle of her fetish staff. The warrior woman nodded, then looked at Tyressa "This one is your son?"

"Yes."

"He has played honorably and well."

Tyressa ruffled Jerrad's dark locks. "He's always liked games."

"That you have raised him to treat honorably with strangers says much, Tyressa of Silverlake." The Kellid leader glanced at the game again, then looked into Tyressa's eyes. "These areas we have agreed belong to the Wolfmanes—we will allow you to use them through winter. Then next spring, if your son can beat my champion at *lerkot*, we shall extend the time to the spring following."

"You are most kind, Chieftain Darioth." Tyressa smiled. "As I said before, you and all the Wolfmanes are welcome here, to visit or trade as you will."

"I will tell the others." Darioth nodded toward Jerrad and said something in the Kellid tongue. His opponent gathered up the slate gray stones and put them in a pouch, which he handed across. "Practice, Jerrad of Silverlake. Others will come to test your prowess."

"Thank you."

Darioth grunted, then turned and strode toward the opening where the gate would go. The other Wolfmanes followed her, with the crone shaking her fetish staff here and there. Jerrad had no idea what that was meant to do, and no real desire to find out. That the Kellids were fierce and at home in the wood was more than enough for him to know.

Tyressa gave him a quizzical look. "She was a hair's breadth from driving us from Echo Wood. She laid claims to almost *all* the land, and half of the lake. Do you have any idea what you've done?"

"It's good, yes?"

"Very good." Tyressa shook her head. "They were willing to give us your sister's weight in skins for her. That's on par with the Murdoon offer."

"I won't tell her."

"No, don't." His mother sighed. "It's not news she'll take well."

Serrana sat beside her brother in their darkened tent. "Are you awake, Mouse?"

"I am now."

"I can't do it."

"What?"

"Live here." A muffled sob escaped her. "I'm not like you."

He frowned in the darkness. "What does that mean?"

"You know. You've always been . . . different." Serrana sighed. "I was raised at court. I never liked it outside. Maybe the gardens, just when flowers were blooming, because they were pretty; but everything here is wild. You see that, right?"

He sat up on his canvas cot. "Yes, it's rough out here."

"Rough?" She grabbed his forearm and squeezed tight. "You've been chased by goblins and wolves and kidnapped by the fey. I have farmers who want to trade cows for me, and the Kellids . . ." Her voice broke and her hands left him. "I thought they were going to kill me."

Serrana began to sob, shaking the cot.

Oh, by the gods, what do I do? "Shh, Serra, everything will be fine. You'll see. It'll all work out."

"No it won't! Not for me, Mouse. Not for you, either. Once you're a few years older, Mother will be trying to marry you off to make alliances, too. The nixies hate me and the sprites hate you. And those are the least of our worries."

"What are you talking about?"

She sniffed, and her silhouette swiped at tears. "Baron Blackshield can't let us win. You were there. Mother threatened him with an Ustalavic invasion. We took woodsmen who were working for people who were paying him. Mother's made peace with the fey and the Kellids. She's taken the steps to make Silverlake viable, which means Blackshield has to move soon to stop the threat."

Jerrad's eyes tightened. He couldn't fault his sister's logic, but this level of anxiety wasn't like her. *She's been talking to someone. Sunnock, I'd bet.*

The simple fact was that Baron Blackshield hadn't visited, nor sent spies, nor even sent a message concerning Silverlake since their arrival. *And while it's true that our alliances threaten him, they also make it very difficult for him to threaten Silverlake.*

"He's not the threat you think he is, Serra."

"Fine, you can believe that. It changes nothing. This is an evil place, Mouse." Hands moist with tears grabbed his hands. "I don't want to die here. If I stay, I will. I know I'm no good. I can't do anything right. I couldn't even gather mushrooms without someone putting a knife to my throat. But what will it be next? The nixies drag me off to drown? The sprites decide you're no longer fun, so they come after me? Why do you want to see me die, Mouse? Why?"

Huh? Jerrad squeezed his sister's hands. "I don't want to see you die, Serra. I don't."

"Then will you help me?"

"Help you do what?"

"I can't stay here. I can't. I want to go home."

"There isn't any home to return to."

"I can petition the prince. He can keep me in his palace, as a hostage against Vishov perfidy."

Perfidy? "What makes you think that will work?" Jerrad squeezed her hands hard. "Serrana, what is it?"

"You have to promise to tell no one."

"I don't know if I can."

"You must." All warmth drained from her voice. "I can't have you fail me now. Promise."

Knowing he'd regret it, Jerrad said, "I promise."

"I had a message from home. I got sent Ailson Kindler's new book, *Winds of Mercy*."

"What? How?" Jerrad cursed silently. "It was Lord Sunnock, wasn't it?"

"That doesn't matter. The book is the sequel to ours. In it, the character who's me returns to Ustalav as the prince's hostage. It's barely part of the story, but that's the key, don't you see? It's a message, from the prince himself."

"Are you mad?" He tore his hands from hers and scrubbed them over his face. "If mother finds out you read another of those books . . . ."

"She won't if you don't tell her."

"You're asking me to lie to her."

"No, just *not tell her*." She grabbed Jerrad's biceps and squeezed hard. "Just like I haven't told her about the little book *you've* been reading, Mouse, and the things you've been doing."

"What? How?"

"Keep your voice down." She sighed. "Jerrad, I don't want to do this, but I *will* die if I stay here. Tell me you'll help me."

I need to figure this out. He groaned. "Don't do anything weird. I need to time to think."

"Then you'll help me."

"Maybe."

"I knew it." She planted a kiss on his cheek. "Thank you, Mouse. You're the best brother. Sleep well."

She vacated his cot, and he slid down under the covers. *As if I'll sleep now. Or ever.*

Chapter Twelve
A Dream Rooted

Tyressa Vishov stood on the battlements of Silverlake and surveyed her empire. The longhouse's completion enabled half the families to move in, with stout wooden walls to ward them and a pitched roof above their heads. She'd chosen the lucky families by lot. A few people suspected she'd not put her family's name in the sack with the other wooden chits, but no one *knew* for certain. A few of the woodsmen had given up their billets to losing families, claiming they weren't ready yet to surrender the freedom of the stars for a roof, but that hadn't fooled many people, either.

Those who hadn't won still lived in tents, but they were tents on raised wooden platforms, with low walls and wooden frameworks. They shifted supplies into unoccupied tents on such platforms, save for the perishables, which were stored in one of the three root cellars they'd dug. Next up would be the stable and expanding the smithy, then more permanent smoke-houses, a communal barn, a wharf, and the walls looking down toward the lake.

She looked up at the dark sky and the stars glittering in its inky depths. Silverlake had made major strides, but to take any serious pride in them would invite the gods' mockery. Two months into a twenty year sentence was hardly a victory. Chances were good that the winter would destroy them. Or spring floods, or summer storms, or any of a thousand forms of disease and pestilence. Silverlake could best be described as hanging on by its fingernails.

She glanced down at her hands. *I have no fingernails.* Two months had roughened her skin. It had cracked and chipped her fingernails such that her fingers bled more often than not. Her clothes hung loosely on her, and she'd had to cut new holes into her belt. And it wasn't that she'd not been eating, but that she never had a moment to rest.

Though creating Silverlake brought with it an unending string of problems, there *was* one benefit: jobs could actually get done. She had no trouble remembering what the site had looked like when they first arrived—or, worse yet, the quagmire it had become after the rains. Mud and bracken predominating, with the wood close in on all sides, she'd though Mudflat might have been a better town name.

Yet now, it had come to resemble a town. *At least a large field camp.* Section by section, the longhouse had been built. Palisade walls with sharpened logs and two wide doors on big iron hinges had been set in place. People had gathered large stones to mark off a green near the longhouse, and to draw boundaries between their homes. They did that not out of possessiveness, but because it allowed them to obey civil convention. They respected each other's privacy, though no one could keep a secret for long in Silverlake.

People had done all this. They had taken nothing and made it into something. Yes, the wood was still green and would have to be replaced with more seasoned wood, but that would have to wait. For the moment they made what they needed most urgently, and were happy to have it. What others had said was impossible, they were making possible. They took pride in that notion.

As well they should. Their everyday efforts were all that stood between them and death. And people weren't just out for themselves. They worked together, not expecting an immediate return, but knowing that what was good for one person in the community would be good for all. It made Tyressa proud of all this, and all them. *We have come very far.*

Tyressa shivered, not from the cold, but from recollection. She'd stood atop battlements—true battlements—far taller and made of stone. She'd watched companies of men, her husband at the head, marching off to war. The Vishov family estates had been much more vast than the holding to which she lay claim here in Echo Wood. With the help of estate managers and vassals, she had overseen it all for her father and then brother, but even that duty had not prepared her for raising a town from the ground up.

A town. Not even a city. And she wanted Silverlake to be a city, a grand glowing city of which Thornkeep would be its shadow. That had been her goal when she set out, and her desire to attain it had grown when she saw whom Baron Blackshield had taken to wife. She wanted grand stone towers and paved streets, bright pennants flyings and bridges soaring above streams.

I want it to be perfect.

Just for a moment she understood the impatience of kings and conquerers. *And men like my brother.* They had the vision of a perfect city, a perfect society and civilization which could stand as a beacon for all who dwelled near the Inner Sea and beyond. It was ambition, but noble and pure, meant for good.

But built on a foundation of impatience.

With eighty people, she'd created a wood and earth town. With eight thousand or eighty thousand, she could have created her shiny city, but every bit of pain and hardship her eighty had known would be multiplied by thousands and tens of thousands. People would die for her ambition, and more would die the grander it got.

Patience, Tyressa. Silverlake would grow. She had twenty years to make it grow. The longer it took to build, the longer it would take to destroy. She would not let it fail.

"Excuse me, my lady."

Tyressa turned and found Lord Sunnock mounting the ladder to the catwalk. "How may I help you?"

"I think it's I who can help you." Sunnock quickly rubbed his hands together to remove mud she'd tracked onto the ladder. "I thought to head into Thornkeep tomorrow morning."

"Ever the optimist that Baron Creelisk will recall you?"

"I've petitioned him for aid for Silverlake." Sunnock leaned on the wall and looked out into the darkness. "I know you hold me in contempt for not helping out more, but I do what I can. I believe my master will approve the latest requests. I must remind you, however, that you are not my mistress."

"Of this I'm well aware."

"And my master tasks me with certain duties."

"And what would those be?"

"I would never ask you to betray a confidence." He glanced at her, his face shrouded in darkness. "But I'll do you a favor. I am concerned about your children. Your daughter, specifically. She's no better suited to life here than I am."

Tyressa's breath caught in her throat. Ever since her encounter with the Kellids, Serrana had been detached. She still did her chores, pitching in around the camp, but she did them emotionlessly. Tyressa would have welcomed an outburst of anger or happiness. Instead the girl seemed far away.

Tyressa felt she was dying inside.

"What is it you propose? Take her to Thornkeep, ask Lady Ivis to care for her?"

"That would be an option, but I fear not one which anyone would like. However, I think she would enjoy a journey to Thornkeep. It's a bit more civilized than Silverlake."

Tyressa slowly shook her head. "I can't authorize that sort of a trip. I can't designate anyone to act as her bodyguard—we need everyone here."

"I would be happy to see to her care."

"The offer is appreciated, and rejected." Tyressa's eyes tightened. "It would be inappropriate for a young woman to be in your company alone."

"It might affect her price in cows and pelts."

"Droll, but your offer is unacceptable."

"Your son could come as well."

She considered that for a moment. In the past two weeks brother and sister had grown closer—or at least, if they were fighting, they were doing it where she couldn't see or hear them. Jerrad she could trust in Thornkeep, but she couldn't believe he would be able to keep his sister out of trouble. *Especially if it involves goblins or mud.*

"I have two problems with allowing Serrana to go to Thornkeep. The first is that this would be a privilege for her—one she has not earned. As you acknowledged yourself, you're seen as being less than useful here. But I'm not your mistress. My daughter, however, is my responsibility. To reward her for doing the minimum asked of her would destroy morale."

Lord Sunnock nodded. "Very astute observation, my lady. Your other objection?"

"A simple trip to Thornkeep would delight my daughter, and destroy her when she had to return here. We would give her hope, then crush it. I fear that the only thing she will settle for, the only thing she will joyously embrace, is a return to Ustalav. Since that won't be happening, to indulge her would be cruel sport."

"What if it *could* happen?"

"What do you mean?"

Sunnock stroked his chin with a hand. "The prince has great affection for you. By extension, for your children. At Baron Creelisk's orders I took a chance—a chance more slender than that last paring of moon in the sky above. I've generated a number of reports which paint progress here in less than glowing terms. I've not lied *per se*, but have left the impression that you are, well, manfully embracing your duty. Silverlake, however, is slow to thrive, and your daughter . . . well, it doesn't look good for such a flower in this place."

Tyressa folded her arms over her chest. *You cannot be thinking* . . .

"Baron Creelisk is going to petition the prince to allow him to give your daughter—and your son, of course—sanctuary in his estate. He will . . . ."

"No."

"No?"

"Never."

"I've not finished."

"Yes, you have." Tyressa thrust a finger off toward Thornkeep. "How can you imagine I would agree to that when Lady Ivis lives not ten miles from here? I won't have Creelisk do to my daughter what he did to her."

"I have no idea to what you refer."

"No?" She snorted. "Her father and brother went off to war. Her mother sickened—black boils—and died. Ivis grew ill as well. Your master took her in, saw to it she survived the illness."

"Hardly the hallmark of someone not willing to aid those given to his care."

"Then he seduced her. She was barely older than my daughter." Tyressa shivered. The affair had been something of an open secret among girls at court, simply because Lady Ivis had taken on airs. When Creelisk tired of her, he informed her family of what she'd been up to. For that reason her father was more than receptive to an invitation to marry her off to a bandit lordling far from home. "He'll never get his hands on my daughter."

"It was my impression, my lady, that he was hoping she would find his son Ranall favorable."

"I'm certain he may even believe that himself, but once he saw her, realized how innocent she is, I doubt he could avoid temptation." *Or be unable to convince his son that inheriting his father's mistress was anything but the boy's good fortune.* "No, that will not be happening."

Sunnock turned fully to face her. "Are you certain you're not speaking for yourself, and not your daughter?"

"I don't follow."

"You struck this deal with the prince. You made the commitment to be here. All of those who accompanied you did so as volunteers. Even the locals who've come to help have made a choice. But neither of your children could make that choice, could they? Do you hate the idea that they might be able to regain the life your rash decision denies them? Do you believe that anyone back home holds them to blame for what your brother did?"

"They blame me."

"You were his advisor, after all."

Tyressa balled her fists, but hid them at the small of her back. "Just as you are not privy to your master's every thought and whim, so it was with my brother. Perhaps I *should* have seen what he was doing. Mayhap I *could* have seen. The fact remains that I never did.

"As for your suggestion that my children would be seen as being free of guilt, you underestimate the depths to which people have already descended. Ailson Kindler was persuaded to write her book at the behest of a patron, I know it. *Who* I cannot say, but someone paid her to disgrace my family. Someone that unscrupulous wouldn't hesitate to hurt my children."

"And yet, wouldn't they be safer far from this place?"

An icy serpent slithered through her guts. "Far from this place, I can't keep them safe."

"But can you keep them safe *here*?"

"There are some who might interpret that as a veiled threat."

"Thankfully you're too intelligent to do so." The man's silhouette opened its arms. "I say to you truthfully, I bear neither you nor your family any ill will. Perhaps my master's motives are tinged with ambition. If your daughter and his son were to fall in love, then the estates he holds in stewardship for the Vishovs might join the Creelisk holdings. At the very least, it would be Vishov blood overseeing them. It would be a way to guarantee the outcome for which you labor here."

Tyressa's hand rose to her throat. *Is life here too hard for my children? Serra would jump at the chance he offers. And Jerrad . . .* "Your suggestion is not an easy one to dismiss."

"Nor to accept." The man shrugged. "Perhaps I *am* too abrupt in bringing this to your attention, or in asking for a decision. My offer stands, whenever you deem it advisable to move your children to safer environs. I do understand your reasons. I merely hope you understand my reasoning in return."

"Yes, thank you, Lord Sunnock." Tyressa exhaled heavily. "I'll think on this, and perhaps give you an answer in the morning."

"If it pleases you, my lady." The man bowed and slowly descended the ladder.

Tyressa turned and leaned against the palisade, staring out at the dark wood. *Have I trapped my children here?* She knew, of course, that she had. But the cruelty of that act came only with the meanest reading of circumstance. The children couldn't stay in Ustalav. The prince had been forced to show disfavor, which meant all of the Vishovs' friends and allies would have to follow suit. To do anything less would leave them open to charges of treason, and to be implicated in helping her brother through a campaign of whispers.

When she'd come up with the plan, people had thought her brave and even noble—at least to her face. Most considered what she was doing a futile act fueled by guilt and desperation. They'd be happy if she succeeded, and would welcome her back with affirmations that they knew she'd been innocent. In reality, they probably all devoured copies of Sunnock's reports, tingling delightedly at every suggestion of disaster.

"Plenty of fodder for their dreams: floods, fey, barbarians, and an old enemy in the nearest town. Just the kind of things Kindler would weave into another story." She turned around and looked out at the town. "But those haven't defeated us. Gods willing, nothing else will."

Then a man's blood-curdling scream split the night and ended in a gurgle.

The gods' will, it seems, is to test me yet one more time.

Chapter Thirteen
A Dream Uprooted

Jerrad couldn't tell from which direction the scream had come. He'd been huddled beneath a blanket reading the wizardry text. Something about the words didn't require light for him to read—which made sense. Many of the spells were centered around illusions and projecting images into a subject's mind. The whole book, he decided, was primarily a practical text on illusion, and he devoured each lesson as the book choose to reveal it to him.

Don't move. He closed the book and trembled. *Someone just had an accident. It can't be anything bad. Just stay here.*

Someone else screamed.

Serra!

He threw off the blanket. Silhouettes ran through the night—some normal people and some small, like children, but with enormous heads and ridiculously large ears. He resisted the urge to duck beneath the blankets again, and instead cupped his hands around his mouth. "Goblins!"

Jerrad grabbed his belt and fumbled with the buckle for a heartbeat or two before realizing he didn't need to wear the belt. His hand drifted down to the dagger, and he drew it just in time for one of the goblins to bound into his tent, peg teeth flashing.

Time died. The goblin had daubed its face with reddish mud and some yellow paste probably made from flowers. It had tied feathers to its biceps and just below the knees. A mangy skin made up its loincloth and the short cloak it wore. It had a rusty knife tucked into a slender belt, but never made to draw it.

The goblin hissed and leaped for him. Clawed hands reached for Jerrad's throat. The young man thrust the dagger forward—less as an attack than an attempt to fend the goblin off. His dagger plunged into the goblin's throat right above a necklace of bones. Hot blood shot up Jerrad's sleeve, and the goblin's dying spin tore the slicked knife from his hand. The creature stumbled and fell against Jerrad's cot.

The goblin's claws rent the pillow asunder, then the creature slumped amid a blizzard of feathers. It sighed as if settling down for a welcome nap.

Jerrad stared at his gore-drenched hand. A feather landed on it, drinking in the goblin's blood. *What have I done?*

Then he heard another scream. *Serra! I have to find Serra!* He dropped to a knee and yanked the dagger from the goblin's throat. Trailing feathers in his wake, he ran into the night, and heard her scream a third time.

There!

Serrana ran pell-mell through the camp in a panic. She headed mostly west, angling toward the furthest of the root cellars. He raced after her, slashing goblins and pushing them out of the way. He didn't hurt many, but caught a couple solidly. They'd either not seen him coming or didn't care as long as there was loot to carry off. Odd, capering victory dances took precedence over fighting, adding absurdity to the night's horrific chaos.

Ahead, his sister tripped and fell against a pile of wood scraps. Three goblins moved at her. Two had knives.

"Hey!" Jerrad thrust his left hand high in the air as the goblins stared at him. *This better work!*

He cast the spell he'd been trying to perfect beneath the blanket. A brilliant light flared from his hand, rendering the goblins in silver and his sister in icy blue. One goblin screamed, dropping his knife, and clawed at his own eyes.

As darkness returned and a wave of fatigue washed over him, Jerrad let his run carry him into the nearest goblin. He bowled the creature over. His foe sank teeth into Jerrad's left shoulder, but the boy barely noticed. Hand tight on the dagger's sticky hilt, Jerrad stabbed again and again. His thrusts ruined the goblin's belly, but he didn't stop stabbing until the jaws slackened.

He pitched the body off and rose, blood coursing down his arm and dripping from the blade. He gave Serra a smile. "It's okay."

Her eyes grew wide and her voice rose with fear. "Jerrad, look out!"

He spun right into an avalanche of goblins. His knife sank into something solid and warm, but it didn't matter. A skull clipped his jaw, cracking teeth together. With horror contorting Serra's face, Jerrad sank beneath a wave of rending claws, biting teeth, and goblin flesh.

Tyressa leaped from the battlements and landed in a crouch. She gathered her skirts and pulled the rear hem up between her legs, tucked it into her belt at the belly. Cool air chilled bare feet. Another two steps and she picked up a stout stick. Two more and she levered a hatchet free of the chopping block where they killed chickens. With one stroke she slashed the stick into a sharpened stake, then stalked into the night.

More screams drew her onward. She heard someone yell "Goblins!" and thought it might be Jerrad. *At least he's alive.* She killed the urge to run to him. Panic would slay her, and then she'd be no help to anyone.

The first goblin flew at her out of the darkness, screeching as it came. Tyressa twisted, thrusting with her left hand. The stake caught the goblin in the chest, but a skin vest prevented it from penetrating. The creature giggled at its good fortune, then grew quiet as an overhand blow with the hatchet split its skull.

Off to the right, one of the woodsmen cleaved a goblin in half.

"To me!"

The man looked up as she wrenched the hatchet from the skull, then ran to her, nodding as he came. "Goblins."

"I see. I'd prefer highwaymen."

"My lady?"

"Bigger targets, and they don't bite." She raised her voice. "To me, Silverlake!"

Tyressa had meant the call to draw the settlers to her. A few came, one with an arm hanging limp and blood pouring from his shoulder. More quickly, however, came the goblins, chittering and gibbering, snarling and giggling insanely.

Off to the north one section of the wall ignited in a wash of flames. Goblin silhouettes writhed across the landscape. They piled up against the longhouse, standing on each other to get in the windows. Knives cut some, broomsticks thrust others away. Yet more ran around carrying off even the most inconsequential of trinkets. One had even slapped a boot on its head, lacing the floppy helmet on beneath the chin.

All this Tyressa took in with emotionless clarity. She didn't even allow herself anger, because letting in one emotion would open the way for others. She thrust and cut within her guard, remaining safe as her husband had taught her to do, yet missed no opportunity to kill. The hatchet's dull end pulverized what the blade wouldn't slice. A slap with the flat shattered bone. Goblins reeled away trying to press their faces back into shape.

The wounded man went down, and the goblins dragged him away. Tyressa closed ranks with the others. More goblins came in a wave that broke against the ferocity of the settlers' defense. Blood splashed. Sweat stung the countless scratches on her legs and forearms. Bones snapped. They weren't hers, but one solid hatchet stroke sent a shock wave up into her shoulder, and the dying goblin carried the hatchet away with it.

"They're running, my lady."

The woodsman was right. *But that's* not *right.* Tyressa frowned, wiping her brow and smearing blood across it. The goblins *had* thinned, scattering in all directions, but more were upright than dead or dying. *Why would they break off the attack?*

Then she felt it, through her feet. Tremors in the ground, matching heavy footfalls. Something crashed through the darkness, coming up from the lake. She couldn't tell what it was, other than big. Whatever it was, the goblins knew better than to be anywhere near it. And she'd have followed their example, except that she wasn't going to let anything drive her from her home.

Welinn huddled just inside the southernmost portion of the wall, cloaked darkness. He could see plenty well through it, as could all the goblins. The problem was, he couldn't see anything *but* goblins. Attacking, looting, setting fires, dying, all he saw were goblins by the legion.

That wasn't the way it was supposed to have worked. He, being of the Brambleclaw Tribe, had gotten the blessing of his chief, then gathered a company of goblins. He'd told them all the things the manlord wanted, especially about the scaring and the girl. The scaring would be what earned him extra money, so he had stressed it to his fellows.

He'd had a special thought in that regard. The manlord had wanted the attack to come on the moonless night, but that made no real sense if scaring was the object. If men couldn't see the goblins, how could they be scared? They couldn't, so the plan had to be modified so there was enough light to allow the scaring.

The Brambleclaws had taken the news about scaring to heart. More than one approached him asking if they could invite a cousin, since more would be scarier than less. Welinn had accepted the first few offers, then started refusing, but no one had listened to him. Cousins had invited other cousins, and it looked as if every goblin between Thornkeep and Silvershade Lake had joined in.

Then he saw it. One of the goblins had gone to far with scaring. *He invited Grakka.*

The creature looked like an ogre, but Welinn had heard it was of mixed blood—human or elf, though looking at it the goblin couldn't have told which. The ogrekin lived alone in the wood, having been driven from or escaped from Mosswater. It came dragging the lower half of a sapling—complete with root ball, as it stalked up the slope from the lake. The footfalls sounded as thunder and the ground shook.

Too much scaring. The goblin made himself as small as possible. He waited for Grakka to pass, then Welinn snuck around the corner and darted into the night. It didn't matter how much gold money the manlord would give him, it wouldn't be enough to lurk within the ogrekin's bloody domain.

Jerrad rolled and tried to heave a goblin off him. He might have succeeded, he didn't know. His push included his knife, but he didn't hear a grunt or scream.

Then again, being at the heart of a ball of yowling, gouging, gnawing goblins meant he couldn't make sense of much at all.

I have to get free. He fought panic and bit. He drove his knees into things. He smashed his head backward into something which crunched. His left elbow slammed against hardness, and his left hand closed on something squishy. He yanked. That got a howl, then teeth closed on his right wrist and his knife went flying.

He lashed out with everything he had, but the goblins weighed him down. Any time he sent one flying, two more would pile on. He couldn't get a decent breath. And something had a hand on the side of his head, trying to work his head up to expose his throat. He fought it. Claws sank into his scalp. Blood ran. The grip slipped for a second, then moved down and hooked beneath his jaw.

Then it was gone. Something hit with a solid thunk, and that goblin vanished. Then another thump, and another. Weight left his legs, so he kicked. He arched his back, then twisted, trying to get his hands under him.

Another thump, and more weight evaporated.

And then he heard her voice. "Get. Off. Mouse!"

Jerrad wriggled from the pile. As he stood, two goblins came for him. An arrow splashed back to front through the throat of the furthest, then struck the other in the back of the head. The razored broadhead skewered the left eyeball on its way out. The goblin stiffened, viscous fluid streaming down its face, then flopped to the ground.

Beyond it stood Kiiryth, another arrow already fitted to his bow. He gave Jerrad a nod, then turned and sped another shaft into the night.

Between them stood Serrana, a four-foot length of pine sapling clenched tight in her fists. She whipped it up and around, spraying blood and goblin brains all over, then crashed it down. The blow pulped a goblin's bulbous head. The club rose again and struck the same goblin.

"Serra. *Serrana!*"

She looked up at him, feral fire burning in her eyes. Lips peeled back in a snarl. She flashed a grin, then whirled and battered another dead goblin's skull into wet mush. "Get. Off. Mouse!"

"Serrana, its okay, they're off me."

His sister stopped for a moment, a thick, dark slurry running down over her hands. "Mouse?"

"Yes, Serrana. You saved me."

"I saved you."

Kiiryth closed with both of them. "There are more to save. To the longhouse, now."

Maraschal Sunnock stood alone in the chaos within the longhouse. He'd gone there to give some last-minute orders to his servants concerning the next day's journey. He'd heard the scream and seen forms running through the night before someone had closed and barred the door. And even when a goblin thrust its face through a window, he still couldn't believe it.

This is wrong, all wrong! His mouth went dry. *I wasn't supposed to be here.*

"You, help us!"

Sunnock looked up. One of the woodsmen had joined two other men at the door, pushing back against a horde of goblins. Boards began to creak. Nails squealed and worked free of the wood. The man waved him forward and, dazed by disbelief, Sunnock joined him.

The second his hands touched the door's wood, fear burst within his heart. Until that moment, the attack had been an abstract thing. Here, leveraging his muscle against that of the goblins, he could feel their insistence. They were avatars of gluttony and hatred and greed. A knot in a board popped free, striking him in the face. He stared out through it, eye to eye with a goblin.

Sunnock spun, slamming his back against the door. People warded every window, stabbing and battering goblins, shoving them back into the night. But there, toward the center, children huddled with older folks. Faces ashen with fear, they looked toward him. His presence gave them hope. They counted on him. He was their salvation.

For a heartbeat before he realized the pressure on the door had slackened, Sunnock felt like a hero. He understood that all the gold in the world couldn't buy the sensation of having someone look upon you with gratitude for saving her life. He was all that stood between them and the end of everything. His selflessness would live on forever.

And it was that thought, as yet untainted by wondering how he could turn that gratitude to his own advantage, which occupied his mind the very moment the massive root ball exploded the door. Sharp oaken splinters pierced him through and through. A heavy board crushed his skull. His lifeless body flew into the room, bouncing and rolling to the edge of the circle of people he had saved.

He never heard the terrified screams attesting to his failure.

Jerrad arrived at the longhouse's far end just as the huge, ugly beast struck his first blow. Wood shattered. What had once been the door was now a jagged hole. People screamed from beyond it.

Jerrad choked down fear. "What is that?"

"Some unholy creature gotten on someone by an ogre." The archer's eyes narrowed. "Not full-blooded—usually called ogrekin—but just as nasty as the purebreds."

The ogrekin tugged its club free. Eight feet tall, with flesh the color of a bruised mushroom, the creature bulged with muscle. The sheer power it could generate was terrifying enough, but its face could only be described as blasphemous. One pointed ear sat lower than the other, and the pale blue eye on the left had to be three times the diameter of the brown one on the right. Yellow teeth were jumbled in a jaw that gaped open, and the nose had been broken so many times Jerrad had to cant his head to make the nostrils line up right.

Kiiryth's bow came up. The bowstring twanged as he loosed an arrow. It pierced the monster's left shoulder, the broadhead emerging out the back. Blood ran in rivulets down the arm and dripped from the arrow's tip.

The ogrekin didn't give the wound so much as a glance.

Tyressa, butcher knife in one hand and fishing spear in the other, appeared and whistled loudly. "You're not welcome in my town."

Mother! Jerrad started toward her, but Kiiryth grabbed his collar and held him back.

"You'd only slow her down."

The behemoth looked at her. Contempt further warped its face. It snarled, flashing a tangle of uneven teeth. The ogrekin reached for her with its left hand.

Tyressa ducked beneath the attempted grab and circled around toward the monster's back. It turned to keep with her, but its grip on the club slowed it. By the time the ogrekin had pulled the club from the longhouse, Tyressa had darted in and slashed the thing's right heel. Black blood sprayed from a deep cut over the tendon.

Tyressa danced wide, carrying her outside the range of the ogrekin's swinging club. The club came around and slammed into the longhouse's wall. It splintered boards and snapped the corner post. The longhouse shifted, the wood closing like jaws on the club, clinging to it with a fierce tenacity.

The ogrekin snarled and set itself, muscles bunching in shoulders and back. The monster heaved, trying to free the weapon. Wood groaned. Some nails squeaked as they came free, but the building didn't release the club on that first attempt. So the behemoth planted its feet and hauled back for all it was worth.

The damaged tendon popped. The creature's right foot slid out from under it. The ogre landed hard on the base of its spine. The tremor rattled teeth in Jerrad's head. The monster threw its head back and howled in pain.

And a little bit in fear.

The people of Silverlake boiled from the longhouse. Woodsmen chopped into the ogre's shoulders and wrists. People stabbed it, using knives, scythes, and even sharp sticks. Kiiryth shot arrows into any exposed flesh. Even Serrana charged in, battering it with her blood-stained club.

But Tyressa slew it. As others hacked at its limbs, Jerrad's mother leaped onto the ogre's chest. The monster's head came up. It hissed a challenge. Tyressa roared back, the stepped on its throat and thrust the fishing spear straight through the larger eye.

The ogre thrashed, ripping the spear from her hand and tossing her into the crowd. Its death throes crushed one man and broke several others. The people withdrew, weapons ready, as the monster thrashed out the last seconds of its life, then cheered as it lay still.

Tyressa emerged from the bloodthirsty throng bruised but otherwise unhurt.

Jerrad stared at her, and wasn't alone. *You're my mother, but* are *you my mother?*

Tyressa bent, resting hands on knees. She breathed heavily for a moment or two, then let her skirt hem slip down and straightened up. She looked around, then nodded.

"This is a terrible night, but you've all done well. See to yourselves. See to our wounded. Then we shall attend to our dead." She wiped her bloody hands on her skirts. "This is a night we mourn now, but shall celebrate in the future. And because of you, Silverlake will *have* a future."

Chapter Fourteen
To Begin Again

Aside from the dozen gravestones evenly spaced against the south wall, Silverlake bore little evidence of the previous month's attack. Many people had wanted to mount the ogrekin's skull on a post above the gate, and flank it with goblin heads, but Jerrad's mother had vetoed that idea—wisely, as far as Jerrad was concerned. Goblins and ogres would certainly see it as provocation, and the fey weren't likely to think much of the idea either.

Jerrad walked along the wall, stooping to rip weeds from the grassy mounds. Each of the dead had been given identical stones, quarried nearby and finished by two stonecutters from Thornkeep. The markers—white, slender, and rounded—bore the name of the deceased, birth and death dates, and the simple legend "Silverlake Mourns for Thee." It didn't matter who they had been, or their station in life, all of them had been treated equally.

Even his servants hadn't protested Lord Sunnock being treated as an equal with commoners. Unkind Silverlakers suggested that Tyressa's decree that each of the deceased be treated equally was so Sunnock wouldn't be given a small wooden marker which would decay quickly. Many folks, especially those who had seen him using his body to secure the longhouse door, counted him a hero and credited him with saving their lives. In their minds, his modest marker didn't lower him—everyone else's identical markers elevated them.

Some people suffered had wounds which would handicap them for the rest of their lives. Broken bones had been set to mend, but no one yet had a cast off. Cuts had long since scarred over, but the attack had done more significant damage. Not a night went by when two or three people didn't wake screaming from a nightmare—Jerrad included. When the slivered moon came again, Silverlake braced for another attack.

But the goblins didn't return.

In the week after the attack, the settlers completed work on the lake wall. Not only did they raise the palisade, but they dug a trench deep enough that even an ogre would have been stuck in it up to his eyes. They sharpened and included plenty of wooden stakes, both pointing up and slanting down. Anything which fell into that pit would remain there until rescued.

That precaution meant the only practical way to get from the shore and into the town was to pass north or south and assault the gates, leaving attackers open to archers along the walls. To make that defense work, the citizens of Silverlake began practicing archery two hours a day. A bowyer and two fletchers took up temporary residence to create the necessary equipment.

Jerrad had hoped that Kiiryth would teach the people how to shoot, but two Wolfmane hunters appeared. Without any prompting or promise of pay, they began to give people little tips about shooting. They even took some of the better archers out into the wood to bring back rabbit, deer, and other meat. While they steadfastly refused to move in on a permanent basis, they showed no signs of leaving, and gladly accepted gifts of skins and what other things Silverlakers could spare.

Jerrad understood the reasons behind his mother dictating that everyone learn to shoot. Aside from the need for archers to defend Silverlake, the training gave them the ability to do something to defend themselves. They easily saw signs of their improvement, and to be invited by a Kellid to go hunting took on the honor of being knighted in some civilized land. Having a bow in hand and the weight of a full quiver at the hip calmed many.

Serrana seemed never to be without her bow, or at least a leather bracer on her left forearm. Since that night she'd not worn any of her finer gowns—and the one she'd had on during the attack had been burned. She most often wore homespun tunics and skirts, and for hunting would wear trousers. At first some of the other women had been scandalized over this, but "hunting trousers" soon made up a part of every woman's wardrobe. Some even made a small ceremony of awarding an archer her first pair to coincide with her first kill.

Once the wall had been completed, progress on Silverlake slowed. Part of it was because of the deaths. The dead accounted for a seventh of the population, and the wounded half again that many. Not only did they leave the workforce, but the necessity of posting guards and caring for the injured pulled even more people out. The woodsmen had to travel further into the wood to harvest lumber. That made them more vulnerable to attack, which in turn meant they worked more slowly and cautiously, shrinking output.

Repairs to the longhouse stalled because some people believed it was haunted. Tyressa ordered it razed, then had it rebuilt closer to the front gate and oriented north-south. She had the door placed in the eastern wall, facing a large green and away from the gates. The second longhouse—which had only yet been framed—had been started on the opposite side of the green, with its door facing west. They'd rebuilt the first with much stouter walls and loopholes for shooting any invaders.

Despite some setbacks, Silverlake's population had grown past what it had been the month previous. The stonecutters and fletchers brought their families in to join them. Fishermen who seasonally based themselves in a camp on the lake's south shore relocated. Their choice was one of convenience, since the rains had washed most of their camp away. Then again, as one of them allowed, with goblins massing in the area, Silverlake looked very inviting.

"Jerrad, have you forgotten?"

He looked up at the sound of his mother's voice, raising a hand to block the sun. "No, I was just finishing up weeding."

"Be quick. I'll be in the tent." Tyressa turned and walked off.

He watched her go. Though she had been gifted a pair of hunting trousers by several grateful women for having slain the ogrekin, Tyressa never wore them. She didn't carry anything more than her skinning knife. She remained stiff and wary, ready to react at the slightest sign of trouble.

And she's still disappointed in me.

She'd not discovered that he'd been teaching himself wizardry until a week after the attack. Serrana had spent most of that time sleeping or crying, sometimes both. Tyressa had done her best to tend to her daughter's needs as well as those of the larger community, but she was only human. She only had so much emotional energy, and had said to him, "At least I don't have to worry about you," more than once during that time.

Then, in one of her crying jags, Serrana had described everything which happened that night. Jerrad's mother had picked up on the spell he'd used. She immediately woke him out of a sound sleep and demanded to know why he was being so stupid.

He learned, then and there, that while the author of his grimoire thought the idea that a wizard would be somehow hurt by his magic was silly, his mother feared mightily for his safety. She'd stared at him in horror one moment, then hugged him tightly the next, her tears soaking his tunic.

As much as she was scared for him, what hurt her most was his betrayal of her trust. He tried to explain that he wanted to see if there was any truth to his ability to work magic before he worried her. She latched onto that, using it as proof that he *knew* magic was dangerous and that he shouldn't have been playing around with it without her express permission. He attempted to point out that a spell had allowed him to save Serrana, but

Tyressa countered that if it had failed, she'd have lost *both* of her children.

She capped that with a coolly delivered, "I expect that sort of irresponsibility from your sister, but not you. I thought I could trust you."

That had sunk the knife in and Jerrad had started crying. He didn't want to, but he couldn't hold the tears back. "I just wanted to help," was all he managed to squeak out past the lump in his throat. He balled his fists and pounded them against his thighs, wanting to scream, but refusing to do so.

That was when his mother sat him down and hugged him. She kissed his head and brushed away tears. Her "I know, I know," melted into whispered apologies from each of them. She held on tight, and he clung to her until both of them had stopped shaking.

Then, after he blew his nose, she demanded he tell her everything. He had, save for the part about Kiiryth having given him the grimoire. He told her that he'd been running from sprites and stumbled into a hole where he found it. He wasn't sure what it was, so he started and reading, and . . .

From that point forward, as others gathered to practice archery, Jerrad reported to their tent to study and work spells. Not many of the Silverlakers complained about his not joining them for practice, since bows meant for war proved a bit stout for him to draw, and yet he was a bit older than the children who practiced with bows suitable for shooting varmints. Tyressa also hired Kiiryth to instruct him in archery and other woodland skills, which mollified anyone inclined to protest his special treatment.

He joined his mother in the tent and produced the grimoire. "Is it okay to practice?"

"Read for the moment. The Kellids have been more inquisitive of late." His mother scratched the back of her neck as she studied a map of the settlement. "We can't afford to alienate them."

Because of their history, the Kellids had little liking for magic, and even less use for practitioners thereof. Jerrad hadn't known that at his first encounter with them, but Oreena had explained things after his mother took her into their confidence concerning his abilities. Had he used magic to win the game and the shaman detected it, it might have been barbarians storming Silverlake, not goblins.

That made Jerrad mindful of the grimoire's first admonition concerning magic, and glad he'd observed it. Cheating wasn't really in his nature, but he could see how magic would make some things very easy. Pretty quickly he realized that this was what his mother feared: that with power could come an erosion of his compassion and sense of duty to others.

He seated himself on a camp stool and opened the grimoire. He flipped first toward the back, to see if any new pages had materialized. None had. "There's nothing new."

"Then you might read something else."

Jerrad dropped to his knees and studied the spines arrayed in a small bookcase. Half the books had come with them from Ustalav, while the rest had been traded for or, in the case of the book he pulled from the bottom shelf, *rescued*. Back in the woodsmen's camp, Pine Callum had been tearing pages from it and using them to light fires. Gods alone knew where he'd gotten it, or why he chosen to destroy it rather than selling it off, but he'd been forced to leave it behind—along with plenty of other things—when his workers confronted him about his crooked accounting.

Jerrad placed the book in his lap and brushed his hands over the cracked leather cover. The title had been incised on the front and spine, then had gold leaf applied to it. He knew the book to be Syrin Gorthath's *Brief History of Brevic Noble Houses*, but the lettering appeared to be gibberish.

Jerrad closed his eyes and recalled to mind visual pattern he'd associated with one of the simpler spells from the grimoire. It started as shards of stained glass, which he fitted together in his mind, but the magic happened when he forced the pieces to overlap, freeing a riot of colors. He watched them swirl and his flesh puckered. He waited for the tingling sensation to roll all the way up his spine, then opened his eyes.

The words on the book shimmered as if beneath an inch of water, then surfaced clearly and cleanly. Jerrad opened the book, which took him straight to page two hundred and seventeen. The words had no need to shift on the page. He could understand the language easily, and that comprehension extended beyond the written word to the spoken as well.

That's why she wants to keep me away from the Kellids. Tyressa sincerely doubted Jerrad's ability to maintain a straight face if he were to overhear cutting or cunning remarks shared between the barbarians. They'd certainly note his reaction and quickly enough figure out what was happening. Given their attitudes toward magic, that wasn't in Silverlake's best interest.

This book had been written in Varisian, a language which was common enough in Ustalav, but which Jerrad had never needed to learn. When you were noble, people were always happy to speak your language.

Brevic history consisted of a lot of struggles for supremacy between the various powerful families. The author detailed every plot, every blood relationship, every instance of bastardry and murder as could be believed, and hinted strongly at things he couldn't prove. The narrative suffered from later references to material that had long since gone up in flames, but reading it expanded Jerrad's understanding of politics.

Saving his place with a finger, he looked up at his mother. "May I ask you a question?"

"You'll make up the time any answer takes. I won't have you distracted."

"Yes, Mother."

"Well?"

Jerrad sighed. "It's just that in reading this history, it makes me wonder. Did uncle Harric do it? Did he really try to overthrow Prince Aduard?"

"It would not be wise to measure Ustalavic politics by a Brevic yardstick."

"But that's it. The great houses of Brevoy and ours in Ardis—they're all trying to rekindle glory from the past. Is that why he did it? Did he think he could really succeed?"

His mother pulled another stool around and sat, taking the book from him and tossing it on her map table. "Your uncle—my brother—always suffered from one fault. For him, it was enough to come up with the plan. He never wanted to put the work in to make the plan come to fruition. Were he here, we'd have the most beautiful maps of Silverlake ever. Piles of them, one per season. He might even commission a model of what Silverlake the city would look like. You and I—anyone really—would be amazed. And Harric would convince us that we were looking upon a vision from the future. Though he might not have a taste for actual hard work, he was brilliant in his ability to persuade others of his vision."

She took Jerrad's hands in her own. "Someone, or several someones, shared with him a plan for replacing Prince Aduard. They let Harric convince himself that their vision was his own, and then he set about gathering others into a conspiracy. At least one of them informed the prince. Harric was arrested and tried, and refused to name any other conspirators."

Jerrad nodded. "If you had known, would you have told the prince?"

A tiny shudder ran through his mother's hands. "I ask myself why I didn't know. I should have. Had I, I would have done everything I could to talk him out of such foolishness. I never had that chance. And if I couldn't, well, I don't know, Jerrad. I think I would have told the prince, but I just don't know."

Before he could ask who she suspected had worked with Harric, the alarm bell in the heart of the green began clanging loudly. Both of them stood and headed out.

A breathless man met them just outside the tent and pointed back toward the gate. "Edge of the woods, my lady. Armed men, a whole army of them, and they've come under a banner of Ustalav."

Chapter Fifteen
A Visitor From Home

Tyressa ran to the wall, threading her way through crowds of archers. Serrana had an arrow nocked and started after her mother, but Tyressa stopped her with a raised hand. "Wait."

"Mother, I can hit an apple at the edge of the wood from here. You'll be a target."

"Just wait. Get people arranged. Come up on the wall when I give the signal."

Serrana nodding and turned. "You heard her. Form ranks."

Tyressa climbed the ladder and joined the sentinel above the gate. Out at the forest's edge stood a small group of huntsmen in greens and browns, each armed with a short bow. They flanked a young man in a bright red tabard. He bore the standard of Ustalav, a scattering of red stars on a field of purple, above a stag's rack in black and a central tower. Below it hung a second banner.

She looked at the guard. "The lower banner, the white lion rampant—does it have a gold collar?"

The man squinted, then nodded. "'Pears so."

I'd not have thought . . . She pointed down toward the green. "Go tell them to stop ringing the bell and get ready to open the gates."

"Yes, my lady."

Serrana looked up from the ground. "Is it an army from Ustalav?"

"Not quite an army, but from Ustalav. From Ardis." Tyressa folded her arms around her middle. "It appears Baron Creelisk himself has come to pay us a visit."

As the news spread, Silverlake dissolved into a strange sort of social chaos. Many people scattered to their homes to pull on their finest clothes. Serrana did so, donning a lovely yellow gown which now strained at the shoulders. She even slashed the sleeves open, less to accommodate the new muscle she'd put on than to show off the bracer on her forearm.

Others, including Jerrad, wore their everyday clothes. If they chose to add something, it tended to be a pair of boots or a furred vest which the person had created using skins he'd harvested with his own hands. People proudly displayed fruits of their labors, and more than one wore the bows and arrows with which they had become practiced.

The herald, guarded by the huntsman, approached and announced that Baron Creelisk was coming. Within the hour he appeared, riding a black horse. One of his sons—the eldest, Tyressa thought, but could not be certain—rode beside him on a brown horse. Behind them came a dozen heavily laden wagons, followed by thirty soldiers on foot and twice as many tradesmen.

I don't understand. Not at all. She descended the ladder and called her daughter's servant, Aneska, to her. "Find your mother and tell her to organize the families. They're to move from the outlying tents into the longhouse. Everyone is to squeeze in so we have room for our guests."

"Yes, my lady."

"Serrana, you will greet Baron Creelisk, then conduct him to my tent. I shall receive him there."

The girl nodded. "And you'll change?"

"Why would I . . . ?"

"Mother, this is Baron Creelisk. You must." Serrana shook her head. "You must make the right impression."

"Yes, of course." She gave her daughter a smile, then retreated to her tent. She knew what her daughter intended by reminding her to change, but the nature of the "right impression" would be something they differed over. Serrana, and those who dressed as she did, wished to show that they remembered Ustalav fondly. They wanted to display their loyalty. The others wanted to have their independence noticed. They could live without Ustalav, and would be happy to do so.

But what is it I wish to convey? Tyressa shuddered. In even asking that question she found herself falling back into an Ustalavic mindset—the sort of thing that made survival at court even possible. Back across the river, nuance was everything. The color of flowers in a vase, or the number of petals on each, could convey a different message. A courtier summoned to the prince's presence could read in his attire and the room's decorations everything the prince would never deign to say.

As quickly as she could she located the hunting trousers she'd been given and replaced her skirt. From her belt she hung the hatchet and the butcher knife she'd used on the night of the attack. Had it not been awkward and unnatural, she'd have even carried the fishing spear. Instead she returned the Brevic history to the shelf and sorted a sheaf of notes into distinct piles on the map.

Cheering heralded the party's arrival. Tyressa half-expected thunderous hoofbeats leading to the tent and Creelisk stalking in, incensed that she'd not greeted him at the gate.

Calm yourself.

The baron did not appear. The noise from outside shifted toward the south. It took Tyressa a moment, then her eyes tightened. *Well played.*

She didn't need to venture out to understand what was going on. In fact, Baron Creelisk's action meant that she *couldn't* leave. Before coming to see her, he diverted the company to Lord Sunnock's grave. He'd unfurl some banner over it, or sprinkle earth from Ustalav. He'd do it in silence, pretending to have a private moment while in clear view of everyone. No one who watched him, who saw the signs of grief on his face, could bear him any ill will.

While he played at his charade, she sat and quickly wrote out plans for a larger memorial, to be placed on a small hill to the south. They'd create it in the spring, and expand Silverlake in that direction as well. The fallen would be disinterred and reburied beneath a monument grandly celebrating their sacrifice.

She'd just laid her quill down when Creelisk appeared at the tent's opening. She'd seen him two years earlier—at her brother's execution—and he hadn't changed at all. Of average height and yet cadaverously slender, he had curiously droopy jowls which he sought ineffectively to hide beneath a beard. His coal-black hair matched the hue of his eyes, but she was certain he dyed it. The lines around his eyes and on his forehead betrayed his true age, though his cold gaze had an ancient sense about it. He wore black clothes trimmed with purple. The white lion had been embroidered over his heart, complete with the gold collar that only the head of his family could wear.

"Please, my lord, enter."

"So kind, as always, Lady Tyressa."

"Out here, I have no rank."

The man smiled carefully, tugging off his black gloves. "In Thornkeep, and even to the west, they call you *Ogrebane*. Even discounted, the stories are enough to earn you any title you want."

Tyressa nodded simply. "And you, my lord, know the truth of things. I put it all into the letter I sent."

"I appreciated that very much." He hooked the toe of his boot through the legs of a camp stool. "May I?"

"Please."

He sat and did not appear to mind having to look up at her. "To be frank, I didn't think Sunnock had it in him to be a hero. In fact, I sent him here because he had a streak of cowardice which, I assumed, would keep him safe. Here, he would also have less of a chance for embezzlement—the cowardly form of theft. Giving his life for others simply wasn't in his portfolio."

"People are full of surprises. One never knows what they'll do under stress."

"Succinctly put."

"May I ask why you've come?"

Creelisk chuckled. "To pay my respects to an old friend."

"Will you be taking his body back to Ardis?"

"I think not. Lugging a corpse to Ustalav is going to be an untidy affair. But there's no hurry. That's not a decision that needs to be made right now."

Tyressa folded her arms over her chest. "You make it sound as if you plan an extended stay."

"I have, though exactly how long is in question."

"You've brought enough people to double our population. We're not eating overmuch at the moment, and saving as much as we can for the winter. If we feed all of you, we'll die out here. But then, that's to your benefit, isn't it?"

Creelisk nodded. "I anticipated you reaching that conclusion. It's what I would be thinking. That's why the wagons are laden with all the supplies you last requested through Sunnock. In fact, I doubled them. I suspect Sunnock had confederates who were siphoning off some of the things which were sent in this direction. Also, based on your report of the attack and the aftermath, I guessed at the nature and number of artisans you would require to repair things. While I see you've made great headway, these people will be yours to keep."

Tyressa sat. "Your doing this makes it more likely Silverlake will thrive."

"I don't care if it thrives; it's merely important that it *survives*." Creelisk hunched forward, resting elbows on knees. "You know well I've long coveted Vishov lands.

Now I find myself steward of them, and I'm content to wait twenty years for them to become mine. The problem is that it's very apparent that's not going to happen. Things have changed in Ustalav."

"How so?"

The man's dark eyes narrowed. "It's the romance of the thing here, of Silverlake. You recall how someone paid Ailson Kindler to write that tripe which disgraced your family and embarrassed the prince?"

"That's why we're here."

"Yes, well, someone else paid that scribbler to write another of her so-called novels, with a heavily disguised Silverlake as one of the settings. The book, *Winds of Mercy,* is already wildly popular. In it, the character who represents you—who represented you in the last book—does battle with a goblin king and slays him. So when news of your battle here reached home, it struck many as if you'd proved your innocence. Slaying that ogrekin was your trial by combat. Because you're now seen as an innocent victim, people look to see who's benefited from your hardship."

"And they point at you."

"They do."

"Forgive me, my lord, but the opinions of others have rarely mattered to you in the past."

He sat up. The corner of his mouth twitched in an approximation of a smile. "The reaction within Vishov lands had been especially *vehement,* shall we say. People talk of refusing to pay taxes and instead sending grain and gold here, to Silverlake. As I couldn't stop such a movement without slaughtering masses, I placed myself at the head of it."

Tyressa smiled and looked beyond him. "And the artisans, they were among the most vocal in their support of Silverlake?"

"I found it convenient to offer then a chance to join you." He opened his hands. "That, however, was not the reason *I* had to come."

"No?"

He shook his head. "Your letter, filled though it was with dire news, had a spark buried within it. I read no despair in your words. Stress, yes, and the presentation of a thousand challenges, with the line of them never to end. You reported facts without panic, and asked for aid within reason. And yet, I sensed a need."

"A need for . . . ?"

"In you, nothing. It was something I felt in my heart." He opened his hands. "To put it plainly, I found myself envying you."

"Envying? You've not read well the reports of mud and goblin guts."

"The fact of it is this: I inherited my title and holdings in Ardis after my brother died. My adult life, the last thirty years, has been spent administrating. I hear reports, I make reports, I give orders, all with mind-numbing regularity. Everything runs well, save when highwaymen set up shop or barbarians come raiding. Yet even those things occur within predictable patterns. I will pass my lands and title on to Ranall, and once I'm dead, there will be nothing in the world by which I'll be remembered."

He stood and pointed back toward Sunnock's grave. "Can you imagine anyone mourning my passing? No, please, don't offer a polite protest. My wife won't—don't pretend you don't know of my seeking carnal pleasure outside the marriage bed. My children may. No one else. No one will think of me as they do Sunnock, believing they owe their lives to me.

"I've come to ask you to let me be part of Silverlake. Let me help you however I can. I'll freely give you all the Vishov resources you want. I'll match them with my own. While I will have to return to Ustalav for the winter, if Ranall chooses to remain, I'll see to it that you want for nothing."

Tyressa sat stock-still. Had she had the leisure to imagine a conversation with Baron Creelisk, never in a thousand eons would she have imagined his saying what he just had. Conniving, vicious, the leading candidate for being one of Harric's conspiratorial friends; all of these she would have applied to him and known they were true. His offer came as such a reversal that it defied belief. Knowing him, she was certain the rose he offered had a thorn, but she couldn't see it.

"Your offer is most generous, my lord. I scarcely . . ."

"You cannot believe it. I know. You don't trust me. No, I've earned that, I've earned it many times over." He clasped his hands at the small of his back. "What I would propose is this: In these wagons I have all the provisions I mentioned, plus more. Enough for a grand feast. It should take a day or two to prepare. I assume there are local dignitaries you'd wish to invite to join us, and everyone needs time to settle in. The second longhouse should be finished—that could be the cause for celebration, in fact.

"Take your time to think. Judge me by my actions here. Take a week or a month. Even to the first snow.

Unless you tell me to leave, I shall be here until then. If you see that my intentions are true, you'll have no better partner in raising Silverlake."

Tyressa stood slowly and offered the man her hand. "I can promise only to judge you fairly."

"I can ask no more of you, Tyressa of Silverlake." He smiled a bit more broadly, and maintained it for a heartbeat or two. It almost seemed as if he was having to learn to smile for the first time. "I admire what you've done, and before I die, I would help you make it so much more."

He shook her hand, then turned and walked from the tent.

Tyressa, alone with her thoughts, wanted to sit down, but refused. She forced herself to clear the papers from the map and study it. She made herself look at it as it was, not as Creelisk's help would make it.

That gave her perspective.

But I wonder if it's enough perspective?

Chapter Sixteen
The Measure of a Hero

Jerrad sidestepped the staff-thrust. He slapped the baton in his left hand against the wooden shaft, then whipped the other baton down and around, aiming for a knee.

Kiiryth leaped away and spun the staff around his back, transferring it from right hand to left. He arced it in with a sweeping blow at Jerrad's midsection, but the boy ducked low beneath it. He tucked and rolled forward, then lashed out at the half-elf's right shin.

Kiiryth drew his leg up, letting the batons sail past, then snapped a kick into Jerrad's side. The blow landed solidly, pitching the youth six feet away. As he came down, Jerrad tucked his right shoulder and rolled, coming to his feet a couple steps later. He brought the batons up in a guard.

The half-elf, leaning on his slender staff and breathing heavily, peeled a lock of white, sweat-stuck hair from his cheek. "You're getting better."

Jerrad swiped a sleeve over his forehead, but kept his eye on his teacher as he did so. "I better be. You've had me going through the same basic forms for the last week, two hours a day with you, and an hour by myself. I know I'm faster."

"You're getting hit less often."

"But kicked about the same amount." Jerrad rubbed his forearm against his ribs. "I'm still not seeing how this will make me a good archer. You said you'd explain that."

Kiiryth nodded. "You've come far enough to understand the answer. When you look at it objectively, what's an arrow really?"

Sweat stung Jerrad's eyes as he frowned. "A stick with a sharp end, I guess, that can kill at a distance."

"It can *hit* at a distance."

"You do well with the killing."

"Wolves and goblins are small enough that the arrows open big holes. Something the size of an ogre, well, I've seen ballistae whose bolts would only be an annoyance." The half-elf walked over to the base of a birch tree, reached down, and tossed Jerrad a skin of water. "Once you've shot all your arrows, what have you got?"

He caught the skin, then glanced a the half-elf's bow. "A stick?"

"A stick, just like the one you've got in each hand."

"But if I kill at a distance, as archers can do, I'm not going to have to worry about beating something with a stick."

"So much to learn. Let's look at what you just said." The half-elf stroked a hand over his chin. "Can you guarantee that you'll never face more enemies than you have arrows?"

"No, not really."

"And if your bowstring breaks . . ."

"I have a stick."

"Which is easier to find: a strung bow and sheaf of arrows or a stick?"

Jerrad held his hands up. "I get your point."

"But we're not done. You're learning to be a wizard. You'll find magic can be very effective for killing."

"That's just the problem." Jerrad drank from the skin, then splashed a little more water over his face. "The only thing the book teaches me is how to fool people and make light. It's all illusion. I can't do anything."

"Ask yourself this: in battle, which is more important—the ability to kill, or the ability to survive?"

"That's obvious."

"Only if you have the right answer." Kiiryth sat and leaned back against the tree. "If the enemy wants to destroy you, you win by surviving. Bards would make you think that battle is all about killing, but there's so much more. Deception, eluding, evading—they're all part of it."

"You're talking about running. That's cowardice."

"Is it?" The half-elf pointed north and slightly west, toward the Worldwound. "In the Crusades, a very brave commander took his force toward a demonic horde. Scouts reported that the horde outnumbered his troops five to one. Terrain gave him no advantage. To stay where he was would be to condemn his troops to death or worse. So, he had his men pitch their tents and light fires. He had volunteers stand watch and change the guard. Then, in the darkness, his troops slipped away. Is that cowardice?"

Jerrad rubbed a hand over his forehead. "That's different."

"That's not an answer." Kiiryth held up a hand. "Now, this commander, he didn't flee, he stayed behind with the volunteers. His subordinate commanders, without his knowledge, hooked east and north. They fell upon the enemy from behind, catching them unawares. They inflicted a serious defeat on the enemy—all because they benefited from deception. They slaughtered three times their number of demons. Would that be a cowardly act?"

"No, of course not. But . . ."

"Wait, one more thing." Kiiryth half-smiled. "The commander gathered the volunteers and fled from the demonic host. They led them south and west, which helped the others win their victory—the swiftness of the demonic pursuit was what strung them out, over-extended them and made that victory possible. But the commander didn't know what his subordinates had done. When pursuit flagged, he and the volunteers launched a suicidal attack against the demons, to prevent them from pursuing the others—or what's what he thought he was doing. Had he continued to run, he and his men would have been safe. Instead, most of them died, and a few were captured, hauled off and made to endure endless torments and tortures. Was that cowardice or bravery or stupidity?"

"No, no, stop." Dropping the batons, Jerrad pressed his palms against his eyes. "You're confusing me. You take a cowardly act, then wrap it up in heroism, and then box it all up in wasteful stupidity."

Before he knew what was happening, and before he could open his eyes, the staff's butt end smacked him squarely in the sternum. Jerrad stumbled back and landed solidly on his bottom, his head pitching back to smack a tree. Above him squirrels chittered mockingly, and one dropped an acorn that plunked off his head.

Kiiryth towered over him, the staff ready to poke him again. "Deception is more important in war than killing. Creatures will fight hardest when they believe they have no hope of surviving; and when given the chance to survive will run away without a second thought. If you can make someone think he won't win, but he can escape, he'll escape. And even if he changes his mind, if guilt and duty drive him back, all the energy he used to escape will be gone. Every meal eaten, every arrow shot, just gone. So when you have to engage him again, you'll have him at your advantage."

For a heartbeat or two, Jerrad entertained the idea of using magic to blind the half-elf, then gathering up his batons and knocking him down. *But he's anticipated that.* Kiiryth stood between Jerrad and the abandoned sticks. Even blind, he'd be able to thrash the boy solidly.

Jerrad looked up. "Was the commander a coward? A fool?"

"Not in my eyes."

Jerrad caught a hint of something in the half-elf's voice. "You were there, weren't you? You've been in the Crusades."

Kiiryth's eyes focused elsewhere for a moment, then he nodded. "I was. I fought. I scouted. I knew the man of whom I speak."

"Did the demons kill him like they killed my father?"

"There are many ways to die out there." Kiiryth turned away. "And worse things that can happen to a person."

"What do you mean?"

The half-elf sighed. "I saw things up there which would have made the ogrekin your mother killed flee in terror. Horrible things, demonic things with otherworldly powers for which many men do foolish things. At least when you and I die, we don't surrender who we were."

He came back around to face Jerrad. "We need to deal with one more issue. You want to kill at distance. Do you know why?"

"It's the best way to stop the enemy from hurting me and everyone else."

"That's a valid reason, but it's not *your* reason."

"What do you mean?"

"Think back to the night of the attack. What did you feel when you stabbed that first goblin to death?"

Jerrad fell silent and hugged his knees to his chest. He forced himself to think back. He saw the surprised look on the goblin's face. He could feel its warmth, smell its fetid breath and the weight of its body. He'd wanted it to leave him alone—*which is different from wanting it dead.*

He felt the blood spraying up his sleeve again, all warm and sticky, matting the hair and tickling the inside of his elbow. And when he stood, its blood ran from his arm. It didn't drip, it flowed like a river. Splashing down over a face frozen in pain.

"It was an accident." He looked up. "I wondered what I'd done."

"Killing a thinking creature isn't like killing wildlife. Hunt down a deer and you harvest it. You use everything: meat, bones, antlers, skin. If there's anything left over, bird, beasts, and bugs will finish it. Nothing goes to waste."

Jerrad shook his head. "Not the goblins. Not the ogre." Silverlakers had gathered all the goblin bodies and burned them on a huge pyre. The ogre they dragged out onto a raft and sank in the deepest part of the lake. They worked hard to rid the settlement of any sign of the enemies that had attacked.

"No. We don't eat them. We don't harvest their parts. Well, there may be some that do, necromancers and the like, but we show them that much respect. Not because we think they deserve it, but because it makes us think we're better than perhaps we are." Kiiryth's expression tightened. "Do you want to know why the grimoire hasn't taught you any combat spells?"

"Because it doesn't contain any?"

"No. It's because you're not certain you really want to kill anything. That's far from bad; its good you struggle with it. Killing shouldn't come easy to anyone—*especially* not those who can use magic."

Jerrad wanted to protest, but he thought for a moment. *If being able to work miracles makes me believe I'm better than everyone else, then other thinking creatures become as insignificant to me as wildlife. Killing them won't cause me any concern.*

"I'll have to think about this."

"That's a good answer." The half-elf gave him a nod. "Now, do you want to know why I'm teaching you to fight with sticks?"

"Because I can always find a stick?"

"No. Because whether you want to or not, there will be times you have no choice but to kill. I want you ready."

Jerrad rested his forehead against his knees for a moment, then climbed to his feet. "Better to have a skill and choose not to use it."

"That's the spirit." Kiiryth levered the batons up with his staff and flicked them at Jerrad. "We'll start with the first form again."

"Right. Just one thing."

"Yes?"

Jerrad stared down at the ground. "If the grimoire does teach me a fighting spell, do you want me to tell you?"

Kiiryth leaned on his staff and chewed his lower lip. "I'd like to know—but *not* the nature of the magic itself. You should tell no one."

"Not even my mother?"

"That's not a judgment I can make, but certainly no one else. Your mother is wise. She knows that secrecy can be a source of great power."

The youth nodded. In the week since Creelisk had arrived in Silverlake, his mother had told him to go into the wood to read and practice magic. She'd even stepped up the schedule of Kiiryth's tutoring him as a reason why he was removing himself so much from Silverlake. She clearly didn't want Baron Creelisk aware of his abilities. While the baron had been polite and even solicitous of Jerrad, something about him creeped Jerrad out.

"Master Kiiryth, has my little Mouse learned anything?"

Serrana, bow slung over her back, dressed in hunting attire, came along the trail which wound around the low hills surrounding the bowl in which they fought. Ranall Creelisk followed in her wake. He'd likewise donned hunting clothes of dark brown and green, and carried a boar spear. Taller than his father, well built, clean-shaven, and, by all accounts, handsome, he smiled at Jerrad and Kiiryth. *He smiles enough to be a halfwit.* Jerrad wanted to believe Ranall was addle-pated, but his brown eyes brimmed with intelligence.

Except when he looks at my sister in adoration.

Kiiryth bowed. "My lord and lady, you would be surprised at Jerrad's skill. He's an apt pupil."

Ranall's smile broadened, revealing even teeth. "You're teaching him to fight with batons. Since I was his age—and even younger—I begged my father to let me learn that technique. He maintained that nobles don't fight with vulgar weapons, but it always struck me that in even the most dire of situations, one can lay hand to sticks."

"Your insight does you credit, my lord."

Jerrad stared daggers at Kiiryth. "I thought we were practicing here."

"Yes, please, don't let us interrupt you." Ranall took a step back. "If you wouldn't mind, could we watch? Just for a bit?"

Kiiryth canted his head. "If my pupil has no objection."

Jerrad was about to voice an objection loud and long, but a sharp glance from his sister warned of dire consequences if he refused. "Okay. But, you know, stand back. I don't want anyone to get hurt."

Ranall reached out with a hand to guide Serrana back toward him, and she didn't seem to mind one bit. Jerrad shivered and focused on Kiiryth so he wouldn't puke. "I'm ready."

"Commence."

If Jerrad had imagined that the half-elf would go easy on him in the presence of witnesses, the first sharp attack dispelled that notion. For a heartbeat Jerrad felt betrayed, as if Kiiryth were trying to impress the spectators, but the youth forced that emotion away. He made himself focus on fighting the same way he did on magic. *No emotion, just results.*

Jerrad ducked beneath blows and leaped above others. He parried with one baton and crossed both to block. *Click-clack.* He jumped back as the staff whistled past his midsection, then lunged forward, stabbing with both batons, forcing the half-elf to retreat a step.

Jerrad fought faster and more fluidly than before. He didn't even imagine that he matched well with Kiiryth, but he was infinitely better than he'd been on the first day—and certainly the best he'd been yet. *I might get hit, but not easily.*

Kiiryth brought the staff around in a circular blow which Jerrad leaped above, then the half-elf retreated. He planted the staff on the ground and bowed his head to his opponent. "Very good, Jerrad. Very good indeed."

Ranall applauded. "That was magnificent. Even at court, during entertainments, never have I seen such a display."

Jerrad smiled, refusing to even blink though sweat stung his eyes. "I have the best teacher in the world."

The young Lord Creelisk nodded. "Might I beg an indulgence, Master Kiiryth? Would you teach me how to fight like that? I'll convince my father that here, in the wood, where sticks are plentiful, it would be a useful skill. He'll still think it vulgar, but I suspect he'll acquiesce."

"I should love to accommodate you, my lord, but the fact is that, within the week, I must away. I'll be gone a month, no more."

Jerrad's mouth hung open. "What?"

"There are tasks which demand my attention, Jerrad." The half-elf extended the staff toward the youth. "In my absence, perhaps you would undertake training Lord Creelisk in the basic forms. You know enough to do that. I would consider it a favor, and it would allow you to continue your practice."

"I don't know."

"Please, Jerrad, I would be in your debt." Ranall looked from him to Serrana and back. "Your sister has been a wonderful hostess, but I'm sure my constant reliance on her is a burden. Besides, she has archers to train and things to hunt. I will be a very serious student."

Serrana's incendiary gaze made only one answer possible, so Jerrad nodded. "It would be my pleasure."

"Thank you, Jerrad, you are very kind. And you, Master Kiiryth." Ranall's smile lit up that small segment of the forest. "I had never imagined that here, so far from Ustalav, I would feel so welcome and so much at home. I don't know how I can ever repay your kindness."

Jerrad would have offered a suggestion, but another acorn bounced off his skull, and the resulting laughter kept still his tongue.

Chapter Seventeen
Things Arcane and Odd

Jerrad froze as Nelsa Murdoon lifted a hand. She'd crawled to the crest of the hill, and he wasn't far behind. He didn't like being on his belly on wet leaves terribly much, but that kept their approach quiet. It also made him feel stiffer and more sore than he should have been from his last lesson with Ranall—who had learned much in just two weeks.

Nelsa looked back at him, smiling. She held up one finger, then nodded.

He worked his way up to her left and peered beneath a pale green fern leaf. His stomach fluttered, but he fought down panic. *There's no mud, and I have a stick in my belt.*

Their position overlooked one end of an oblong depression. A single goblin bent down and smoothed a leather mat out. It had a series of concentric circles drawn on it and eight lines radiating out from the center as if it were a compass. Strange line drawings—animals mostly—filled the circles, drawn in black and a rusty brown Jerrad took to be blood.

The goblin himself—and since he was naked, gender was relatively easy to ascertain—capered over to the leather satchel from which he'd drawn the mat. He pulled out four leather bags, each tied securely. Clawed fingers made short work of knots. The goblin carefully poured the bags' contents out, one bag per quadrant of the mat. The goblin flicked his fingers through the piles of bits, spreading them out, but didn't seem to put them in any particular order.

Bones. Little, tiny bones.

The goblin returned the pouches to the satchel and tossed it off toward the depression's far end. He returned to the mat and bowed once at each edge, then began to prance around to the left. He seemed to be stepping to a tune Jerrad couldn't hear. The jerkiness of the moves left Jerrad happy he couldn't hear it, but as he watched, he thought of magic, and carefully started slotting puzzle pieces together.

The spell he invoked was one of the most simple, but the one with which he'd had the least amount of success. According to the grimoire, the spell would give him a sense of magic in the area. The few times he'd had any success with it, he heard what he took to be as a thin echo of a spell having been cast.

Not so this time. The goblin's spell came discordant and loud, blasting into his head with harsh noises. Clicks and screeches ebbed and built, then twisted back on themselves, as if one strain mocked another. It sounded black and cold and *wrong*.

Around and around the goblin danced. He took to hopping whenever the rhythm doubled back, then spinning when sounds hissed like steam escaping wet wood on a fire. His hands came up as the volume increased, then came down again, twisting on wrists, stirring the music into its darker tones.

Nelsa reached over and clutched his hand. A tiny tremor ran through her grip. Jerrad squeezed her hand in return and gave her a brave smile. She didn't see it, so riveted was her gaze on the mat and the dancing goblin.

Then Jerrad saw what she'd seen. The bones had begun to rattle and bounce, as if they'd been set on a drumhead. They crashed into each other, usually flying away, but not always. Some of them stuck. Tail pieces came together. Legs assembled themselves. Ribs leaped into place between spine and breastbone. Tiny teeth shivered into jaws and skulls popped themselves into place.

Four skeletal mice began to dance, aping the goblin's every move. They raced around the mat, leaping, spinning, jumping forward and back. Watching them, Jerrad wanted to laugh, and would have, had the cacophony not raked his mind with cold thorns.

Then the goblin spun one last time and slammed his hand down on the mat's heart. The mice exploded into a blizzard of ivory. The goblin pulled his hand back, and sat abruptly at the mat's western edge. He hunched forward and began mumbling to himself.

The jangling noise of the magic began to fade. Not entirely, but to the same sort of hushed echoes Jerrad had heard before. The goblin's mumbling rose above it, but made no sense at all, and didn't appear to betoken another spell.

Jerrad smiled and constructed his own magic, using the spell that had allowed him to read the Brevic history. A shiver ran down through him. Nelsa squeezed his hand as it passed.

The goblin peered closely at the scattered bones. "Little mices tell me true, what will we be going through?" He repeated that same rhyme over and over—so much so that Jerrad felt he'd understand it even without the use of magic.

The goblin got up and circled the mat, pausing to look at the array from each of the cardinal points. As nearly as Jerrad could make out, he seemed overly concerned with where all four of the skulls had rolled together, right on top of the three-headed jackal symbol for Lamashtu. Worship of the Mother of Monsters was hardly unknown in Ustalav, as she often featured as the patron of villains in fairy tales and bards' stories, and Jerrad recognized the mark easily.

That all four skulls had landed on that symbol clearly shocked the goblin. Several times a hand would creep slowly toward the quartet, then he'd yank it back and suck at his fingers.

Nothing shifted on the mat, so the mice remained mute on the matter, or so it appeared to Jerrad. The goblin apparently got no satisfaction. He circled the mat once more, then reached for one of the smaller bones. His hand hovered as if the bones radiated molten heat. He sat back for a moment, then came around to the western side again. He grabbed the mat by its corners and shook it, much as a servant might shake dust out of a rug. The bones flew off. No fires ignited, nothing even smoldered, but the goblin circled far from where they'd landed. He rolled up the mat, then retrieved the satchel. Without casting a glance back, he headed south, toward the Dismal Caverns.

Jerrad and Nelsa watched him go. Jerrad realized that he was still holding her hand. He wanted to let go, but she hung on. She wasn't squeezing it tight, as she had before, just maintaining a reassuringly firm grip. He found himself smiling, and when she finally looked at him, she wore a similar grin.

They had to let their hands go to retreat back down the hill. Jerrad did so reluctantly, then closed his fist to retain the last hint of her warmth. They slid down the hill as quietly as possible, then retraced their steps to the next hill. After that, though they were heading north back toward Silverlake, they swung west. They used a new path for their return, frustrating anything that might have been waiting to ambush them on the path they'd taken south.

About a mile on they stopped, fairly confident they had reached a safe distance. There wasn't any logic behind that decision—Jerrad just knew he *felt* safe. And he felt he would burst if he didn't say something.

"When you said you wanted to show me something, I couldn't have even guessed. What was that?"

Nelsa shrugged. "I mean to tell you, I ain't exactly sure. Now, plenty of folks know the Bonedancer goblins live in the Dismal Caverns. Won't be long before you'll hear plenty of tall tales about folks adventuring down in there, pulling out treasure as if them caverns was a warehouse in Mosswater. And from what you said about the attack, a passel of them goblins was Bonedancers. I was only meaning to maybe show you some goblin tracks, but that was . . ."

"What was he? Was he a wizard?"

"Priest, most like. Goblins don't have much truck with magic what ain't got a god's-mark on it, or so I'm given to believe." She frowned, and Jerrad thought she looked cute the way she concentrated. "I been to Thornkeep a time or three. I seen people cast bones that way and read fortunes."

"That way? With the dance?"

"No, and they weren't starkers neither." She shook her head. "Not sure that's something I ever want to see again."

"Me, neither." Jerrad's flesh tightened at the nape of his neck. The echoes of that discord would be enough to give him nightmares. "If he was casting a fortune, he didn't seem very happy with the result."

"I don't expect so. I don't know about all that, but four skulls together can't be a good thing. You know, my pa does a bit of trading with the goblins, mostly to keep them from deciding to rob us blind. I learned some words. I could teach you."

Jerrad almost told her he didn't need any lessons, but two things stopped him. He had no idea how Nelsa would react to his learning to be a wizard. More importantly, if he said no, she might not come around as much. "I would like that. It would be very helpful, you know, with Silverlake."

"I reckon we can commence lessons inside the week. I have to tell pa what I'll be doing."

"Good. Good." Jerrad glanced back toward the Dismal Caverns. "What are you going to tell your father about what we just saw? I don't know what I should tell my mother. If she knew, she might worry."

Nelsa nodded solemnly. "We didn't much learn anything, anyway. A goblin cast some bones, didn't like the way they fell, then pitched the whole lot of them away. All in all, not much to be worrying about, is it?"

"Nope."

She grabbed his hands. "Okay, so we agree. We don't tell about this unless we both figure someone needs to know, right?"

"Right."

They both fell silent, holding hands. Jerrad's heart began to pound a little faster. He felt awkward saying nothing, but was sure that if he said something—*anything*—it would break the magic of the moment. He would have been content to stand there forever.

He looked up at her, and caught her, just for an instant, looking at him the way his sister looked at Ranall. Then she blushed and dropped one of his hands, and turned away. His heart caught in his throat, and he couldn't get rid of the stupid grin on his face.

He looked down. "I guess we should be getting back to Silverlake."

"I'm of a mind that you're right."

They started walking, still holding hands. They kept holding them until the flatter land got bumpy. They needed both hands to scramble up the hill. Neither reached for the other's hand after that, which settled some cold in Jerrad's belly where there had been warmth.

"I can walk you back to your family's compound."

"No need. Mulish is at Silverlake. He'll take me back."

"Right. Of course. I should have . . . Um, what does he think of Ranall? I mean, your father suggested that he could marry my sister, but she seems to have her heart set on Ranall."

She laughed lightly. "I'm going to trust you with a secret."

"I'll keep it."

"I know." Nelsa smiled. "Won't be for long. I reckon that by the time Silverlake has its harvest feast, the news will be out. Mulish might even save it for announcing then. Since everyone will be there."

"Right." Baron Creelisk had suggested to Jerrad's mother that they use a portion of the supplies he brought for a welcoming feast. She'd thought about it, then put the matter to a vote of the settlers. She asked if they would prefer to feast now, in the summer, or save those treats for a more traditional harvest feast. Included in that latter idea, though never explicitly stated, was the possibility of canceling the feast if it looked like Silverlake would need the supplies to see it through the winter.

"Mulish, he's pretty stubborn on many things. Long about when he was all of five, maybe seven—he keeps getting younger when this is brought up, you see—he announced to the family that he was going to take himself a wife from Katapesh. Don't no one recall where he learned that name." She shook her head. "One time a bonecaster in Thornkeep said Mulish was an old soul born in a young body, and that his last life had probably been down in Katapesh. I don't know that's true or not. Pa thinks the fortune-teller heard the story about Mulish and thought she could earn some coin telling us all about his past."

"So he never really was interested in my sister."

"Well, I'll tell you this, he's allowed as how she's easy on the eyes."

"I won't tell her he said that."

"That ain't the secret." Nelsa lowered her voice and leaned in closer. "Mulish, he's going to up and head down to Katapesh come the spring. Now, while he's here, he'll give Ranall a bit of competition. He thinks its funny and it keeps Pa from suspecting."

Jerrad smiled. "I promise, I won't say a word."

"I trust you." She winked and Jerrad felt heat rise to his cheeks. "And just so you don't go thinking I hide things regular from my folks, it's my ma that told me about Mulish's plan. She wanted me to distract my pa if he started getting ideas."

"A wise woman, your mother."

"Yours is sharper than new-honed knife. My pa's said that and ain't nobody found no reason to disagree." As they emerged from the woods, Nelsa nodded toward the settlement. "Lots of people have dreams, but not many of them can make them come true."

"She's got the help of a lot of friends, like you and your family."

Nelsa smiled, then squeezed his hand and kissed him on the cheek. "Helps she has a smart son with a honeyed tongue."

Jerrad wanted to say something, but his mind completely blanked.

She released his hand, but pressed a finger to his lips. "Don't need to say nothing, Jerrad Vishov. Times no words at all is better than the best words. I'm content with this being one of them times."

Chapter Eighteen
Forging Alliances

M other, we have a problem."

The urgency in her daughter's voice made Tyressa look up from the map table. "Is someone dead? Is someone bleeding?"

"Not yet. You better come." Serrana pointed at the hatchet. "You'll want to be wearing that, too."

Tyressa grabbed the belt from which the hatchet hung and looped it over her shoulder, then threaded her way to the second longhouse's door. Everyone living there appeared to be going about their afternoon duties—consisting largely of childcare and meal preparation. Outside, the two women headed for the gate, and people drifted with them.

More of them were armed than Tyressa found comfortable. Not because she didn't like them carrying weapons, but because they were milling about. *We may have taught them to shoot, but we've not taught them to be warriors. That will have to change.*

Through the gates, she followed her daughter along the winding track heading west, eventually leading to the road that ran near the Murdoon estate. Slightly south of where the road disappeared into the forest, a crowd of Kellids had gathered. The Wolfmane tribesfolk weren't arrayed as warriors any more than her people had been, but given their history and training, any battle between them would be short, swift, and bloody. *And not decided in our favor.*

"Wait, Serra. What's happening? Why is Aneska standing there with Lekar?"

"That's the problem. She went hunting with Lekar. About the time I expected them back, so Lekar could continue training people this afternoon, Selka said the other Kellid wouldn't be returning to instruct anymore, and that Aneska would go with him to be his wife."

"Is she with him willingly?"

The girl wouldn't meet her mother's gaze. "I don't know."

"How can you not know? She's your servant and—I thought—your friend."

"I've been spending much of my time with Ranall. Aneska and I don't talk as much as we used to. Hardly at all now."

An angry spark flashed through Tyressa. "I'm not asking if you're still friends, I'm asking what you observed. You have a role here, and not just because you're my daughter. We all have to be responsible for each other. Was she complicit in this? Is she consenting, or is she under duress?"

"Like I said, I don't know."

"You and I are going to have a long talk, young lady."

"Mother."

Tyressa had expected defiance from a child trying to be an adult. Instead, she got pain and fear from a young woman who clearly felt as helpless as a child. "I'll do what I can," she told Serrana. "You go back to town and don't let anyone do anything stupid."

"Yes, I understand."

Tyressa continued toward the Wolfmanes, taking some heart in the fact that a carpet had been rolled out, flattening grasses. Darioth sat on one end with her back to her people. Tyressa also recognized the crone from their first meeting, and both Lekar and Selka, the two hunters who had been helping train the Silverlakers. Aneska stood next to Lekar, the Kellid's arm draped possessively around her shoulders. Darioth had added a gold bracelet and a bejeweled cloak clasp to her clothing, making Tyressa feel somewhat underdressed.

If they meant to kidnap the girl, they would just have taken her. Their ways are not our ways.

Tyressa paused at the carpet's edge. "Greetings, Darioth of the Wolfmanes. To what do I owe this honor?"

"I would trade with you, Tyressa of Silverlake." She waved Tyressa to the other end of the carpet. "My nephew will take this woman to wife. We shall agree upon a bride price."

Not our ways, but not wholly foreign. Tyressa sat cross-legged, matching Darioth. "I'm honored that you come to negotiate. You have me at a disadvantage. You have the girl. Knowing of Lekar's strong will, I don't imagine he will surrender her if we cannot reach a settlement."

"It might seem that way to you, Tyressa; but I would remind you that you have gotten much labor from him and Selka. Your people have gained skills which they will not forget. Those skills guarantee their survival, and that of their children. Your people will have a future because of what Lekar has done. Would you deny him and his bloodline the same future?"

"I would never denigrate his efforts on our behalf." Tyressa glanced back at the town and momentarily ignored the small knot of people heading toward the meeting. "I was under the impression that we had generously demonstrated our gratitude. If we have not, then the fault is mine. We can negotiate recompense for that slight."

Darioth smiled. "Your generosity has been without fault. It is that nature of your people which shows through this girl, and what has made us value her greatly. You will find that we will be generous, honoring any reasonable request."

Tyressa smiled easily. The Kellids had the girl and weren't going to give her back. The invitation to trade for her, while honestly offered, was not *fairly* offered. The Kellids could just steal Aneska away, and the Silverlakers couldn't stop them. Moreover, if the compensation Tyressa asked for fell outside of reason, she'd insult Darioth and might provoke the Wolfmanes to attack.

And that's all immaterial because I cannot sell one of my citizens.

Lord Creelisk's voice came softly urgent. "Lady Tyressa, may I have a word?"

Tyressa bowed to Darioth, then stood. "I would seek counsel."

"I will wait here."

Tyressa walked back down the hill, past where Baron Creelisk waited, forcing him to follow her. His son and the captain of his guards, Ellic, came along with the baron. She stopped with her back to the Kellids. "This is not a good time, my lord."

"I know, but what I have to say is important." He straightened up. "Everyone in Silverlake is agreed. We will not let them take her."

Ellic nodded. "My troops are arming themselves and ready to strike."

"You, Captain, will return to Silverlake and tell your men to stand down."

"My lady—"

"Captain, what part of what I just said gave you any indication this was a matter open to negotiation? Go. Now."

Creelisk stayed the man's departure. "Lady Tyressa, as I said, Silverlake has agreed."

"This is not a matter to be decided by the town."

Creelisk arched an eyebrow. "I was under the impression *all* major issues were decided by the town. In the matter of the feast, the town voted . . ."

"This is different. When you say the town has decided, how do you know that? Did you poll everyone—save *me*—and reach a consensus? Or did you just tell them 'we must' this and 'can't allow' that? In a moment of fear, did you ask them to think, or did you offer them a plan which meant they didn't *need* to think?"

"This is not the first time I've been in this sort of situation, Tyressa."

"You could have been in it a thousand times before, my lord, but it would not mean you're right in *this* situation." Her nostrils flared. "Why are you still here, Captain Ellic?"

"Sorry, my lady."

Creelisk's face darkened. "This would establish a horrible precedent, Tyressa. If we don't fight to defend our citizens, then bandits, Broken Men, and anyone else wandering through will take them. We need to send the Wolfmanes a message, and through them, a message to everyone else."

"You'll perhaps someday forgive me for saying this, my lord, but when the only tool you possess is a dagger, then every problem you face appears to need bloodletting."

"You can't seriously be telling me that I'm wrong about this."

"Your analysis of the problem is crystal clear, and accurate." Tyressa shook her head. "Your choice of solutions is foolish. Fighting the Wolfmanes will do one thing only: start a blood feud with the Kellids. The killing will never end."

"But if you give in, they won't respect us. They'll make other demands. They'll come and take others." He pointed back at Silverlake. "The next one they come for could be your daughter."

"It could be *me*, my lord. I understand that."

"And you have a solution that will prevent this from ever happening again?"

"I believe I do. You'll remain here. Ranall, you'll come with me, but you will say nothing."

Creelisk grabbed her arm. "You're not giving them my son."

"No, my lord, have no fear." She turned and started back up the hill. "Come."

Ranall fell in a step back and half a one to the left. "Just one thing, my lady. You're not going to get me a Kellid wife, are you?"

Tyressa shot him a quick glance. "You'd never survive a Kellid wife, Ranall. Have no fear. I just want you to listen for your father, and for everyone else."

"As you desire."

Tyressa returned to the carpet and sat again. "Forgive me. Some believed there were matters that required urgent discussion."

"The burdens of leadership."

"So wisely put." Tyressa pressed her hands together. "I'm confident that what you will offer us for Aneska will be magnificent, for she is magnificent. She is my daughter's friend. Having her away from us will create a vast void."

"We will do our best to fill it."

Tyressa looked past Darioth and studied Aneska's face. She watched her for a moment, then made her decision. *If it pleases the gods, let this work.*

"Before I can negotiate fairly, Darioth, I need to ask the girl two questions. Here is fine. May I?"

The Wolfmane Chieftain nodded.

"Aneska, answer me truthfully: Do you go with Lekar of your own free will?"

Aneska smiled quickly and rubbed a hand over her belly. "I do."

"Good. I'm pleased for you." Tyressa returned the smile, openly and genuinely. "Then all I have to ask of you is what you think is fair compensation for you?"

The girl's eyes widened in surprise—as did those of many of the Kellids. Darioth covered her reaction the most quickly, and the crone reacted with a toothless smile. Aneska looked up at Lekar, and he down at her. His fingers tightened on her upper arm, more reassuring than restraining, Tyressa thought.

The girl shook her head. "I'm sorry, Lady Tyressa. I don't know what would be fair compensation."

"I understand, child." Tyressa kept her smile broad as she shifted her gaze to Darioth. "That Aneska goes of her own free will and is happy is all the compensation I can ask. I hope she is as beloved among the Wolfmanes as she is within Silverlake."

"Of course she shall be." Darioth nodded solemnly. "My nephew will see to that."

"In this I trust, Darioth of the Wolfmanes. And, Aneska, know that you are still one of us. If you or your family need for anything, or simply wish to come visit, you will always be welcome."

"Thank you, Lady Tyressa."

"You'll want to bring Lekar into town and let your parents know. I'll tell them right now, but you will be back within the week, yes? Then we shall celebrate your wedding, or even arrange for it here, if the Wolfmanes so desire."

"Yes, my lady."

Tyressa stood, then bowed to Darioth. "As always, it is a pleasure to see you. Thank you for everything."

The barbarian chieftain rose and returned the bow. "The people of Silverlake are wise and fair. It is little wonder they will prosper."

Tyressa turned and walked away. Ranall fell in behind her, remaining silent. They walked down the hill in silence and didn't even pause when they reached where Baron Creelisk stood. He caught up after a step or two, but Tyressa didn't bother glancing at him.

"What did you get for her?"

"Nothing, my lord."

"*Nothing!*" Creelisk sputtered for a moment or two. "Nothing? Not a skin or an arrow? Have your senses completely abandoned you? Nothing?"

Ranall laughed quickly. "She actually got *everything*."

"Talk sense, boy. How can nothing be everything?"

"My lady . . . ?"

"Please, Ranall. I wanted you there to hear. Explain what you heard?"

The young man remained silent for a moment, then began in an even and strong voice. "The danger you saw, Father, is because the Kellids are a fiercely proud people, skilled at fighting. You saw them as all Ustalavs have seen them since our nation was carved from lands they claimed—reavers and bandits, savage opportunists whose morals are beyond our ken."

"I know the history, Ranall."

"My point, Father, is that Lady Tyressa realized that their weaknesses are their pride and their love of freedom. The Kellids knew that they were claiming Aneska as chattel. Had Lady Tyressa negotiated for material goods, she'd have been selling them a slave. While they would have gotten what they wanted, Lady

Tyressa would have been diminished in their eyes. She would have denied the girl freedom—a girl who is now counted as a Wolfmane. That would have sowed seeds of distrust that might eventually lead the Wolfmanes to attack Silverlake."

"But they made an offer, didn't they?"

"Yes, yes they did. And in this, Lady Tyressa was more brilliant."

Tyressa shook her head. "I was lucky."

"Lucky was what Aneska said, my lady. Brilliant was in how you used it."

"I'm waiting, son."

"Yes, Father." Ranall paused as he leaped over a small stone half-buried in the grass. "Lady Tyressa asked the girl to put a price on herself. The Wolfmanes would have been honor-bound to meet that request if reasonable; and Lady Tyressa could have negotiated it down were it not reasonable. But the girl said she couldn't name a price."

"So you gave them the girl for *nothing?*"

"I gave the girl her freedom of choice. The Wolfmanes saw her as a prize of great value, but because it was her desire to join them, I demanded nothing."

"You *are* mad."

"No, Father, she's not. Remember, the Kellids are ferociously proud. What she did was create an obligation of infinite size. They can never truly pay it off, so they will forever in Silverlake's debt."

"Wait. Stop."

Tyressa stopped and turned back to look at Creelisk. The baron stared at the ground, hand to forehead. "Yes, my lord?"

"You found a solution where you turned an enemy into an ally without any loss of status or power?"

"And without any blood being shed. Yes, my lord."

His head came up. "I owe you an apology."

Tyressa blinked. "My lord?"

"When I came here, I feared finding a settlement little better than a gathering of mud huts, with people in rags, half of you dead, the rest ill and dying. When Silverlake wasn't that, I reminded myself that you, Tyressa, had managed the Vishov estates. It became easy for me to ascribe Silverlake's condition to that: a well-managed estate in the heart of a nation at peace."

He swept a hand out toward Silverlake. "This sort of situation, I thought it would be beyond you. You show me depths I had not imagined before. I apologize for having believed so little in you."

That was unexpected. Tyressa nodded. "You are most gracious, my lord. If the truth be told, I would have believed of me what you did right up until I found myself on top of that hill. I don't know that I had this in me all the time, or if it's grown in me since being here. But I will tell you this: I mean for Silverlake to thrive. Not just so my family can return to Ustalav, but so the people who have put their trust in me can thrive as well. This is a duty I hold to be sacred, and one I will fulfill until I succeed or die trying."

Chapter Nineteen
The Asp

Baron Anthorn Creelisk strolled through Silverlake's gates as dusk trailed into night. He waved away the guard who would have followed him. "I shan't be long."

"Yes, my lord."

Creelisk headed off along the path running to the north and then back east, outside the wall, and down toward the lake. He made his way casually, hands clasped at the small of his back, as if a man lost in thought. Most of the Silverlakers regarded him politely, but didn't interact with him overmuch. Their loyalties lay with the Vishov family, so on one level or another, they regarded him as an enemy.

Tyressa Vishov had surprised him in her treating with the Kellids. He would have loved to know what she would have done had the girl said she didn't want to go to the Kellids. The impasse he'd described would have then been in place. He had to allow that she might have been able to find a way to resolve the issue without bloodshed, but that he put down to a minimal chance of success. Most likely she would have had to fight, which would have killed people in the short term, and allowed Silverlake to wither.

That would have been an outcome that would not suit him. Not anymore. He had contingency plans in place to reinforce Silverlake if necessary, but he much preferred to remain in the background. If he were seen as having too much of a hand in Silverlake's fate, it would put the whole of his plan in jeopardy.

He paused at the top of the hill overlooking the lake. The setting sun cast a long shadow out before him. The silhouette of his head touched the waters gently lapping at the shore. He watched red and silver lights dancing on the water.

Silvershade Lake had a certain beauty to it which Creelisk could recognize despite having spent his life in more settled and civilized lands. Echo Wood had an elegance and power that mocked the empires of men. Hundreds of settlements might well have been raised down through antiquity where Silverlake now stood, and when they fell, the wood simply reclaimed them. It hid the accomplishments of men, appearing innocent and inviting when the next company of settlers arrived.

The harsher bits of Ustalav allowed no one such illusions—places like Carrion Hill, for example. It existed at the southern edge of the Furrows, a desolate land scarred with trenches from a generations-old war, and often still sterile because of the destruction. Anthorn's father had taken him there when he even younger than

Jerrad Vishov. He'd pointed to the devastation and told Anthorn that it had all be caused by a civil war which pitted brother against brother.

The old man's meaning was clear: were Anthorn to plot against his brother, only ruin would result. He told his father he understood.

I just didn't tell him what *I understood.*

The lesson he'd taken from that landscape was simple: never engage in a war unless you've guaranteed the outcome before the first arrow flies. While that lesson might have served as the brake to ambition for another, it challenged Anthorn. He never looked upon others as allies, but as enemies or weapons or both. He resolved not to make the mistakes that had killed so many in the past, but that was far cry from resolving to see to it that no one died.

Ascending to the pinnacle of Creelisk power had not been difficult. Anthorn had secured—by bribes, extortion, and apparent friendship—enough support to unseat his brother. He'd have happily murdered him, but his brother did him the favor of falling from a horse and dying.

He closed his eyes, raised his face to the sky, and smiled. Had anyone been watching him from the wall, they'd assume he was luxuriating in the beauty. And he was, in a way, just not the beauty of the lake. It was in the memory of his brother's death. His brother had died riding, which was something the man had always enjoyed. The fact that his death was in character with who he was elegantly killed rumors of foul play. Anthorn was able to assume the throne without having to destroy conspirators or gossipmongers.

The smile still curving his lips, Creelisk opened his eyes again and walked down to the shore. The rustling hiss and slap of water pleased him with its calm regularity. It, akin to people, was a predictable force. Recognizing strength and momentum allowed one to manipulate anything or anyone. A nudge might do. A shove in an extreme case. An encouraging word and a heartfelt expression of sentiment worked for people.

His son, for example, was so simple. Like all young men, he chafed to be out from under his father's shadow. Tyressa had used that by picking Ranall to accompany her to talk to the barbarians. And Ranall had repaid her when he came back and deigned to educate his father about her brilliance. Ranall was proud of her because he was proud of himself.

Which is why I said what I said to her. The baron bent, picked up a flat stone, then skipped it across the water. It vanished into shadow before it sank beneath the waves. *The praise I gave her, he took for himself.*

Creelisk would be certain to praise his son in the coming days. Not effusively, that had never been his way. He'd just approve of more things. He'd tell Ranall that he could remember when he'd just been a boy, and now he was all grown up. He'd play the proud father, and Ranall would take to it like a newborn calf to a teat.

Creelisk would also praise Tyressa in front of Ranall. That praise would reach her ears via his son and her daughter. That means of transmission would benefit him. Because both of the children had developed an affection for each other, they had a vested interest in seeing to it that their parents became friends. Anything Creelisk said about Tyressa would be embellished to the point where he'd vomit were he asked to repeat what they reported.

Oddly enough, he needed Tyressa to see him as an ally if his plans were to succeed. She was rightfully suspicious, since he *had* coveted Vishov lands. He didn't mind that level of suspicion, however, because it blinded her to the enormity and depth of his planning. In fact, he felt insulted that she believed his ambitions were so paltry as to begin and end with owning her family's land.

He started walking south along the beach, treading carefully over the rocky patches between the high water mark and where the water currently sat. A few people gathering firewood from the piles on the beach gave him nods as he passed. He smiled indulgently, which is what they expected of nobility, then continued on into darkness.

Tyressa Vishov, despite her being stronger than he'd imagined, presented him little difficulty when it came to analysis. She'd proposed the creation of Silverlake to save her family and its legacy. This remained her goal, which meant she was incredibly shortsighted. In twenty years, Silverlake could grow to be the biggest city in Echo Wood. He doubted it would even take that long, but her focus was on survival, not the acquisition of power. *Even though the latter would make the former far more certain.*

The daughter had surprised him. According to the reports Sunnock had sent along, she wanted nothing to do with Silverlake. Creelisk had fully expected she could be lured back to Ustalav easily enough. He'd brought Ranall for that purpose, and had sent books and other mementos through Sunnock to make her homesick.

Either Sunnock had been incredibly dense in his reportage, or the girl had changed significantly in the wake of the goblin attack. Creelisk believed the attack had been a turning point in her life—as it might have been in anyone's. Once you killed, things changed. So it had been for him, and so it apparently had been for her. People in Silverlake compared her favorably to Garath Sharpax, saying she was a worthy heir to his legend.

Though he'd not accounted for that possibility in making his plans, it served him very well. Having Serrana Straightarrow be the daughter of Garath Sharpax and Tyressa Ogrebane would cast Silverlake into a different light. Whereas many Ustalavs had felt sympathetic toward the effort to save the Vishov family, now Silverlake became a noble Ustalavic outpost sunk deep in Echo Wood. It would become not a place that people hoped would survive, but one where they invested their pride.

So when it's destroyed . . .

Creelisk briefly considered the boy, Jerrad. From the tales circulating in Silverlake, Jerrad's only talent lay in finding bogs and running afoul of goblins. His need to be rescued from those encounters made him comical at best, and pitiful in truth. Even Ranall, who spent time training the boy to fight, said little of him save that he tried very hard.

He's of no use in this affair. But as soon as the thought formed, Creelisk caught himself. Having the boy as a survivor would generate a certain amount of sympathy. *Were I to take him under my wing, return him to his estates, I would rightly be seen as the protector of the Vishov legacy.*

Creelisk considered that for a moment, then shook his head. He'd have the Vishov estate when the family was all dead. While Jerrad might be easily manipulated, if he *were* to grow a spine, he could be a difficulty. *No, best he dies here with the rest.*

Creelisk stopped and looked back. Judging by how the torches along Silverlake's walls appeared to be little more than sparks, he'd gone a thousand yards along the lake's shore. He waited, stilling his breath and listening. He heard crickets chirping and the lonely calls of waterfowl echoing over the water, but nothing else.

He dropped to a knee at the water's edge and tugged the glove off his right hand. A gold ring fitted with a knuckle-sized ruby encircled the fourth finger. He reached over and twisted, sliding the ruby up and around, revealing a hollow beneath it. Turning his hand over, he shook the contents into the gloved palm of his left hand, then closed the ring again.

With thumb and forefinger he plucked up a greasy black lock of hair. One of the Silverlakers had cut it from the dead ogre's head. It had cost Creelisk three gold pieces, though he'd gladly have paid a hundred times that much for it. The previous owner had seen it as a souvenir, but for him it became the key which unlocked Silverlake's destruction.

A destruction they've carefully constructed for themselves.

He brought his hand down into the water. The hair softened, the water imbuing it with a semblance of life. It brushed against the backs of his fingers. He let it soak thoroughly, then curled it tightly and tucked it back in the ring's hidden compartment.

He smiled. He'd had the ring made for him especially by a necromancer whose blatant disregard for ethics meant Creelisk got all he paid for without pesky questions being asked. This part of the plan had cost him a ridiculous amount, but as with the hair, some things were worth more than gold.

He tightened his grip, sank his fist in the water, then closed his eyes and concentrated. Within his mind, the pieces of the various spells locked within the ring appeared. All sharp-edges, like shards of glass, and blacker than the night, they spun and twisted and floated. He reached out to one, stopping its motion, then slid another into position. They snapped together, then he added another piece, and another, until they formed a rigid blade. He caught the blade in his mind, feeling it, *knowing it*, drawing on its essence. Then he focused the magic down through channels in the ring and into the hair. The rigid blade became fluid and jetted like blood from his fist. It pulsed into the lake, black ink in clear water. It washed over the ring, then resolved itself into hairlike fibers which spread out and flowed down.

Creelisk bowed his head as a momentary fatigue shook him. He'd used the ring's magic before to animate the dead, in order to familiarize himself with its workings, but those times he'd been closer to the body, often able to touch it. When he'd worked at a distance, it had seldom been more than the depth of a grave, and many of those had been shallow.

But this, this is different.

The Silverlakers had made a good decision in choosing to sink the ogrekin's body in the lake. Were other ogres to find it, at some point or other it would occur to them that the people in Silverlake had killed their compatriot. While most ogres wouldn't waste sentiment on another of their kind, a community of ogrekillers was a threat to everyone. It could not be allowed to stand.

Hiding the body deep in the lake would keep it away from ogres, but the Silverlakers didn't understand that their watery grave didn't mean the ogrekin would be hidden forever. The lock of hair, because it had come from the corpse, had a connection to the corpse. And the lake's water, which touched the ogrekin, likewise had a connection to it. To accomplish his goal, Creelisk merely had to use those connections to link the corpse with his magic.

His fingers tingled up to the knuckles, and he smiled. He'd not expected the link to be that strong, at so far a distance, but the corpse would be fairly fresh. The depths would retard putrefaction, so save for bits gnawed off by fish or cut off as mementos by Silverlakers, the ogrekin should be in fairly good shape.

He pulled his hand from the water. The ruby glowed lightly, and Creelisk hid it once again within his glove.

He withdrew from the lake's edge and concealed himself in a tree's moonshadow. *He should be coming right... about... now...*

Something bobbed to the surface thirty feet from shore. It came in, water draining from a head and broad shoulders. The left hand had two fingers remaining, the right three.

Water sheeted off as the creature limped from the lake. It dragged its right foot, but that didn't concern Creelisk. He didn't need speed or agility from the undead ogrekin. He just needed it following his command. It would deliver a message, and that would be enough.

He remained in shadow. "I who raised you now command you. You are to go to Mosswater. Consume what you must only when you must, to sustain yourself. Once in Mosswater you will conceal yourself until I give you further commands."

The ogrekin did not turn to look at him, nor did it acknowledge him in any way. The end of the fishing spear remained stuck in the one eye. It limped on, shifting its course slightly south, then again west, heading on a fairly straight course for the Mosswater ruins.

Creelisk smiled and rubbed his left hand over the ring. He'd set things into motion. Barring unforeseen interference, nothing could stop his plan from working. He looked up at the stars twinkling in the cold sky. "If you could see me, Father, I think you'd be amazed at how well I learned the lesson you worked so hard to teach."

Chapter Twenty
The Perils of Curiosity

Something about the goblin and what it had done with the bones kept at Jerrad like an itch on his back that he couldn't ever scratch. The magic had felt so wrong and so evil that he wanted nothing to do with it. At the same time, its being that evil meant that to ignore it would be an irresponsible act which could jeopardize Silverlake.

Armed with two sticks, he ventured back to the hollow where he and Nelsa had seen the goblin. He used every ounce of woodcraft that Nelsa, Kiiryth, and his desire to avoid the fey had taught him. Out of respect for his skill, or simply because they didn't notice his silent passage, squirrels ignored him. He didn't see or hear any fey—especially sprites.

The absence of goblins also gave him heart.

He hadn't told Nelsa what he was going to do, even though he'd made up his mind to do it the last time they'd explored the wood together. He wasn't afraid she'd talk him out of going, or point out that what he was doing was decidedly foolish and certainly dangerous. He wasn't even afraid that she'd have followed him. He *knew* she'd have led the way, even though she thought the expedition was foolish and dangerous.

He keenly felt the lack of her company as he slipped from shadow to shadow. Nelsa wasn't easy to peg. Smart and adventurous, she tended to think about things almost as much as he did. It wasn't that she couldn't be emotional—though nowhere near as much as his sister—but she let her mind take a run at things before she defaulted to her heart. She was more like his mother in that way, though her laconic sense of humor wasn't anything like his mother's.

My mother's sense of humor has been missing since the attack. It had died about the time she killed the ogrekin. The advent of Baron Creelisk and the need to prepare for winter hadn't given it any chance to come back. He missed hearing his mother laugh.

I miss my mother.

A little indignation shook him. He was thirteen years old. *Almost halfway to fourteen.* He wasn't a mouse. He'd killed goblins. He could work magic. He didn't need his mother.

Still, he missed her. While anger had prompted her to monitor his training; the result had been that they spent two hours together every day. She'd taken delight in his successes and consoled him over his defeats. She'd offered advice and chastened him when he got arrogant or lazy.

Jerrad understood that she had to be mother to him *and* to the whole of Silverlake. He didn't really want to be sharing her with everyone else, but they needed her as much as he did—or more. Whereas he was nearing manhood, Silverlake was still in its infancy and wasn't anywhere near weaned.

It was with that in mind that he'd decided on his mission. He needed to show his mother that he could help with Silverlake, and that he wanted the settlement to succeed as much as she did. He also needed to make sure she knew it wasn't because he planned to return to Ustalav when the twenty years was over. He'd decided Silverlake was going to be his home—he wasn't in exile, he was right where he was meant to be.

Part of that decision came from the heart. He really liked Echo Wood. As much as he enjoyed traveling over the Vishov holdings, they lacked something. Ustalav was a nation that had long ago been tamed. The only vitality came in political intrigues. There was nothing wrong with his old home, but it lacked the wonder of Echo Wood. In Ustalav he was a Vishov. Here, he could be *anything*.

Practically speaking, however, he didn't expect there would be anything to go back to. Serrana and Ranall seemed quite cozy with each other. It wasn't going to surprise him if before winter, or in the spring, or at the height of next summer, Ranall asked for his sister's hand in marriage. They'd return to Ustalav, probably live on the Vishov estate, then take over the combined family estates once Baron Creelisk died.

That he'd be shouldered out of his birthright didn't bother him at all. He and his sister might fight, but they shared the same blood. Just as his mother had been supportive of her brother through to the bitter end, so he'd support Serrana and she'd support him. If he'd ever doubted that she would, he only had to think back to her beating goblins to death to save him.

Jerrad reached the hollow and crawled up the hillside. He listened, but heard nothing. Peeking over the berm, he saw nothing. He pulled himself up in a crouch behind a fern and studied the situation a bit longer. He couldn't see a single thing out of place.

He moved into the hollow slowly, stopping every step or two. Both Kiiryth and Nelsa had taught him that most creatures saw movement more easily than they saw stationary items. When he paused, he studied the area, moving his eyes only. Everything remained clear, so he completed his descent.

He crossed to where the goblin had flicked the bones off the mat. A few leaves had blown over the area. He dropped to knee and brushed some aside. He had to look closely, but he managed to spot bits of white bone against the darker leaves and loam.

His eyes sharpened. He reached toward one of the mouse skulls, but froze before he touched it. He opened his palm, recalling that the goblin had reacted to the bones as if they were embers. He felt no heat, so he touched the skull with his finger.

Nothing.

Tentatively he picked it up between thumb and forefinger. He was ready to drop it in an instant, but he caught no hint of warmth. The bone felt cool and damp, even a bit greasy. He put it in a pouch on his belt, then added a couple more long bones.

He retreated from the hollow and made his way north. He didn't follow either his entry path or the one he and Nelsa had used to leave the hollow previously. He picked out as difficult a path as he could, choosing a route that should be harder for short-legged goblins. He even found a stream, went south against the current, then west and around north again to throw off pursuit.

Confident he'd not been followed, he crouched in the wind-scoured bowl at the base of an enormous, old pine. He pulled the skull out of the pouch, laid it on the ground, and covered it with both his hands. Then he closed his eyes and blended the colors, invoking the spell that let him sense magic.

He caught the magic from the skull. It felt faint, like the last wisp of fog burning off the lake in the morning. He almost couldn't feel it, so he concentrated. More of its nature came to him, as if the skull was a bell still vibrating after long ago having been struck.

Wait.

He turned away from the skull, but the sense remained. No matter which way he turned, it permeated the air.

It's not the skull. It's the land, the wood itself. Jerrad frowned. The spell wasn't working on the skull, but it appeared as if the wood knew what he sought and was giving it to him. *But why?*

Then an even greater vibration pounded into him, not from the skull but from the north and west. It hammered through his chest like a thunderclap. He shied from it and tumbled back, bowled over as if in a goblin stampede. Something tightened around his chest. He couldn't breathe. *It's like I'm under the pile of goblins again.*

After a moment, the pressure eased. Jerrad slowly rolled to his knees and shrank down to make himself as small as possible. He waited and listened. Nothing came to him save for the normal sounds of the forest. Even though something had shaken him, he couldn't remember having *heard* anything. He just knew it felt wrong—just as the ritual magic had felt wrong—*but scaled up to be a mountain instead of an anthill*.

He quickly tucked the skull away. Remaining low, scuttling forward on all fours, he moved in the direction from which he'd felt the vibration come. He became hyper-vigilant, taking nearly an hour to cross what couldn't have been more than a hundred yards. His travel brought him to the edge of a steeply walled ravine.

At first he couldn't be certain what he was seeing, but he resisted the urge to venture down to get a closer look. The ravine didn't have much of anything in the way of old-growth trees. Bushes and saplings grew there. Many of the smaller trees appeared to have been shoved aside. The bushes had been uprooted in some cases and trampled underfoot in the rest. It looked as if something enormous had stalked through the ravine, leaving a trail there the way Jerrad would in meadow grasses.

He paralleled the trail for a bit, then started down a game path. He kept low and quiet, taking forever to descend. Sweat rolled down his cheeks. He didn't swat at a mosquito intent on landing on his temple. He held his breath as he waited in a cloud of gnats. His lungs burned by the time his quarry's trail cut across the game path.

He might only have been in Echo Wood for less than a season, but he'd learned enough tracking to have his guts get squishy. A big left footprint, as long as his arm, had sunk a handspan deep in the moist ground. It looked terribly familiar. He'd seen that sort of track before, in Silverlake, after the attack.

An ogre?

That realization paled compared to the second one. The right foot hadn't left a print. It had just gouged a wide track through the leaves—a track as long and as wide as a shallow grave. The creature was dragging its right foot. Where the left foot planted, the drag marks stopped for a bit as it heaved that leg forward.

It can't be the ogrekin. It's dead. His mouth went sour. *But dead doesn't mean gone, does it?*

Jerrad glanced at the sky, shading his eyes with a hand, then looked at shadows. He couldn't be certain, but he was pretty sure the trail started in the direction of the lake, and appeared to be headed west toward the Murdoon compound. Unbidden came to mind the broken corpses the Silverlakers had dug out of the longhouse ruins. All too easily Jerrad was able to put Nelsa's face on one of the corpses.

He couldn't let that happen. The very idea of Nelsa lying dead took his breath away again and made him feel queasy. She couldn't die. She had too much life in her—but he would have said that of any of those who had died at Silverlake, too.

He had only one course of action. He steeled himself and followed the track. He couldn't tell exactly how old it was. Leaves on broken branches had begun to wither. Animal tracks overlaid some of the footprints.

The weather for the past several days had been cool and sunny, but in the ravine's shadowed depths, the sun hadn't been able to dry out and crumble the tracks' edges. Jerrad was willing to bet the tracks were at least a day old, but not more than a week.

Reanimating a corpse . . . He shivered. *I don't even know spells that kill. How powerful does a necromancer need to be to do something like that?* His stomach twisted in on itself. Dealing with the ogrekin had been bad enough, but a necromancer who could raise it was worse. Though he had no practical knowledge of necromancy, countless fairy tales had made clear the evils of that dark art, and the twisted nature of the magic made it easy to classify as such.

Jerrad considered trying his spell again, but held off. He recalled his mentor's caution about magic always being detectable. As long as he had the tracks to follow, he didn't need magic. He did, however, slip the two sticks from the quiver he wore across his back and made ready to fight if he had to.

The trail remained painfully easy to follow. The ogre made no attempt to conceal his passage. Where the ravine split, with one branch heading more south, it went in that direction. This made Jerrad feel better, since that meant the ogre wasn't headed directly for Nelsa's home. Still, its path would cut across the road up from Thornkeep, and a right-handed turn would aim it at the Murdoons again.

He tracked the monster to the road, which was nearly a mile since he'd found the trail. The ogrekin didn't appear to hesitate or hurry in crossing the road. Jerrad located the crushed blossom of a night-blooming flower in a track, suggesting the thing traveled at night. *No wonder no one has seen it.* Then again, even though Jerrad was crossing in mid-afternoon, he couldn't see any traffic north or south.

He followed for another half-mile, to the place where the ogre turned west and dragged itself up a hill. Unless it was going to curl up and around to the north, its path wouldn't take it anywhere near Nelsa. In fact, the ogre's trail hadn't deviated much off a southwesterly course for as long as he'd followed it, leading Jerrad to guess it was bound for Mosswater.

He cautiously concluded the necromancer had to be an ogre calling the dead ogrekin home. While he didn't have anything to compare the magic's sense to, the sheer strength seemed monstrous enough to pin on ogres.

That meant Silverlake's effort to hide the fact that they'd killed the ogre had gone for naught. He really needed to get back to Silverlake and let everyone know about the danger.

But what if it's a false alarm? He looked up the hill. It could easily be that the magic ran out, and the ogre's body lay sprawled on the other side of the hill. The goblin's magic had certainly run its course—why wouldn't the same be true of the ogre magic? *If I go back, sound the alarm, and it turns out to be nothing . . .*

He shook his head. It would take too long to track this thing back to Mosswater, but at least he could see its path from the top of the hill. That would be good.

He scrambled up in the monster's wake. The way the ogrekin's left foot had dug deep holes in the hillside helped him immeasurably. He moved from one to the next, pausing to rest and listen. He watched the sky for carrion birds, but saw none. When he felt it was safe to move on, he worked his way further toward the crest.

He reached it and smiled. In the distance lay a town he took to be Mosswater. From afar he had trouble seeing much more than a tower here and there, but they clearly stood out. He eyeballed the distance as roughly a dozen miles as the crow flies.

And longer as the ogrekin tumbles.

The ogrekin had come up and over, then really gone over. A couple of deep holes marked the first few steps it had taken, but after that flatted bushes and snapped trees marked its passage. Clearly it had stumbled and rolled. If Jerrad wasn't mistaken, the gray, flappy thing impaled on the sharp end of a sapling was a strip of the monster's hide. As the ogrekin had made its uncontrolled descent, sharp branches and rough stones had flayed it.

If I bring a scrap back . . .

Jerrad started down cautiously, but sand and gravel shifted. A stone turned beneath his sole, and Jerrad lost his footing. He somersaulted, then bounced into the air and landed hard. His sticks went flying. He clawed at the ground as he slid, but that just slewed him around. Stars exploded before his eyes as his head bashed something, then his ears popped and he rolled again.

He slid to a stop at the base of the hill, and instantly knew something was wrong. Blood leaked from a cut on the back of his head. He felt dizzy, but that cleared easily enough. The main problem was that he lay on a bed of dry leaves when those stuck to his forehead and cheeks were still wet. Nine feet further on, past scraggly thorn bushes, a wrought iron fence separated him from a dusty cobblestone street.

No forest. Iron fence. Dry leaves not wet leaves. Not good.

The sun had begun to sink in the west. The long shadows thrown by tall buildings stabbed toward him. He was looking at buildings that hadn't been at the base of the hill, or anywhere close to it. *Not within a dozen miles, in fact . . .*

Jerrad's breath remained locked in his chest. *Echo Wood wanted me to follow the ogrekin. I did, but apparently not fast enough. So the wood gave me a little push . . .* He shivered.

All the way to the middle of Mosswater.

Chapter Twenty-One
A Lovely Place to Visit

Baron Blackshield is going to be very angry. And that is the least of my worries.

Jerrad lay very still. Every stupid thing he'd done to get him flat on his back and bleeding in the middle of a city which ogres had conquered two generations ago pummeled him. Every single step he'd taken in the ogrekin's wake counted as a stupid thing. And his decision to revisit the goblin site and to start studying magic went for bonus dumb.

Stupid Mouse. Really, really stupid.

The only reason he didn't cry in frustration was because that would be stupider than everything else combined.

I am dead. I am so dead. He pressed a hand to the back of his head to slow the bleeding. *When I die here, my mother will hire a necromancer to bring me back to life, just so she can punish me.*

He looked to the right and left. He lay at the base of a cemetery hill. Most of the markers had been knocked over, and several of the graves lay open. He found it easy to imagine corpses digging themselves out of the ground. Stories he'd heard of Mosswater suggested the ogres ruled it by day, but at night the bodies of those who hadn't escaped wandered the streets. That included adventurers who had died there since, which, as nearly as he could remember, pretty much consisted of *every* adventurer who had ventured into Mosswater searching for treasure.

He couldn't solve the big problem of being in Mosswater, so he focused on the little problems. He needed to bandage his head and get somewhere with less exposure. *No reason to make this easy for the ogres.*

As he focused, he found it a bit easier to keep his fear under control. The ache in his head became a bit more apparent, but taking care of that would have to play second fiddle to his getting out of the graveyard.

Without lifting his head too much, he surveyed the street. Where the cobblestones had subsided, the dry, cracked surface of mud puddles provided plants some purchase. In the last fifty years trees had grown up, splitting foundation stones in several place. Ivy clawed at walls. Some plants had even grown up through building roofs, loosening clay tiles that had shattered on the street below. A little wind whipped dust into a tiny cyclone that skittered along the road.

Things looked pretty well wrecked, save for one squat, round building with a slender, cylindrical tower rising from its middle. The sun silhouetted the tower, but in its shadow Jerrad couldn't see any debris or other major signs of destruction. If things hadn't despoiled the building, it probably meant it was protected somehow. He might not be able to get in, but he was willing to imagine other things had learned to stay away.

He studied the street, then came up on a knee. His head swam, but things came back into focus again. He staggered over to a monument, hid behind it, then continued on toward the cemetery's ruined gate. He huddled down against a thick stone pillar and watched the streets again.

His new vantage point afforded him a better view up and down the road at the cemetery edge. West and east, at the road's far ends, ogres patrolled singly or occasionally in pairs. They looked less like military than stray dogs poking about. The problem was that even as far away as they were, they still looked *huge*.

He watched a little longer and waited. Once it looked as if the coast was clear, he darted across the street and into shadows. He huddled beneath a window. His left hand came away bloody from his head, so he put more pressure on the wound. He checked behind him for any signs of a blood trail. He didn't see anything, but he was pretty sure plenty of things in Mosswater could smell him out easily enough.

I'm not getting out past roving ogres with an open wound. What I need right now is a place with an entrance small enough that an ogre can't follow.

He came up and looked inside the window. The shutters had been shattered, but the casement remained intact. It still had patches of the bright blue paint that had decorated it. Sunlight slanted in from west-facing windows, revealing five skeletons lying side by side.

They'd died holding hands. A sixth skeleton had most of its bones arranged in a chair. The arms had fallen off, scattering bones around the chair's legs.

They couldn't escape, so he killed his family and then killed himself. Jerrad closed his eyes and murmured a silent prayer for mercy on the man's soul. *If the ogres come to Silverlake, I hope no one has to make that sort of decision.*

He crouched again. He'd come as far as he had not because he wanted to, but because he'd wanted to protect Silverlake and Nelsa. *If I give up, if I allow myself to die here, people* will *have to make that sort of decision.* He pictured families in the longhouses all lying down together and his mother being the one to dispatch the last survivors before taking her own life.

"That's not going to happen."

Jerrad worked his way west for half a block, remaining low and in shadow until he stood across the street from the unmolested tower and its open arched doorway. Blue tiles defined the arch, and the wall's light brown paint had barely faded. More curiously, scattered bones and detritus described an arc roughly ten feet out from the wall. The bones of heavier creatures had gotten closer to the wall, but none had penetrated to within three feet of the arch. Jerrad spotted bones from a variety of vermin, goblins, humans, and ogres. All the bones had a glassy sheen to them, as if they'd been polished by a jeweler.

Jerrad invoked the spell that allowed him to recognize magic. Instantly a bold image pulsed out from the tower. Metaphysically, it felt like a stiff wind, and in his mind it appeared as a stout wall of stone. He reached a hand out and could feel the breeze, even though it didn't disturb the hairs on the back of his hand. From the way the bones lay in the street, it appeared as if the most force came through the archway.

He took another look at it and noticed something curious about the tiles. They appeared almost identical, white on dark blue, in an odd sort of floral pattern. The only difference between them occurred in the pattern of the leaves on the interior side of the design. At a casual glance they might just have been an artistic flourish by the artisan who made them, but the pattern repeated itself on the right and left without being mirrored.

Jerrad cast a spell—not the one for finding magic, nor the one that let him understand other languages, but a minor one that combined elements of the two. The book had claimed it would help him read magical writing, but so far, given that his was the only magical text in Silverlake, he hadn't had the opportunity to try it out.

Sure enough, the anomalous squiggles resolved themselves into letters. He read it carefully and whispered to himself. "You may not enter."

Jerrad stared at the words and mulled them over. The presence of the tiles suggested the spell was of long standing. When casting it to protect the tower from marauding ogres, would the wizard really take the time to decorate?

He wouldn't. The spell effect extends into the street, which is impractical in a thriving city. What if the breeze would just keep people out when he didn't want to be disturbed? And when the ogres came and the city fell, the wizard just intensified the spell?

Jerrad, though he knew comparatively little about magic, felt certain the spell had been cast by a wizard. It felt familiar, and sounded proper. He imagined that any creature approaching the tower would feel the wind. It would blow harder and harder until it knocked him back or, by picking up dust and grit, would scour flesh from bones. The smaller creatures likely had been tossed at the building by ogres or others trying to work their way in. *For fun or testing.*

He remembered the expression on the ogrekin's face. *Definitely for fun.*

Jerrad sighed. He had two problems. First, the spell was enormously powerful, and he couldn't match it. Second, his arsenal of spells didn't include any counter-magic. *I don't think card tricks are going to work, and making myself look like an ogre might fool ogres, but the tower's magic doesn't seem to like them very much.*

Something snarled down the road. Jerrad looked back toward the cemetery. Two ogres, every bit as lumpen and ugly as the ogrekin that had died at Silverlake, and yet half-again as large, had gotten down on all fours and were sniffing the ground. One touched a bulbous finger to a spot on the road, then stuffed the finger into its nose and rubbed it around. It looked up and pointed.

At me.

Panic burst through Jerrad, crushing his heart, freezing his lungs. The ogres sniffed again, then began sidling forward. They had his blood scent. He couldn't outrun them, and even if he'd not lost his sticks, he couldn't fight them. *And hiding mouselike isn't going to work.*

"But maybe there's a chance I can get them to reconsider." Jerrad stood and concentrated, weaving a spell he'd not practiced much, but one which had impressed his mother when he'd showed it to her. As he emerged into the sun's dying light, magic transformed him. As far as the ogres could see, he was a tall man with a shaved head, wearing a golden robe with inset panels of lapis. Golden rings glittered on every finger. The jewels set in them cast rainbows. He was handsome and stern, hawk-nosed and scowling.

This better work. His stomach in knots, Jerrad spread his arms and faced the ogres. "Come on. It's taken you long enough to find me." He didn't mind that his voice didn't match the image. That would likely confuse the ogres even more. He didn't want them thinking, he just wanted them scared halfway to death.

He beckoned them toward him, all while inching his way back toward the tower's arch. The wind whistled in his ears. Dust kicked up, stinging his eyes. He stopped before the magic could shred his clothes and peel the flesh from his bones, but hoped the rising howl would convince the ogre that he was working the magic, not the tower.

"Why are you so slow? Are you cowards?" Jerrad screamed at the top of his lungs. "Cowards!"

The ogres glanced at each other, then turned toward him and roared defiantly. They rumbled forward, running on feet and knuckles. Cobblestones shattered, shards dancing behind them. They leaped over holes in the road and jostled each other to win the race. One ogre had a third eye, bloodshot and tiny, below its left one. The other had only one, about the size of a dinner plate, save that it wasn't entirely round. Nor was it centered—the opposite side of its face was all a bulging tumor. Each ogre snarled, flashing twisted teeth.

Next time, scare them to death, not just halfway.

The lead ogre shrieked at him.

Jerrad couldn't help it. He'd tried to be brave, but his nerve broke. Yelping, he leaped back. He knew the tower would kill him, but better that than the ogres. The wind pressed hard against his back as he raised his hands in a feeble gesture to ward off certain death.

One ogre lunged at him. The other leaped high, fingers reaching. They'd likely collide in their haste, but that wouldn't do Jerrad any good.

I'm sorry, Mother. I'm sorry I wasn't more like my father.

The three-eyed ogre reached him a heartbeat before the other ogre, arms outstretched. The magical wind howled. Gray flesh burst into a red mist. The wind devoured the first ogre's arms up to the elbows. Wet bones danced off the cobblestones in time with the wind's howl. The ogre bounced back, triple-gaze darting from one stump to another. Blood jetted from the ragged openings. It beat its arms against its chest, coating itself with blood, then slumped down and twitched.

The pressure at Jerrad's back broke. The boy stumbled backward, arms flailing to keep his balance. *What's happening?*

The other ogre's leap had carried it high into what seemed to be dead air, for it flew over Jerrad's head. Then it descended. The wind buffeted it, bouncing it up, removing a layer of hide as it did so. The ogre flailed, then came down again. Flesh dissolved, muscle evaporated, then the wind lofted it high. Each descent hastened the ogre's destruction. Soon bone showed, and shortly thereafter the ogre's struggles ceased. The wind's play did not, however, until the bones had flown into dust which flowed down the street.

Jerrad stared at where the first ogre twitched in the street. Looking up again, the youth found himself beneath the arch. The wind's tune still echoed, but as he took another step backward, the sound trailed off. He retreated a few more steps and found himself in a courtyard garden with a small fountain burbling away.

"Why am I not dead?" He'd foolishly hoped he could frighten the ogres. With a moment to think, he found he couldn't recall a single story where ogres had ever been afraid of anything. *The piles of bones outside should have told you they weren't afraid of this tower.* That he wasn't dead made him happy, though he felt close to dying of mortification at how stupid he'd been.

I don't understand. He walked to the fountain and bent over to drink. The water's surface shimmered, showing him as himself one moment, then as he appeared in the illusion he'd cast.

He sat on the fountain's edge. "It couldn't have been as simple as disguising myself with an illusion, could it? 'You may not enter'—was that a clue? Can you only get past if you aren't yourself? Did no one else ever puzzle that out before?"

He tore the left sleeve off his tunic, soaked it in the fountain, and pressed it against the back of his head. The cool water trickled down his back, prompting a smile. *I'm still alive. That counts.*

He refused to believe so powerful a magic would have so simple a key. He returned to his original premise, that the spell was a warning for people not to disturb the tower's resident. Yet the presence of a clue suggested he didn't mind some people coming in. And, as keys went, casting that simple a spell meant almost anyone who knew magic could have made it through the arch—which pretty much negated the arch's usefulness.

Unless.

Jerrad stood and looked up at the tower. It occurred to him that perhaps his safety wasn't due to a simple disguise spell, but rather to *that specific* spell, taught the way he'd learned it. "The grimoires—the wizard who wrote it lived here. I got in because the tower thinks I'm one of his pupils."

That also explained the nature of his illusion. He'd not had time to think, so he pulled together an image that felt right. Based on the sense of the author he'd gotten while reading and studying, he'd imagined what his mentor must have looked like, and clothed himself in that image.

His mind raced. Had it been dumb luck that brought him to the tower? Or had the wizard distributed copies of the grimoire assuming his students, at a certain point, would find him? He wondered if the wizard was still alive, or if casting the guardian spell had been his last act.

Jerrad looked over at an open doorway further along through the garden. *Only one way to find out.* He knotted the sleeve around his head. *I'm sure there are lessons here for me to learn. I only hope I'll survive them.*

Chapter Twenty-Two
A Lovelier Place to Escape

Jerrad stopped at the open doorway. Blue tiles decorated it, but they contained no hidden message. He still had a sense of magic all around him, but it was impossible to pinpoint anything.

He moved slowly as he entered the tower. Everything appeared remarkably clean—the magic wind apparently had the added benefit of keeping the dust down. The main floor had fairly open architecture in the front half. Furnished with an eclectic mix of dark wood and light, some things heavy and others delicately wrought, the decor's unifying feature was gold and lapis trim. It matched the image Jerrad had conjured, further confirming in his mind that the tower belonged to his invisible mentor. As nearly as Jerrad could tell, the tower's treasures came from all over the world.

Whoever he was, he traveled widely or bought from those who did. Jerrad had to imagine the wizard had chosen every piece himself, simply because some things looked so junky that no one in his right mind would pay for them. *Then again, nothing about this collection suggests he was in his right mind.*

The only aspect of the decorations Jerrad couldn't figure out were the lanterns hanging from the ceiling. The big, brassy affairs were designed to move along a circular track that started at a wide hole in the ceiling and curved around from the left all the way to the right. Even standing on his tip-toes he couldn't touch one of the lamps. He figured they went around on the track and disappeared up through the hole, only to appear again down it and around to complete the circuit. At the moment, however, all were still.

At the room's heart, a bit forward of the hole, a staircase spiraled up to the towers other floors. Jerrad wended a twisted path toward it, passing here and there as items caught his eye. Though the collection featured all sorts of items, he didn't see anything that would provide him an immediate means of escaping Mosswater. The only weapons proved to be ceremonial or miniatures, none of which would be the least bit useful against the ogres.

Jerrad really had no desire to ascend the stairs, but the main floor had no books on it. Given that he'd decided the tower had been home to his magical mentor, he hoped he could find another grimoire which could teach him a spell or two that would get him out of Mosswater and back to Silverlake. He was willing to settle for even a magic gem or bottle or anything that could produce a localized version of the guardian spell, which he could use for personal defense.

He reached the base of the stairs and something rattled above. It was a small sound—not the clank of armor, or the sound chains made as some creature tested its strength against them. At first he thought one of lanterns nearest the stairs had made the sound, but they all remained still.

Jerrad crept up the stairs, peering upward as he went. He stopped as the rattling sounded again and studied the floor below. Nothing. He started up again, into the dim recesses of the tower's upper reaches. The air smelled dry and had a hint of leather, which he hoped meant books. It also had other scents—floral mostly—but nothing he associated with malevolence.

He came up high enough that eye level was equal to the room's floor. He couldn't see very much more than shelves lining the walls and the undersides of tables and a stool or two. Here and there the sun's dying light—which had squeaked past shutters—reflected from an alembic's curved side. The lanterns and track also circled the ceiling in this chamber. The stairs curled further up into the tower, but shadow hid whatever was up there.

The rattle sounded again, snapping Jerrad's head around. There, on the east side of the room, one of the lanterns shook and glowed. A soft green light pulsed, growing brighter with the rattling, then dying as silence resumed. The lantern's outer cylinder, which had slits in it to let light out, didn't give him a good look at what was inside.

On cat's feet he entered the room. Though he'd never seen a wizard's library before, he couldn't have mistaken it for anything else. Aside from shelves full of books, the tables had jars filled with ingredients. Mortars and pestles, bowls, pitchers, and vials lay everywhere. A small stove had a distillation coil next to it—that much he recognized from a still some of the Silverlakers had created.

Again the lantern rattled. As Jerrad approached it, he noticed something odd. While it hung from the track like others, a brass tube about a foot in diameter led from a hole in the wall right up to the lantern's side. Around the pipe he caught the guardian spell's whistle.

He reached the cage. *Could it be a pigeon, maybe?* Jerrad smacked the heel of his hand off his forehead. *Stupid Mouse, pigeons don't glow.*

"Hello?"

The lantern remained still and silent, with no hint of light leaking out.

Jerrad climbed up on a stool to bring his face up level with the lantern. He rapped on the metal shell. "Hello?"

Light blazed.

"Ow." He recoiled and grabbed the lantern so he'd not fall off the stool. The lantern shook, and something bounced around inside. It didn't seem to be very heavy, and it made little snarling sounds that suggested it wasn't very happy, either.

Jerrad blinked tears from his eyes. "Look, I'll help you get out of there if you promise not to blind me again."

The lantern remained dark and quiet.

"I'm not going to hurt you."

No response.

Jerrad rubbed his hands over his face. "Fine, stay trapped. You're probably some demon that will rip my face off anyway." He climbed off the stool and started looking at the books while he still had a little sunlight. He didn't see anything that came even close to the slender volume he'd been using. "If I can't find something, I'm stuck here forever."

The lantern's light strengthened to an emerald glow. Jerrad took advantage of it quickly, looking around for anything that resembled his grimoire. "There, got it." He made his way around a table to the northern wall and slid a small book from between two larger volumes.

He flipped through the pages. *Blank*. None of them had writing, not even incomprehensible gibberish. "But it *feels* like my grimoire. It's hopeless."

"Release me. I'll help you."

Jerrad smiled and tucked the grimoire inside his belt. He returned to the stool. "How can I help?"

"The bars of this cage are too close. I can't escape."

The youth didn't see any bars, and assumed they had to be inside the outer shell. He reached up and around, slipping the two spring catches that held the cylindrical shade tight to the lantern. It came off easily. He set it down, puzzled.

"What cage?"

The sprite in the middle of the lantern spread her arms. "*This* cage." She stood just over half a foot in height and had beautiful leaf-like wings which were dark green at the points, fading to a lighter green at her back. Her eyes had an emerald hue, and her red hair fell in ringlets to cover her breasts. Her skin had a slight greenish cast to it, making it appear that she had been carved from a pale jade.

Jerrad couldn't see the cage to which she referred. Three posts connected the lantern top and bottom, but nothing else stood between her and freedom. He frowned, then renewed the spell which gave him a sense of magic.

"That's it." He smiled.

She folded her arms and snorted. "My plight amuses you?"

"No, no, it's not that. I think I have it figured out." Jerrad smiled. "I'm Jerrad, by the way."

She eyed him suspiciously. "You can call me Lissa."

"Good. Lissa, I think you're seeing an illusion which makes up your prison. The magic seems strongest in the lantern's top. I'm going to guess that there's an enchantment there which projects the illusion keeping you in."

She stared at him for a moment. "You're saying there's no cage?"

"I'm saying the wizard really liked illusions." Jerrad shrugged, thinking better of explaining why he thought that. "The illusion is strong enough in your mind to keep you in, but I think I can put my hand in there and pull you out."

"And slice me up through the bars? They're as sharp as knives!"

"If there are bars, I won't be able to reach in and pull you out."

She frowned. "You may have a point there. I think I'll close my eyes."

"Might help." He rubbed his hands together to warm them. "I'm ready."

The sprite nodded, then closed her wings about her. Her light died, plunging the room into darkness. Jerrad reached out, letting his fingers slide slowly along the lantern's floor. He felt the sprite leap into the back of his hand and grab his cuff, then he slid his hand out again.

She leaped into the air, wings spread and light blazing.

"Ow, blinding!" Jerrad pulled back, hands rising to shield his eyes. The stool tottered. Too late he grabbed for the lantern and missed. The stool slid over to bang off the bookcase. Jerrad slammed hard into the floor.

A green blur circled the tower, then shot down the stairs, leaving Jerrad utterly alone in the dark. Lissa's ghostly afterimage lingered in his eyes, and shutting them did nothing to get rid of it.

He pounded his fist on the floor. *I should have known. Sprites hate me. I try to do something nice, and I get abandoned. I'll die here hungry and alone and ignorant.*

Tears welled in his eyes. He swiped at them angrily, then sat up. She'd fooled him, and he'd let himself be fooled. He knew he should have been angrier at Lissa than he was at himself, but that wasn't how the voice in his head was apportioning blame. He was as trapped in the tower as the sprite had been in the lantern. *I'm so stupid.*

He sat in the dark for a bit, then started thinking to distract himself. It wasn't hard for Jerrad to piece together what had happened to the sprite, or to many sprites in the past. The tube constituted some sort of trap by which the sprites became caged in a lantern. He figured that some magic which no longer functioned moved the lanterns along the circuit, providing light for the tower. Once a sprite made the full circuit, they probably went out the way they came in. The wizard likely had some magic that made them forget what they'd been through, so they'd not warn others.

It struck Jerrad that this was a clever use of spells, but he didn't like the way the sprites became enslaved. It might have been that the wizard trapped them when they came to steal things from him, and a little involuntary servitude was the penalty he meted out. The gods knew that Jerrad could have wished for that sort of justice heading the way of the sprites that picked on him, but it still seemed harsh.

Now, if I could find a way to get the ogres into these lamps . . . He laughed at himself, feeling a little better. That would require magics well beyond his abilities. He suspected the reason the slender volume he'd pulled off the shelf had blank pages was because he wasn't ready to handle those spells. *My mentor thinks those spells would kill me. Without them, even odds for starvation or ogres doing the job.*

In a rush of wings and a burst of green light, Lissa bobbed up through the stairwell. She appeared to be the same as she'd been in the lantern, save that she had a wicked little recurve bow in her left hand and a quiver of needle-like arrows hanging at her right hip. "I found it."

That was one of the miniature weapons displayed below. "You're not here to shoot me, are you?"

"No. I don't often need rescue. Never before, really. But I understand gratitude." She held the bow up. "This my grandfather's. He lost it before Mosswater fell. The family scoured Echo Wood for it. They looked everywhere—except here. I came. I found it."

"Great." Jerrad smiled weakly. "On your way back to your family, would you mind killing some ogres?"

"I'm a good shot. This is a great bow." She shrugged. "But these arrows won't stop ogres. Or the animated skeletons."

"No, of course not. Silly me."

"Why do ogres concern a wizard like you?"

"I don't, um, I'm not . . ." Jerrad sighed and killed the illusion.

"Hey, where did you go?" The sprite darted in toward his face, gasped, then backed off. "You're Ogrebane's son.»

"Guilty." Jerrad frowned for a heartbeat. "Probably would have left me here faster if you knew that from the outset, right?"

"I barely recognized you. No mud." She shrugged. "A deal is a deal. You freed me. I'll free you."

"Thank you."

"Once you're out of Mosswater, you're on your own."

"Get me on the road to Thornkeep and that'll be good."

"Done and done."

Jerrad followed the sprite down the stairs, using her light for navigation. She moved quickly, so shadows shifted. He barked his shins twice, but bit his tongue. Though Lissa's idea of gratitude clearly differed from his, he didn't think pointing that out to her right at the moment was a good idea.

They paused in the archway, and Jerrad's heart sank. Though there wasn't much light by which to see, a number of shapes large and small shambled through the night. Skeletons—mostly adult humanoids, but some decidedly shorter—limped along in threadbare clothing. Occasionally they had a dark patch of dried scalp with a long lank of wispy hair. Though they didn't appear to move very quickly, Jerrad ascribed that more to lack of targets than inability to run.

"First trick is getting out of here." Jerrad took a good look at the tiles on the inside of the arch. "A bit more light would help."

Lissa obliged him. A number of the skeletons oriented toward her glow and marched into destruction via the guardian spell. "You might want to hurry," she offered.

"I know." He cast the translation spell. The legend on the tiles read, "May the wind speed your journey." That gave him heart, which increased when he noticed two tiles opposite each other, about waist height. Their decorative element translated as a glyph for wind.

"The spell was meant to keep folks out, but battering legitimate visitors wouldn't make sense." He shifted the grimoire around and tucked it in at the small of his back, then reached a hand for one of the wind tiles. "I bet if I touch this . . ."

"Wait." Lissa lowered her light. The skeletons lost interest. She flew over to the opposite wind tile. "Straight down this road. Cross the stone bridge. Turn south."

"How far?"

She gave him an appraising look. "Probably too far. I'll distract those I can."

Jerrad nodded. "Thank you."

She nocked a needle-like arrow. "Now."

He touched the wind glyph and jetted forward. The gust of wind carried him beyond the ring of debris. He stumbled as he landed, but somersaulted and came up on his feet. Jerrad ducked a swipe from a bony claw, and not because it was particularly slow. *The spell* is *speeding me.*

He started running. Lissa sped ahead of him a yard in front and two above, bright as a full moon. Her light rendered the skeletons as luminescent jade carvings. He spotted them easily and gave them a wide berth. He leaped over stone blocks with ease, and quickly was able to gauge how far a jump would carry him.

Barely a hundred yards from the tower, an ogre spotted him. She shouted, a mixture of surprise and outrage. More shouts answered her from down the street. The earth shook as the ogres—curious, hungry, or just murderous—came to the street.

Lissa dove fearlessly at them, weaving her light into a glowing knotwork. Ogres would reach for her, but she'd elude them, then pop up right in front of their faces. She loosed arrows to pierce them tongue and throat, adding pain to their shouts.

As bold as she was, her quiver had few arrows, and pain enraged rather than discouraged ogres. Her flying through the branches of a tree, or down through an arch, might lure an ogre into a collision, but the pack of them gathering in Jerrad's wake had their target in sight. She couldn't distract them, so flew ahead to light his way.

The wind made him faster than the average ogre, but a couple of the tallest pounded after him. Their long strides ate up ground. They got close enough that he could hear fat folds slapping against each other. He dared not look back, and instead put his head down and pushed himself for more speed.

Ahead loomed the bridge Lissa had mentioned. The stone arch wasn't very long, and spanned a dry canal. Jerrad aimed himself straight at the middle. *On the other side, I turn right.* He glanced toward the street running south and smiled. *No ogres.*

That momentary distraction almost doomed him. He raced up the bridge and, at the last second, realized the center had fallen away. Without a good chance to measure the distance, he leaped and hoped for the best.

He cleared the hole, but slipped as he landed. He bounced off the balustrade and tumbled to his knees. He spun around, facing his pursuit. The ogres were far closer than he'd dared imagine.

Lissa darted down. "Run!"

"No." Jerrad forced panic away and cast his illusion spell. *This should buy me time.*

The ogres chasing him never saw the gaping hole in the bridge. Jerrad's spell concealed it within an illusion crudely matching the surrounding surface. The first ogre stepped through it and fell. His face hit the edge closest to Jerrad, scattering teeth in a rattle. The second ogre couldn't stop either and crashed down onto the first. Voices roared from beneath the bridge, and ogre blood splashed darkly against the bridge's stone railing.

Jerrad got to his knees and ran off the bridge. As he turned south, he got a shadowed view of the ogres. At least one more went through the hole, but it appeared as if she jumped instead of being pushed. Then something that looked terribly armlike rose back up and the ogres crowded on the bridge started to jostle and claw for it. Another ogre went through the hole—clearly pushed—and the snarling became blood-curdling.

Lissa paced him, keeping her light low unless she needed to warn him of a hole or skeletons. He avoided pursuit, and as he reached the edge of Mosswater, the wind spell slowly faded. He stopped where weeds had conquered the road and turned toward the sprite.

"I just wanted to thank . . ."

Lissa circled him once, then vanished to the east like a dying star.

Jerrad frowned. "That's right, go tell your squirrel buddies I'm coming." He wanted to be angry, but decided instead to be pleased she'd at least kept up her end of the bargain. *I couldn't have gotten this far without her.*

Jerrad headed south as quickly as he could. That wasn't as fast as he wanted to be. The spell might have sped him along, but it also tired him out. And made him thirsty.

I wonder if there's a spell in that grimoire for conjuring up water. He reached back for the book, but it wasn't there. He couldn't remember dropping it, but quickly figured it had flown free on the bridge.

He look a last longing glance at Mosswater, then shook his head. *Not going back for that.* He pointed his nose south and started running again.

After an age, he burst through the last hedgerow and sprawled on a clear stretch of road. His chest heaved. He knew he had to get up and keep running, but he needed just a moment to catch his breath.

The ground shook. For a heartbeat, he feared ogres had somehow raced past him and cut him off. He dragged himself to his feet and looked for cover.

Wait, that's not ogres. Those are men on horseback.

Relief flooded through him. He staggered toward them, holding up open hands. "Please, help me."

The patrol's leader reined up short, and Jerrad recognized him. His heart sank.

"Jerrad Vishov. How curious to find you here." Baron Blackshield scowled at him. "You've broken one of my rules, and for that, you shall pay dearly."

Chapter Twenty-Three
The Scourge of Silverlake

Tyressa forced her hands open as Baron Blackshield and his riders came through Silverlake's gate. The shadows from torchlight deepened the angry lines on the man's face, but Tyressa hadn't suffered under any illusion that he ever smiled sincerely. *I don't want to be around when he does.*

"To what do we owe this pleasure, Baron Blackshield? The Master of Thornkeep raised a hand and impatiently flicked fingers. One of his subordinates came around to his side. A hooded figure, bound hand and foot, lay athwart the saddlebows. Even before the rider grabbed the back of the boy's tunic and unceremoniously dumped him to the ground, Tyressa's hand rose to her throat.

Jerrad.

Serrana, slinging her bow, ran to Jerrad and yanked the hood off. "Mouse's breathing."

Jerrad gave his sister a sharp look, the white of his eyes contrasting sharply with his dirty face. "I'm okay."

"He's got a cut on his head, Mother."

Tyressa met the baron's hooded gaze. "Do I thank you for fetching him here, or explain to your widow why I killed you for hurting him?"

"Temper, Tyressa of Silverlake. You don't want to start a war with Thornkeep."

"Look around you, my lord." She spread her hands. "You'll notice that my people have organized themselves into squads to search for my son. We outnumber your men here, and with Baron Creelisk's guards, we're a match for your house troops. If there's to be a war, you'll die with the first dozen arrows crossed in your heart."

Serrana stood. "That's a small target, but the yellow will make for easy aim."

Jerrad, slipping his bonds, held a hand up. "He didn't hurt me, Mother. I fell and bashed my head. He found me and brought me here."

"There, you see, Tyressa. I did him no harm."

"Then I thank you."

"Gratitude may be premature." Blackshield dismounted and pulled a coiled bullwhip from his saddle. "I wish you to think back to when you first came here. I told you there were rules. Primary among them was that Mosswater was off-limits. I told you that trespassers, if they survived, would be severely punished. We found your son escaping Mosswater. He admitted it."

"Is that true, Jerrad?"

"I can explain, Mother."

"Later, Jerrad." She shifted her gaze back to Blackshield. "I recall your warning."

"Had we found anyone else, we would have brought him to Thornkeep, tied him to the pillory, and administered the punishment." Blackshield smiled. "Because he's your son, we brought him here. It's important you all see him punished. A hundred lashes with this whip."

"A hundred lashes? You can't!" Tyressa's hands curled into fists. "You don't administer that punishment to everyone. Treasure-hunters break your rules all the time."

"Treasure-hunters don't lie to me about how they came to be in Mosswater. Your son claims he got lost and just found himself there, then ran for his life. He didn't even have the intelligence to snatch a handful of loot along the way. Treasure-seekers do just that, and then buy their way out of the punishment."

Baron Creelisk stepped up to Tyressa's side. "How much?"

Blackshield shrugged. "Ten gold crowns a lash."

Serrana stood and brought her bow to hand. "A thousand gold? No one has ever paid you that."

"Market prices wax and wane." Blackshield let the whip's coils snake to the ground. "That's the going rate now."

The search parties shifted position, moving to surround Blackshield's entourage. Serrana's hand dropped to an arrow. Two of Creelisk's solders closed the town's gates.

Tyressa smiled. "I believe there's room for negotiation."

Blackshield chuckled. "You don't honestly imagine I can allow this challenge to stand."

"Is it worth dying for?"

"I dispatched one of my riders back to Thornkeep. If I don't appear by dawn, he'll issue orders in my name that will make you prey. Your supplies will never leave Thornkeep. Your people will be ambushed. Workers will be hired away or their families will be threatened. And arson . . . amazing how fast things can be made to burn. My life is immaterial, but my good will is vital if Silverlake is to last twenty years."

Jerrad limped between his mother and Tyressa. "Mother, I *did* break the rule. I was wrong. I'll take the punishment." He tugged off his shirt, revealing the blood that stained his spine. "You can bind me to the bell post."

Creelisk reached out and stopped the boy with a hand to the shoulder. "Jerrad, a hundred lashes could kill you. If it doesn't, it will leave you crippled and scarred."

The boy looked up, tears having tracked down through the dirt on his cheeks. "But no one else will be dead."

Ranall Creelisk pulled off his tunic. "I'll take ten of those lashes."

Blackshield arched an eyebrow. "Really, my lord . . ."

"I'll pay for the privilege. A crown a lash."

Jerrad shook his head. "Ranall, no."

"I can't have my teacher crippled, can I?" Ranall smiled. "You can work on me, first, tire your arm out."

Baron Creelisk nodded at his son. "And then me."

"My lords, I would not shed noble blood."

Tyressa's nostrils flared. "Then you will lash me for my son's indiscretion."

"And me, for my brother."

Mulish Murdoon stepped forward. "Can you be giving me a nice scar so's I can be drinking off the story for the rest of my life?"

Selka of the Wolfmanes slipped between Mulish and Ranall. "Haven't you got a bigger whip?"

One after another, the citizens of Silverlake demanded that they get lashed as well. They all pushed forward and in. Blackshield's horses shied at the press of people. The baron's face remained impassive, but the whip's impatient twitching betrayed anxiety.

"There are more than a hundred of you here. You mean that the boy won't be punished."

Jerrad straightened up. "I'll take the first and last." He walked through the parting crowd to the bell post and grabbed on tightly. "You'd best get started if you want to be home by morning."

Blackshield stalked through the crowd, stopping a good twenty feet shy of where the boy waited. He whirled the whip overhead, then brought it forward, testing its weight. It cracked sharply, once, twice, and Jerrad flinched each time.

Tyressa's broken nails dug into her palms. *Oh, Jerrad.*

Blackshield stepped closer, bringing her son within range.

"Just like Mosswater, you brought this doom on yourself, boy!"

The whip whistled and cracked.

The blow knocked Jerrad into the post. It marked him with a dark welt from right shoulder to left hip. Blood oozed. Jerrad clung to the post, his knees buckled, but he didn't go down. He arched his back and his fingers clawed splinters from the wood. Muscles bunched in his throat as he strangled any outcry.

Then he gathered one foot beneath him, and the other. A fist pounded his thigh. He hid his face from everyone, walking north into shadows.

Tyressa wanted to run to him, to cradle him in her arms, but she held herself back. Instead she nodded in his direction, then walked forward, her head high. She placed herself where he had been, then pulled her tunic over her head and swept her dark mane out of the way.

"Be quick, my lord. The night's chill rises."

The whip ignited fire in her back. It exploded through her, a thousand flaming needles driven deep. She cried out, sharply and quickly. She had wanted to remain silent, but couldn't. *It's okay. Jerrad showed them how to be strong. I've show that to be mortal is not a vice.*

She clutched her tunic to her chest and walked away. Ranall replaced her, and after him came Serrana and Baron Creelisk. After them followed the original settlers, the woodsmen, the newcomers and locals, all mixing with each other. Some made brave requests as she had, others remained silent. The Wolfmane hunter just glared. Those who didn't cry out got solemn nods from the others—but no one was berated if they gave voice to their pain.

Tyressa slipped her tunic back on and stood beside her son, watching each of the citizens step up to be whipped. Blackshield delivered more than a hundred lashes that evening. About a third of the way through, after people he recognized had passed into a stream of anonymous individuals, he appeared to lose heart.

He still struck people, and struck them hard, but the avarice in his eyes had dulled to boredom.

Finally Jerrad returned to the blood-spattered post. He spread his legs and planted his feet. He hung on tightly, but said nothing.

Blackshield coiled the whip as he strode forward. Blood covered his hand. He stepped up to Jerrad, slapped the whip against his back, then dropped the weapon in the dust. "You've ruined the whip. It's yours now. But understand, if you violate the rule—if you stir up the ogres—I'll be back with another whip, and as Silverlake shared your punishment now, so they will share its full brunt then."

He turned and nodded to Tyressa. "I am told, Ogrebane, that bog mud will take the fire out of your back. Mark what I told the boy. The ogres destroyed Mosswater. Silverlake would be as nothing against them."

"We have no intention of incurring further ogre wrath, my lord." Tyressa walked with Blackshield to his horse. "Safe journey home. My respects to your wife."

Blackshield hauled himself into the saddle and departed. Soldiers closed the gates behind his company and Tyressa breathed more easily. Then she realized the citizens of Silverlake stood around looking at her expectantly.

"There are no words to thank you for your bravery this night. I would thank you for saving my son, but I know we would all have done this for anyone's son, or daughter, or any citizen of Silverlake. We came here as a way to redress an injustice done in Ustalav. Now, here, we have fought another injustice. Silverlake may be small. It may be one of the youngest towns in the world; but no place has more honorable or brave citizens. Remember this night well. Twenty years from now, and a hundred twenty years from now, stories will be told. Many will be those who claimed to have been here, but only the most courageous will bear the mark. Wear it proudly, my friends. No matter where we've come from, today we are all from Silverlake, and that is a claim that will spark envy in faint hearts, and tell others everything they need to know about you."

Tyressa noticed, already, that young men and women had slashed the backs of their garments. At first she thought it was to relieve the pressure of cloth on wound. Then it occurred to her that they wanted to display the mark. *They* are *wearing it with pride.*

She worked her way through the crowd and found Jerrad. "If you don't mind, I should like to speak to my son alone."

Jerrad looked up at her, his eyes wider than they'd been at any time since his return to Silverlake. "I'm sorry, Mother."

"It's not about that." She led him to the longhouse and their quarters at the far end. Tyressa sat him on a stool, freed the makeshift bandage from his head, then took up a razor and began to trim blood-matted hair away. "It's a nasty cut. I'll have to sew it shut."

"Yes, Mother."

"I thank the gods it's not worse. What happened out there?"

"If I tell you everything, I'll violate a promise."

"I think things have gone beyond any promises you've made."

His voice grew smaller and his shoulders slumped. "Yes, Mother."

She used water and wine and a soft bit of cloth to clean the inch-long gash on the back of his head. As she did so she listened to his story of seeing a goblin performing magic, then finding evidence that the ogre-kin they'd slain had been reanimated. To that he added magical transportation to the heart of Mosswater. That would have been the most difficult part of things to swallow, save that he'd previously told her how Nelsa Murdoon was able to find shortcuts which seemed to defy the actual geography of Echo Wood.

He didn't flinch much when she pinched skin flaps together and began stitching. "What happened to the grimoire?"

"I dropped it when I was running. I wanted to go back, but Lissa told me to keep running. I did."

"I see." Tyressa sighed. "So, tell me what you did wrong."

"The sun will be up soon."

"The sun can take care of itself. What did you do wrong?"

He shrugged. "I guess I shouldn't have kept a secret from you. And I should have told you about the bones when we found them. I just didn't want to get Nelsa into trouble."

"That's something I'll need to discuss with her mother." Tyressa resisted the temptation to slip her arms around him and hug him. "What else?"

"When I found the ogre, I should have come back and told you."

"Do you know why you didn't?"

Jerrad sighed. "I guess I wanted to be . . . I wanted to do my part for Silverlake."

"No, no, let's go back to that first part. What did you want to be?"

"I wanted to be a hero. I wanted to do something that everyone could look at and . . . There are so many people doing so much. Mulish and Ranall, they're both . . ."

"Older? Better trained?"

"I guess.»

She leaned forward and kissed the back of his head. "There was a time, Jerrad, when I was sewing up a cut just like this on your father's head. And he made a comment. He said, 'You know, for every scar I have from battle, I have five from trying to do stupid things before I was ready to get them done.' Jerrad, I know you want to be all grown up. You want to be a hero because it's in your blood and, frankly, Silverlake needs heroes. It's not an easy life out here. People do need someone to look up to. They need someone to be a leader."

"I don't think I'm cut out for that, Mother." Jerrad sniffed. "I'm not a hero."

Tyressa's heart ached. "A hero does heroic things. You may not have gotten any jewels or gold from Mosswater, but you *survived*. You were smart and clever and, yes, a bit lucky, but you survived. More importantly, here, facing down Blackshield, you did the most heroic thing I've ever seen."

"That's not true."

"It is. Do you know why people took lashes? Not out of pity, but so they could show they were as brave as you were. You accepted an unjust punishment so they wouldn't get hurt. They honored that. You may see

Mulish and Ranall as heroes, but they acknowledged your heroism tonight."

"Really?"

"Doubtlessly." She knotted off the thread and trimmed the end with her teeth. "What happened here tonight may be more important to our survival than anything else we face. Tonight every Silverlaker accepted responsibility for themselves and the settlement. Because of tonight, twenty years doesn't seem that long at all."

Chapter Twenty-Four
The Messenger

Standing on the battlements near the gate, Baron Anthorn Creelisk watched the people of Silverlake as they bustled through their business. As summer cooled into autumn they worked hard—much harder than he had expected they would. Their industriousness had increased in the weeks after Blackshield had visited.

Above him, a flag showing a black whip slithering across a yellow field fluttered high atop a newly erected flagpole. People still wore slashed clothing to show off the scars they bore. The smartest among them had stitched those rents closed, but they used contrasting thread to mark the presence of their scar. Good-natured backslapping had become a grave insult overnight, and use of any whip, even on animals, all but stopped.

The only exception was the use of the original whip on those who wished to join Silverlake. As the story of Jerrad's defiance spread, a trickle of people who'd had enough of Blackshield and Thornkeep headed to Silverlake. Once they announced their intention to join the community, they'd bare their backs and Tyressa or her appointed lieutenant would hit them with the coiled whip. They never did any damage, but the rest of the Silverlakers treated the newcomers as if their flesh had been laid open to the bone. They gifted them with plaited leather bracelets as a reminder of the ritual.

Creelisk understood the value of the ritual, though he thought the whip wasted on newcomers. He'd truly have lashed them, so their pain would unite them with the others. The courage and determination required to accept scourging would weed out the weak and undesirable.

Aside from that minor disagreement with the ritual— an objection he never voiced to Tyressa—he greatly enjoyed watching the settlement come together. He had no doubt that Silverlake would survive the winter. Because of the citizens' frugality, the supplies he'd bought had hardly been touched. He worked with Tyressa to draw up lists of new supplies to be ordered from Ustalav—a few luxuries like wine, but mostly tools for the spring plantings and emergency rations should the weather turn especially severe. By no means would anyone in Silverlake become fat, but starvation was not going to haunt the settlement this winter.

Just as with the Ogrebane story, the fact that a brave Ustalavic boy had cleverly escaped Mosswater and then defied Echo Wood's petty dictator would play well back home. Creelisk had already chronicled the events in glowing terms. He'd felt it necessary to embellish on the Mosswater episode, having Jerrad liberate gold and jewels which was the motivation for Blackshield coming after him. Extortion made much more sense to people than worrying about ogre raids. Once he'd composed his stories, he used Sunnock's old agent, Pine Callum, to carry the documents west.

The flag snapped like the whip when Blackshield had struck him. Creelisk's flesh tightened involuntarily. He wasn't alone among Silverlakers to have that sort of reaction. Everyone noticed it in others, and they shared a quiet laugh about it. *At least they did amongst themselves.* No one, save his son, laughed with him; and no one laughed *at* him.

But, just for a moment, as the ghost of the lash again burned his skin, Creelisk felt a kinship with the people. For the first time in his life he shared an experience with others in a very direct way. He fully understood pain, but it was an abstraction in others. Yet here they'd all been hit with the same whip. Their blood had mixed on the lash. Some philosophers and magicians would maintain they all were now inexorably spliced together on a metaphysical level.

Because of that tenuous link, he considered whether or not Silverlake truly had to die. His plans had been predicated on the settlement being wiped out. The resulting anger among Ustalavs would set many things in play. Chief among them would be a backlash against the prince for having exiled innocents to such a savage place. The Vishovs would become romantic figures around which people would rally. With the prince afraid of the people, he'd be happy to give Creelisk sufficient troops for a punitive expedition into Echo Wood.

Creelisk would eliminate the ogre threat, liberating Mosswater, and then would have all the vast wealth in that dead city to fund an army which could go back and unseat the prince. In Mosswater he'd find evidence that the prince engineered the ogre raid which destroyed Silverlake. The prince would, of course, deny it, but the people would rally to Creelisk so he could avenge the Silverlakers.

If I don't destroy Silverlake . . . The ends he desired could still be reached. Creelisk would have to work hard to promote the Silverlake saga in Ustalav, as well as devote time and effort to the town. The groundswell of support would be based on the Silverlakers choosing him as a champion. After a half-dozen years, when Silverlake had grown to rival Thornkeep, assassins linked to the prince would have to kill the Vishov family. The advantage there was that he'd have Silverlake as a base of operations.

That will take too much time.

Creelisk smiled at himself. Timing was a consideration, but it wasn't the primary reason for rejecting that plan. If he let Silverlake survive, he would have to place himself in a subordinate position to the Vishovs. Only as an outraged disciple and believer would he be credible. All credit and praise would go to the martyrs.

And I am subordinate to no one.

Creelisk descended the ladder from the battlement and made his way to the small cabin he shared with his son. Built of logs and roofed with wooden shingles, the cabin had none of the elegance to which the baron had long since become accustomed. A row of pegs in the wall served as a wardrobe. He slept on a straw-stuffed mattress resting on a wood and rope frame. A small fireplace built into one wall was enough to heat water for tea, but would hardly warm the place in the winter.

He dropped to a knee at the foot of his bed and unlocked his wooden traveling chest. He moved aside papers and books and found the small velvet satchel in which he kept the ring. He opened the bag and slipped the ring on. Locking the chest again, he stretched out on his bed and covered his right hand with his left, hiding the ring.

Closing his eyes, he arranged the pieces of the ring's magic. This one formed a complex puzzle. The pieces fit into an amorphous capsule which shifted in shape and color. He build it around an image of the ogre's hair, slowly trapping it, then used the hair to cocoon the fragment of bone he'd obtained to increase the magic's power. Then, when finished, the capsule shrank around the lock so tightly that individual strands of hair stood out.

Creelisk watched light glow from the black capsule, then pushed his consciousness into it. The magic, which the necromancer had insisted couldn't be done until Creelisk had doubled his fee, accepted him. A black tunnel opened to swallow him. He fell into it, drawn by an unseen current. He rolled and spun, with the tunnel corkscrewing around, or curving so sharply he thought certain his spine must crack.

Then he plunged completely into a turgid bubble, thicker than blood, but not as stiff as egg white. He found himself suspended in it, like an insect trapped in amber. It had an unpleasant chill to it, but he knew that the temperature was an illusion.

The chill marked the hatred all ogrekin had for men.

Hanging there, Creelisk breathed in. The unseen fluid flowed into his nose. It filled his mouth and throat, then lungs. He forced himself to breathe, purposely pumping fluid in and out of his chest.

And many miles away, the undead ogrekin began to breathe. The creature knew enough to know this was good. It didn't really understand the concept of being dead and then resurrected. It simply knew something wasn't right, but breathing *was*. It opened its good eye, and its momentary pleasure was enough to let Baron Creelisk in.

Creelisk held a part of himself back. He would have found it easy to fully engage with the ogre. He could revel in the incredible physical power. Even the altered perspective of looking out through eyes two feet above his own would have amused him. He could have learned much and accomplished much.

Once my plan is complete, I will have more than enough time to explore.

Creelisk forced the monster to its feet and got it moving forward. Following the orders he'd given it when he resurrected it, the creature had returned to Mosswater, but had hidden itself away until summoned again. It chose to sink itself in a pond at the heart of Mosswater—a good choice, since that eliminated notice and predation. It was no good to have the creature discovered before the right moment.

The ogre emerged from the lake and stood. It threw its head back and howled—which came out as a horrid gurgling until it had expelled the water from its lungs. Creelisk made it roar in anger, and whimper. He would have had it stamp its feet, but Tyressa's handiwork made that difficult. Instead he just limped the ogre around in a circle, looking for any signs of life through the one good eye it had left.

Finally some giant shapes squeezed through alleys and crawled along streets. Creelisk accessed another aspect of the ring's magic so he could converse with the ogres. He got nothing very useful from the sounds they were making—expressions of surprise, mostly, and nothing even hinting at sympathy.

The undead ogre spread its arms. "I am come as a warning. At Silvershade Lake there is a village. Not like this one, but a new one, of wooden walls and wooden homes. Not like this one. Small. So small the goblins decided they would take it. And because it was not a town like this one, and because goblins are not as we are, I went to take what I could. I am an ogre. All is mine to take."

Creelisk let the ogre's hands drop limp to his side. "The humans of Silverlake are not like the humans of this town. They took all that I was. They cut me and stabbed me and killed me. Fearing what you would do if you learned of what they did, they sank me in the lake they now claim as their own."

A very large ogre strode around from Creelisk's blind side. "We chased you away long ago. You are dead, Grakka. How are you here now?"

"It is the magic of the wood. They hurt the wood. If we do not stop them, they will destroy the wood. They will destroy us."

"You are a trick of the wood."

"I am a *gift* to you from the wood. Know this. It was one of their people who came to Mosswater and slew

275

two ogres. Here. In Mosswater, back under the new moon."

The ogres exchanged glances and whispered comments.

Creelisk's inquisitor pounded a fist into the ground. "A trick would know that. The wood knows."

"And gives you this knowledge as a gift. The wood's first gift. But the wood does not ask you to believe me. Send goblins as spies. The Bonedancers must know." Creelisk brought the ogrekin down to one knee. "And you should know this: in two months, on a night of the full moon, they shall feast. Their guard will be down. You can end the threat to Mosswater in a night of blood and killing."

"The family shall speak on this."

"You will destroy them. You must. The wood demands it."

"The wood should do it."

"Through you, it will." The ogrekin rose again and threw its arms wide. "And the wood gives you *me* for strength."

To guarantee my plan will *come to fruition.*

Creelisk sent the ogrekin lurching toward the others. He'd heard legends of cannibalism among ogres, and had made his plans accordingly. He headed straight for his inquisitor, fists raised in an overhand blow. He commanded the fists to fall, starting the fight that would end in a flesh-rending frenzy and feasting.

He moved to pull his consciousness free—

And failed. He pulled again, but the ogre flesh held him.

He was trapped.

His target slouched sideways, letting the blow glance off a shoulder, then shoved the ogrekin to the side. Other ogres sprang in, grabbing his arms and yanking him forward. More hands grabbed his ankles. Their powerful grips crushed bone. His shoulders ached as they twisted his arms around. Those holding his legs began to pull them apart. He tried to fight, but a femur popped free of the pelvis. Then the leg came off.

The large ogre filled his vision. Firmly grasping a handful of hair, he tugged the ogrekin's head up. Creelisk looked into the ogre's eyes, seeking sympathy or compassion, but saw only fury and hunger. The ogre reached out, grabbed the dead ogrekin's head in both hands. He twisted it left and right. Vertebrae cracked, then the ogre tore his head clean off.

Creelisk screamed.

"Father, what is it?" Ranall appeared at his bedside, shaking him by the shoulders. "What's wrong? You were thrashing in bed."

"It was nothing." The baron shook his head, glad to find it still attached. His arms felt numb from the shoulder down, and his neck ached fiercely. *And my hip . . . I'll limp for a while.* "A bad dream. Ogres."

"You're not alone in that." Ranall sat on the cabin's wooden floor. "Having heard the stories, there are times I can't sleep."

Creelisk forced a smile onto his face. "Those stories are designed to create sleepless nights or entertain children."

"And Echo Wood is rife with them." Ranall smiled. "I've already been told to stay inside the settlement tonight because the full moon summons creatures that run and howl like wolves, but aren't wolves at all."

Creelisk kept his smile in place. "As if Echo Wood isn't dangerous enough, the settlers import stories of werewolves from Ustalav. Perhaps they find comfort in the familiar horrors."

"You're likely correct, Father."

The baron raised an eyebrow. "I don't believe it was my crying out that summoned you. You were already coming to see me."

"I was."

"Because?"

His son rose and began to pace—which had always been a sign of something which had been bothering him for a long time. "Silverlake will be hold its harvest feast in two months. I know you have your heart set on returning home before then."

"We have no choice, Ranall. All the signs suggest an early winter. We don't want to be caught on the road when the snows howl down from the north. That's what killed your grandfather. I won't have it happen to you."

"I know. I've heard the story." He turned to face his father. "I'd like to ask you to let me stay. Let me winter here."

Creelisk drew himself up against the cabin's back wall. "Is this about the girl?"

"Yes, but not just her." Ranall glanced down, a smile stealing its way onto his face. "What you've done here, Father, is remarkable. So many people are amazed. You've worked hard and been generous. Some of the people are still afraid of you, but here, away from Ardis, they're seeing a new side of you. You wouldn't believe the number of people who never thought you would have joined to take a lash for Jerrad."

"I couldn't let some bandit lordling believe he had the better of Ustalavs."

"It's more than that." Ranall met his father's gaze. "You are my father. I have always loved you. I will always love you. What you have done for Silverlake has made me proud of you—prouder than I've ever been. It makes me work harder to be worthy of being your son."

Creelisk froze. He heard the earnestness in his son's voice. He parsed the sentence, draining it of its true meaning. He understood it all, including what his son wanted to hear in reply.

He just couldn't understand *how* his son could think that way.

"Ranall, I am far from a perfect man. You've heard stories about me, I know. I've done things—none as bad as the stories would make them out to be, but perhaps not things that would make you proud. But what you've just said, it rewards me for all the aches and pains and, I hope, offsets the less-than-virtuous things I've done."

"Father, if I winter here, I'll know, firsthand, what Silverlake needs. I can help you help Silverlake."

"And you can get to know Serrana Vishov even better?"

"Yes, Father."

"This isn't a decision I can make on the spur of the moment. There are things to be considered—not the least of which is explaining to your mother why I abandoned you in some green hell."

"I'll write her a long letter, I promise."

"You'll do that either way, I know." Creelisk slid off of his bed, stood stiffly, and enfolded his son in a hug. "You make me proud, Ranall. I hope I can become the man worthy of being your father."

His son tightened the embrace and hung on.

Creelisk stroked his son's hair. *And when I lead an army into Echo Wood, I shall see to it that you, my beloved son, are very well avenged.*

Chapter Twenty-Five
The Ritual

Jerrad desperately wanted to be alone, but the second he escaped into the wood, he felt terribly lonely. That made absolutely no sense, and he knew it. He hated having his mood carom between the aloofness someone like Baron Creelisk exhibited and his sister at her neediest. He just didn't feel at home within his own skin, and there seemed no escaping that sensation.

In Silverlake he felt like someone he wasn't. Part of that feeling came from his hiding his wizardry from the others. The magic aspects of things were easy enough to leave out of the story—his mother's version of it did just that. Still, he was deceiving people he liked, and feared their reaction when they learned the truth.

Because he was hiding something from them, life with them became almost unbearable. The people looked up to him, and made wonderful comments about him. They talked about how brave he was, at his age, to face down ogres and Baron Blackshield. Others weren't even fazed by the level of heroism, "given who he came from." The same people who would never have accused him of being even worthy of standing in his father's shadow now talked about how both parents had bred true in the children.

Despite what they all said, he didn't think what he'd done was heroic at all. He'd foolishly followed an undead monster and ended up in Mosswater by accident—or the wood's design, which was worse. He'd survived that first encounter with ogres by pure luck, and had escaped by doing little more than running fast. For him to be considered a hero for that was to consider a hare heroic for outrunning a wolf. No one had ever tried to push that view in his hearing, yet they were happy to make the case for him in that regard.

As for standing up to Blackshield, he really hadn't had any choice. The man wasn't going to listen to any explanation Jerrad offered, and Jerrad couldn't tell him the truth. That would reveal his learning to be a wizard. His mother had revised his tale once he'd told it to her: it became his trailing something large and falling into an old magical portal, perhaps something left behind by the Azlanti even. No one had questioned her telling of the tale, and it remained close enough to the truth that Jerrad was able to answer questions without being caught in a lie.

None of that mitigated the fact that Jerrad had been very foolish. He knew it from the first step. When the people of Silverlake were willing to fight to prevent him from being punished, he couldn't have allowed it. *No one else should have been punished for my stupidity*. So he said what he said, then Ranall stepped up, and all the others did. And Jerrad's claiming of the last lash, too, seemed only fair to him, but others saw it as the boldest move of all.

Part of him understood what was happening. The people had accepted punishment for him because they all felt united. What Blackshield was willing to do to him he could have done to any of them. They hoped that by standing with Jerrad, others of Silverlake would stand with them were the situation reversed. And Jerrad knew he would, simply because they were part of Silverlake.

But to see him as a hero when he felt like anything but a hero—that just didn't work.

He wasn't alone in being treated like a hero, of course. Ranall and Serrana had been elevated in the eyes of Silverlakers. Ranall's stepping up first simply cemented the position his demeanor and attitude had already won him. His affection for Serrana not only endeared him to those who wanted to believe in a fairy-tale romance, but was seen by many as what had saved Serrana.

Before the goblin attack, Serrana had wanted nothing more than to be back in Ustalav. In the attack's aftermath, she focused on learning how to shoot a bow. She went from being moody and useless to focused and lethal. While that made her very useful in Silverlake, there were folks—Jerrad first among them—that weren't looking forward to the moodiness returning to mix with lethal.

The fact that Ranall liked her for who she had become, and yet brought out the better bits of who she had been, gave Serrana a safe haven to discover herself. He gave her something else to focus upon. His willingness to pitch in and do almost anything, coupled with her desire to spend time with him, meant Serrana became a worthy heir to Tyressa's example. More than one person could imagine Silverlake growing into its fourth or fifth decade with Ranall and Serrana as its leaders.

Jerrad picked up a crooked stick and sliced it through ferns as he walked along. He'd grown to like Ranall, and his sister was tolerable, but he couldn't spend too much time with them together. It wasn't that they were too affectionate. They might walk hand in hand in the moonlight, or sit together watching the sunset over the lake. That he didn't mind because they generally sought some privacy for those moments. What he couldn't stand was the longing glances they shared at other times. Their longing annoyed him—in a very large part because he really couldn't imagine anyone looking at him that way.

Well, there's Nelsa, but she's different.

An acorn plonked off the top of his head. He spun around, looking up at a chittering squirrel. Its tail twitched just as a root caught his heels. Flailing, but avoiding a second acorn, he tumbled backward and somersaulted down a hill.

Not again! He covered the back of his head with his left hand and grabbed for anything with his right. Branches broke as he snatched at them. His fingernails scraped bark off roots. Leaves flew up in clouds, plastering themselves over his face. He barked a shin on a tree, which started him on a flat spin. That took him through a blackberry bush—a fact he learned from the scent of crushed berries and the fiery scratches of thorns raking his body.

And there will be mud. There has to be mud.

Finally he rolled to a stop on a flat greensward. Spitting out leaves and loam, he opened his eyes and found himself in a circle of mighty oaks. He glanced back over his shoulder, just to confirm what he already knew: there was no space between the trees to let him roll through there.

Glowing lights swirled around amid the leaves, strobing on and off as they disappeared behind trunks and branches. He heard nothing, even as the lights descended. As the bottommost ranks got closer, others appeared from the shade above. Sprites, hundreds of sprites, spiraled down slowly.

I think I would have preferred mud. He gathered himself into a sitting position, hugging his knees to his chest. *This must be really bad.*

As the first sprites approached the ground, a ring of mushrooms sprang up. They looked sturdy enough—the biggest of them anyway—that he could have sat upon one. He'd never seen mushrooms of the red and purple and blue variety that these were before, and was pretty much certain each was deadlier than a viper.

The first sprite landed atop a purple mushroom across the way. His flesh was the gray of a normal mushroom. His hair, wings, and long beard shared the brown of a dried leaf. Though his glow made it difficult to discern, Jerrad thought he saw wrinkles on the sprite's face. He didn't know what the signs of aging were among sprites, but he was willing to bet this sprite was heading toward the twilight of his existence.

Other sprites seated themselves on the remaining mushrooms, while yet more landed on branches or hovered above the green. Jerrad couldn't begin to estimate how many there were, but felt sure that if they all shot as Lissa had, he'd look like a porcupine before very long.

The older sprite posted fists on his slender hips. "You are Jerrad of Silverlake."

Jerrad nodded. "Butt of jokes, target of squirrels, mud-man. You know very well who I am."

"You, manchild, speak of who you *were*. I, Thyrik, speak of who you have *become*."

The youth frowned. "Then I'm Jerrad of Silverlake."

"Then you are the one we seek." Thyrik spread his arms wide. "Begin!"

A flock of sprites descended from the trees and flew so swiftly around him that any one became a blur, and any attempt to follow them made him dizzy. He closed his eyes for a moment to regain his equilibrium, but that was a mistake. While he wasn't watching, the sprites spattered his face with mud.

His eyes sprang open. He would have cried out save for two things. First, he didn't want to get mud in his mouth, and second, the sprites weren't haphazardly attacking him. Some smeared dark mud over his throat, jaw, and cheeks. Two delicately painted it over his upper lip. Others brought a white mud which they daubed down his nose and across his cheekbones. They spread it over his forehead and coated his ears.

A whirring began above him. He looked up. A legion of sprites descended bearing a construct of branch and leaf. It resembled nothing so much as a pair of their wings, but large enough to be meant for a man. The sprites brought it down and, using thorns, attached it to the back of his tunic.

Others flew down in their wake. They bore a coronet woven of ivy. They settled this on his brow, then withdrew. He expected to hear tiny laughter, as he had to look a sight, but solemn silence greeted him.

Thyrik looked at Jerrad, then smiled. "Now that you have the proper aspect, we may speak as equals."

Jerrad, not certain what to say, just nodded slightly. He didn't want the crown to fall off, and was afraid the mud on his face would flake.

"In Mosswater, in the Cursed Tower, you freed Lissa, and she recovered Alorek's Bow."

"Yes."

"Thank you." The leader of the sprites pointed toward the sky. "Bring her."

Four sprites descended, each holding a vine. Tightly bound and dangling from the ends, Lissa hung her head. Her captors brought her to the ground, then landed and pulled the vines tight so she couldn't wander.

"I don't understand."

"The Cursed Tower is so called because, for many years, sprites would disappear in Mosswater. The tower presented a challenge, for it was full of things we find intriguing. The Lost Ones would return after a time they could not remember. The only evidence of their disappearance came from a complete aversion to the tower itself. Even before the ogres took Mosswater, we forbade sprites from traveling there."

"I had to get my grandfather's bow."

"The prisoner will be quiet."

Jerrad thought for a moment, and a few ideas came together. It had to have been that the wizard captured the sprites and used them for light, then released them after a time. He clearly did use some sort of magic to make them forget their captivity and instill their leeriness concerning the tower. Those who were captives at the time of the conquest . . .

He looked up. "Did a group of Lost Ones return all at the same time when Mosswater fell?"

Thyrik's eyes narrowed. "Yes, but this is not at issue. You rescued Lissa, therefore you have a say in her punishment."

"I freed her from a brass lantern. She, using the bow she recovered, freed me from a city of ogres. I don't know who Alorek was, but I can't imagine him wielding that bow with more courage or skill." Jerrad shook his head. "If she is to be punished . . . What is the punishment?"

"She will be banished."

Lissa struggled against her bonds at that pronouncement.

"I see." Jerrad considered for a moment, then nodded. "Then banish who she *was*, not whom she has become. As I am not who I was in your eyes because I rescued her, neither can she be who she was, because she rescued me."

Thyrik looked past Jerrad. "You have heard. In light we welcome Lissa, and in dark send her away. How say you?"

In turn each of the sprites seated in the circle let their light blaze or extinguished it completely. Jerrad had no idea if a simple majority would win the day, or even if the ballot would bind Thyrik. As it was, less than a quarter of the sprites went dark. When things came back around to Thyrik, the elder sprite shined brightly.

"Release Lissa. Return the bow to her." Thyrik bowed toward Jerrad. "Your wisdom does you credit."

"As you forgave me, how could you do less than forgive her?" Jerrad smiled, and mud cracked on his cheek. "Were I was wise as you suggest, I'd think you led me to the answer you wanted."

"Were you not at least that wise, we would not have granted you wings." Thyrik again looked up into the branches. "Bring it."

With Lissa in the lead, a half-dozen sprites flew down. Between them they held a web woven of vines. They set it in front of Jerrad. On it rested the grimoire he'd lost in Mosswater.

"This is yours, yes, Jerrad Wisewing?"

"Yes." The youth stared at it, then looked up. "You risked much to fetch it from Mosswater."

Lissa fluttered over and landed on Jerrad's shoulder. "I told them of the fun we had with the ogres, and Thyrik couldn't resist."

"Angering ogres is a dangerous game."

Thyrik shrugged. "When are ogres ever not angry?"

"Good point."

"One we trust you will bear in mind in the future, Wisewing." Thyrik's wings fluttered, and he rose in the air. "May your way ever be in the light."

"Thank you."

All around him the sprites took to the air, Lissa among them. They circled the grove quickly, a cyclone of light, then withdrew upward and scattered amid the branches, leaving him kneeling there, alone. When he moved, the wings fell to clutter and the coronet became brittle and rough on his head.

He remained on his knees. Save for the mud on his face and the withered ivy wrapped around his head, he couldn't be sure he'd not imagined the whole thing. He rubbed at the back of his head, just to see if he'd not bashed it again when he fell and dreamed the whole encounter. All he succeeded in doing was breaking the crown apart and tangling twigs in his hair.

He climbed to his feet, measured some shadows, and started back toward Silverlake. He wasn't sure quite what had happened, but he felt pretty certain it wasn't bad. Even if all it did was earn him a reprieve from squirrels and tripping roots, he'd take it.

Chapter Twenty-Six
At the Murdoons

Tyressa accepted the wooden tankard full of mulled cider from Moll Murdoon and raised it in a salute. "To great health and mild winter."

Nelsa's mother nodded, and they drank. Beyond them, in the back corner of the Murdoon's cleared property, members of the Murdoon Clan and a gang of people from Silverlake pulled ropes and pushed poles to raise the front wall to the new barn. The workers cheered as it came upright, then others scrambled around, pounding nails to keep it in place.

Moll Murdoon wasn't what Tyressa had expected. Given Tunk's bluff exterior and rustic manners, she'd visualized her as an equally large woman, with apple cheeks, bright eyes, and broad hips—and saddled with a grandchild on each. She'd thought the woman would have years of hardships etched on her face, and perhaps a body stooped with decades of hard labor.

Instead, she found a woman her own size, with sharp brown eyes and hair black as night. Tyressa guessed the color came from dye, but the hair's natural waves and sheen defied age. Though Moll's hands hinted at her true age, absent a look at them, Tyressa would have assumed the woman still hadn't seen forty winters. *Or, if she had, they were mild indeed.*

Moll turned to glance at the barn. "Your people are making short work of this. Tunk didn't want to ask for your help, given that Mulish said he has no interest in your daughter."

"We're more than happy to help. Mulish has been wonderful working around Silverlake. And his taking a lash . . ."

Mulish's mother nodded. "Highlight of his life so far, though the scar isn't quite what he wanted."

"Why did your husband think we'd not agree to help?"

"Lady Tyressa . . ."

"Just Tyressa."

"I was raised to know better, but have lived here long enough to accept." Moll smiled easily. "My husband has lived his whole life here, not just in the wood, but within the Murdoon clan. They're fiercely independent and proud. In fact, had Nelsa not run across your son in Thornkeep, I doubt you'd ever have met any of us."

"You're not from here. I'd guess the south . . ."

"Osirion, yes. I started life named Malkia." The woman set her tankard down, linked her hand through the crook of Tyressa's arm, then began to stroll away from where others were preparing food and drink for the workers. "My father was a merchant—still is, if he yet lives—in a family trading firm. My uncles and cousins and grandfather and father all went off on trading jaunts. They returned with wonderful stories. I listened, entranced, and wished to see those places. My father wouldn't hear of it, so I stowed away on a ship and came north."

"That's quite an adventure.»

"An adventure, yes, but not of the sort sung of in songs. I was headstrong, but young and innocent. I ran afoul of a variety of characters." Moll hesitated for a moment, then nodded. "I arrived in Thornkeep in a coffle. I was auctioned off in town, to Blackshield's predecessor. Fortunately for me, Tunk had been in town, witnessed the sale, and decided I should be free. He and his brothers arrived to rescue me about the time a line of guards stood between me and freedom. We won our way free, and Tunk named me 'Moll' so if anyone came asking for Malkia, he could say he'd not seen her in years. I've been with Tunk ever since."

"I think you leave much unsaid, but I can see where Nelsa gets her spirit."

"Nelsa is the answer to my mother's prayer that I have a child as trying as I was." She squeezed Tyressa's forearm. "Echo Wood was not where I expected to find myself, but I have no regrets."

"But you've not seen your family since, have you?"

"I imagine they believe I'm dead." Moll shrugged. "It's probably just as well. This is a green land with fierce winters. This would be the greatest of hells to my people."

"It's the same for most of those I know in Ustalav. Not because of the cold, just because of the raw wildness of the frontier. They'd look at this place and see nothing. I look at it and see everything." Tyressa pointed toward the barn. "Two months ago that was just a field. A year ago, I imagine, it was woods that you harvested to get the lumber for the barn. Through sweat and strength you're making something where nothing existed before. It's as close to being a god as any person should get."

"Sagely stated. This is why Silverlake will endure." She nodded toward where Nelsa and Jerrad hauled sloshing pails of water over for the workers to drink. "We should speak of the secret our children shared. About the goblins."

"They both want to be adults, yet it frightens them. And, I can't blame them for wanting to keep a secret. At the moment they learn something important, they realize how foolish they've been to take the risk. They expect to be punished, so they hide something we need to know."

"Of course." Moll shot Tyressa a sidelong glance. "I believe they feared we would stop them from running about together."

"I probably would have, too. Not to punish your daughter, but to protect her. I could never forgive myself if she came to harm because of Jerrad's actions."

"I don't believe that would ever happen." Moll nodded. "Even though he's new to magic, he seems quite responsible."

"What do you mean?"

Moll patted Tyressa's arm, and Tyressa dearly wished she could get her arm free. "You do well to protect him, Tyressa. Nelsa had guessed. I told her to say nothing, but your reaction confirms it. And just so you know,

Nelsa is that way inclined, too, but of a sorcerous bent. She gets it through Tunk's grandmother. How do you think she found the hollow where they saw the goblin?"

"And how she makes it through the wood so easily."

"Exactly." Moll sighed. "To tell you the truth, I'm pleased that what she felt is true. Her brothers are all blind to magic. She's proud, but has no one who understands. She could use a confidant."

"As could Jerrad." Tyressa looked at her. "Who teaches her?"

"She has some of her grandmother's books. Tunk won't send her away, so she learns by herself—sorcery is in the blood. Having someone else to compare her progress with might spur her on."

"Jerrad as well. Should it worry us that their friendship could develop into romance?"

"*Could?*" Moll laughed. "I know she's already taken with your son. Look at them now. I don't know if he's confided anything to you, but their willingness to keep a secret so we'd not separate them speaks volumes."

Tyressa nodded. "It does. I don't want him—I don't want *either* of my children—to suffer heartbreak."

"No mother should, but no mother can prevent it. First romances often go that way, alas."

"Not mine." Tyressa smiled. "First and only."

Moll's smile wizened. "What of you now, Tyressa? Tunk's youngest brother has to be your age. His wife passed two years ago of fever. He's got two children almost Jerrad's age."

"Oh no, I couldn't."

"I understand that Silverlake is your responsibility, but having someone to share the burden with . . ."

Tyressa laid her hand over Moll's and squeezed. "You're wise and you're right, but I can't. I'm still married."

"I thought you were widowed. That's what most seem to think."

"Everyone but me." Tyressa glanced down, a lump rising in her throat.

Moll shifted her arm and brought it around Tyressa's shoulders. "You can tell me. You best, in fact, so I can keep the Murdoon women away with their hints and suggestions."

"I would bore you."

"I doubt that, Tyressa of Silverlake."

Tyressa studied the ground. "My husband was in service to my father when we met. We fell in love instantly, denied it for as long as we could, then announced it to the world. Of course, the match would not do, since I was noble and Garath was common. I was a prize chip in the political games around Ardis. My father was so against the match that he threatened to exile Garath, and I said I'd go right along with him."

"So you had the ogrekilling spirit from your youth, then."

"I don't like being caged." Tyressa sighed. "My mother found a genealogist who was able to prove that Garath Sharpax was really a member of the Vishov family. He's a seventh cousin or something. I think she actually paid to have the document forged, but suddenly Garath became useful. He was a leader in ways my brother was not, so all was well and we were wed. I even got to remain a Vishov."

"A true romance."

Tyressa nodded. "It was. But it's been ten years since Garath went north to fight in the Crusades. It wasn't the first time. He found court life cloying, but he always promised he would come back to me. He always had. But then, in the Worldwound, there was yet another big incursion. So many soldiers just vanished. We widows and widowers were so many, and we had nothing to mourn, nothing to fill graves. Each one of us told the other that we had to hope. I told a thousand people that my husband might not make it back, but that they had to believe theirs would. He was their leader and, as his wife, that was my responsibility to the families they left behind.

"Then my own mother died, so I served my father in her stead. Then he died, and my brother required my services. And then . . ."

"You've never had a chance to mourn."

"No, it's not that." Tyressa brushed a tear from her cheek. "I've never had a chance to stop believing. Because if I do stop believing, I'll make a lie out of his promise to return."

"You can't do that."

"I won't let myself do it. I've never given up." Tyressa pointed east toward distant Silverlake. "I undertook Silverlake so my husband would have a place to come to. I wanted him to make it home, and maybe, just being closer to where he was lost . . ."

Tyressa squeezed her eyes tight, but tears escaped nonetheless. *She has to find me pathetic.* To cling to a promise which, every year, became yet more impossible to believe; it was the gateway to madness. To undertake the establishment of a town in the vain hopes that after fifteen or twenty or forty years a man who was most assuredly dead would somehow find his way to her was completely insane.

Moll hugged her tightly. "I believe you are a very lucky woman."

Tyressa pulled back. "How can you possibly say that?"

"You've had what so few women have ever had: a man who loves you enough to promise to defy death to return to your side. I dearly love my husband, and I know he loves me, but when he says he'll return after slopping the hogs, I know there's only half a chance he will, and that falls to nothing if he suddenly decides something in the wood needs hunting. Now, that's his way. I accept that, and I even love him for it. But to have a man who made that promise and kept it before, that's special. Were I you, I'd have turned a mountain into a hole quarrying stone for Silverlake."

"You don't think I'm mad?"

"Pity that you're not. It helps living here in the wood." Moll gripped her shoulders. "Now you'll forgive me if I tell you the things your husband will say when he comes back. You're a marvel, Tyressa of Silverlake, Ogrebane, Mistress of the Whip Banner."

"You're much too kind."

"Not by half. You think about all that. You've carved a place from wilderness. You've twice faced down Baron Blackshield. You've killed goblins and dropped an ogre with a fishing spear. You've got a daughter who could put an arrow through a crow on the wing at a hundred paces. You've got a son who stumbles into Mosswater and emerges with a small cut. Save that I've been hearing this all from sources I trust, I'd be thinking you were one of the tall tales my kin brought back from their trading trips."

You cannot possibly see me that way. "You make it sound better than it is."

"If your husband doesn't return, it'll only be because he'll be afraid he's not good enough for you." Moll gave her a wink. "And, for my money, anything that stands between him and you lacks any prospect of a long or happy life."

"Thank you."

"You're welcome, dear."

Tyressa wiped away tears. "Do you ever feel the need for someone to say that sort of thing about you?"

"I have seven sons, a daughter, and a husband. I live in a compound with all of them, plus uncles, aunts, cousins, and a few strays that might or might not be distantly related to someone. There are times when I start to mutter in Osiriani, and everyone knows to stay out of my way. Then, when this happens or that, and only I can fix it, I learn everything about me that I told you about you."

"If you ever need a friendly ear . . ."

"Thank you, dear." Moll hooked their arms together and steered them back toward the food tables. "I think it's about time for me to make my first visit to Silverlake. I'll need to consult concerning the harvest feast. Your invitation was generous. You do know there are nearly half as many Murdoons as you have in Silverlake?"

"There wouldn't be any Silverlake without Murdoon help, so all are invited."

"This invitation may be something you come to regret, Tyressa." Moll freed her arm and scooped up the tankards, returning Tyressa's to her. "But with the Murdoons present, I guarantee, this feast is something you'll never forget."

Chapter Twenty-Seven
Broken Men

Jerrad glanced back over his shoulder at Nelsa as they traipsed through the wood. "Anyway, thank you for not laughing."

"Called you Wisewing, a sprite did?"

"Yes, and I wasn't, you know, using magic to translate. He spoke in our tongue." He stepped over a tree which had fallen across the game path. "I didn't have any mud in my ears, so I'm sure that's what he said."

"Do know that I hain't never heard of such a thing. Now, there was Osric Slopebrow over to Thornkeep said he seen sprites in one of their circles, but that was after a big rock bounced off his skull and left quite a dent."

"I didn't hit my head."

"This time."

"Nelsa!"

"Tell me it ain't true. Now, I ain't saying you don't recollect about the sprites right, just that some of what you say tallies with at least one other story." She caught up and grabbed his left arm, tugging. "We go up and over here."

"Okay." Jerrad nodded, happy she was content to leave her hand hooked inside his arm. "You believe me, right?"

"Well, I might take it as a tall tale, but you hain't been tripping nearly as much as in the past. The squirrels ain't chittering at you, and you're steering clear of mud." She cocked her head to the side. "Take me for a fool, but I'm thinking the sprites ain't picking on you like they was before."

"I'd never take you for a fool." He laughed a little. "I'm glad you're learning sorcery. I have to say, I never noticed magic around you."

"I don't know near as much as you do, and never thought to work it around you. Then that goblin started his dancing, and I wanted to see, so I start seeking out the magic and its coming off you like you was on fire."

"I would have told you, but my mother said I shouldn't tell anybody."

"Ain't the thing just anybody should know." With an empty wicker basket hanging from her hand, she pointed toward the right. "There, in the shade on that hill."

Jerrad smiled. "So, that's the secret."

Nelsa's smile lit up her whole face. "Finest blackberry bushes in the whole of the wood, right there. My aunt will make up some tarts that are the best in all the River Kingdoms."

"We get to eat while we pick, right?"

"Got to make sure they taste right."

"Let's go."

They climbed up along the hill's crest and came down beside the thicket. They both shrugged off the baskets they'd worn on their backs and used their heels to carve a flat spot on the hill to set them up. Nelsa then scouted down the hill a bit and returned.

"I don't see no bear sign. Iffen a bear does come along, we'll hear the crashing. Grab the baskets, head up to them rocks over there. If it gives chase, we leave the berries."

"Got it." Jerrad nodded, then moved upslope and started picking. He pulled up the bottom of his tunic to make a pouch, securing the hem in his teeth. That freed both of his hands to pluck plump berries from amid leaves and thorns. He did his best not to crush them, but quickly enough blue juice stained his fingers.

He returned to the basket and unloaded his tunic. Berry juice stained it. He sucked on his fingers, enjoying the tart taste, then returned to harvesting. He looked down, intending to ask Nelsa how she was doing. As he turned toward her, a ripe berry hit him square on the cheek. He expected to hear squirrel chatter, but instead only caught her laughter.

He blushed and swiped at the stain. He plucked a berry some bird had half eaten and flung it down toward Nelsa. He missed and she didn't even have to dodge.

"You're needing to work on your berry-flinging skills, Jerrad."

He shrugged. "I don't think I've ever thrown a berry before."

That brought Nelsa's head up. "Ain't your first time picking berries, this?"

He shook his head and began harvesting one-handed, holding the hem of his shirt up with his left hand. "I would go picking on the family estate. I went alone, or sometimes the scullery maids would help. They ate plenty of berries, but didn't throw any."

"Ain't nothing else for to do with the half-bit ones. Mulish says it spreads the seeds around, so it ain't a waste. Ma always makes us wear the raggediest clothes we have. Said it was so the thorns wouldn't have much to pick at. Still and all, the best stains made their way into quilt squares."

"You're not looking raggedy today."

"You, neither." Nelsa dumped her small basket into the larger, then walked over to him. "Them there scullery maids, did they ever do this?"

Jerrad looked at her as she brought her hand up and fed him a berry. For a heartbeat he froze, then chewed. "Um, no, thank you, they never did."

"Then they never would have gone and done this." Nelsa leaned in and kissed him on the lips. Warm and light, the kiss sent a jolt through him. She rested her hands on his shoulders, holding him still, letting the kiss linger. She pulled back, then licked her lips.

"Nelsa."

She shook her head. "You don't need to say nothing, Jerrad. I been wanting to try that out. I reckon it leaves something to be desired."

"No!" He reached out and took her face in both hands. "It was wonderful." He kissed her again, closing his eyes. He hoped he matched her warmth, but kissed more heavily. His stomach tightened, thinking he'd gotten it wrong, but she didn't pull back, or push him away.

Finally, he broke the kiss. Then he remembered to breathe. "Was that okay?"

She nodded, brushing a hand over her lips. "That weren't bad at all." Her eyes flicked up. "You dropped your load."

"What?"

"Your berries.»

Jerrad looked down at the carpet of berries around his feet. He squatted immediately and she did as well, so they almost butted heads. He brought his tunic up into a pouch again and started filling it.

Nelsa helped. "If them maids didn't kiss you, where did you learn that?"

"I haven't kissed anybody else, if that's what you're asking." He shrugged. "I saw Ranall kissing my sister. Kind of hard to miss. They're stealing kisses all the time, seems like. It wasn't like I stared or anything, but it seems pretty simple."

"Not according to my aunts. They say you can tell a man by how he kisses."

He looked up. "Really?"

"Not sure *what* you can tell. Might take some more kissing."

The berries all gathered from the ground, Jerrad stood and started picking from the bush. "Um, if you wanted, you could kiss me some more."

Nelsa joined him. "Only if you wanted to kiss me some more."

"Yes."

"Good. Don't think I know anyone else needs kissing."

"Me, neither."

"Good."

"Good." Jerrad smiled, but wouldn't do more than glance sideways at Nelsa. His insides were fluttering, kind of the way they did when he was afraid, but this was different—not mousy at all. Fear made his chest tight and heart heavy. Now he was afraid his heart was just going to sprout wings and fly on out of his chest.

They kept picking, not saying a word. Jerrad didn't want to spoil the moment. His lips still tingled with their kisses. He wanted to kiss her again, but feared she'd changed her mind and wouldn't want anything to do with him. He wanted to believe that was nonsense, but he feared making a mistake that would drive her away.

But what if she wants me to kiss her again and I don't? His breath caught in his chest. Then he snorted. *This is Nelsa. If she wants another kiss, she'll let me know.*

"What is it?"

"I had a silly thought." He turned past her and unloaded his tunic into the basket. "It wasn't anything, really."

She smiled at him as she emptied her basket. "Were you thinking another kiss should be in the offing?"

Jerrad blushed. "I was, and if . . ."

She clapped a hand over his mouth and crouched. He grabbed her wrist, but before he could pull her hand away, he heard voice. Men's voices. He gave her a nod. They gathered up their baskets, retreated to the rocks and hunkered down behind them.

Four men—Broken Men, unkempt and emaciated—came around the base of the hill and worked their way up. Two of them were bare-chested. Ribs stood out, as did patches of snow-skin and scars. Some were clearly from burns, and others blades. The scars Jerrad most easily recognized wrapped around their bodies. *They've been whipped.*

The man in the lead pointed at the berry bushes. "Told you I saw them."

The two men with tunics pulled them off and spread them out. The men began picking blackberries and relaying them by the handful to the tunics. Though the men were wolfishly lean, they picked without eating.

Jerrad started to stand, but Nelsa pulled him down. "Don't."

"But the near tunic, it's purple and red—Ustalavic colors. He's from my home."

"Ain't proof of anything but what he took that off one of your countrymen." She shook her head. "There's camps of Broken Men all down the Crusader Road. Whole men go amarching north, and pieces of 'em come limping south. Take another look. Ain't a one of 'em wouldn't gut you to get your shirt or shoes."

Jerrad again peered out through the space between the rocks. The men did look well used. The man who had found the bushes and the largest, the one with a rag looped around his shaved head to hide a missing eye, moved as close to normal as any of them. The other two picked berries slowly, like they were moving underwater. Their eyes didn't focus on much. They didn't notice when berries bounced to the ground. They just dumped handfuls on the tunic every couple of minutes, whether they had one berry or dozens.

He reached out and found Nelsa's hand. "I look at them and I think my father might have known them. They could have been his men."

"If they was, I'd wager they'd give their lives so he wouldn't be dead." She squeezed his hand. "Those that come here to the wood, they're the ones not ready for polite company. May never be. And ain't a good idea for us to see how close to polite they are."

"We'll at least tell our parents that they're out here, yes?"

"We'll mark where they're camping, figure out how many there are and all. Hain't never had much trouble with them. I don't reckon Silverlake should."

Jerrad nodded. Even though he wasn't very big, he felt pretty certain he could subdue any of them using his sticks. He wouldn't attack them, any more than he'd beat a starving dog. It struck him that this is exactly how he was seeing those men. *They may look like dogs, but they* are *men. Broken Men.*

"Can we leave them food?"

"Not a good idea." She gave him a hopeful smile. "Might could be we give 'em tracks to follow to sweet water and an old orchard. But not now."

"No, not until we've reported back."

Below, the men laughed. They gathered the corners of the tunics and started back downhill with their bounty. Not all of the twisted scars decorating their backs looked old.

Nelsa glanced in their baskets. "I reckon we have our fill. Should be enough left for them to come back."

"Thank you."

"Just the neighborly thing to do." She kissed him again, too quickly, and smiled. "And since we're going back early, we'll be having us some free time. I'm thinking we can work out a way to best spend it."

Chapter Twenty-Eight
Visions of the Future

As the days wound down to the harvest feast, Jerrad found his role in Silverlake's society shifting. While he'd never really been seen as an authority figure, people had treated him as if he was Tyressa's heir. With Ranall and Serrana getting closer, that honor had shifted to the two of them. He knew lots of folks were hoping and wishing they would wed, since that gave them leadership in waiting in case anything happened to his mother.

Though he'd not expected it, Serrana rose to the challenge. She'd gone from never wanting to be in Silverlake to acting as if there had been no life before the settlement. When he'd told his mother of the returning crusaders, Serrana was even more vehement in expressing distrust for the Broken Men than Nelsa had been. She stressed Silverlake's need for self-reliance, and plenty of citizens were happy to follow her example. As a result, their efforts to help the Murdoons harvest berries and nuts produced a crop twice what the clan had ever gathered by itself.

Jerrad didn't so much get forgotten as relieved of responsibilities he'd never really realized he'd been given. Silverlakers didn't needle him about spending time with Nelsa. At most they mentioned that they thought she was a nice girl, or they'd give him something they'd made and suggested she might like it. Women tended to do that a lot with soap they'd scented with flowers and herbs. He didn't really understand, and Nelsa might sniff and smile, but Moll Murdoon seemed very pleased and asked for thanks to be passed along.

In a quiet moment it occurred to him that his life had returned to how it had been in Ustalav. No one was expecting anything of him. The difference was that in Ustalav they dismissed him because he was just a child. Here they seemed to believe that if there was anything amiss, he'd handle it or let everyone know what was going on. He'd gone from being a mouse to something else. *But what is that something else?*

That confident trust left a mark on him. He might still wander the wood as he had done before, but he didn't allow himself to daydream. He looked out for things, like signs of Broken Men or goblins or ogres. Absent finding anything like that, he gathered food, marked out hardwood stands, and located lots where windfalls or spring floods had deposited firewood.

One thing had changed significantly for him. Wandering south of Silverlake, in the shadow of a hill, he found a small patch of land covered in mushrooms.

None had grown too big, or had odd colors. He spotted three varieties—two good for eating, and one that could be brewed up into an earthy tea that settled the stomach no matter how sick the person was.

He bowed in the general direction of the mushrooms. "Thank you." Then he dropped to a knee and harvested two thirds of the plants. The rest he left for the sprites. He imagined they'd eat some, or other creatures would; but some of the remaining ones would be used to populate new patches.

He reached into a pouch on his belt and pulled out a handful of dried berries. These he piled in the middle of the area he'd cleared. This time it was berries. Other times he'd left some bread or cheese or roasted chestnuts. The sprites didn't seem to care for cheese much, but everything else vanished without any tracks being left behind.

He tucked the bag of mushrooms into his knapsack and slung it over his back again. Pushing on, he came to one of the sprite bogs. With autumn coming on, and the leaves becoming a blazing canopy of red, gold, and brown, the bog looked even less inviting than it had before. The leaves that had gently drifted down to the surface floated limply. Holes had opened in their surfaces as they slowly dissolved. Even though he approached the bog from upwind, he couldn't miss the stink.

He'd been to this bog before. With Nelsa's help, he'd filled a clay brewer's jar with mud and lugged it back to Silverlake. The settlers had long since been taught about the dangers of roast-weed and avoided it, but having a supply of the mud available wouldn't hurt.

Besides, if it soothed roast-weed, Jerrad wondered if it might not also be good for treating frostbite.

As he got thinking about that, he thought about another affliction: snow-skin. It had nothing to do with snow, or even the cold, but earned its name because patches of skin became numb, then flaked off in white bits resembling the large, feathery snowflakes that fell in the dead of winter. The only treatment came through mixing animal fat—the more rancid the better—with ashes and fermented tea leaves. It didn't seem to cure the disease, but just paste the flakes on the flesh so they weren't falling all over the place.

He eased himself halfway down toward the bog, planting his right foot firmly about a yard above a huge roast-weed plant. He shucked off his backpack and pulled another bag from it. He opened that bag wide and placed it on the ground.

Taking a deep breath and letting it out slowly, he mentally assembled the colorful mosaic he associated with the spell he'd most recently learned. Fog formed around his hands, starting as a cloud, then tightening down into gloves. He was fairly certain that unless someone could recognize magic, they wouldn't see a thing. The ghostly gloves slipped forward and off his hands. He brought them down to a roast-weed plant and quickly stripped it of leaves. He stuffed them into the bag and returned to harvest more. The stem bled a milky white liquid. The leaves did likewise, but not enough to soak through the bag.

He collected about a pound of leaves, dunked the ghost hands into the bog, then used them to pull the bag's drawstrings up and tight. He knotted them, then dispelled the hands. He pulled another bag from his pack, turned it inside out, scooped the bag of leaves into it, then knotted it securely closed. He stuffed the bag into a separate compartment in his pack, to separate it from the mushrooms.

It had occurred to Jerrad that snow-skin might flake off because the flesh around it was numb. He hoped that a highly diluted roast-weed tincture might stimulate the skin and bring it back to health. Because he had the sprite mud, he knew he could counteract the burning effects if he made the solution too strong.

Try as he might, he couldn't put the Broken Men out of his mind, nor could he feel anything but sympathy for them. Silverlake's woodsmen reported that crusaders had pilfered some wood from their lots—more as a report of a nuisance than any threat. They took to piling trimmings and short boards in a stack for the men to take. Fishermen had noticed Broken Men trying their luck with string and hook, or trying to net fish at some of the stream outlets. They didn't report any overwhelming success, and were willing to leave the crusaders all the small cutthroat that came up.

Something in the way others saw the Broken Men struck Jerrad as wrong. Silverlakers seemed to feel pity for the men. Not a huge surprise, since the ones he'd seen looked pretty pitiful, but that sentiment came tinged with disapproval. Whoever the men were now, they had once been strong warriors who had neither defeated the enemy nor died trying to kill them. The silent judgment seemed to be that these men must have been cowards on one level or another—were they not, they'd not be in such a bad state now.

That's a nasty little piece of circular logic.

Jerrad saw it differently. The warriors he'd met, both in his grandfather's court and in Baron Creelisk's contingent, weren't as much at home in the wood as he was. Even when the sprites had been bedeviling him, Jerrad could identify good mushrooms from bad, could have found his way home, and could have found enough food to last him until he made it home. If the warriors of Silverlake couldn't do that much, why would anyone expect crusaders to be able to do more? *They were trained to make war, not to forage in a foreign land.*

A branch snapped off to the west, beyond the far lip of the bog hollow. Jerrad came up a bit. *What's he doing out here?*

Baron Creelisk, apparently unarmed, walked through the wood with his head down and hands clasped at the small of his back. He seemed many miles away, lost in thought.

And truly lost. I've never seen him out this far. Jerrad climbed to the top of the hollow, then walked around the south end. "Is everything alright, my lord?"

Creelisk's head snapped up immediately. He turned slowly toward Jerrad, a smile struggling to curve his lips upward. "Master Vishov. It's good to see you. I was taking a walk so I could remember Silverlake well. Have you been successful doing whatever it is you're doing?"

"I'm gathering mushrooms and anything else I can find. It's all for the harvest feast."

"Of course." The man's eyes narrowed. "I'm grieved I shall not be able to join you. I should very much like to see how the custom plays out in so rustic a setting."

Jerrad shrugged. "Nelsa says the Murdoons have a family feast. Usually do it at the solstice just to break up the winter. Reminds them that spring's coming, and they're looking forward to ours as a way to welcome the winter. Why do you laugh, my lord?"

The man held his empty hands up. "Forgive me, but as you were speaking, you sounded more like a Murdoon than you did a Vishov. I found myself wondering if Ranall's speech would take on more of a pragmatic structure."

"I guess that's a good question."

"And I shall have an answer come next spring."

Jerrad arched an eyebrow. "You'll be returning to Silverlake, then?"

Creelisk nodded, gathering his hands at the small of his back. "Had I had time to make the proper preparations, I should have arranged to stay through the winter. I plan on wintering here next year. With any good fortune, I may convince Ranall's mother to join us. Even if she doesn't come, I'll see to it that a great deal of supplies are delivered in her name. I also have it in mind to bring a printing press and vineyard cuttings, so we can plant for a wine crop. Do you think those are good ideas?"

"I'm sure if you think they're good, they are, my lord."

The man half-grinned. "I asked your opinion, Master Vishov, because I truly seek it. You must understand that when you've reached my years, you view things through an ever-narrowing window. I can only contrast what *is* with what I have seen in the past. You, your sister, my son—even your mother, remarkably enough—have the vision to see this place as it can be. Might I ask you to indulge me?"

"As you wish, my lord."

The baron stroked his chin with a hand. "In your mind, where do you see Silverlake in five years? I mean, it will physically be here, of course, but, well—take this glade. We're well south of Silverlake, but how will this place be? Will the trees have been taken for building and fire? Will people level the hills and plant crops? What is it you see for the future?"

Jerrad's brows arrowed together as he concentrated. "Well, there's an old quarry. That's where Thornkeep got most of its stones. If we get some more stonecutters, we can build real walls. And there's mud here, white mud, which I think is really good clay. With some potters, we could make and sell urns and bowls and all sorts of ceramics. The Murdoons say the earth is good, so we can grow crops, maybe send things back to pay for the ones you've brought in. Five years, I guess, we could be five times as big as we are now, maybe twice that."

"The size of Cesca, then."

"Yes, my lord."

The man slowly nodded. "I cannot say I disagree with your vision."

From his tone, Jerrad couldn't tell if that was a good or bad thing. "Is that how you see things, my lord?"

"Yes, son, I do believe so." Creelisk looked past him, focusing distantly. "In five years, Silverlake would rival Thornkeep—nay, it will have surpassed it. People will start flocking to the Whip Banner come spring, and others will trade with Silverlake preferentially over

Thornkeep. Blackshield's domain will wither. In fact, the night he scourged Silverlake was probably the last chance he had to save his realm."

"I think my mother would rather find a peaceful solution than fight with Blackshield."

"I'm certain she would, were that opportunity given her." Creelisk shook his head. "I can see from your expression this talk is unsettling. You'll forgive me. As I said, I can only see things through the past. Politics colors everything. Surely Blackshield can be made to see reason and bloodshed can be avoided."

"Yes, my lord."

Creelisk smiled, but it didn't carry up into his eyes. "I thank you for your opinion, Jerrad. Back in Ustalav, when I speak to others who might wish to travel here, I will share your vision for the future. I'm certain you will inspire many to visit the wood."

Jerrad bowed his head. "Thank you, my lord."

Creelisk waved vaguely back toward Silverlake. "Please, don't let me detain you."

"You're most kind, my lord. Enjoy your walk." Jerrad retreated quickly, putting two hills between them before he slowed down. He shivered. Something about that conversation seemed wrong. He felt as if the baron intended two meanings for every word, and one of them wasn't good.

He almost doubled back to trail the baron. Had it been just curiosity, he would have done it. But because he felt something was wrong and didn't wholly trust the man, he'd be spying. That just wasn't an honorable thing to do to a friend. Were he discovered doing it, his mother would be disappointed, and his sister would see him as having interfered with her relationship with Ranall.

"Whatever he's doing, it doesn't matter. He's leaving soon." Even if he was lying about something, like returning in the spring, it wouldn't matter. Unless he categorically refused any request by Tyressa for supplies—thereby endangering his own son—there really wasn't anything he could do to affect Silverlake.

Confident in his analysis, Jerrad headed back to Silverlake. The town would take care of itself, of that he was certain. He didn't know if his vision was right or wrong, but he was willing to bet more on the former.

Silverlake is the future, my *future*. Jerrad smiled to himself. *And there's nothing I won't do to make the vision come true.*

Chapter Twenty-Nine
Wheels Turn

Creelisk waited until he was certain the Vishov boy had departed. There was something odd about the boy—more than just his being a product of that bloodline. He considered the possibility that Jerrad might have somehow detected the true nature of his ring. Though the baron was by no means a scholar of the Vishov family, he couldn't recall ever having heard of the Vishovs being magically inclined. Nothing the boy had done since Creelisk's arrival even hinted at magic—but then, the baron was willing to admit to himself, he'd really not paid Jerrad that much attention.

It hardly matters. Even if the boy were able to work magic, he had no one in Silverlake to properly instruct him. Moreover, the child was guileless. Had he somehow detected the reanimation magic and traced it back to the baron, he'd have reported it immediately to his mother. That she had said nothing to him about it, nor reacted to him any differently than she had at the start, suggested she'd been told nothing of the kind.

Creelisk thought for a moment. If Jerrad was able to work magic, it made him a bit more valuable. Were he saved from the doom that would descend inside the week, he could be trained and become an engine for vengeance. A wizardly avenger would certainly attract attention and support for Creelisk's endeavor.

The problem was simply that magic made the boy unpredictable. Creelisk was fairly certain the ring's magic couldn't be traced back to him, but that was by no means an absolute truth. If, at some point in the future, Jerrad *did* learn the truth, he'd become a serious threat to the Creelisk bloodline.

No. Even if the boy could work magic, the danger of keeping him alive greatly outweighed the risk of leaving him to whatever fate had in store for him. And if by happenstance Jerrad managed to survive the slaughter— especially through the use of magic—Creelisk could always welcome him home, and provide him training so they could avenge their dead. *I could arrange for him to be managed and, if needed, destroyed.*

Dismissing that matter from his mind, Creelisk wandered deeper into the woods. He came to the edge of a ravine, near where he'd found a strip of the ogrekin's flesh hanging from a branch previously. The sun and air had dried it down into a curled piece of leather no longer than his little finger. He pulled it from a pouch on his belt and tucked it through the loop of his ruby ring. Then, seating himself between the roots of an old oak, he triggered the ring's magic.

This was the greatest of the ring's magic, the whole point of the gambit. He needed a way not only to control a single animated creature, but to allow that control to spread from there to the living. The necromancer had called it his life's work—ironic, given that Creelisk had the man killed shortly after the ring's delivery.

Though parts of him still ached from having been linked to the undead ogrekin as its fellows tore the creature apart and devoured him, the baron marked that as a sign that the linkage critical for the success of his plan had been established. The verbal argument he'd made for the ogres to attack had only been to align their thoughts. They were thinking what Creelisk wanted them to think as they consumed the ogrekin.

They had ingested carrion with which he had a magical link. As he invoked the ring's power, pushing it through the lock of hair, the bit of bone and scrap of skin, it connected with those other bits that yet existed inside the ogres. A sliver of bone worked down between tooth and gum. Some hair as yet undigested. A bit of meat or fragment of nail that had lodged in some intestinal pocket, escaping evacuation. All of these resonated with magic.

The magic flowed through them and into the ogres' blood. Where the undead flesh had gone to strengthen muscle or grow new brain tissue, there it was the magic moved. In the ogres' minds, the magic touched upon the dreams and fantasies of conquering Silverlake. It kindled fears of the humans who dwelt there. It triggered hunger for manflesh. It recalled the glorious tales of Mosswater's fall and assured the ogres that their conquest of Silverlake would be just as memorable.

And in one ogre, more intelligent than the rest, it suggested that their attacking and feasting on the night of the human feast would, in fact, be a joke of the highest order.

Each day, as he took his walks so he "could remember Silverlake," he made time to inject himself into the ogres' minds. They resisted at first, but it became simpler and simpler. As the magic brought their thoughts to him, he remembered and reinforced things. He let each ogre know that its particular thoughts were right. He let them believe that if they didn't destroy the men, the men would destroy them. And if the ogres *did* destroy the men, they would be counted as the greatest among ogres.

This time, as always, he finished by sending the feeling that the night of the full moon was the perfect time for them to do their work. He slipped the image of that bright, cold orb into their blood-spattered fantasies. He had no doubt they would do what he desired, on the night he desired.

Which means I only have a short time to finish my work.

Creelisk returned from the wood and immediately sought Tyressa. He found her in the longhouse, seated at her desk amid an ocean of notes and diagrams. He smiled at her. "I would not disturb you were it not important, Lady Tyressa."

She looked up, her eyes red with fatigue, and managed to smile. "I welcome the distraction."

"Your devotion to Silverlake, your level of sacrifice, speaks to your character. I tell you truly that I can think of no other person from Ustalav who could have created and held together this community."

Tyressa stood. "My lord, you will be leaving in less than a week. There is no need for flattery."

He shrugged. "Perhaps there is. I ask an indulgence of you."

"What would that be?"

"When I return to Ustalav, I shall head for Caliphas. I shall speak to the prince, about you and Silverlake. I will tell him that a great injustice has been done to you and your family. I'll ask that he transfer control of Vishov lands to someone else."

"Because, my lord?" Tyressa fingered some papers. "I hope you've not found my requests for materials and supplies to be onerous."

"On the contrary, I find you being more conservative than is prudent." He brought his chin up. "This creates a problem for me because people will judge me by what gets sent. They shall assume I wish to doom Silverlake so your family's holding will fall to me."

"I could inflate numbers."

"But you know that even were I to give you everything, I should still be judged this way. I cannot win." Creelisk glanced down at the wooden floor. "Neither can the prince.

"The fact is, my lady, that while many welcomed your exile, not everyone did. Your being here is seen as an injustice. As stories of your successes circulate, Silverlake will be seen as a point of pride for Ustalavs, and more proof of your virtue. Thus the injustice of your exile will be made more apparent. The prince, I believe, needs to look upon Silverlake as an Ustalavic colony. He needs to support it. The lords of the River Kingdoms might not be pleased, but Silverlake could add stability to the area and serve as a bulwark against the ogres of Mosswater raiding further east."

"Then the indulgence of which you speak is . . . ?"

"Allow me to speak to the prince on your behalf. If you would be so kind, please write him a letter sharing with him your dreams for Silverlake. You know politics and the court at Caliphas well enough to know the letter will not remain secret. Let those who would learn its contents and dream of joining you discover through your words the wonder that is Silverlake. As more people support you and dream of your city, so must the prince support it."

Tyressa nodded slowly. "I don't deny your read of the politics or nature of secrets at court. I won't say I'd not considered writing such a letter. A report on our first year, perhaps."

"Events would warrant earlier reportage, my lady."

"I will accept your judgment in that regard." She hugged her arms around her stomach and met his gaze. "I must ask you something."

"Please."

"I would not discount or denigrate what you have done here. Your counsel has been wise and I shall never forget you and Ranall taking lashes. For me to do that was expected since I was his mother, but for you to do it—that meant more to the people than I could ever have possibly imagined."

Creelisk pursed his lips for a moment. "It was the first time I felt I had been accepted by the people."

"You made yourself one of us. I don't doubt that you are." She raised an eyebrow. "I do have to ask, however, why you would invest so much of your personal prestige in Silverlake."

"You want to know what kind of return I expect to see from my investment."

"I wouldn't have put it in quite that pragmatic of a way."

"But that *is* how you meant it. No, please, take no offense." He smiled. "If you didn't ask that question, you would not be the person who could have created this place. So I'll answer you squarely. I have two main reasons for aiding you. The first is simply this: just east of Cesca, on the West Sellen River, I shall establish a ferry service and trading post. I'll pay well for furs and other goods, yet charge an absurd amount for drayage of same across the river. I'll ferry settlers over for modest fees, charge more for those returning to Ustalav, and make a considerable amount of money through arbitrage. My risk will be minimal, and the return will be incredible. I will also establish a trading post here to serve the needs of settlers and hunters, lumberjacks or returning crusaders."

"You could better assure your plan's success by maintaining control of Vishov assets."

"I could, but I'm sure whoever the prince places in stewardship can be bought and, if he proves greedy and tries to renege, things will have become lucrative enough that I can convince the prince that only *he* can properly protect your interests. He'll take over, or he'll pardon you and place the Vishovs back in charge, where you should be."

"Elegantly explained and well thought out."

"My walks have given me time for reflection." He held a hand up. "Lest, however, you think me someone whose only interest is in gold, I should mention the second reason: my son."

"Everyone here is quite fond of Ranall, my lord."

"I know. Time once was when I would have been envious of him, but age tends to strip one of vanity. The fact is that he's asked me to let him winter here. I think, unless your daughter were to chase him with arrows all the way across the river, he would never leave Silverlake. I have to say, this does not displease me. In fact, it makes my heart soar."

"I don't understand, my lord."

"I would have thought that if anyone would, it would be you." The baron opened his hands. "As we have just discussed, Ustalav is a land of many political intrigues. Such intrigues killed your brother. Had mine not died, he doubtless would have preceded your brother to the gallows. Were you to look at the generation of noble scions which includes my son, I believe Ranall would stand out as being inspirational, or at least sufficient for some to pin their aspirations to. I don't want him caught up in webs of deceit. I'd rather him here, taking his chances in a land with goblins and ogres and petty tyrants with whips, than in a truly dangerous place like the prince's court.»

"I see." Tyressa shuffled some papers, then looked up. "You know that there will be those who claim we've taken your son as hostage against you giving me what I want."

"I'm certain that's true. In fact, I considered asking you to entrust Jerrad to my care, to take back to Ustalav for the winter, to counter such a claim. I would see to it he had the best tutors, of course—and they would come back here next spring to continue his education. But I won't ask for your son to accompany me."

"It would break my heart to let him go."

"And his to be sent away." The baron nodded. "So, I shall just entrust my son to you. If there were an announcement next spring or summer of troth being pledged—preferably to your daughter—it would put the lie to those rumors and make Silverlake that much more of a fanciful place."

"That would please me, my lord."

"Me, as well. It would give me an agent I could trust here in Silverlake." He half-bowed. "Ever the pragmatist, I am."

Tyressa shook her head. "I don't believe that of you, my lord. I wondered why you came when you did, but I've watched you here. Even were the night of the whip forgotten, you would truly be seen as one of us. You've sweated and toiled by our sides. Your hard work has benefited Silverlake greatly. It saddens me that you will not be here to join us in celebrating all we have done."

"I wish I could remain." He straightened up. "But I return to our home to make preparations, so next year I can return and, perhaps—just perhaps—I'll never have to leave again."

Chapter Thirty
The Interloper

I didn't realize you didn't like him." Jerrad reached deep into the shadeberry bush to pluck the purple berries. "Should I have noticed you didn't like him?"

"Not particularly." Nelsa shrugged. "Something 'bout Baron Creelisk weren't right. I like his son fine. Now don't you get pouty, I don't like him like that."

"That wasn't me pouting, that's me disappointed in myself." He pulled his hand out of the bush, dumped a handful of berries in his basket, then held his hand out toward her. A small droplet of blood welled up near the base of his thumb. "Leaves still on the bushes and I don't find a thorn. Bushes bare but for berries and I get stuck."

"Shadeberry bushes are tricker than blackberry bushes." She leaned over and kissed the tip of his thumb. "There. Better?"

"Yes, thank you." He wiped the blood off on his trousers. The weather had turned cold, and a frost had settled over Echo Wood for the two nights before the harvest feast. The berry bushes stood on the north side of hills, so never really warmed up. With the frost, the berries went from a bright red to a deep violet. Nelsa insisted that meant they'd be sweeter than ever and that her father made a wonderful berry wine out of them.

"Will we get enough for your father?"

"More than last year. No real frost." She smiled. "May make only a bottle or two, but that will be enough."

Jerrad thought for a moment. "Next spring, if we came back here, chopped out some terraces and planted more bushes, we'd . . ."

". . . attract plenty of bears." Nelsa laughed, and Jerrad liked the sound. "We'll get a lot more roast-weed, too."

"Maybe roast-weed will be useful." Jerrad shrugged and started gathering more of the pea-sized berries. "What was it you didn't like about the baron?"

"Didn't see him that much, but he reminded me of a wild dog. My pa says that once a dog gets out away from men, he sheds polite and becomes more wolf. Any dog is three generations from having a curled tail and a quick bite." She emptied her hands into her basket, save for one berry she tossed toward Jerrad.

He snapped it out of the air. The berry burst between teeth, tart as ever, but with the sour definitely cut by sweet. He fished the seed out of the pulp with his tongue, then spat it off to the west. It bounced off a broad roast-weed leaf and disappeared amid the patch.

"It still tastes pretty sharp."

"Pa ferments it in an old oak barrel."

"That must help." Jerrad nodded. "I don't know that I see the baron as going feral all that easy, but maybe

I'm judging him by Ranall. Doesn't seem that a man like Ranall could have sprung from a bad man's loins.»

"Don't folks say doesn't seem like you could have sprung from Garath Sharpax's loins?"

"Ouch."

Nelsa set her basket down and took his hands in hers. "You never heard me say that. I hain't never even thinked it. Fact is, I look at you and reckon your pa had to be pert-near the greatest hero ever to have got you on your ma. And to have kept up with your ma, too. Truth be told, you Vishovs give us Murdoons a run for our money."

Jerrad squeezed her fingers. "I know you don't see me the way others do. I guess it's just that I've been thinking about my father lately. I don't remember him, not at all. And, well, I see the Broken Men filtering south for the winter. I see how torn up they are. I keep wondering if what happened to them happened to my father. You see the ones that aren't looking at anything . . . I guess that wanting to help them out was hoping maybe someone would have done that for my father."

"And that's a noble sentiment, Jerrad. I reckon your ma was right in deciding not to bring them in to the harvest feast. They're wild dogs, too, and you see that. Remember, though, she said Silverlake will do more for them if the winter is bad. My pa allowed as how we'd do the same."

"I know. Not like they're not doing good." Freeing a hand from hers, he pointed back toward the north. "I haven't seen nearly as much goblin sign on this side of Silverlake as I have south."

"South is closer to Bonedancer land."

"But down there I see tracks going north and back south. Here they just go north and don't come back."

"Better wild dogs than no dogs at all." Nelsa glanced down in his basket, then up toward the sky. "I reckon we can almost fill that basket by the time we have to head to Silverlake."

"We have plenty of time before the sun goes down. Folks won't be eating until the moon's full up."

Nelsa sighed. "My ma and aunts and all said I have to wear a dress for the feast. Your sister's lending me one of hers. They want me there early so they can make me beautiful."

"Huh? How?"

She fixed him with a sharp glance. "I ain't sure how you meant that, but I know how I heard it."

"No, no, I just meant you're always beautiful.» Jerrad's cheeks felt like they were on fire. "That first day, there in Thornkeep, with you thrashing goblins. I've never seen anyone prettier. I don't think I ever will."

Nelsa watched him closely, then slowly smiled. "Iffen you was a summer or two older, I'd be thinking you were snake-tonguing out them words. But, being as how you're redder than a ripe shadeberry, I'm taking you at your word." She leaned in and kissed him on the cheek. "Thank you."

"It's the truth." He smiled and wanted to go for a kiss on her lips, but heard sounds from the north. He crouched, pulling her down with him.

Four of the Broken Men had spread out in a line heading southwest. There could have been more— Jerrad could see two clearly, and caught flashes of color deeper in the wood marking two more. The closest appeared to be the one-eyed man from the previous day. He wore mail belted at the waist, with the coif up over his head. He carried a battleaxe, and a short sword hung from his belt.

"I don't think they saw us," Jerrad whispered.

Nelsa slowly dragged her basket to her. "More wild dogs, and with sharp teeth. Probably turn bandit for winter."

"They wouldn't if they had another way to survive."

She frowned. "They're soldiers. They live by the sword."

"But they were crusaders. They held the demons back. That has to count for something, doesn't it?" He sighed. "I bet if we try to talk with them, we'd agree on . . ."

Nelsa squeezed his forearm and pointed. "Isn't that . . ."

The second man wasn't a man. Kiiryth, arrow nocked in his bow, raised a fist. The one-eyed man stopped, then whistled low. The other men stopped. Kiiryth darted forward, staying low, then rose up and shot.

A low rumbling roar came from the west. A loud crashing sound accompanied it. The men shouted and started running toward the bushes.

The ogre, a warty brute with pink scar tissue where half her scalp should have been, burst through the underbrush. Her two eyes were both big as saucers, though one sat high on the left and the other low. Pendulous breasts and thick rolls of fat quivered and swayed as she raced away from her pursuit—and right at Jerrad and Nelsa.

The arrow had taken the ogre through the neck, but little enough black blood had flowed from the wound. It hadn't slowed her down. Nor had it dampened the fury in her eyes.

"Nelsa, run!" Jerrad stood and stepped forward, putting himself between her and the galloping behemoth.

"Jerrad, no!"

"Run!" *No place for a mouse here.* He met the ogre's hateful gaze, then curled his lip in a sneer. He forced away the fear as the monster roared a challenge. She didn't even bother to snap a tree off to use as a club. She balled fists as big as his chest and came straight at him. Her footfalls shook the ground.

Jerrad let the mosaic flow together, reaching out with a bare hand. He magically stripped a roast-weed stalk of leaves and swiped them across the ogre's eyes. As the monster rose above him, fists poised to smash him, Jerrad stuffed the leaves up the ogre's nose.

A hand on his collar yanked him out of the way. The ogre's pounded the ground, cratering the dirt where he'd been standing. Her momentum carried her past, and she stumbled, then pitched headlong into the shadeberry bushes. Thorns tore at her flesh. She rolled over, her eyes already swollen. Pus ran as tears and the eyelids crusted. Gallons of mucus squirted from her nose despite the nostrils being almost swollen shut. Blood tinged the glistening fluid and oozed from countless scratches.

Nelsa dragged him back up the hill. "Are you hurt?"

"No. Thank you." He got his feet under him and kissed her. "You saved me."

"I prefer hauling you from mud."

Kiiryth appeared, cast a glance at the ogre, then pointed up the hill at the youths. "Go! You need to get to Silverlake. Warn them."

Jerrad stared at him. "You're with them. You're one of the Broken Men."

"That's not important right now. Get going!"

The archer moved with them, urging them along. By the time they reached the top of the hill, four other men had reached the ogre. She still thrashed, but hadn't gotten up again. Led by the one-eyed man, they started cutting their way through the berry bushes to hack the ogre to death.

"Kiiryth, tell me what's happening."

"Something has the ogres riled."

"Was it my going to Mosswater?"

Kiiryth smiled. "Not hardly. That was months ago. Ogres are a bit more impulsive. We've been picking off goblins who were scouting for them. It would appear the ogres are heading out in force to raid, and Silverlake has to be a prize. Even if none of the goblins mentioned an ogre dying there before, they've certainly talked about the place. Faster."

The trio raced through the wood. Jerrad hoped the wood would be kind and open one of the shortcuts, but they had to speed over every hill and through every hollow they'd traversed on their way north. No roots tripped them, no branches lashed them, but Jerrad wasn't moving as fast as he wished.

"Why didn't you tell us you knew those men? You were a crusader like them, right?" Jerrad glanced over his shoulder at the half-elf. "If you had vouched for them, we could have helped them."

"Not everyone sees themselves as deserving help, Jerrad."

"But they're heroes. They saved us from demons."

"You think they're heroes. They only see themselves as survivors." The half-elf's eyes tightened. "For them, the heroes are the comrades who died so they could live. They owe them, and it's a debt that can't ever be repaid."

They're in a prison of their own making. Jerrad shivered. *I wonder if Silverlake will become something like that for my mother?*

They sprinted out of the woods and toward the settlement. Torches lit the walls. The Whip Banner flew flanked by streamers and ribbons of orange and yellow, teased by the wind coming off the lake. A line of people and two wagons were wending their way toward the front gates.

"That's my family." Nelsa started waving her arms. "Ogres! Ogres!"

The three of them redoubled their speed. Jerrad kept looking back and then toward the west and Mosswater. He didn't see any ogres, and the way the Murdoons waved back at them hinted at nothing even approaching alarm. Even the guards on the walls waved happily.

They reached the gates near collapse. Jerrad grabbed Captain Ellic's arm. "Ogres! Ogres are coming."

"Where? How many?"

"I don't know." Jerrad looked at Kiiryth. "How many?"

The archer shook his head. "We've killed one, a scout, to the north. The others will be coming up from Mosswater. Probably a dozen, maybe more. And given what a single one did here last time, chances are it isn't going to be humans feasting here tonight."

Chapter Thirty-One
Cruel Steel

The alarm bell's frenzied tolling brought Tyressa at a run. She gathered her skirts in her hands and cut through the gathering crowd. She reached the front gate as the Murdoon caravan cleared it. Tunk and Moll stood with their daughter. Both Nelsa and Jerrad dripped with sweat and were breathing hard.

"What is it?"

Captain Ellic nodded at Kiiryth. "He knows."

"Ogres are heading this way. We've been finding signs of goblins up north as well, and killing quite a few of them."

"We?"

Jerrad nodded toward Kiiryth. "He's one of the Broken Men."

"I have comrades in a camp to the north.

"'Not your own master' makes sense now." Tyressa folded her arms over her chest. "We've seen signs of goblin activity south of here, but nothing overtly hostile."

"Ogres are bad enough. If they bring goblins, that will just make it worse." Kiiryth jerked a thumb toward the north. "We found one ogre. I put an arrow in it. Jerrad incapacitated it."

She grabbed Jerrad's shoulder. "Are you hurt?"

"No, Mother. Nelsa saved me."

The girl snorted. "Only after he faced it off and told me to run."

Tunk patted Jerrad on the back.

"What makes you think they're headed this way?"

Kiiryth dropped to a knee and drew a map in the dirt. "No reason to find the one we did where we found it if they aren't. She was scouting along the northern flank. If they'd hit the Murdoon place, she wouldn't have come that far east, and the Murdoons wouldn't have gotten this far."

Tunk shook his head. "We didn't see anything on the way but a Thornkeep patrol. They kept their distance."

Tyressa glanced at the ground. "And no scout would be this far north if they were headed for Thornkeep. Could be the one you saw was just that, a scout confirming goblin reports before they go after the crusader camps. I'd love to believe it's nothing more, but we have to act."

The Murdoon patriarch nodded. "Best if we Murdoons come in here and help defend. If that scout just got lost and they *are* hitting our place, we'll see the fire from here."

"Your help will be greatly appreciated." Tyressa turned and saw the crowd that had gathered near the gate. She stepped over to one of the Murdoon wagons and climbed up on the seat. "There are signs that ogres may be raiding in the area. Silverlake might be a target. Everyone should arm themselves and report to your militia captains. The captains will report to me. The other thing I need—and I will ask you, Oreena, to take charge of this—is for the captains and crews of our fishing boats to take on board the children and get them out of here. Head south, and stay on the water until morning, when you can get a better look here. We'll fly the Ustalav banner to let you know it's safe to return. Go."

People scattered. She climbed off the wagon and returned to the gate. "Jerrad, you listen to everything Oreena says. I'm counting on you to help with the children."

The look he gave her sank a dagger into her heart. "I'm not leaving."

"Jerrad."

"No." He pulled himself up to his full height. "I'm not a child. I may not be big and strong like Ranall, and I may not shoot like Serrana, but I can run arrows to those who need them. I can help folks who are wounded. I can do a lot of things that will need doing. I may not be a hero, but I can do the things a hero needs done so he can be one."

She reached toward him with her left hand, but held back, balling her fist. "Jerrad, I need you to listen to me . . . ."

Tunk Murdoon gave her son a nod. "Jerrad, I'd be obliged if you'd look after Nelsa for me."

The girl spitted her father with a fiery glance. "I ain't going."

"You'll go if I tell you to, young lady."

"I ain't going."

Tunk looked at his wife. "Talk sense to your daughter."

"She's *my* daughter now, is she?" Moll dropped to a knee. "Remember dear, ogres are hard to kill, but easy to confuse."

"Yes, Ma." Nelsa smiled. "I reckon I can do that."

Tyressa shook her head. "This isn't a joke."

"Mother, I know." Jerrad tapped a finger against his breastbone. "I know how dangerous ogres are. And I've seen the crusaders out there. Kiiryth said they don't think of themselves as heroes because all they've done is survive. I don't want to be out on the water or anywhere, thinking that if I'd been *here* you and Serra and everyone else would have lived. I don't want you to die to give me a chance to live. I have to have the chance to fight so others can live."

She covered her open mouth with a hand. *As adamant as his father.*

She chewed her lower lip for a moment, then pointed back toward the lake side of the settlement. "You two will be back there with the reserves, running arrows, doing what has to be done. Here's where I'm going to trust you two. You better not fail me."

Both of them shook their heads.

"If—*if*—things go badly and the ogres win, I want you to get as many people out as you can. Don't be stupid. You don't have to be heroes. You *will* have to keep your heads about you. Can I trust you to do that?"

"Yes, Mother."

"Yes, my lady."

Tyressa pointed east. "Go."

The two of them ran off past where mothers were bundling their children up in the warmest clothes they could find and entrusting them to the fishermen. Tyressa watched them go, pride warring with terror in her breast. She turned back, her expression grim. "Captain Ellic, we should have scouts out in the woods. Not too far but . . . ."

"I'll ask for volunteers."

Ranall stepped up. "I'll go."

Mulish Murdoon joined him. "I know the wood fair good."

"Three should be enough." Kiiryth fitted an arrow to his bow. "I'll go as well. When it gets dark, you two pull back to the wood's edge. I'll give you a sign if I see anything, then can lead them off while you get back here."

Ranall nodded, then walked to where Serrana stood. He spoke to her in whispers while they embraced and kissed. Mulish gave his mother a hug, and shook his father's hand. "Be leaving something for me to eat when I get back."

Tyressa wanted to tell them to stay put, to remain safe behind the walls. But she knew that if she did that, then some sort of surprise might cause everyone to die. Those three men might well perish, but for the good of the rest, she had to deploy them.

She shivered. *Now I understand the true burden you faced, Garath. To consign men to death . . . You can tell yourself they might live, but that's no solace when they die. How I underestimated the burden you carried.*

Once the three of them had headed out to the wood, Tyressa ordered the gates closed, but left the smaller sally port open. The archer company captains joined her as the children followed Oreena and the fishermen through the sally port and around to the boats. "Serrana, your company will be at the main gate. Selka, company two will have the south wall. I want one squad from three on the north wall, but the rest of you remain in reserve to reinforce the walls or to shoot if the ogres get through the gate."

Serrana, looking far more grown up than her mother liked seeing, unslung her bow. "When do we light the range fires?"

Tyressa glanced at the sky. "First ogre or sundown."

"It'll be done."

Tyressa caressed Serrana's cheek. "I'm sorry."

The girl arched an eyebrow. "For?"

"I brought us out here to save the family. I knew there would be dangers, but I underestimated them. And there were times when you were, well, whining about wanting to return to Ustalav. I almost sent you." She hesitated. "Now I wish I had."

"I'm glad you didn't."

"You would have met Ranall anyway, I'm sure.»

"Not that, Mother." Color rose to Serrana's cheeks. "I know I was horrible then. The person I am now *would* send the old me back to Ustalav. Back there, I had no responsibility. Here I do. I think I finally understand how you and Father work. Life isn't measured in the things you do, its value comes from the things you do *for others*. When those goblins went after Jerrad . . . well, he's *my* brother. If anyone gets to kill him, it's me."

Tyressa laughed. "Now you know how I felt about you some of the time."

The girl smiled. "I love you, Mother."

Tyressa gathered her into a hug. "And I, you. Shoot straight."

"Keep the arrows coming."

Tyressa hung on just a bit longer, then let her daughter slip from her embrace. The archers climbed up the ladders and mounted the battlements. A lump rose in her throat. She watched Serrana position her troops, then turned away.

On the ground inside the walls, workers hastily dug a double row of postholes in a deep loop running from one side of the gate around and up to the other. Into the inside holes they set five-foot-tall posts, and into the others, posts half that tall. Others brought over sharpened logs which had holes drilled halfway into their underside. They fitted them over the posts, creating a ring of sharpened stakes pointing at the gate. Men could easily slip between them, but creatures as large as ogres would have a harder time of it.

Especially at a charge.

Closer in, men sowed caltrops around the longhouses to a depth of six feet from the wall. They'd been simply formed of two foot-long lengths of iron. The smith had bent each rod ninety degrees in the middle, then fused the joints. He'd shaped and sharpened all four ends until they had barbed tips like fishing hooks. No matter how the caltrop hit the ground, a foot of sharp steel pointed upward, and ripping it free would do more damage than the point did going in.

Near the longhouse doors, a two-foot wide path zigzagged between the caltrops. Tyressa negotiated it without difficulty and quickly changed. She removed her skirt, pulled on the hunting trousers, and donned a mail surcoat. She cinched it up with a broad leather belt, distributing the weight between her hips and shoulders. She slid a dagger into the sheath at her left hip. Then she strapped on leather bracers with cylindrical pockets running the length of each.

She opened a box on her desk and filled each of the eight pockets with slender, metal spearpoints. They'd been fashioned very carefully, after the design of the militia's arrowheads. They closely resembled a drill bit with two razored edges spiraling the length. Every two inches or so, to the inside of the spiral, the edge had been notched and bent inward. The bent portions of the blade functioned first like a fishhook's barb, making the points brutal to yank out. More importantly, when they lodged in muscle and that muscle contracted, the notches drove the head deeper. An ogre's vital arteries might be well sheathed with fat and muscle, but those points would grind their way in and find them.

Even if we're long dead.

Garath had once showed her arrowheads from the Worldwound with a similar design. They looked brutal and cruel, at least as painful as they were deadly. It didn't surprise her that demons would use such a thing, and she said so.

He'd shaken his head. "We created these, to use on them. And their human allies."

"But . . ."

Her husband held up an open hand. "Anyone who says war is about nobility has never been knee-deep in blood. The only thing war teaches is how to kill, the faster and nastier the better."

She took a ninth from the box and fitted it into her spear shaft. "But can we be fast enough?"

The alarm bell rang mournfully.

Tyressa looked at the longhouse captain. "Once I'm out, close-bar and block the door. Don't open it until you know they're all gone."

"Yes, my lady."

She exited and listened to the bar slide solidly in place. She jogged toward the gates, just in time to see a fire arrow arc through the dusky sky. She hurried up the ladder and reached her daughter's side.

The burning arrow had landed in a fire pit roughly two hundred yard out from the wall. It lit the wood and oil piled there, then the fire ran along three channels. One led east back toward Silverlake and ignited a smaller fire a hundred yards out. The other two channels ran north and south, bringing the fire to larger pits with smaller, satellite pits closer to the walls. The fire ran around the fort on three side, leading down to the shore.

Its light made it easy to see Ranall and Mulish sprinting back to the road and toward the fort. Of Kiiryth, Tyressa could see nothing, but she wasn't looking that hard for him. There at the wood's edge appeared one ogre. Then another, and another. Tall and broad, or hunched and twisted, they emerged onto the cleared plain before Silverlake.

Serrana looked at her mother. "I see at least a dozen. Probably more waiting."

"Yes, with bone armor, iron-bound clubs, and giant metal hooks." Tyressa's eyes narrowed. "One did so much damage here, and now we have a dozen."

If Serrana offered a comment, Tyressa never heard it. The ogres roared in unison and then, as one, began their charge to Silverlake.

Chapter Thirty-Two
Cold Manners

"Very kind of you to invite me to dinner, Baron Blackshield." Anthorn Creelisk raised the cup of dark wine in a salute to his host. "I had thought only to pay a courtesy call upon your household. To be invited to dinner, and to have your lovely wife here to serve us wine, is a most unexpected and quite welcome turn of events."

"How could I not invite you to dine with me? And you must call me Tervin." Blackshield smiled, saluting with own cup. "I don't believe I ever apologized to you for the stroke to your back. I fear it may have been harder than I intended, as I was not yet fatigued."

"No matter. I survived." Creelisk sipped his wine. *Doubtless your wife has told tales which sped your arm.* "I found that whole exercise fascinating. You sought to break people, and you only unified them. That could be seen as an unwise move on your part."

The younger man stared at him, his head canted slightly to the side. "This would be because . . . ?"

"Because Thornkeep is a cesspit where the largest chunks float to the top. If anyone here were to make a profit, the only thing they would be assured of was your coming to take your cut of it. Your household troops are only adequate to fend off bandits and the occasional Broken Man. The mercenaries here might back you, or might work against you."

"You provide an interesting analysis of my city, my lord."

"And this after only four hours spent watching and listening." Creelisk sipped the wine. Though full of flavor and with a spicy finish, it was drier than he normally preferred, and not nearly as sweet as he liked. "You are in a precarious position, and Silverlake sounds good to many by comparison."

"You're suggesting that what I did will cause them to supplant me? If you're foolish enough to believe that, you're foolish enough to underestimate Echo Wood." Blackshield set his cup down on the wooden sideboard. "The sting they felt from my whip will be as nothing compared to the winter. They lost blood and pride to me. They'll lose fingers and toes to the dark months. Tracks to Silverlake are barely passable now. Snow will bury them. They'll eat through their stocks before spring, and we'll be here to sell them grain and anything else they will need. At prices that will have them begging for the lash."

Creelisk looked up at the heads mounted around the room. "Your hunting trips must give you much idle time to indulge in fancy."

"Fancy? Are you to tell me Tyressa Vishov can control the snow?"

"No, but I *can* see to it that supplies get through." Creelisk smiled. "And when I say 'through,' I mean 'by bypassing Thornkeep.'"

"You'll find that the bandit infestation is a severe problem in winter, my lord."

"You'll find, Tervin, that bandits can be bought off."

Confusion registered in the other man's eyes. Creelisk's smiled broadened. *Now I have you.*

Before his host could say anything, the shriveled man that served as his castellan, Cranstin, entered through the previously closed door. "Forgive me, my lord, but there is urgent news."

"Yes?"

"A patrol has come back from the northern branch of the Dagger Road. There are signs of ogres heading east in force. Unless they're hooking around, they're not going to kill the Murdoons."

"How many?"

"At minimum a dozen."

"And Mosswater Road—have the patrols returned from there?"

"They report no activity, my lord."

"Have everyone put on alert. Send a runner to the Blue Basilisks . . ."

Creelisk held up a hand. "You might take a moment to consider some things, Tervin. We might discuss them in private. Certainly, your man might as well alert those who need to be alerted, but you'll want to choose your course of action carefully."

Tervin waved the castellan away. "Go. I will bring further word . . ."

"Soon." Creelisk nodded. "Very soon."

Ivis, her hands full of the wine pitcher, looked to her husband. "Shall I leave you to serve yourselves?"

Creelisk held his cup out toward her. "No need. I recall your ability to keep secrets, my dear. You're welcome to hear this."

Tervin nodded as his wife refreshed the baron's cup. "I would tell her of anything you said regardless." He moved to make certain the door had closed firmly behind Cranstin, then turned back to his guest. "Unless I've missed something, your son is at Silverlake. The ogres must be bound for there. You put his life in jeopardy."

"As you have so aptly pointed out, the winters here are harsh. My son, by choosing to stay behind, put his own life in jeopardy. Who am I to argue with fate?"

"I had been given to understand you were bloodless . . ."

"Just pragmatic, Tervin. Even if you were to gather up all the able-bodied troops you have here, organize them, and ride to Silverlake, you'd have, what—fifty men? Thirty? Against a dozen or more ogres? And while you rode there, perhaps another two dozen monsters come from Mosswater and sack Thornkeep? Your best force would be insufficient to save Silverlake, and likely insufficient to guard your own town. Since there could be a threat against your town, riding to die at Silverlake would be foolish."

"But I must do *something*."

"So send a patrol. Gather intelligence. Once you know there's no threat to Thornkeep, by all means, ride as fast as you can to Silverlake. Either you will contribute to its salvation, or you will avenge the people and send a full report to me in Ardis."

Blackshield stared at him. "You won't come with us?"

"As much as the fate of my son concerns me, it is the fate of Thornkeep which concerns me more." Creelisk swirled the wine in his cup. "Consider the two possible futures. Let us look at the unlikely case in which Silverlake is able to defend itself and drive the ogres off. The town will be broken."

"Are you certain? Last I recall, everyone there was armed and willing to fight."

"You had best hope the town is broken. You will offer succor, and your kindness will be noted. The town might continue, but it will never grow. Anyone who would think of settling there would have to fear another attack. At the very worst, Silverlake becomes a Vishov family compound, much as the Murdoons have established. While they may never be friendly toward you, they're not in a position to be your rival, either. That is the best case for you."

Blackshield recovered his wine and drank. "I see your logic, but I don't agree with your conclusion. It strikes me that, by your reasoning, the best case scenario for me is for Silverlake to be completely obliterated."

"You might think that. You're wrong." Creelisk drank, trying unsuccessfully to identify the vineyard where it had been produced. "In fact, that might be the worst possible case for you."

"But you just said a rival would be eliminated."

"Ah, but a big one would be created." Creelisk faced the man and smiled broadly. "If the ogres slay all of

Silverlake, I shall petition the prince to give me an army with which to avenge his good friend, Tyressa Vishov. He will grant my petition. I will summon volunteers to join me to avenge Silverlake and my son and his fiancée, Serrana. I shall cross the river and have to secure a base of operations. Thornkeep will be it. I might well be forced to depose you. From there I will undertake a campaign which will destroy the ogres and retake Mosswater."

"The last time that was tried, the effort was abandoned within weeks."

"You underestimate my resolve. Of course, I will find it necessary to pacify the whole of Echo Wood and, in honor of my friends and to pay homage to my ruler, I will create a new River Kingdom, called Vishovia. Perhaps only a province of Ustalav. I'll see how the political winds are blowing at that time. Either works. But, using the money that can be taken from Mosswater, and with volunteers who will happily settle here to make the dream of Silverlake a reality, this whole area will be under my control."

"Very ambitious, my lord."

"Just to suggest something you may puzzle over on your next hunt, ask yourself this simple question: What would happen if, after I conquered Echo Wood in the name of a popular heroine who has been seen as being unjustly accused of treason, I were to discover evidence showing that the prince himself—the two-faced man that he will be seen to be—had her falsely accused? Because of that treachery on his part—his betrayal of a good friend—the beloved heroine of Ustalav was ripped limb from limb and devoured by ogres. What do you think the people of Ustalav would demand of me then?"

Blackshield drained his cup. His hand shook as he passed it to his wife. "You said you *might* have to depose me."

"Yes, yes I did." Creelisk finished his wine and held it up for Ivis to replenish. "You've stopped drinking, my lord?"

"I fear the discussion requires a clear head."

Creelisk nodded when Ivis only poured a half-measure. "You have the very good fortune, Tervin, of having married a woman of Ustalavic nobility. She was known to be friends with Tyressa Vishov at court—or rather, we can make it so. Her public grief and her admonishing you to avenge her friend, as well as the devastated tone of your report about what you found at Silverlake, would cause me to see you as an ally in this undertaking. You would mourn your friend, wouldn't you, my dear?"

Ivis set the pitcher on the sideboard. "As if my life depended upon it."

"A very wise choice." Creelisk smiled over the rim of his cup. "Were I to be called away to permanent residence in Caliphas, Vishovia would need its own county governor. Who better than someone who knows the area and is tied to Ustalav?"

"Would not the story of me having plied the whip counter any positive feelings for Silverlake?"

Creelisk laughed aloud. "I admire your reasoning, but your naiveté is quite endearing. The perception of that act is determined by the story spun by the survivors. Were I the only one, I would point out that a dispute had arisen within the community and you were invited in to adjudicate the problem and administer justice. That the Silverlakers trusted you that much speaks well to your character."

"How will you get that story spread?"

"I go back to the woman who set all these things in motion." The baron of Ardis sipped wine. "Ailson Kindler started this all with her novel, *Winds of Treason*. I don't know who paid her to write it, but that was a masterful stroke. I, myself, paid for the sequel, which has been quite popular. I've also paid for a number of bards and minstrels to sing of Silverlake. Writers are notorious whores. I'll pay the Kindler woman to grind out another of her insipid ramblings. Call it *Winds of Courage*. I'll be seen to weep as I read in it of the death of my son. And, best of all, my political foes will support any move that will send me back to Echo Wood."

Tervin scrubbed hands over his face. "You've told me what happens to Thornkeep if Silverlake *does* survive seeing the ogres off. I don't disagree with your assessment. But, I must ask: what happens to *your* intentions if Silverlake drives off the ogres? You have no sympathy, no army, no plan."

"That, my dear Tervin, is why you have risen as high as you ever will." Creelisk opened his arms and slowly pirouetted. "This is the best you will ever know. The plan I have detailed to you is simply one of many. It is the one which is in play. If things do not go according to *that* plan, there are others."

"If Tyressa Vishov survives, I could tell her all that you said."

"She wouldn't trust you. Were I questioned, I was simply responding to your question of what would happen were my son to not survive the winter. All other political speculation is merely your fancy, and a false attempt to get me in trouble." Creelisk arched an eyebrow. "And I would tread carefully, my lord. After all, it was you and your men who found Jerrad Vishov as he left Mosswater. You grabbed him and brought him directly to Silverlake. If there *are* ogres attacking the settlement, it was *your trail* they followed. I do believe that is a fact you would rather have remain hidden. It will make your life so much easier and, in the long run, much more profitable."

Tervin Blackshield stared down at Creelisk. "I have to say, I'd not considered that. A failing to not see through your webs of deceit."

"Don't fault yourself, Tervin." Creelisk started to chuckle, but it became a laugh which he quickly brought under control. "A provincial like you could never understand the politics involved in the Ustalavic court."

"Very true." Tervin smiled. "But then, I don't have to. For that, I have my lovely wife."

Creelisk glanced over at Ivis. She smiled at him. He remembered that smile, but had never seen it quite so cold.

Tervin advanced and plucked the cup out of his hand. "She told me you could never be trusted. And she told me many more things. Things about you, and what you did to her. This is why, when she insisted we invite you to dine—and insisted on poisoning your wine—I agreed."

355

Creelisk suddenly felt how light his head had become, how weak his knees. Something clenched hard in his chest, and he stumbled.

Tervin reached out, taking his wife's hand in his own. "Fear not, my lord. We'll see to it that your body is found at Silverlake, where you also died. And I promise I'll be eloquent when I vow to avenge you and all the others of Silverlake. I'll make your dreams come true."

Chapter Thirty-Three
Quenched in Blood

Jerrad dropped a spare quiver with several archers, the last being his sister. "Here, I'll bring more."

Serrana acknowledged him with a nod. "Lots more."

Tyressa glanced at him. "Remember, you organize survivors, if needs be."

"Yes, Mother." He turned from her and stared out into the night. Ranall and Mulish had gotten inside the closer ring of fires and were sprinting to the gate. Guards and archers shouted encouragement.

Beyond them, ogres emerged from the forest at a gallop. Most ran on two feet, but several whose arms dwarfed their legs came on feet and fists. Muscles rippled with each pounding step, fat rolls surged. Tremors built as they approached, vibrating up through the palisade to the catwalk.

As Tyressa climbed down the ladder, Serrana raised a fist. "Wait for the signal. You're not shooting through the armor. Find meat or blind them."

Below, Ranall and Mulish made it through the sally port. Several of Ellic's men slammed it shut, dropped a bar across it, and blocked it with a small log angled down into the ground. It paralleled the two larger ones securing the main gates. The two men each grabbed weapons—a bastard sword for Ranall and short spear for Mulish—and slipped between the sharpened logs to stand with other defenders.

Jerrad shouted down to them. "Where's Kiiryth?"

Frustration flared Ranall's nostrils. "He told us to run. We thought he'd be behind us."

Jerrad's hands tightened into fists. *If anyone can survive out there . . .*

Nelsa pointed further west. "In their wake. Goblins and goblin dogs."

Like the vermin they were, goblins flooded the fields behind the ogres. Most ran toward Silverlake, ululating war cries scaling up until they became inaudible. The others rode on hairless rodent-things with whiplash tails. Open mouths revealed a tangled mass of sharp teeth. *Once the ogres batter their way in, they'll pour through like locusts.*

"Shoot!"

At Serrana's command, the archers of the first company loosed their arrows. The shafts vanished in the night, then reappeared quivering in the target or glancing off bony armor. One of the two lead monsters, stuck in both eyes and with the left thigh bristling with arrows, stumbled and went down. The one following leaped over the rolling body. Despite more arrows peppering his hide, he kept coming.

The ogre lowered his shoulder and smashed full speed into the gate. The bar holding it shut splintered, but the two angled posts kept the gates shut. The impact shook the whole wall. Two archers fell, but Jerrad and the rest caught hold of the wall, remaining upright.

The ogre rebounded, stumbling back as if drunk. As he came around, arms up to maintain balance, Serrana sped an arrow into his right armpit. Black blood splashed. The ogre clamped his arm down tight and sat abruptly.

"He's done.» Serrana's lip curled back in a sneer. She nocked an arrow, twisted to track a target, then let fly. "One less goblin."

Out at one of the fires, a trio of ogres hung massive disks on thick chains over the blazes. The disks caught, and in the brief second before ignition turned into conflagration, Jerrad saw enough to realize the disks were tree-trunk slices the size of cart wheels. The ogres, once the flames had engulfed the disks, whirled them around themselves in a circle. The flames all but died, but the disks' edges began to glow the angry red of hot embers.

The ogres released the missiles. One flew awry, plowing into a mass of goblins. The chain sailed through them, snapping a handful in half. The burning disk crushed several more. Wounded goblin dogs yelped. Riderless beasts turned and began to devour their former masters.

The other two disks crashed into the gates. One hit high on the right, blasting through the door. Wooden splinters sprayed into the settlement. Several fighters reeled away, stuck through. Mulish snapped off a splinter in his shoulder, then yanked one out of his father's hip.

The last disk hit low on the left, undercutting the gate. The wooden gate split apart where the post had been supporting it. Pieces of door tumbled into the courtyard. The post fell down onto the burning disk.

Another ogre hurled himself at the door. Wood shattered. A piece of the right door sailed into the settlement. It skipped off the longhouse roof and spun down onto the green. The ogre stumbled, but tucked his left shoulder. He rolled through the gap in the door and came up inside the compound, a hideously expectant grin on his malformed mouth, letting his momentum carry him forward into battle.

He impaled himself on a sharpened log. The point shattered bone armor, driving broken ends back into his enormous gut. The log punched through his stomach, splashing the contents of his last meal onto the ground. The bloody point emerged from his back, just left of the spine.

The ogre looked down at his ruined middle, then lashed out with the twisted metal hook in his right hand. The sickle-shaped hook most closely resembled an oversized baling hook. It had been bent out of wrought-iron railing, the end wrapped tightly around a piece of wood for a grip.

Tyressa ducked the swipe, but another man who was wiping ogre blood from his face, caught the hook in the side. The metal ripped him front to back, from flank to spine, tearing through mail, flesh, and bone. As he screamed, Tyressa thrust her spear into the ogre's throat and yanked it back, leaving the point buried in the monster's flesh.

More ogres rushed the gate, and the goblins followed closely.

"Serrana, here." Jerrad pulled the sack of roast-weed leaves he's salvaged from the longhouse off his belt. "Get these on fire. The smoke will hurt the goblins.

His sister glanced at him, then nodded toward the burning disk. "Throw toward that."

Jerrad hauled his arm back and threw. The bag arced up and started down. Serrana tracked it, then shot. The arrow snagged the bag and pinned it to the disk.

It took a moment or two for thick white smoke to seep from the bags. It remained low to the ground and swirled around ogres and goblins alike. *This has to work.*

One goblin on a goblin dog leaped through it. The dog landed, then leaped sideways, spilling its rider. The animal went down, rolling onto its side. Its tongue had swollen and begun to ooze pus. Its lungs worked harder and harder, but nostrils had closed. The rider regained his feet, but his eyes had already closed and begun to crust over. An arrow took him square in the forehead, pitching him back onto the disk. His body sizzled, but it also smothered the fire on the bag.

"More arrows, go!"

Jerrad slid down the ladder with Nelsa close behind. He grabbed two sticks from where he'd thrust them into the ground. She snatched up a cudgel, slipping her hand through a rawhide loop, then twisting the club to tighten it around her wrist. Jerrad started toward the lake end of the settlement and small blockhouse that served as Silverlake's armory.

The ogres had crowded through the gate and paused, finding themselves hemmed in. Jostling knocked several forward. One twisted between the stakes. Two others got knocked onto them, but one only got stuck through the thigh. The last took the shaft through his lower abdomen, puncturing rolls of fat before bursting his bladder.

More goblins poured into Silverlake, easily passing between the poles. Arrows from the reserves cut down their first ranks. Goblins tottered and died, their bulbous heads having made excellent targets. The back ranks slowed, trapped between ogres and defenders, then turned toward the walls.

Here they come. Jerrad set himself, holding two slender sticks against a knot of knife-wielding, shrieking goblins.

Nelsa laughed. "We have them. Ain't no mud."

One thrust at Jerrad. He twisted back to the left, letting the knife slide past his belly. He snapped one stick down on the goblin's wrist, then thrust with the other. He hit the goblin clean in the throat. Knife falling from a numbed hand, the goblin fell back choking.

Nelsa reshaped one's skull with savage blow. It crumpled. Another leaped above it, knife raised for an overhand stab. She took a half step forward, grabbed its throat in her free hand, then turned. She dropped to a knee, speeding the goblin's arc. It hit full force, face first. Its neck snapped loudly and the body bounced limply into shadows.

A third, rushing at her back, stiffened as Serrana's shot took it in the right shoulder and angled to emerge at the left hip. The goblin skidded past Nelsa. Jerrad darted forward, knocking aside the knife-thrust by a fourth. He swept its legs with his right foot, and Nelsa whirled, cracking its skull with her club.

Jerrad looked up to give his sister a nod. "Serrana, behind you!"

An ogre had leaped up and caught the wall's upper edge. He loomed above her, a fist raised for a crushing blow.

Serrana spun, leaped back, and loosed an arrow. She hung in the air as the shaft caught the ogre under the chin. It ripped out the left cheek, shredding the ogre's tongue. Blood and spittle hung in a mist.

Then the fist came down. The blow narrowly missed Serrana, but swept two other archers into the night. They tumbled through the air, arrows spilling, and descended into the melee at the gate.

Serrana fell and landed awkwardly. Her right leg snapped, audible even above the growls and shrieks. Her body bounced, but she never lost her grip on the bow.

"Serra!" Ranall's shout cut through the din of battle. His blade flashing left and right, he cut his way through goblins to reach her side. Legs spread wide, both hands on a blade running with dark blood, he snarled at gathering goblins. "Come and die."

Nelsa dragged Serrana back, while Jerrad pointed up past Ranall. "The ogre!"

The ogre came up over the wall. With a nightmare-inducing grin, he drooled blood and landed with both feet on the catwalk. He crouched, preparing to leap down and perhaps crush Ranall. Ranall brought his sword up in a guard, but there was no way that slender blade could save him.

Before the ogre could leap, wood splintered and snapped. The catwalk support gave way beneath his bulk. The ogre, falling, grabbed for the top of the wall to support himself. He succeeded only in impaling his hand. Worse yet for him, as he fell, his broad leather belt snagged on the wall itself. His feet dangled shy of the ground and his pierced hand hung him up.

Ranall thrust up into the creature's belly. He avoided the kicking feet, dancing back, then in again to stab. Three times, four times, Ranall perforated the ogre's gut. Foul fluids gushed while the monster roared with outrage. The ogre stopped trying to kick the man and instead drove its heels back against the palisade itself. Bark flew and wood splintered.

"Jerrad, get Serrana and Nelsa to safety. The wall's going to come down."

"No time. Goblins!"

The ogre's predicament fascinated the goblins for only as long it took for a murderous mob to gather. As Ranall turned away from the dangling ogre, a wall of goblins surged forward. All knives and claws and teeth, they came howling gleefully.

Jerrad lashed out with his sticks. He might not have been fast enough to beat Kiiryth, but the goblins came in carelessly and slow. He parried thrusts, then struck back. He shattered jaws, crushed cheeks, fractured wrists and arms. He struck without thinking, knowing he couldn't help but hit targets, so many of them came at him.

To his left, Ranall's blade crunched bone and slid wetly from bodies. Nearest Serrana, Nelsa smashed goblins with her club. Bodies dropped heavily. Goblins snarled and whimpered, then gurgled and died.

Something grabbed Jerrad's ankle. Before he would pull back, the goblin bit him through his boot. Another rushed forward, his knife stabbing. Jerrad twisted, but not enough. Steel burned, slicing him over the ribs. He elbowed the goblin in the eye, then cracked another across the head. That one went down, then another hand grabbed his free leg.

He begin to fall on his back. "No!"

A goblin surged up through the pile, spitting out boot leather through bloody lips. He raised a knife above his head in both hands. He graced Jerrad with a red grin, arching his back, ready to pin Jerrad's heart to his spine.

The knife descended.

Chapter Thirty-Four
Etched in Pain

Ogres squeezed slowly between the sharpened logs, whereas goblins poured over and around them. Tyressa thrust up at an ogre, aiming to punch through a gap in its bone armor, but a goblin deflected her spear upward. The point skittered along armor, then plunged into the ogre's neck. Blood squirted, just missing Tyressa as she pulled back.

Despite warriors trying to hold the line, the ogres penetrated Silverlake's first line of defense, heading for the western longhouse. Enormous flat feet stomped on caltrops. Metal spikes punctured dirt-black soles. One ogre bellowed, then jumped up and down clutching his foot. Caltrops clung to it like ticks. His necklace of skulls bounced as he hopped. Then he came down on more caltrops. He flailed his arms against the pull of gravity, and crashed down on his right flank in the metal-strewn field.

Another ogre sank an enormous baling hook into his ankle and pulled him back. *It's not a rescue. She doesn't want him reaching the longhouse first.* His thrashing body picked up more caltrops, clearing a path to the prize. Her hook rose and fell again, taking the first ogre in the hip and dragging him backward out of the way.

Triumphant, she darted in. The shutters over the longhouse windows clacked open. A bristle of spears thrust outward. Some of the shafts snapped as their points caught on the ogre's armor. Others found gaps, sticking the monster in thighs and shins. As the spears withdrew, the points remained in the ogre's flesh. The ogre plucked one out as if it were a thorn, then shrieked and went at the longhouse again.

Fear fluttered in Tyressa's stomach. *How can we stand against them?* Yet as soon as the thought came, so did the answer. *We will because we must.*

Tyressa replaced the point she'd left in the ogre. She quickly grabbed another and jammed it deep in a passing goblin's neck. She brought her spear up and around, using the steel-shod butt end to dent one more goblin's head.

The biggest ogre she'd ever seen thrust aside two smaller of his kind and marched through the gate. Leg bones had been laced into an armor ladder covering his chest and ample gut. His skull necklaces had each been strung with different types of skulls. The smallest, worn closest to his throat, featured goblins. The largest, which hung down to his belly, had skulls from wild beasts. The middle string contained human skulls. The only sense she could make of how they'd been arranged was that he kept families together, with children's small skulls strung between parents'.

One blow with his iron-wrapped club shattered a sharpened log. A large piece flipped up into the air, then bounced down and rolled over some goblins. Blood and unrecognizable bits sprayed into the air in its wake.

The head of the snake.

Arrows flew thick and fast, but not nearly enough to kill this giant. The arrowheads were too small to penetrate deeply and would take a long time to work into muscle and blood vessels. Ogres would die in torment from them, but not nearly soon enough.

"Archers, take the goblins!" Tyressa turned and trotted back around toward the green. She whirled her spear around, clearing a circle in the goblins. They didn't so much withdraw—happy though they were to leave wounded and dying kin on the ground—as they ran off to easier targets. *Or to escape great danger.*

Tyressa turned and shook out her shoulders. The big ogre, by intent or happenstance, had followed her to the green. She pointed her spear at the larger of the ogre's two eyes. "You're mine."

It didn't matter if the ogre understood her words or not. He had enough arrows sticking from his ears that she couldn't even be certain he'd heard her. But the dark eye tightened. The ogre barked a sharp command which slowed two other ogres. They took up positions between him and the longhouse, grinning lopsidedly.

Their master aped that grin and laughed.

In the handful of heartbeats before they joined combat, Tyressa saw things with frightening clarity. Had her enemy been just a man, the laugh would have been bluster and bluff. Coming from a man, she'd describe it as evil; yet his willingness to meet her in single combat would suggest honor. She, defending her home, would claim righteousness favored her. They both would believe that this would give her an advantage.

The ogre's laugh suggested none of that. The ogres had come to Silverlake in a mass for nothing more than a midnight raid on a fully stocked larder. First in would feed well. The ogres were foxes, and Silverlake was one overlarge henhouse.

And I'm an amusement, a bantam defiantly crowing at the fox.

Twice her height, three times her width and four times her weight, the ogre pounded the ground with his club. Tyressa felt the ground shake and took a step back. The ogre offered a comment in his foul tongue and his two compatriots laughed.

Oh, for a gust of the wind that sped you from Mosswater, Jerrad.

As he lifted his club again, Tyressa darted forward. She feinted toward his middle, so he swiped with the club. She dodged left. As it swept past, she thrust. She stuck him inside his elbow, unfortunately shy of the artery. The point went deep and remained in when she yanked back. She whipped the spear around, shifting it to her left hand, and cracked the steel end off the monster's knee. It shattered the scapula serving as armor, but did no real harm.

Tyressa rolled forward, passing beneath the club's return strike, then reached her feet and faced the ogre again.

A guttural comment from one of his two compatriots stung the ogre more than her assault had. The monster's eyes tightened. He backhanded the sharp-mouthed ogre, knocking him closer to the longhouse, where he drove a caltrop into his heel. The third ogre laughed at the second. For a moment it appeared they might fight one against the other, but their leader snapped an order which silenced both.

Tyressa cut right as the ogre thrust the club at her. The blow missed, but dented the alarm bell and crushed the posts holding it up. She lunged forward, driving the spearpoint into the ogre's left foot. She ducked beneath the club's sideswipe, then pulled back and put another point on her spear.

Though huge, the ogre moved more quickly than she might have guessed possible looking at its robust belly. Tyressa kept working to her right, forcing the ogre to pivot on his wounded foot. She jammed another spear-point in that ankle, drilling in below the shinbone. The ogre's frustrated attempted to hit her constantly forced him to flex his elbow.

Deeper and deeper, little spear point. Find something.

The subordinate ogres started chattering again. Her quarry becoming more angry. He turned toward them, cursing savagely, and exposed his back to her.

Tyressa smiled and saw her chance. She started forward, then something clutched at her leg. A wounded goblin had grabbed on and wrapped itself around her calf. Even as she sought to bring her spear down butt-first to crack its skull, the goblin's legs caught her other ankle.

Tyressa went down.

And her foe, alerted by wild gesticulations, turned back and raised his club.

The face of the murderous goblin rising above Jerrad evaporated in a hail of black needles. Skin peeled back, disappearing in a green-black mist. The ears vanished and, just for a heartbeat, the big gold earring on the left hung in the air. Facial muscles flew to bits. The jaw gaped. The goblin jerked backward as if it had run into a wall.

Lissa, blazing with golden light, flew up, drew Alorek's bow and loosed another needle shaft. Above and around her, coming over the south wall in a river of golden fire, sprites flew into battle. Their volleys dropped goblins and forced them to the east, where human archers spitted them with clothyard shafts.

Jerrad punched and kicked right and left, knocking goblins back. "Lissa, what are you doing here?"

"Killing goblins." She circled around him once. "Try to keep up, Wisewing, or we'll have to give you a new name."

The sprites carved a trough through the goblins, scattering them and their hellish hounds. A path littered with writhing and bleeding creatures led to Silverlake's green. An ogre turned from the longhouse and two confederates to raise his club and smash . . .

Mother!

Jerrad ran, knowing he had to save her. *But how?*

Then it came to him. As he leaped over dying goblins, he cast one spell after another. He dropped his voice as low as he could and growled, "Touch her and your life will be pure torment."

The ogre's club continued to rise, but he came around to face Jerrad. The youth could read nothing on the monster's face. He hoped for fear and would have settled for surprise. What the ogre should have seen was the illusion Jerrad had used to enter the tower, but with the gold blazing as if it was molten.

Jerrad thrust a hand at the ogre and triggered a blast of light. The monster's pupils contracted, but he didn't even raise a hand to shield his eyes. Instead he pointed the club at Jerrad and snarled an order at his subordinates.

The nearer of the two ogres started for Jerrad. Before it took a full step, a man came running down the slope of the longhouse roof. The one-eyed man launched himself at the ogre, a battleaxe drawn back in both hands. He brought it down heavily, cleaving the ogre's skull down to the neck, then ripped the axe free as he rolled to his feet.

It's Kiiryth's friend, the Broken Man!

The Broken Man came fully around as the second ogre reached for him. The axe took the monster's hand off at the wrist. Then from behind it, up at the roof's peak, Kiiryth shot. The arrow drilled into the back of the ogre's neck. The creature rose up on its toes, back arched, then collapsed in a tangle of limbs.

Jerrad turned. His mother had regained her feet, crushing a goblin's skull with her heel. Her spear spun up and around, then she nodded to the ogre and beckoned him forward. "Your fight is with me."

Then something slammed into Jerrad's back, driving him face-first into the ground.

Tyressa let her spear rise to whirl above her head, then brought it down to circle her waist. Blade and butt flashed past as the weapon spun. The ogre's eyes narrowed, and he moved left warily. Tyressa accommodated his choice, reversing her earlier course. She came at his right, avoiding the club, feinting at his hand and forearm.

373

Tyressa could read neither fear nor intelligence in the ogre's eyes. *Animal cunning, maybe.* The ogre watched her the way a cat might study a feisty mouse. She caught no curiosity, just annoyance at having to delay feasting.

Lips peeled back in a fierce snarl, the ogre hammered the ground with his club. The tremor coaxed a dull clank from the broken bell. Tyressa slowed, stepping warily, remaining just out of range.

The ogre slammed the club down again and again. Stones and bits of broken post danced. He began to beat a steady rhythm, hitting harder and harder, sinking depressions into the ground. With his free hand, he imitated her invitation.

The club fell again, and Tyressa darted forward. Before the ogre could heft the club, she lunged, stabbing deeply into the creature's groin. Blood spurted, and she pulled back, but the spearpoint didn't release cleanly. It hung up for a second, trapping her in place.

The ogre flicked his left hand in a swat. Tyressa caught only a glancing blow, but that was enough to toss her across the green. She hit and bounced, rolling to her feet. She reached over to grab another spearpoint, but her bracers were empty.

She brandished her spear, bringing the iron-shod end into play. The ogre laughed, lifting his club. Both were metal-wrapped wood, but his club mocked her stick. *I can hit him a thousand times and do no harm, but even grazing me with that club . . .*

The ogre raised the club high, pumping his arm victoriously as he advanced on her. His gaze measured the distance between them. He might miss once or twice, but he *would* kill her.

Then an odd thing happened. As he brought the club to the apex of its arc, it fell free of his right hand. The fingers twitched like the legs on a dying spider. The ogre brought his hand around to look at it, but the forearm flopped limply at the end of his arm.

The spearhead. It found a nerve.

The ogre's expression melted from triumphant to disbelieving. He started to turn back to grab for his club again, but his foot didn't fall right. It smeared a goblin into a bloody paste, and slipped wide. His knees wobbled, then he sat down abruptly. Mud splashed—mud mixed of dirt and the blood pulsing from his groin. He tried to drag his right hand over to staunch the wound, but it still refused to work. His head slumped forward. He stared down at the weakening jets of blood, then leaned back and collapsed.

Teeth sank into Jerrad's shoulder. Something tugged, flipping him over. He caught a fleeting glimpse of a goblin dog, then it was gone. Nelsa had her legs wrapped tight around it. She'd trapped its throat in the crook of her left elbow. Her right hand raised a knife. She plunged it between the hairless beast's ribs. Blood bubbled from punctured lungs.

Jerrad scrambled to his feet again and ran past her, scooping his sticks up. He raised them in a guard, snarling at a goblin brandishing two knives. Its eyes narrowed.

Then an arrow struck the goblin in the left temple. The creature spun around on one foot as if drunk, then pitched over backward. One knife landed beneath its body; the other stuck straight up in the ground.

Jerrad backtracked the arrow's path. Kiiryth gave him a nod from the longhouse roof. Then he turned and shot again, this time toward Silverlake's gates.

Jerrad looked around for another threat, but saw none, and so let the illusion fade. The sprites spiraled up and out of the settlement like sparks rising from a fire, headed west. A couple of archers had mounted the walls and shot out toward the forest as well. The reserve archers raced forward.

He turned to Nelsa. "How is it possible they're all gone?"

"Beyond my ken." She smiled. "How's your shoulder?"

"Hurts as much as my ankle and my ribs." He gave her a grin. "Thank you for saving me."

"I was saving a tall man in fancy gold." Nelsa kissed him on the cheek. "If I'd knowed it was you, I'd have knowed you didn't need saving."

Ranall appeared through the ranks of reserve archers streaming toward the gates. He carried Serrana, her arms around his neck and her face buried against his chest. Her right foot hung at an odd ankle, but she still held on to her bow.

Ranall walked past Jerrad and carried his sister to Tyressa. He set her down on the ground and knelt beside her, holding her hand.

Their mother bent over Serrana and stroked her brow. "We'll get that seen to, and your cuts, too, Jerrad. Very soon." Tyressa slid a knife from her belt. "But first, we slit every goblin throat and make certain the ogres are all well and truly dead."

Chapter Thirty-Five
Homecoming

Tyressa's eyes burned and arms ached. She'd have been happy to ascribe the latter pain to the exercise of making sure all the enemy were dead, but she was beginning to feel the effects of the ogre's blow. She hadn't allowed herself to feel the pain until dawn thrust rosy fingers through the low clouds. With its light came a true accounting of the damage done.

So much destruction.

Kiiryth came around the longhouse corner and tossed her a waterskin. "It does appear that the Bonedancers made up the majority of the goblins. A human tribe would be devastated, but goblins breed fast enough . . ."

"I know. We'll have to deal with them in another couple of years." She smiled. "We'll have walls of stone by then."

"That will keep more than goblins out."

"Only those we don't desire to let in." Tyressa nodded to him. "That doesn't include you or the Broken Men. Without your help . . ."

The half-elf shook his head. "We didn't give you much more than a warning." He jerked a thumb toward the west. "The Kellids showed up and attacked the goblin flank and rear because of how you'd dealt with them. The sprites came because of Jerrad. The work you did in preparing and organizing your people was what occupied the ogres enough for everyone else's efforts to matter."

"You may see things as you will, but I know the right of it. You and the other Broken Men, to get where you were, had to fight through the goblin horde, and more than one ogre fell to your people."

"Not *my* people, Lady Tyressa."

Her eyes narrowed. "That's right. You will do me the service of sending your master to me, so I may thank him."

"I don't think . . ."

"Kiiryth, do this."

The archer watched her for a moment, then nodded. "I'll convey your message."

"Thank you." Tyressa drank from the waterskin and went to toss it back, but the half-elf had already vanished.

In the battle's aftermath, the people of Silverlake converted the eastern longhouse into an infirmary. She slung the waterskin over her shoulder and entered, pausing for a moment for her eyes to adjust to the lower light. The most seriously wounded had been placed in the north end. No one expect any of the eight people there to recover consciousness, much less recover. Families and friend sat with them for comfort. Tyressa had been of mixed feelings about summoning children back so they could watch parents die, but who could tell what solace the injured might take from a child's words or the splash of a tear?

She turned toward the south end, where Serrana sat propped up on a cot next to Tunk Murdoon. She'd broken an ankle and he his leg. Moll and Ranall stood watchful guard over them. Mulish, his thigh wrapped in bandages, sat on a stool between the cots.

Tyressa smiled, but allowed a bit of her weariness to show. "I apologize for being so poor a host and having so poor a feast."

Moll shook her head. "As I told you the first handful of times you apologized, you need not apologize. Echo Wood defies those who would predict the future. It mocks those who plan. I don't think there was any malevolence on the wood's part in letting this happen, but the events have given the wood a sense of your measure."

Tunk nodded. "Means either winter will be uncommon mild, or fiercely cold—no middle ground. Also means you've won the right to be here."

Tyressa closed her eyes for a moment. *The way we know we exist is to survive an attempt to destroy us?* The sentiment sent a quick chill through her, but a burning pride chased it off. Since before her arrival, since her brother's treason, people had been trying to destroy her and the Vishov family. *Even my brother was doing that.*

But now we've won. She nodded, opening her eyes again. *Not victory, not really even a reprieve, just the opportunity to continue.*

"I can truthfully say we'd not be here without your help—the help of the whole Murdoon clan. You were the first people who greeted us as friends." Tyressa smiled broadly. "This we will never forget."

Tunk threw her a wink. "And, next year, we'll be having your feast, without a night's entertainment?"

"I will do all within my power to make it so."

She excused herself and wandered through the building, thanking and reassuring the wounded and worried. Neither the Kellids nor the fey had allowed their casualties to enter Silverlake for treatment. Tyressa assumed the fey had their own ways of handling injury, and that the Kellids just didn't want to acknowledge having had any of their own blood shed. The wounded were evenly distributed amongst the people, with the archers having fared the worst.

Having completed her rounds, she walked out onto the green. People were piling goblin bodies on sledges to drag them west, to the field where they'd be burned. Others hacked the ogres to pieces so their parts could be buried separately and distant. If any ogre was going to summon them back from the beyond, she was determined to make the task as difficult as possible.

Silverlake's dead had been laid out near the southern wall and shrouded with tent cloth. They'd be buried there temporarily. Next spring, as Silverlake expanded, Tyressa would have them moved to where she'd had the parlay with the Kellids. She'd already dubbed the place Memorial Hill, and her only regret was that it would have room for many more bodies.

"Kiiryth said you wished to see me."

She didn't turn toward the voice. "I wasn't certain you wanted to be seen."

"Neither was I." The one-eyed man emerged from the longhouse shadow. "How long have you known?"

She looked him up and down. *Far too gaunt, hair pared to a faint white stubble, one eye gone and so many more scars added.* Even his voice had changed, become more tentative. He met her gaze, but not with his chin up.

"Not until you leaped from the roof to save our son."

Garath glanced toward the far longhouse. "That man wasn't . . ."

"An illusion." Tyressa's eyes tightened. "Perhaps like the promise you made to return me."

Garath looked at her, then down. "All that kept me alive these last years was my desire to fulfill that promise. I was captured and tortured, Tyressa. You can't imagine . . . I'd personally angered one of the powerful demons, and he found it entertaining to invent new punishments for me, always healing me just enough to keep me from crossing death's door. Eventually, I managed to escape, along with a few other prisoners. We came south. We were bound for Ustalav, then heard you were here."

"You should have come here immediately. You said you'd come back."

"I wanted to but . . . ."

"What?"

His hands curled into fists. "I truly am one of the Broken Men, Tyressa. My mind is not always my own. Seldom, in fact. I may not be as bad as the worst of my brothers, but there are times a wolf would be better company. I didn't want to be a burden. The men with me, the nightmares, the memories. I'm not fit to be a husband or parent."

"Yet you had the presence of mind to send Kiiryth to watch over Jerrad."

"That was vanity." He wiped his nose on the back of his glove. "In that prison-hole, Tyressa . . . I let myself imagine a perfect life. To be so close, and yet unworthy . . . I still had to know. Serra, our Serra, I could at least guess at. But our son. I had to know."

"You could have come here and known."

"Could I?"

The pain in his voice clawed her heart. That she might have rejected him was pain she could understand. No so rejection by his children. Their memories had been reshaped or replaced by stories. *The man before me is not the Garath Sharpax of legend. But then, who could ever be?*

Tyressa made herself smile as tears came. "You are not absolved of your promise to me. You have fulfilled it. You *have* returned—wait, let me finish. You seem to think you've done something wrong. You think you need to apologize for being the man you've become. But you did nothing wrong. And were I to treat you as if you did, I would not be worthy of your return."

She pointed toward where men were dragging away pieces of the ogre he'd slain. "I don't know if you consider yourself to be Garath Sharpax anymore, but I do know this: Garath Sharpax would be proud to know the man who acted as you did."

Tyressa extended a hand toward him. "And I will be happy to welcome that man home as my husband."

Jerrad grabbed the goblin by the wrists and Nelsa got it by the only ankle it still had. They swung it twice, then released it. It landed on the pile, then slid half-way back down until an arm got trapped between a pair of legs.

Others dragged more bodies from the sledge, so the two of them backed off to the piles of firewood people had gathered and began shoving sticks in wherever they would go. Some of the lumbermen brought over long poles, which they leaned on the pyre and used to prop some of the bodies in place.

Nelsa pointed back toward Silverlake. "Looks like the wee ones are back." With Oreena leading them, Silverlake's children marched in an orderly file around toward the gate. "Not sure if I'd have been more scared on the boats or in the fight."

Jerrad shrugged, then rubbed at his sore shoulder. "The good thing is that the fear will fade."

She frowned. "I ain't sure there's going to be a lot of forgetting going on."

"No, you're right. Just folks won't remember as strongly." He nodded toward the kids. "They'll be looking at the result of the storm, which is better than having been in the thick of it."

"I reckon that winning makes for better remembering anyway." She snapped a stick in half, then twisted both halves deep into the pyre. "How scared were you?"

"Plenty, I guess. When Serra fell, and when my mother was down. Those scared the life out of me."

"But never for yourself."

"I must have been. I guess I was just too busy to notice." Jerrad smiled. "How about you?"

Nelsa straightened up proudly. "Weren't a lick of fear in me."

"No? Really?"

"Really."

"Why not?"

"No need wasting fear on an outcome what was decided in our favor. Them ogres was damned fools attacking the home of Jerrad Wisewing Ogrebane."

"Ogrebane is my mother's name."

"And you laid claim on it coming out of Mosswater. You killed how many?"

"I don't think luring them to a magic death counts."

"I don't reckon any ogre looking for a vendetta would be that particular." She started ticking things off on her fingers. "You got two to start, and at least one more when you were escaping."

"Fleeing. For my life."

"You say fleeing. Sprites say you rescued a sprite maiden from a city full of ogres. Then there's the goblins you've killed, and . . ."

Jerrad raised both hands. "Hold up. You're making it sound like I'm a hero."

"You are. That's why I wasn't afraid. I was fighting side by side with a hero."

"No, no, I'm not a hero . . ." He shook his head adamantly. "I'm not a hero. I'm not . . ."

" . . . Not your pa?" She reached out a hand and caressed his cheek. "Your pa may have been the bravest hero in the whole world. Could be that had his shadow just touched any of them ogres, their hearts woulda seized on up and they'd have died stone dead. But just because that's what he would have done don't mean what you did wasn't heroic."

"But I didn't do anything more than anyone else."

Nelsa arched an eyebrow. "Everyone fought, that's true, but didn't nobody go running at an ogre armed with nothing more than a magic costume. You up and made yourself a target. That saved your ma. And as I understand it, heroing ain't about doing the most killing, it's about seeing that folks don't get theirselves killed. Now if you care to explain how you ain't a hero, I'll just listen, then tell you how wrong you are."

Jerrad glanced down, watching field grasses slowly rise after having been stepped on. "For as long as I can remember, I've been invisible. I wanted to be. That was safe. Invisible meant no one would see me try the things my father would do. No one would see me fail. No one would have proof I wasn't a hero."

"Jerrad, it's not that you're not a hero. It just that you ain't your pa." She took his head in both hands and kissed him softly on the lips. "Give yourself some time to think on it, and you'll see how right I am."

"Thank you." He pulled her into an embrace. He hung on tight despite the soreness and pain from his injuries. Holding her just felt better than his wounds felt bad.

One of the lumbermen pointed back toward Silverlake. "Ain't that Lady Ogrebane waving your way?"

Jerrad glanced over. "Appears to be."

Nelsa slipped her hand into his. "Looks like she wants us back there."

Hand in hand, they ran back toward the settlement, the dawning sun rendering Silverlake as a silhouette. That hid its imperfections, and gave it sense of peace.

Jerrad waved back at his mother. "We're coming!"

"Hurry, Jerrad." His mother urged him on. "There's someone here you need to meet."

About the Author

Michael A. Stackpole is an award-winning game designer, computer game designer, graphic novelist, screenwriter, podcaster, editor, and novelist. He got his start writing solitaire adventures for *Tunnels & Trolls*, so it was a distinct pleasure to return to a world of pure fantasy for this book. Mike lives in Arizona, teaches writing classes through the Piper Center for Creative Writing at Arizona State University, and swing dances in his spare time.

Acknowledgments

The author would like to thank Pierce Watters, James Sutter, and his agent, Howard Morhaim, for making this deal possible. In between drafts of this novel, the author traveled to Austin, Texas and taught two days' worth of writing classes with his friend, Aaron Allston. During that trip he was able to figure a number of things out about the story, thanks to many insights Aaron offered in his classes. He'd also like to thank Kat Klaybourne, Chantelle Osman, Jami Kupperman, and Paul Garabedian for keeping him sane while he wrote the book. (Tough job, which is why it required four people.)

Glossary

All Pathfinder Tales novels are set in the rich and vibrant world of the Pathfinder campaign setting. Below are explanations of several key terms used in this book. For more information on the world of Golarion and the strange monsters, people, and deities that make it their home, see *The Inner Sea World Guide*, or dive into the game and begin playing your own adventures with the *Pathfinder Roleplaying Game Core Rulebook* or the *Pathfinder Roleplaying Game Beginner Box*, all available on **paizo.com**. Those readers particularly interested in the region explored in this book should check out the setting book *Pathfinder Online: Thornkeep* or explore, fight monsters, and build their own settlements in the *Pathfinder Online* massively multiplayer online roleplaying game.

Ardis: Former capital of Ustalav.

Azlant: The first human empire, which sank beneath the waves long ago.

Azlanti: Of or pertaining to Azlant; someone from

Azlant.

Broken Men: Derogatory River Kingdoms term for deserters and former crusaders heading south from the Worldwound.

Caliphas: Current capital of Ustalav.

Carrion Hill: City in Ustalav.

Crusader Road: Local term for the branch of the Sellen River flowing south from near the Worldwound to the Inner Sea, and used for travel by crusaders headed north. Also called the River Road.

Crusades: An ongoing military campaign against the demons of the Worldwound.

Demons: Evil denizens of the plane of the afterlife called the Abyss, who seek only to maim, ruin, and feed on mortal souls.

Demonic: Of or related to demons.

Dismal Caverns: Notorious subterranean goblin den south of Silvershade Lake.

Druid: Someone who reveres nature and draws magical power from the boundless energy of the natural world (sometimes called the Green Faith, or the Green).

Echo Wood: Large forest in the eastern River Kingdoms, along the border with Ustalav.

Elves: Long-lived, beautiful humanoids identifiable by their pointed ears, lithe bodies, and pupils so large their eyes appear to be one color.

Fauns: Fey creatures with the upper half of humanoids and lower half of goats.

Fey: Creatures deeply tied to the natural world, such as dryads or sprites.

Furrows: Region of Ustalav heavily scarred by a past

civil war and haunted by the ghosts of the dead.

Glow Water Lake: Lake near the former town of Mosswater.

Goblin Dogs: Grotesque creature combining the features of dogs and canines, often used by goblins as mounts and companions.

Goblins: Race of small and maniacal humanoids who live to burn, pillage, and sift through the refuse of more civilized races.

Half-Elves: The children of unions between elves and humans. Taller, longer-lived, and generally more graceful and attractive than the average human, yet not nearly so much so as their full elven kin. Often regarded as having the best qualities of both races, yet still see a certain amount of prejudice, particularly from their pure elven relations.

Inner Sea: The vast inland sea whose northern continent, Avistan, and southern continent, Garund, are the primary focus of the Pathfinder campaign setting.

Katapesh: Mighty trade nation south of the Inner Sea. Also the name of its capital city.

Kellids: Human ethnicity from the northern reaches of the Inner Sea region, typically viewed as uncivilized, superstitious, and violent by other cultures.

Lamashtu: The Mother of Monsters, goddess of madness, monsters, and nightmares.

Mendev: Military nation on the eastern border of the Worldwound, devoted to keeping the demons from spreading out across the world.

Mosswater: River Kingdoms city on the shores of Glow Water Lake, destroyed by a savage ogre attack fifty years ago.

Necromancy: School of magic devoted to manipulating the power of death, unlife, and the life force, particularly undead creatures.

Nirmathas: Fledgling forest nation constantly at war with its former rulers.

Nirmathi: Of or pertaining to Nirmathas.

Nixies: Humanoid water fey.

Ogres: Hulking, brutal, and half-witted humanoid monsters with violent tendencies, repulsive lusts, and an enormous capacity for cruelty.

Ogrekin: The offspring of ogre and human relations. Somewhat smaller than true ogres, but still larger than humans, and often just as unpleasant as their monstrous parents.

Osiriani: The native language of Osirion.

Osirion: Ancient nation south of the Inner Sea renowned for its deserts, pharaohs, and pyramids.

Redcap: Fey creatures that look like tiny, angry old men with bloodstained, pointed caps and metal boots.

River Kingdoms: A region of small, feuding fiefdoms and bandit strongholds, where borders change frequently.

Satyrs: Male fey with horns, the legs of goats, and a reputation for seduction. Related to fauns, but a distinct breed of their own.

Sellen River: Mighty river that spans the continent of Avistan from north to south, making it useful for travel and trade.

Silverlake: New River Kingdoms settlement founded on the shores of Silvershade Lake.

Silvershade Lake: A lake near the edge of Echo Wood in the River Kingdoms.

Sorcerer: Someone who casts spells through natural ability rather than faith or study.

Sprites: Small, winged fey known for the magical lights and capricious pranks.

Taldane: The common trade language of the Inner Sea region.

Thornkeep: Town on the western edge of the River Kingdoms, surrounding a fortress of the same name and ruled by the bandit lord Baron Tervin Blackshield.

Ustalav: Fog-shrouded gothic nation with a reputation for strange bests, ancient secrets, and moral decay. Rife with superstition and often said to be haunted. Also the term for an Ustalavic national.

Ustalavic: Of or related to the nation of Ustalav.

Wizard: Someone who casts spells through careful study and rigorous scientific methods rather than faith or innate talent, recording the necessary incantations in a spellbook.

Worldwound: Constantly expanding region overrun by demons a century ago. Held at bay by the efforts of the Mendevian crusaders.

When murdered sinners fail to show up in Hell, it's up to Salim Ghadafar, an atheist soldier conscripted by the goddess of death, to track down the missing souls. In order to do so, Salim will need to descend into the anarchic city of Kaer Maga, following a trail that ranges from Hell's iron cities to the gleaming gates of Heaven itself. Along the way, he'll be aided by a menagerie of otherworldly creatures, a streetwise teenager, and two warriors of the mysterious Iridian Fold. But when the missing souls are the scum of the earth, and the victims devils themselves, can anyone really be trusted?

From James L. Sutter, author of the critically acclaimed novel *Death's Heretic*, comes a new adventure of magic, monsters, and morality, set in the award-winning world of the Pathfinder Roleplaying Game.

The Redemption Engine print edition: $9.99
ISBN: 978-1-60125-618-8

The Redemption Engine ebook edition:
ISBN: 978-1-60125-619-5

The
Redemption
Engine

James L. Sutter

PATHFINDER
CAMPAIGN SETTING

THE INNER SEA WORLD GUIDE

You've delved into the Pathfinder campaign setting with Pathfinder Tales novels—now take your adventures even further! *The Inner Sea World Guide* is a full-color, 320-page hardcover guide featuring everything you need to know about the exciting world of Pathfinder: overviews of every major nation, religion, race, and adventure location around the Inner Sea, plus a giant poster map! Read it as a travelogue, or use it to flesh out your roleplaying game—it's your world now!

EXPLORE YOUR WORLD!

paizo.com